Redfield Farm

A Novel of the Underground Railroad

Judith Redline Coopey

Copyright© 2010, Judith Redline Coopey. All rights reserved.
ISBN (13): 978-0-9789247-4-4 / ISBN (10): 0-9789247-4-6
Library of Congress Control Number: 2010921472

This is a work of fiction. Any resemblance to actual persons, living or dead, is purely coincidental. No part of this book may be reproduced or transmitted in any form or by any means, electronic or mechanical, including photocopying, recording, or by an information storage and retrieval system — except by a reviewer who may quote brief passages in a review to be printed in a magazine, newspaper, or on the Web—without permission in writing from the publisher. For information, please contact: INDI Publishing Group, www.INDIPublishingGroup.com.

Published by INDI Publishing Group in association with the author, Judith Redline Coopey

Interior design by OPA Author Services, Scottsdale, AZ
Cover design by Albert Chui

ATTENTION CORPORATIONS, UNIVERSITIES, COLLEGES, AND PROFESSIONAL ORGANIZATIONS: Quantity discounts are available on bulk purchases of this book for educational or gift purposes, or as premiums for increasing magazine subscriptions or renewals. Special books or book excerpts can also be created to fit specific needs.
Contact: INDI Publishing Group: www.INDIPublishingGroup.com.

Printed and bound in the United States of America.

For Lou

Acknowledgments

Thanks to the following people who read, helped, critiqued, and kept me going.

Mary Agliardo
David Bradley
Kathleen Davis
Rebecca Foust
Linda Kehoe
Pamela Leipold
Genie Robine . . .

. . . and my friends at the East Valley Writers Group, especially Charles Baudo, Libby Farris, Gerri Green, Dave Lettick, Jay Strisik and Ted Tenny.

Chapter 1

1903 . . .

Jesse died today. Right here on Redfield Farm, where we grew up. I'm glad it was here and not someplace out west, where they didn't know him and there was no one to grieve. Worse yet, no one who knew him when he was young and on fire. I'll probably follow him in about two years. Always did. Born there. Grew up there. Grew old there. Two years behind Jesse.

We'll bury him in the Friends Graveyard at Spring Meadow. With Mama and Papa and Abby. He'll be happy there with the rest of the Friends. And the silence. Jesse always did love the silence of Meeting. Said it moved him. Now he can have it forever.

He sure kicked up enough dust around here when we were young. Kept us on edge for most of our youth with his hatred of slavery. Don't get me wrong. I hated it, too. But Jesse's hate didn't just smolder under his hat. He acted on it, from the time he was a boy.

. . . 1837

The first I knew of it was back in 1837, when I was nine and Jesse eleven. Redfield Farm sat, as it does now, on a hill overlooking Dunning's Creek in Bedford County. The hill slopes gently, giving a wide view of the creek as it curves to the north. The field was pasture then. Cows crowded under the shade of the few trees, swishing flies in the afternoon heat. Jesse and I

1

trotted barefoot down the hill, he with a fishing pole, I with a pail for picking berries.

"Ooooh, Jesse! There's a snake!" I jumped as it slithered across the path.

"Don't step on it," was all he said. That's how Jesse was. Unconcerned. He was ahead of me, strutting along, pole in his right hand, worms in his pocket, straw hat on his head.

I ran a few steps to catch up. It seemed I was always following a few steps behind Jesse. I spent my life there. "Why are you always so in a hurry?" I jumped to miss a cow pie.

"Don't get much time to fish."

That was true. Farming was a round-the-clock responsibility, not limited to adults. My brother was expected to put in a man's work every day. This summer afternoon, when the hay was in and the corn was growing meant almost a vacation, with only the morning and evening chores to do. Jesse wasn't one to miss an opportunity.

It was then I saw her. Well, I can't say I really *saw* her—just a glimpse. That's all I needed to know it was Pru Hartley, sneaking around, watching. Always watching. I didn't know why I disliked her so. Maybe it was how she looked. Unhealthy. Scrawny. Pale. Maybe it was that sneakiness I couldn't abide, or the promise of trouble that trailed after her. Whatever it was, her presence never failed to raise the bile in me.

"Jesse!" A loud whisper. He turned. I jerked my head toward the other bank and mouthed her name. Pru wouldn't ever show herself if she thought she could get by unseen. Jesse nodded. We swung to the right, following the path along the creek.

"You gonna fish here?" I wanted to know. The blackberry bushes were farther downstream, near the woodlot, but I didn't like to get too far separated from Jesse in case there were snakes. I didn't like snakes. Still don't. Anyway I didn't want to run into Pru by myself. She had an annoying way of waiting until you got busy with something and then appearing suddenly, like a ghost.

"Not here," Jesse replied. "Too much sun. Down in the woodlot, where it's shady. Fish aren't dumb. They find shade when it's hot."

I hopped up, pail in hand. "Come on, then. I can see those juicy blackberries from here." I skipped along the creek bank, and stopped to pick a few black-eyed Susans to decorate my apron pocket. I liked the way they dressed up my plain brown dress and apron. Papa would have said it was vain, but I thought, since flowers were God's creation, He must like fancy, just a little bit.

I was already in the blackberry patch at the edge of the woodlot, my first berries plinking noisily onto the bottom of the pail, when Jesse wandered past on the bank, looking for a place to drop his line. I lost track of him working to fill my pail, alert in case Pru tried to sneak up on me. When I did look up, Jesse was nowhere in sight. My pail was almost full, so I set it down near the path and started out to find him. Then, on second thought, I took the berries with me. No telling where Pru might be, but she'd steal your berries rather than pick her own. That was sure.

Then I saw Jesse, crouched, hiding behind a fallen tree, his abandoned fishing pole propped on a 'Y' shaped branch. His annoyed hand swat gave me notice to be quiet. I stopped and looked around for what made him hide. Stepping off the path, I crept up close.

"What is it?" I whispered

He pointed to a bend in the creek, all shaded, where the branches of a maple tree nearly touched the water. At first I didn't see anything. Then I made out a man's legs standing in the stream, the rest of him hidden behind the leaves. The legs were clothed in torn, ragged breeches, but the exposed skin was unmistakably black. I inhaled sharply. I'd never seen a black man before. As we watched from behind the log, the legs moved cautiously out from the shelter of the maple branches until a tall, dark-skinned Negro, dressed in rags, stood, clearly visible, not twenty yards away.

We watched in silence, wild eyed, our alert senses sharp. There were two of them—young, strong and full of caution. They moved along in the calf-deep water, looking around, making their way downstream, away from us, their backs glistening in the sun. We stayed hidden, barely breathing, for long minutes after they disappeared.

"Do you think they're runaways?" I whispered.

"Of course they're runaways."

"Where are they going?"

"I don't know. North. Away from slavery." Jesse had a way about him, even then, like he knew everything.

"Where north?"

"Canada, probably. They don't have slaves up there."

"We don't have slaves here, either. Why don't they stay here?" My eyes scanned the bushes on the other side of the creek. Pru was hiding out somewhere over there. I wondered if she'd seen the Negroes.

Jesse was annoyed with my ignorance. "Too close to slave catchers. They might get caught."

"Slave catchers?"

"People who hunt them down for a bounty."

"Bounty?" Now I was really beyond my ken.

"Money. Their owners want them back, so they advertise and offer a reward. Slave catchers make a business of it."

Across the creek I caught a glimpse of Pru, her white-blond head giving her away even behind a bush. My attention came back to Jesse. "That's mean. How are those two going to get to Canada without getting caught?"

"People help them."

"Which people?"

"People like us. Friends. Friends and others who think slavery is an abomination."

I was amazed at his command of big words. Abomination. I'd heard it before—at Meeting—but I had only a vague idea of what it meant. I wouldn't be confident enough to use it. But Jesse would. He'd stand up in Meeting—all eleven years of him—and talk, lecture, harangue Friends into the right path.

Shake his finger at 'em. Get red in the face with righteous indignation.

We waited until the two Negroes were out of sight and hearing before we went back for Jesse's fishing pole. He had a fish on his line. He unhooked it and dropped it into a net bag hanging from his back pocket.

"Get your berries," he directed. "Let's go."

Eying Pru Hartley's hiding place, I shouted, "Why don't you come on out, Pru? We can see you over there!"

Jesse shushed me. He didn't want her to come out. Didn't want to talk to her. I didn't either, but it vexed me, the way she thought she could fool us.

I stepped along behind him, thoughtful on the walk home. It was still hot; the flies buzzed around our faces. Sweat trickled from under Jesse's straw hat. My eyes darted to the bushes on the other side. I knew Pru was over there someplace. Watching. But this other thing was stronger on my mind.

"Jesse, who helps them? Which Friends, I mean."

"Can't say. Wouldn't if I could," he replied. "As few people as possible know. That way we don't have to lie if anyone asks."

"I've never seen a Negro before."

"I have. In Bedford. Some free Negroes live there. And once, when I was there with Papa, I saw a slave catcher on his horse, leading a shackled Negro on foot. Made my blood boil, I can tell you."

"Oh." I pictured the man, stumbling along behind the horse. "That's cruel."

We came up to the back of the cabin, and Jesse took the fish around to Mother to cook for supper.

"Oh, Jesse, thee is a fine provider," she smiled. "And Ann, thee, too!" she said, taking the pail of berries.

Jesse ran out, heading for the barn to find Papa. I took the berries to the spring to wash the dust off, all the while pondering the plight of slaves. A few minutes later I looked up to see Jesse on the back of Old Hand, one of the plow horses, behind our older brother, Ben. Looking important, Jesse barely acknowledged my wave as the two barefoot boys, legs spread wide over the horse's middle, bumped out of the barnyard and up the road.

I returned to the cabin, where sister Mary set two loaves of bread on the windowsill to cool and little brother Nathaniel played with a cat in the dooryard.

"Mama?"

"Yes, Ann."

"Why do people have slaves?"

"To do their work for them, child. Why do you ask?"

"Jesse and I saw two black men down by the creek. Jesse said they were runaway slaves."

Mother's face showed her concern. "It's a sad practice," was all she said. "Go get the churn so you and Rachel can take turns working it to butter."

"Mama?"

"Hmm?"

Why's Pru Hartley so nosy?"

"Who knows, dear? Maybe she's not nosy. Just curious. Poor child. Doesn't have anything. Now get that churn."

I stepped obediently out the door to the springhouse and lugged the heavy churn for mother to fill with milk. Then we both wrestled the full churn out under the shade of a huge oak in the side yard, and I sat down on a bench to the hated job. It was long, boring, hard work. Even in the late afternoon the heat was oppressive, and the flies wouldn't give me any peace. I counted the required thousand strokes and looked around for Rachel. Even then, at only seven years old, she was a dreamy, engaging child that I would have been tempted to call lazy were I not a properly brought up Quaker girl.

"Rachel!" I called. "Your turn!"

Rachel's response, coming from over the brow of the hill above the cabin, sounded far away. "I'm here!"

'You're there and I'm here', I thought. I continued the numbing work of churning, with only slim hope that Rachel would actually come and relieve me. Blonde and blue eyed, she held a special place in our father's heart. Not that he didn't love

the rest of us. He did. But Rachel didn't have to earn her love. It was her birthright for being beautiful.

I churned on as the shadows lengthened, and Papa, passing me on his way in from the barn, reached down and patted my head. "Thee is our industrious one, Ann," he said. "Thee was well made for a life of work."

I knew it was a compliment, but it didn't feel like one. I wondered how it might feel to be Rachel—light hearted and happy all the time. Everybody's favorite—pretty, smiling, full of charm and laughter, and oft excused for idleness. But I could have a worse lot in life. I could be Pru Hartley, wearing flour sack dresses and fighting with nine brothers and sisters for every scrap.

I felt the butter coming, so I kept up a steady rhythm, though my arms and back ached. I stopped counting when it was clear Rachel wouldn't relieve me. Slowly, slowly the butter came.

"Mama! It's butter!"

Mary crossed the yard with a large wooden bowl and two paddles, and we poured off the whey into a pail for the pigs and cleaned out the churn, piling the butter in the bowl.

"This will taste so good on my fresh bread," Mary smiled. I dragged the churn back to the springhouse for washing while Mary carried the bowl of butter inside.

By the time I was back, the table was set for supper, with two benches on either side. Papa was already seated at the head, and Mother was dishing out stew from the kettle over the fireplace.

Jesse and Ben appeared in the doorway in time to scoop up three-year-old Nathaniel and five-year-old Elizabeth and set them on the end of each bench closest to Mama. The Amos Redfield family sat to eat, three boys on one bench and four girls on the other.

We observed a silent grace, which was way too long, by my way of thinking. I kept looking up to see if Papa had raised his head yet. He finally did, cut off a chunk of bread and slathered it with butter. He took the first bite, the signal that it was all right to eat. We dove in, to the clinking of spoons on pewter plates.

Jesse was bursting to tell his news. He squirmed in his seat, watching Papa for a sign that it was all right to speak. Amos nodded to him.

"There's trouble, Pa," he said.

"What's that?"

"Well you know those two Negroes me and Ann saw this afternoon? The ones I told you about?"

"Yes."

"Well, me and Ben rode over to Uncle Sammy Grainger's to see if we could hook them up, like you said."

"What's hook them up?" I asked.

"Hush now, girl. Let them talk," Mother admonished.

"And . . .?" Amos hurried Jesse along.

"And when Uncle Sammy and us got to the creek, we looked high and low and couldn't find them. So we started back, and then we saw Zeke Barnes sittin' on the fence by the Alum Bank School. He said he was guardin' two Negroes locked in the school for Charlie Marsh and Rad Hartley."

"Locked in the school?"

"Yes, sir. Seems Charlie and Rad come upon those two Negroes right after me and Ann saw them and told them they'd hide them in the school until it was safe. Then they lit out to Bedford to look for a slave catcher they saw there yesterday. He was offerin' a reward for two slaves escaped from North Carolina." Jesse was breathless with telling the story. Then Ben took it up.

"While we were standin' there talkin' to Zeke, along come Rad and Charlie with the slave catcher. He got chains out of his saddle bags and had the two of them chained up in no time. They tried to fight him off, but Zeke and Rad and Charlie helped him. He gave Rad and Charlie a twenty dollar gold piece each! They gave Zeke a dollar for guardin' them!"

"Uncle Sammy was furious," Jesse added. "He didn't say anything, but you know how he looks when he's mad. Like a cock rooster, red faced and raised hackles!"

I listened in silence, my mind racing. So that's what Pru Hartley was doing down by the creek! She'd seen those Negroes, same as us. She'd gone and told her no account daddy about them, and now look what had happened!

Papa listened to the boys' account, expressionless. Once or twice his eyes met Mama's and looked away. He, too, was full of anger—anger that would come out. This week, next week, a month from now, he would stand up in Meeting and hold forth about the evil curse that was slavery.

But Rad Hartley and Charlie Marsh wouldn't be there to hear it. They weren't Friends—at least not anymore. Rad had been read out of meeting for his drinking, and Mama said the rest of the family had fallen away. I pictured the Hartleys, all twelve of them—all tow headed—standing on an overhang above the creek, with the water eating away underneath them, falling away. Still, Friends would be exhorted to have nothing to do with Rad or Charlie. Not to hire them or buy anything from them or loan them anything. There would be a price to pay for their treachery.

Jesse's face was red with anger as he and Ben related the picture of the slave trader riding off toward the south with the two black men in tow, heads bowed, stumbling along, hands shackled behind their backs, metal collars linked by chains about their necks.

I could see it as sure as if I'd been there. My heart quickened. I knew even then that all human beings should be treated with respect, even the likes of Zeke and Rad and Charlie. Even them—and Pru. Hard though it might be.

That was the start of it. The first time I ever heard tell of black slaves running away from their masters and white people helping them do it. Little did I know where the knowledge, and my brother Jesse, would take me.

Chapter 2

1847

Pru Hartley wasn't through with me. Not by a long shot. The Hartley clan lived down over the hill on the other side of the creek. You couldn't see their tumbledown cabin from Redfield Farm, but it was there. The evidence was all around us—a chicken missing from the coop, a sickle left lying around disappeared—Papa said they'd steal anything they could carry. There was plain meanness in that bunch, and, for me especially, Pru. She knew how uncomfortable she made me and relished it.

Mama died in childbirth with her eighth baby when I was twelve, leaving Papa with seven children to finish raising. The baby, a boy, died, too. Mary was sixteen, so she had most of the work, but I did almost as much. Ben and Jesse helped with the farm, and Mary and I cooked, cleaned and looked after the younger ones, Betsy and Nathaniel, without a lot of help from Rachel, who at ten, had a long way to go toward growing up.

Mary was kind, a lot like Mama. I didn't realize it then, of course. It was only later that I would look at her and see Mama in her expression or gestures. But she grew up fast, and by the time she was twenty, in 1844, the young men were coming to court. Once they started standing around looking cow-eyed at Meeting, I knew her time with us was short. A young fellow from Osterburg came along—tall, red faced, good humored. His name was Noah Poole, and he was a Friend. That was a good thing. Amos Redfield didn't hold with his daughters marrying out.

Anyway, it wasn't long before Mary was gone off to Osterburg to be a wife, and not long after that that she was also a mother. So I was left in charge. I thought it temporary, thought I'd be married by the time I was twenty, but I was wrong. I learned 'temporary' can be a very long time.

Rachel never did step up. Bless her, she just came for the fun. I would have liked more help. Sixteen is young to shoulder it all. Rachel wasn't a bad sort—not a mean bone in her body. But she never saw what was right in front of her. The work, I mean. She could sit down beside a pile of clothes to be ironed and tell you all about her visit with Cousin Eva Blackburn and never take notice. Everybody liked her, so I kept still, but I can tell you it was hard.

Now when Papa claimed his seat at the table there was no one at the other end. Three sons on one side, three daughters on the other. Then, one spring evening in 1847, Ben gave out with an announcement.

"Papa," he ventured.

Amos looked at him. "Ben."

"I'm ready to plan to wed."

"Ready to plan or ready to wed?" Jesse chimed in.

Amos didn't respond. Losing a son on a farm was serious business. He looked at his plate. Around the table Ben's announcement was greeted with giggles from the girls, a whoop from Nathaniel, and more teasing from Jesse.

"You old fox, Ben!" he grinned. "I saw you and Rebecca Finley eyeing each other, but I thought marriage was a long way off!" He jabbed an elbow into Ben's ribs.

Ben reddened. "Well, I'm twenty-five. Best get started," he muttered.

I agreed. It had been a long time coming, too. How was I supposed to get married with both of my older brothers still single? At nineteen, I had designs, but it wouldn't seem right to just up and leave. Anyway, I said *I* had designs. Didn't say anyone else had.

Amos nodded gravely. "Where do thee think thee will take up?"

"Conway has his farm for sale. Plans to go west. I've got some money saved. I can pay for half now and half in three years. He says it suits him."

"Ain't much of a farm," Amos observed.

"I plan to make it a horse farm. Raise horses, breed 'em, sell 'em. There's lots of pasture land, and on the big field I could grow oats."

Amos smiled. "Specializing, are thee?"

Ben looked down. "Yes, sir. Rebecca's brother, Elias, wants to go in with me."

"Is he putting up any money?"

"Not yet, but he's got some breeding stock. That working pair of his is as fine a team as I've ever seen." Ben's eyes lit up when he talked about horses.

"You gonna have riding horses, too, Ben?" The idea of horses to ride, not just for work, appealed to Nathaniel.

"I'd like to. Maybe later."

"Enough of this horse talk, Ben. You just said you were getting married," quipped Rachel. "When?"

"We'll announce our intention at Meeting this week, so it'll be about two months, if all goes well."

"Two months! Are you sure you can wait, brother?" Jesse teased.

Ben reddened again, and I smiled to myself. Having Ben and Rebecca Finley living a half mile away was a fine arrangement. But having Rebecca's brother, Elias, working with Ben was even finer. Elias was part of my design. We'd known each other all our lives, and been paired off in the minds of many since Mary wed. We were friends, but I hoped someday we'd be more than that.

Amos moved back from the table, stood and offered his hand to Ben. "Be fruitful and multiply" was all he said before taking his hat from a peg by the door and stepping out into the spring evening.

Rachel, Betsy, and I rose and cleared the table. I handed Nathaniel a bucket to fetch in water from the spring. Jesse clapped an arm around Ben's shoulders and walked him out the back door. When the water was hot enough to wash dishes, I left Rachel and Betsy to the task and climbed the narrow, curving steps to the loft, passing through the boys' room into the room we three girls shared. There were two beds: Rachel and Betsy slept in one; I had the other to myself since Mary left. Lined up along one wall were three wooden trunks, one for each of us.

I opened mine, rummaging through clothes: two grey dresses, two bonnets, a shawl, stockings, under things and a quilt top I'd pieced. Maybe with a little help and hurry, it could be a wedding gift for Ben and Rebecca. I inspected it with a new eye. It would do, but I'd have to hurry to finish it in two months. I heard Jesse downstairs teasing the girls about getting the dishes clean. I called him.

"Coming, Mother," he replied, bounding up the stairs two at a time.

"Where's Ben?" I asked, looking behind him.

"Gone to see his sweetie," Jesse grinned.

"I thought I'd finish this quilt for a wedding present. What will you give them?"

"Natty and I'll build them a settle for sitting by the fire. One like Uncle Sammy's that makes down into a table. I have some wood drying in the barn that'll do."

"I'll set Rachel and Betsy to stitching pillow cases and maybe a table cloth. Jesse?"

"Hmmm?"

"Nothing. I was just wondering. What do you think of Ben's plans? For the horse farm, I mean."

"Sure," Jesse replied. "Everyone needs horses. And you know Ben. He'll work so hard, it'll have to succeed."

"And Elias?" I tried to mask my intense interest.

"He'll be good at it, too. You've seen the two of them after meeting. Heads together, talking horses all afternoon. Elias knows good horses, and if I'm not mistaken," he said slyly, "he knows good women, too!"

"Jesse, hush!" I swatted at him with the quilt top as he ducked down the stairs. I sat alone in the gathering darkness, feeling warm and happy. Life promised much.

May and June sped by with the planting and haying. There was never a shortage of work on a farm, but hopefully many hands to lighten it. Farm families rotated around the community, helping each other with the plowing, planting and haying. The women pulled together to feed the hungry workers. Older girls tended the little ones. Older boys helped the men.

Some of the Hartleys always showed up, looking for a free meal for little labor. Pru's brothers all had names for trades: Smith, Weaver, Miller, Cooper and Sawyer, and the sisters all had names like Faith, Charity, Honesty and Truth. Jesse called them the virtue sisters. Said the whole family ought to live up to their names instead of always looking around for something to steal. I didn't like it when the Hartleys showed up. Especially Pru. Her eyes followed me wherever I went. Nothing I did escaped her notice.

The chance to get together with family and friends balanced the heavy toil. At haying, Ben and Rebecca were the butt of many a good natured joke, but they just looked at each other and smiled. I took advantage of such gatherings for the chance to be near Elias Finley. I was always first to go round with a bucket and dipper to offer a drink to the workers, and I saw to it that Elias got his share of whatever was being served—and a double helping of shortcake, pie or cobbler for dessert.

Elias understood my intentions and discouraged me not at all. He was just twenty-one, hard working and serious. Not silly or dumb like Jesse could be at times. A little shy perhaps, and slow to move, but to my mind, a fine catch. I was careful not to let my feelings show, and most folks barely noticed, but Pru Hartley got that knowing look in her eyes when she saw us together.

Ben's wedding day dawned warm and sunny at the end of June. The hay was in, and there was rest from the heavy labor. Jesse acknowledged this to Ben with a wink. Ben reddened.

I'd sewn him a wedding shirt that he wore under his new grey suit, made by a tailor from Menallen Monthly Meeting. I thought he was handsome without being prideful, tall and slender, with thick brown hair and friendly blue eyes.

He rode to the meeting house on Webster, his fine black riding horse. The family followed in the wagon. At Dunning's Creek Meeting, we met the Finley family, mother and children in a sturdy wagon and Rebecca seated sideways behind her father on his best horse. She, too, seemed beautiful to me. Red-haired and brown-eyed, her face was young and alive. I scanned the crowded wagon for Elias. Then I saw him riding up behind on a spirited chestnut stallion. It did make my heart flutter to see him sitting tall on such a fine animal.

The Meeting House was cold, damp, and smelled of old wood in spite of the fine weather. At the end of the Monthly Meeting, Ben and Rebecca stood before the congregation, hands clasped, looking shy and uncertain. Ben vowed to "take this, my friend, Rebecca Finley, to be my wife, promising with the Lord's assistance to be unto her a loving and faithful husband until death separate us." Rebecca's vows were accented by a cough and the creaking of wooden benches. The couple then signed the certificate, first the groom, then the bride, using her married name: Benjamin Redfield—Rebecca Redfield.

After their signatures came those of all who attended, family members signing on the right. The paper was stiff and the pen scratchy. I signed below Elias Finley: Ann Redfield—briefly allowing myself to dream that someday I would be writing Ann Finley—then I handed the pen to Rachel.

The celebration at the Finley home was joyful as only a Quaker celebration could be: no music, no dancing, no drinking, no loud or unseemly conduct, but food, goodwill and fellowship in abundance. Ben was attentive to his bride, forsaking all of the "horse talk" and quietly accepting the congratulations of Friends.

Jesse and Elias were not quite so staid. Elias fell to bragging about his chestnut stallion, and Jesse never could let a challenge go by. They were soon arranging a race, discreetly away from the wedding celebration but known to all but the elders of the company, who would have cast a stern eye on such goings on.

Jesse, Elias and most of the young men drifted off in the direction of Dunning's Creek, where there was a great flat field with a quarter mile track down one side, known among the youth of the community as "Saratoga." Horse races, though strongly frowned upon by our elders, were often held accomplished here.

Jesse had no horse of his own, but that slowed him down not a whit. If Elias could brag, he, Jesse, was determined to "slow him down to a walk." Ben's horse, Webster, stood patiently by, grazing, awaiting his master. Jesse quietly took hold of his bridle and led him off some distance before mounting. Elias cantered casually ahead. They were followed, in ones and twos, by the unmarried young men of Dunning's Creek Meeting, bound for "Saratoga," bent on having some fun.

In those days I missed little that concerned my brother and nothing that concerned Elias Finley, so I took due note of their departure. I loved a good race myself, unseemly as that might have been, but I couldn't conceive of a good excuse to slip away. So I stayed at the party, refilling the dishes and helping the Finley girls (there were four others besides Rebecca) keep the food coming.

I saw Smith, Weaver and Miller Hartley, who had missed the wedding but not the feed, wander off after the young men. They were quick to gamble, so I was sure they'd be taking bets. As I brought out another platter of chicken, I noticed Pru standing near the barn, watching the goings on. Gathering gossip, I'd bet. She smiled and waved almost gaily to me, though I couldn't see what she was so joyful about. She wasn't even invited.

About forty-five minutes later, quietly, almost abashedly, the boys were back, but there was no shouting, taunting or celebrating. Something had happened. I watched Jesse whisper to Uncle Sammy Grainger. I couldn't hear what he said, but I knew it was serious.

I stood by, waiting for Jesse to notice me, but he didn't. He went from Uncle Sammy to Papa, spoke softly to him, and walked back to where the horses were tied. Ben's Webster was the only riding horse in the family, and he would be needed to carry the bridal couple home, so Jesse climbed into Papa's wagon and drove the team quietly out of the yard. Consumed with curiosity, I hitched up my skirts and ran alongside.

"Jesse! What is it?"

"Go back to the wedding, Ann. This doesn't concern you."

His firm countenance discouraged me, so I slowed my pace and turned back toward the party. As I walked in front of the tethered horses, Elias Finley stepped down from his mount and flipped the reins over the rail fence.

"Elias? What's wrong with Jesse?" I asked, delighted at the chance to talk to Elias alone about anything.

"Negroes. Four of 'em, sittin' on a log across the creek, lookin' for a hook up."

"Hook up?"

"A ride on the Underground Railroad."

I knew of it. There was a lot of talk at meeting about helping escaped slaves. I knew the Friends were involved, but speech was guarded and specifics kept secret. They'd say arrivals were expected on third day or fourth day. Help was needed— someone to make a delivery to Johnstown or Claysburg. Nothing more. So while I knew of it, my knowledge was vague.

"What has Jesse to do with that?" I asked.

Elias shrugged. "Hey, got any more of that sour cream pie?" he asked.

Happy to be the focus of his attention, I led him off in the direction of the dessert table, so delighted to have him all to myself, I was tongue-tied.

"You're pretty quiet today," he smiled as he finished his pie, taking my hand in his. I drew my hand away, afraid that Papa might see and consider it unseemly.

"So you and Ben are going to be partners," I said, finding my tongue.

Elias smiled. "That we are." He looked around at the crowded party. "Would you like to take a walk?"

My heart fluttered. Of course I'd like to take a walk. We ambled out the lane toward Enos Conley's woodlot and sat down under a budding oak tree. I watched the gentle breeze ruffle Elias's hair, sending a thrill through me. I spent most of my time with him trying in vain to think of something to say, but Elias seemed to understand and kept up a stream of comfortable conversation.

"We plan to use my working pair to start a breeding line. Ben will be the caretaker and trainer, and I'll be the breeder and seller," he explained.

Elias was so absorbed in the plans for his business ventures, he talked steadily for about an hour. I listened and exclaimed appropriately, truly swept away by the possibilities.

As the shadows lengthened, he rose and helped me to my feet. Taking my hand in both of his, he looked into my eyes.

"I hope this venture with Ben leads to success," he said, "so I can follow in his footsteps in more ways than one." Not a specific promise, but all the assurance I needed to set my mind to planning.

"Oh, Elias. I hope so, too."

As we returned to the wedding party, he tucked my hand over his arm. I basked in the joy of being seen as the object of Elias's affection, and hoped that someday I would play Rebecca's role and Elias Ben's. Our keeping company gave rise among the wedding guests to speculation about another "Redfield-Finley" match, even though we were most likely years from it.

As we rejoined the wedding party I saw Pru Hartley walking off through the woodlot, bold as brass, with a plateful of ham and chicken. Mrs. Finley'd likely never see the plate again, either.

We Redfields hitched a ride home with Uncle Sammy Grainger, since Ben was otherwise occupied, and Jesse wasn't back yet with the wagon. Evening was upon us and the talk was quiet and sparse. There was no sign of Jesse at the house.

Everyone else was bent on retiring, so they didn't notice me slip out the back door and across the yard to the barn. It was dark, but I could hear the heavy breathing of the horses, so I knew Jesse was back. But where was he?

As I turned to leave, I heard a sound like someone bumping his head on a beam. Thunk. It came from the hay mow, so I slipped across to the ladder and called. "Jesse?"

No reply. But I was sure I'd heard it. I set my foot on the ladder and began to climb. As my head came level with the hay mow floor, I stopped, at eye level with Jesse's boots.

"Don't come up here, Ann," he said firmly.

I couldn't keep myself from looking around. The mow was almost pitch black, but I sensed a presence. There was someone else there besides Jesse and me. "Jesse, what is it?"

"Just get down and go into the house. Forget you were ever out here," he said.

"Jesse, is it slaves?"

He stooped down and took me by the shoulders. "Ann, you must obey. Go back to the house. Tell no one you were out here. Now go!"

I backed down the ladder, turned and ran toward the doorway, Jesse's rejection stinging my pride. My heart raced in my chest. Jesse was involved with the Underground Railroad! The realization overwhelmed my other thoughts. I knew it. He was hiding those slaves they'd discovered down by the creek. Pride mingled with fear in my heart. Oh, Jesse. Be careful.

I quietly climbed the stairs and stepped past Nathaniel, already snoring in his bed. In the girls' room I undressed in the dark. Betsy was asleep, but Rachel whispered, "What were you doing outside, Ann? Mooning over Elias Finley?"

"Yes, something like that."

The night was quiet, and I drifted in and out of a light sleep. I heard the wagon pull out of the barn after midnight. I heard it return before dawn. At first light, I got up and dressed, quietly so as not to wake the family. I noted Jesse's empty bed and crept down the stairs. Papa snored loudly in his bed in the back corner of the kitchen. I lifted the latch and stepped out into the morning dew.

Hurrying toward the barn, I vowed to find out what Jesse was up to—how deeply he was involved. This was too dangerous. Let others take the risks. Not my brother.

As I arrived at the barn, the door opened and Jesse stepped out, smiling.

"Good morning, Sister," he said.

"Good morning, Brother."

"Let's have some breakfast."

Chapter 3

1854

So Jesse was in it. He worked hard on the farm—made sure he put in his fair share—but his mind was someplace else. Thinking how he could fight the abomination. I worried for him, but he kept his own counsel. Didn't want any of the rest of us involved. That chafed me. I wanted to know and do and help. Still, life went on as usual at Redfield Farm—to outward appearances, at least.

Amos was not a man given to change. He moved slowly, thought much and acted with deliberation. So it came as a surprise when, one evening in 1854, he announced at dinner that he intended to "build on."

"Build on to what?" Jesse asked, with a wink at us girls. "The barn?"

"The house," Amos replied, ignoring Jesse's teasing.

We three daughters looked at one another in disbelief. Rachel was first to respond. "Oh, Papa! How fine!"

Amos smiled at her. Rachel's opinion always seemed important to him.

Jesse was still puzzled. "Why? Why now?"

"We might be needing a bigger house. One of you might wish to marry and stay here. Take over the farm."

"Oh." Jesse understood that meant him. "I see." It was no secret that Jesse thought about going west, as so many from the Quaker settlement had done. He longed to see what was out there, beyond the Alleghenies.

I smiled to myself, knowing full well Jesse's need to move on. That was what had so far prevented him from settling down

21

and taking a wife, even at twenty-eight. If Jesse followed his dreams west, maybe, just maybe, Elias Finley and I could marry and live in a fine new house. Heaven knew, Rachel and Betsy would marry any day. Will McKitrick fairly fell over himself to be at Betsy's side after Meeting, so an announcement would likely come soon. There were suitors aplenty for Rachel, too. She could take her pick if she ever settled down enough to decide. That was Rachel. Too busy being Rachel.

Nathaniel sat looking at his plate. At twenty, he had no plans about life. So far he had been well taken care of, first by Mama, then by his sisters. Like Amos, he was not one to initiate change and slow to accept it.

"What kind of building on?" he asked, skeptical.

"Two story—big parlor for family gatherings, two upstairs bedrooms. This old cabin will be the kitchen. The loft rooms could still be used. I might like one of them myself." Amos had slept in the main room of the cabin all his life. On a rope bed in the corner. "The rest of you can decide who gets what."

So it was that simple. Prosperity had caught up with the Redfields. Building had to be done in summer, so at the next Meeting it was announced that Amos Redfield was building on, and help was needed when the haying was done.

On July ninth, twenty or so men and boys from the Quaker settlement turned up at Redfield Farm. Amos, Jesse and Nathaniel joined them, and in two days a two story log house was neatly joined to the east end of the old cabin. A week later, a smaller crew came to cover the roof frame with white oak splits.

My sisters and I wore ourselves out cooking and feeding the workers, including, of course, Elias Finley and Will McKitrick. It was a joyous time, full of fun and promise. As I was laying out food on a plank table in the yard, Elias, up on the roof, stopped nailing shingles to call to me.

"Got any more of that peach cobbler, like last time?"

I shaded my eyes to look up at him, smiled and nodded. "Probably not enough for you, Elias Finley."

"I've got a powerful hunger for peach cobbler," he grinned.

Down on the ground, hefting a bundle of shingles to his shoulder, Jesse called, "You've got a powerful hunger for all Ann's cooking, Elias."

"I know a good thing when I see one," came the reply. "And I see one," he continued, smiling down at me.

I blushed and turned back toward the kitchen. Honestly! Elias could be so bold at times, yet he was awfully slow to make a commitment. We were both twenty-six and not getting any younger. What was he waiting for? Everyone in the Quaker settlement paired us off in their minds, but still Elias dallied. I was sure a proposal would come, but when? If asked, Elias said he didn't have much to offer a wife. But he and Ben were building a fine horse breeding business. He had a bright future. I consoled myself with thinking it would be worth the wait.

The morning after the shingles were put on, I looked out the back door to see Pru Hartley standing by the springhouse, one hand on her hip, looking over the new house. That girl moved like an apparition. I never knew where she'd turn up.

"Mornin' Pru. You need something?"

"Not that I kin git here," she replied, her head cocked to the side. "You Redfields'll be gittin' uppity now, I guess."

"Uppity? Why?"

"Fancy new house'n all." She sneered when she said it, like it tasted bad.

I didn't feel like standing around listening to Pru Hartley's assessment of my family, so I turned and went inside. The men were doing morning chores in the barn, and my sisters were still upstairs. Pru stayed in the yard, walked all the way around the house with her head cocked in that put-on haughty way she had. I went back to my work but looked out the window now and then to see where she was, hoping she'd be gone.

Then she came up on the porch and shouted. "You think yer better'n some folk, but yer not! With your big, new house'n all. S'pose you think Elias Finley's gonna marry you? Would've by now if he was gonna. That's my guess!"

Why did she love to plague me so? Why was it her mission to bring me misery? I was tempted to answer her. To ask why she was older than I by a year, had two babies and no husband in sight. But it would just bring more wrath on me, so I closed the door to keep her noise outside. Rachel wandered downstairs, holding her ears.

"Sounds like Pru is full of the 'Old Harry' this morning," she observed.

"I don't know what gets into her. She seems bent on making my life miserable."

"She's miserable herself. Has little to do with you, Sister. You're just a convenient target."

I sighed. "Well, I wish she'd take her misery and be gone. I could do without her."

Now Betsy made her entrance. "What's Pru nattering about now?" she yawned.

Outside, Pru still stood on the porch, bare feet wide apart, elbows akimbo, looking defiant. Amos, Jesse and Nathaniel started in from the barn, talking among themselves. When she saw them, Pru turned and stepped off the porch, hiked up her skirts and all but ran down the hill.

The addition stood tall and large, dwarfing the old cabin. Jesse and Nathaniel chinked the logs to match the old part, and once that was done the whole place looked like it had always been so. The next step was plaster—both the old and new parts.

Plastering was an art, done by hire. For country houses, there was usually an itinerant plasterer looking for work and a place to stay until the job was done.

Amos let it be known he was looking for a plasterer, and within a day one came to the door. His name was Jacob Schilling, of German stock, from Dauphin County.

"What brings you west?" Amos asked.

"I follow the work," was the reply. "If the next job is north, I'll go north. They tell me there's work at Altoona. Brand new city sprung up to service the railroad. Lots of new houses being built. That's where I'm figuring on going from here."

Amos nodded. He showed Jacob Schilling the new addition and explained what he wanted done. They settled on a price, then Amos showed him to quarters in the tack room of the barn.

We three girls watched from the doorway as Jacob Schilling tended to his horse. We all found the handsome young stranger interesting, but none more than Rachel.

"Did you see the muscles in his arms?" she asked. "They fairly ripple!"

"Rachel! Quaker girls do not notice or comment on men's muscles!"

"Some do," Rachel replied saucily. "Oh, Ann. I'm just having fun. You noticed, too. I know you did."

I admitted, reluctantly—to myself—that I had, indeed, noticed, but not in the silly, breathless way Rachel had.

"I worry about you, Rachel. You're too quick to speak and too bold with strangers. I hope it comes to naught, but I worry."

Rachel laughed and tossed her head. "Life is too short to worry," she replied. Little did she know.

Turned out I wasn't wrong to worry. Rachel found Mr. Schilling interesting to the point of irresistibility, and she made up any excuse to be where he was. Rachel, who flitted about from one suitor to another, was fixed on Jacob Schilling. She watched him work; she took him snacks and drinks; she sat across from him at table and listened to his talk as though she'd never heard English before. They took to walking out after supper, long walks in the summer twilight. After the second walk, they came back holding hands, and one evening I saw dried grass clinging to the back of her dress.

I understood her infatuation. Mr. Schilling was worldly compared to the men we knew. He'd grown up north of Harrisburg but wanted none of farm life. He'd even been married before. His wife of two years had died in childbirth. The baby was being raised by Jacob's parents. His wife's death put the wanderlust in Jacob, and he took his trade out to see the world.

Oh, he was attractive, all right. Bright, personable, talkative. I could see it, but still I feared for my sister. If this led to marriage, well,. *No!* Quaker women knew that to marry a non-Quaker was to be disowned by the Society. Rachel wouldn't want that. Besides, what would Papa say? Surely these goings on hadn't escaped his notice.

The plastering took two weeks, during which Rachel was never there for chores, during which Rachel couldn't see or hear anything that was not Jacob Schilling, during which I felt more than a little jealous and more than a little overworked. I worried over and—just a little—resented my sister.

When the work was done, Amos paid Jacob Schilling, and he rode away north, toward Altoona. Rachel was strangely serene at his departure. Relieved at the removal of temptation, I tried to reassert my position as female head of the household.

"There's spinning to be done," I told Rachel the next morning. "Betsy and I are going to wash clothes."

Rachel didn't respond, nor did she spin. She sat around dreamily all day, avoiding my eyes and making a show of writing a letter that I could only presume was to Jacob.

That evening, sitting on the back porch, I shared my frustration with Jesse. "What is she thinking, Jesse? How can she be so silly? Jacob Schilling goes from job to job, loving girls along the way."

"She's twenty-four years old and a woman, Ann. You can't make her over, no matter how hard you try. If she wants Jacob and Jacob wants her, you'll have to accept it. You can't run around protecting her from herself."

I looked down over the hill to Dunning's Creek, misty in the twilight. "I know you're right, but it's hard to stop myself. She's always been a little dithery. You know, so light hearted and happy, one wonders if she really understands what life is about. I worry what a bad match might do to her."

"You can't know it'll be a bad match. It will be what it will be. Besides, he's gone. If you're right about him, she may never hear from him again."

The following Saturday, Jacob Schilling drove up to Redfield Farm in a livery wagon. Showing no surprise, Rachel raced out to meet him, and, as he stepped down from the wagon, fell into his embrace.

"I've come for you," he told her, loud enough for all to hear.

Amos stepped out to confront them. "What's this?" he asked.

"I've come to take Rachel with me, Amos. To make her my wife."

"That's not the way we do things here. Thee have never even asked my permission to court. It takes months to complete a Quaker marriage. Thee hardly know each other."

"We know enough. We'll have no Quaker marriage. We'll go today and be married by a preacher on the way to Altoona."

Amos looked from Schilling to Rachel. "Thee must go inside now. This is men's business." He spoke calmly.

Rachel went to him, reached up and touched his rough, weathered cheek. "I'm sorry, Papa, but I'm going with Jacob."

"Thee will be read out of meeting!" Amos shouted, coming to the end of his patience. "Now go, girl, before I thrash thee!"

I winced. Papa had never raised a hand to any of us. We obeyed out of respect for him, not fear.

Jacob stepped forward, taking Rachel by the wrist. "She is grown, sir. Her own woman. The world is changing, and you must change with it."

He led Rachel to the wagon; she sat up proud, even as a tear found its way down her cheek. Jacob turned to address Jesse, standing behind Amos. "Help me with her trunk?"

"No."

Jacob looked then at Nathaniel. He shook his head.

"All right. I'll get it myself." He stalked across the yard and into the house. Rachel jumped down and raced after him. A few minutes later they came out, lugging the heavy trunk between them. Hefting it up into the wagon almost proved too much for Jacob, but still my father and brothers stood rooted in the dooryard. Jacob climbed up beside Rachel, put an arm around her shoulders and snapped the reins over the horses' rumps.

I watched the wagon disappear down the road. 'And now we are five,' I thought. 'And soon, fewer yet.' I flipped my apron up over my head to hide my tears and went into the house. Betsy followed me, and the men went to the barn.

From that day on, Amos Redfield never liked the new house. He didn't move to one of the loft rooms of the old cabin. He kept his rope bed in the kitchen. One month later, Rachel Redfield was read out of meeting "for marriage by a priest."

Betsy and I each took one of the new bedrooms above the parlor, using the new stairs to come and go. The old cabin, with its uneven floors and curved stairway was left to the men, Nathaniel and Jesse each with a loft room and Papa in the kitchen. Except for cooking and eating, we women spent much of our time in the new part.

As the summer waned, Jesse seemed restless. He didn't sit still for long. Sometimes he slept in the barn or went off alone without so much as a by-your-leave. I suspected he was moving fugitives again, but I kept my peace and Jesse his. Then, one day, he brought in wood and carpenter's tools from the barn.

"I'm going to fix up the little loft room," he announced. He fitted the space under the eaves on both sides with low walls and doors for storage, ending up with a small but airy rectangular room, reaching to the roofline, with a little window on each side of the chimney. He whitewashed the walls, and I found him a braided oval rug for the floor. He bought a bedstead, table and rocking chair at a sale.

It was a cheerful room, but I was puzzled by this domestic turn in a man who cared little for comforts and not at all for beauty. Maybe he was planning to marry after all. Maybe his dreams of going west had died.

Jesse's intentions in partitioning off his room would make sense to me in mid-September when he stumbled home just before dawn one morning after a three day absence, fevered and wild-eyed. Awakened by his arrival, I took a lantern to meet him in the dooryard.

"Jesse! Where have you been?" I held the light aloft and looked into his pale, flushed face. "What's wrong with you?"

"Don't ask," he replied flatly. "Help me to bed. I'm sick."

Leaning heavily on me, he climbed the stairs to the loft, his breath hot on my neck.

"Nathaniel!" he said hoarsely, standing over our sleeping brother.

Nate stirred in his sleep, turned over and slowly woke to the lantern light casting huge shadows on the wall. "Huh? What's goin' on?" He squinted.

"There's a delivery in the wagon outside. Take care of it and the horses," Jesse whispered, his eyes dazed.

Nathaniel rose immediately, pulled on his trousers and boots, and descended sleepily into the kitchen. I heard the door close as I helped Jesse to the bed. He fell heavily, his breathing raspy. I pulled off his clothes, perspiring from the effort even though the room was cold.

"Don't cover me," Jesse protested. "I'm burning up."

As I hurried downstairs to brew a tea for his fever, I was met in the kitchen by Papa and Nathaniel.

"Ann," said Amos. "Thee must help. There is another sick."

I looked from Papa to Nate, then out the window to the barn. No further explanation was needed. I knew.

Chapter 4

1854 – Fall

Jesse's **fever raged for days.** He wavered in and out of consciousness while I worried over him, tried to make him comfortable, tried to figure out what ailed him. Out in the barn, the black man lay just as ill. Tending them both was a huge task, but it was clear that no one else should be exposed, both for the risk of disease and the risk of discovery. The sole responsibility fell to me, and my experience with illness was limited. The Redfields were a healthy lot, isolation doing its part to protect us from most things that went around.

For more reasons than one, I felt it best for Betsy to go stay with Mary for a while, so Amos hitched up the team that first morning and drove her over to Osterburg himself. He returned around noon, solemn faced and looking wary.

"We'd best leave the man in the barn for now. He seems right sick. He should be passed along tonight, but we don't have a choice. We'll have to keep him until he's well. Anything else would be murder, to him and maybe others."

I nodded. I was preoccupied with Jesse, but once I'd done all I could to make him comfortable, I went to the barn with an armload of quilts and a kettle of hot water. I wanted to move the man onto a thicker pile of hay for more warmth and comfort, but he was too sick to move himself and too big for me to move, so I covered him with the quilts and forced some feverfew tea into him.

Jesse lay deathly ill for days. I feared so for him. Why did he do these things? Get himself into such dire straits? He could just as well mind his own business. Come and go on the farm and to Meeting. Why did he have to go looking for trouble? When his fever finally broke, he was still too weak to get up.

The slave's fever raged on. I did my best to make him comfortable in the barn where it was easier to hide him. One never knew when visitors might come to the house, or when Pru Hartley would wander by, watching. Jesse had shivered and shaken quietly, but this one was given to moaning and thrashing. He was too sick to speak, but I felt the fear and helplessness in his eyes as he drifted in and out of consciousness.

After more than a week, when he was well enough to talk, Jesse asked, "How's the Negro?"

"Still awful sick. His fever hasn't broken. All I can say is, he isn't dead yet."

"Can you get him into the house?" It took about all of his strength to say that little.

"I don't know how, if he can't walk. He's terrible sick, Jesse. Sicker than you, even."

"Get Nathaniel to help you. The nights are too cold in the barn. He needs to be in here." He laid his head back on the pillow and rested.

"Where can we put him? I'll have my hands full keeping him quiet."

Jesse nodded weakly toward the storage space he'd built in his bedroom. "Put him in there."

I looked at the solid wall on the south side. "Where?"

Jesse pointed, and I ran my fingers along the wall, until I felt a catch under the molding. I slipped it aside and two of the wide boards swung out, revealing a space large enough for a man to crawl through. The hinges were neatly concealed, and no knob betrayed its presence. So that was the reason for Jesse's 'fixing up!'

After dinner that evening, under cover of darkness, Nathaniel and I went to the barn and told the man we were moving him to the house.

"I'se grateful," he mumbled. "It so cold here. You sure it safe?" It was the first time anything sensible had come out of him.

Nate nodded as we lifted him into a sitting position, then to his knees. He was a strapping young man in his late twenties or early thirties. He leaned heavily on Nathaniel and twice nearly collapsed before I could get my shoulder under his other arm. Together we half carried, half dragged him across the yard and into the house. Truly he was sicker than Jesse.

Getting him up the narrow, curved staircase and through Nathaniel's room to Jesse's was almost more than Nathaniel and I could manage. I'd made a pallet on the floor under the eaves, and when we laid the man down, his heavy breathing filled the room. As long as there was no one around, we kept the passage open for light and heat. I did what I could to make him comfortable, but his condition stayed as it was, wavering between life and death. I feared the move might bring an end to him.

Jesse stayed in bed for several more days, and I waved off visitors with warnings of the fever. We didn't know what to name the illness, but we knew it was bad. I felt a little hot and light headed myself, but that was probably because I was so tired.

One frosty morning, as I went to the springhouse, I was caught up quick by the sight of Pru Hartley, bent beneath a load of firewood, walking up the road.

"Mornin', Pru," I said without enthusiasm, hoping she wouldn't stop to talk. She did. Lowering her load, she looked at me in that sidelong way she had, making me wish I'd slipped into the springhouse unnoticed.

"Mornin', Ann. How's Jesse? I hear tell he's ailin'."

"Getting better now, but it might be catching. Better stay back."

"Uh huh." She stood beside the load of wood, holding her back in a peculiar way. Even under her heavy cloak, I could tell she was with child.

"Pru, are you expecting another baby?"

"Looks like it, don't it?"

"Shouldn't someone else be toting that wood for you?"

"Who would you suggest? One of my brothers? My Pa? Ain't likely." She bent down to rearrange the wood. "House is cold. Pa's drunk. Brothers is gone—sleepin' wherever they can. No one to do fer 'em but me."

It occurred to me to give her a gentle lecture on the fruits of the choices she'd made, but I decided against it. She wouldn't listen anyway.

"You go on home. I'll send Nathaniel down with a load of wood this afternoon."

She brightened. "Now, that's right neighborly of you. I sure could use the help." Then, true to her nature, she added, "Not bein' rich, like you."

My budding compassion faded and I stepped into the spring house as Pru lifted her burden and set out for home.

The Hartleys were part of the landscape of our lives. Rad was a 'good for nothing', as Papa said, and he'd sired ten more like himself. His wife had been pretty once, according to Aunt Alice Grainger, but ten children, though they hadn't killed her, had worn her down. She faded away so gradually, died so quietly, folks hardly noticed, five years ago. Rad went on as before, bingeing and recovering, bingeing and recovering.

The three oldest boys had places of their own, if you could call them that. Smith, the oldest, lived with his wife's folks down by the millpond. Weaver survived doing odd jobs and taking care of the Friends Cemetery. He lived in a shack at the edge of the graveyard with his wife and half a houseful of young ones. Even 'Fallen Away' Quakers were taken care of by the Friends. Miller Hartley came as close as any of them to being of some account. He boarded with Franklin Adams, working on their farm, and, some said, fixing to marry into the family as soon as Frank's oldest daughter, Eve, was ripe. The two youngest boys, Cooper and Sawyer, still lived at home and worked out— whatever odd jobs came their way and didn't disturb their rest.

Pru was the youngest; all four of her older sisters were married and gone. Truth, Honesty, Faith and Charity were scattered about the county, producing babies at an alarming rate, giving whole communities pause about being overrun with 'Hartleys', as the children were known, whatever their last names happened to be.

I watched Pru's progress down over the hill with a mixture of pity and discomfort. There was no changing some people, but it was still hard to understand how they could let themselves get so low. I turned back up the path to the house.

&

"What is this sickness? How did you get it?" I asked Jesse when he was well enough to make any sense.

"In the last station, the whole family was down with it. They thought to get the Negro out before he caught it, and he seemed all right when we left, but he started to cough almost as soon as we were on the road," Jesse explained.

"I got there early in the afternoon the day before, so I'd look like a visitor, but some slave catchers were seen in the neighborhood, so I stayed another day. I was afraid of getting sick but more afraid of the slave catchers." He shook his head.

"I started feeling sick about two in the morning on the way home, but he was already shaking from the chills. I knew we were in trouble."

I felt Jesse's forehead. "If he doesn't get well soon, it'll be too late to send him on. Then what'll we do?"

"Whatever we have to do. First, get him well. Then we'll worry about what's next."

Jesse rallied slowly, staying abed for more than two weeks. One morning, I heard a horse ride up and looked out the window to see Elias Finley dismount. I hurried to the dooryard to head him off.

"Morning, Elias."

"Morning, Ann. Where's Jesse? Haven't seen much of him lately."

"Stay back, Elias. Jesse's sick with a fever. I don't want you to catch it."

"Sounds serious."

34

"It is. Cough, chills, aches. Very sick. We missed First Day Meeting the last two weeks, and we'll miss this week, too, I'm guessing. We don't want to pass it around."

Elias frowned. "No. Guess not." Then he smiled at me. "Looks like you've got your hands full."

I returned his smile. "Yes. We sent Betsy out as soon as Jesse fell ill, so I'm the only one to do it all."

"You look tired."

"I am."

"Well, I just came to tell you and Jesse that I'm going to Chambersburg to stay with a friend of my Uncle James for a while. He has a fine horse farm where I can learn something about breeding. Maybe go on a few buying trips with him. Ben and I need some brood mares."

"Oh, Elias, that sounds fine! How long will you be?"

"A couple of months, maybe. I'll write to you. I should be back before Christmas." He smiled. "I'll miss you, Ann."

"Me, too. It's a long time to be away."

"I know, but if I get what I hope to, it'll be worth it."

His smile contained a promise—or it was just that I wanted it to? "You take care, Elias. You'll be in my thoughts and prayers."

"Yes, and you in mine." He stood there, hat in hand, maybe twenty feet away, looking uncomfortable, as though there was something else he wanted to say. "I'd best be going, then."

"Yes. Good-bye, Elias. Godspeed. Don't forget me." It was a hollow plea, considering how I felt. Empty at the prospect of long days without him.

He turned, his left foot poised in the stirrup. "I could never forget you, Ann."

The words sent a thrill through me. I loved Elias Finley. I always had. He was slow in his ways, but I knew deep inside that he was the man for me. Time was fleeting, but ahead lay the promise of a shared life, a home, babies, maybe even a measure of wealth. I watched him mount his horse, turn and ride out of the dooryard, his shoulders square against the sky.

A trickle of joy began in my feet and spread to my face. I felt warm all over..

Back in the house, I worked in the kitchen, giving myself leave to think about Elias. Sad that he'd be gone so long, but hopeful that his return would bring what I most longed for. I felt like a schoolgirl, all silly and breathless. It was childish, but my dreams overwhelmed me sometimes.

"Ann!" It was Jesse.

"Coming!" Lifting my skirts, I climbed the steep, narrow stairs.

"What is it?"

"He's awake. He's asking for water."

I quickly filled a glass from the pitcher and bent down to crawl into the hiding place. The black man stared as though he'd never seen me before.

"Who you?" he asked.

"Ann Redfield," I replied. "Who are you?"

"Josiah."

"Well, Josiah, you've been mighty sick. It's good to hear you speak. Where did you come from?"

"Virginny. Culpeper County." He pulled himself up on one elbow and drank the glass dry. "More, please."

I struggled out on my knees to refill the glass.

"Where we at?" Josiah asked, peering around under the eaves.

"Bedford County, Pennsylvania." He seemed relieved at that. "That far from Canada?"

"Yes. Pretty far. But you're out of slave territory at least."

"What day this be?"

"Friday, September 29, 1854."

"September? I disremember September."

"You've been sick most of the month. When did you leave Culpeper County?"

"Late July. Saturday night. Wouldn't be missed 'til Monday mornin'." The effort to speak was already taking its toll. He lay back down. Then, feebly, "You Friends?"

"Yes, Josiah. We're Friends."

He closed his eyes and almost immediately went back to sleep. He slept more than he was awake for the next week, and I was gratified to get nourishment into him. His strength slowly returned to where he could stand on his own.

The sickness was diphtheria, I learned when I described it to Aunt Alice Grainger at Meeting. Both men were lucky to have survived. I guessed we'd stopped its spread by staying home. Amos wasn't affected by it. Nathaniel struggled through a mild case, and, if I got it at all, I could barely distinguish it from fatigue.

When Amos brought Betsy back in mid-October, I was hard pressed to hide my relief. "I've been starved for someone to talk to," I told her, "and for help with the work."

Betsy had to be let in on the 'secret' because the 'secret' was still there roaming the house by day and under the eaves in Jesse's room by night.

Her reaction was complete surprise. "You mean we're part of the Underground Railroad? I knew some Friends did it, but I'd no idea my own family . . . Ann! How long have you known about this?" She looked from Jesse to me in disbelief.

"For sure since I was nineteen, but I suspected Jesse for quite a while before that," I said, looking sidelong at him.

Jesse nodded. "I conducted my first passenger when I was seventeen." His answer wasn't prideful. He wasn't one to brag.

"Why, I never dreamed!" Betsy exclaimed, her face pale at the thought of such goings on right here in her own house.

"You're a pretty heavy sleeper, then, sister," Jesse laughed. "It's harder to get things past Ann."

"Who else does this?" Betsy wanted to know. "Are the McKitricks in it?"

"Sorry, Betsy, but the fewer people who know, the better. And the less *you* know, the better." He ducked through the doorway and up the stairs to the loft. That was all he would say.

Betsy, sensible and reliable, took his answer to heart and left the matter at that. Then she took my hand and whispered a new secret to me.

"Will is going to ask Papa for permission to court," she confided, giggling.

"Really? Oh, Betsy! How soon?"

"First day. After Meeting." Her face, always open and easy to read, revealed her delight.

"That means you'll be marrying soon." I picked up a ball of yarn and my knitting needles. I couldn't believe my baby sister was talking about marrying.

"By spring, I hope."

Happy for Betsy, I decided to share as well. "I've a secret, too. Elias has gone to Chambersburg to learn breeding and buy some stock. When he comes home, I'm hoping he'll ask Papa to court, too!"

"Oh, Ann! We could be getting married at the same time!" Betsy laughed. "Whatever will Papa and the boys do? Who will take care of these three helpless men?"

"Somebody needs a wife," I said, loudly enough for Jesse to hear.

"Who!" came the call from the upstairs room.

"You!" We chorused together.

Chapter 5

Winter came early that year. Strong winds from the northwest blew the leaves off the trees by the end of October. In early November, an unseasonable cold settled in, accompanied by gray skies and daily snow flurries. Jesse came in with an all-black wooly-bear caterpillar crawling slowly up his sleeve, signaling a long hard winter.

Work about the farm continued as usual, but with four men to care for and only Betsy to help, some things went wanting. Skutching flax and spinning happened only after the baking, cooking and washing were done. Cleaning was catch as catch can. Betsy was a help, but I didn't blame her if her hands followed her heart and led her to fine stitching pillow cases and linens for her trunk when there was other work to be done. I tried to find time to help her, but short days and little light left sparse time for sewing.

One morning Betsy voiced her regrets. "I'm sorry, Ann. I don't mean to leave it all to you, but my heart isn't in it anymore. All I can think of is making a home for Will." She sat on the floor by her open trunk, fingering a set of fine linen pillow slips she'd made.

I touched her shoulder. "It's all right, Sister. I'd feel the same if it were me." Leaving her there, I stepped into my room, straightened the bed and hustled downstairs to the parlor. A quick survey there added more chores to my list: clean out the stove, trim the wicks, wash the lamp chimneys, sweep the carpet. I sighed. The work was endless.

In the kitchen, Jesse sat in a chair, feet up, comfortable as a count. "Annie, when you're sitting around here with nothing to do, could you mend my saddle for me?"

I laughed, glad to have the old tease back to himself. "Surely, Brother. I'll put that on my list—just after I build a new pig sty. Don't you have aught to do but torment me today?"

"Thought I'd go visiting. Go see Ike Miller—find out what they've heard from Simon. Maybe stop by Mrs. Downing's and praise her pies," he said with a wink.

"You, Jesse! Left up to you, I'd never have to bake another pie!"

He plopped his hat on his head. "I do what I can!"

I shook my head, recognizing the truth in what he said. Jesse was a favorite in the Quaker settlement. A gadabout in winter, hardly a day went by that he didn't saddle up a horse or hitch up the sleigh to go visiting. First Day after Meeting, people were drawn to him. Those who weren't talking to him talked to me or Amos about him.

"He's a handsome one! Be bedding someone soon, I'll warrant!" one old lady whispered to me, as though I were a fellow conspirator.

"A man of principle, not a reed swaying in the wind," was John Barrister's assessment of him.

When Jesse rose to speak at Meeting, the congregation fell silent. He spoke his mind with urgency and a sense of duty that inspired. He could harangue the lot of them and make them like it, because he matched his conviction with action.

After Meeting he was just Jesse, smiling and teasing the girls, bouncing a baby on his knee, wide and generous with his compliments. At least a half dozen young hearts fluttered when he entered a room, and he took care to provide each with a bit of conversation to be taken home, savored and remembered. That Jesse!

Ever the serious Redfield, I envied the ease and lightness with which he moved among the Friends. Strange it wasn't a sister I was closest to, but this brother. While I envied his charm, I knew it hid conviction as hard as Pennsylvania limestone. I wondered if his desire to go west would win out, or would his dedication to the work keep him until it was too late?

He placed a hand on my shoulder, interrupting my thoughts. "Where is everybody?"

"Nate's in the parlor working the accounts again."

Jesse grinned. "I wonder at our little brother."

I knew what he meant. Nathaniel was meticulous by nature, given to keeping records and trying new ways to make the farm profitable.

"I guess if anyone can make this rocky little farm prosper, it'll be Nathaniel." Solitary. Taciturn. Methodical. Like Amos.

"Should I go steal his inkwell?" Jesse was forever trying to put some spunk into Nate. "Where's Pa?"

"Out tearing down the old corncrib. Sawyer Hartley's helping him."

"Sawyer shows some inclination to work now and then. Wonder where that came from," Jesse grinned.

He cut a generous piece of pie and sat down with his hat on to watch me work. Seeing he was in no hurry, I stopped sweeping to bring up what was on my mind. "What about Josiah?"

"What about him?"

"He's about as happy as a crated rooster. I wish we could move him on. Somebody's bound to find out. Loose tongues, you know." I watched Jesse's face. "And with the Hartleys always snooping around. Fine end to things if *they* catch wind of it."

"I think he may be almost whole, but we can't chance sending him on with this weather and the possibility of getting caught," he replied between bites of pie. "The roads are full of slave catchers who'd sell their firstborn for a few dollars. We're breaking the law, Ann, and there are many, including some of our neighbors, who'd be glad of a chance to enforce it."

I shuddered, remembering Charlie Marsh and Rad Hartley promising to help those two poor slaves and then turning them over to the slave catcher for a paltry twenty dollars. The act had brought scorn upon them, and nobody mourned when Charlie was shot a few years later in a fight over a woman. Rad was still around, drunk most of the time and disrespected to the point of poverty. Much good his twenty dollars had done him.

"But Jesse, we can't keep him here all winter!"

"We can if we have to. To send him out now would be murder. We'll hide him as long as we must."

I fretted over keeping Josiah a secret. He hid under the eaves when anyone came, but had the freedom of the house the rest of the time, as long as he stayed away from the windows. Still, it was uncomfortable for me.

"What if someone comes along suddenly? Someone on foot?"

"He can stay close to the stairs and a make quick getaway. It isn't fun, but it's safe enough. Just watch what you say. Don't let anything slip." Jesse took it all in stride. Nothing bothered him.

The Quaker settlement was close-knit, especially in winter. People visited almost daily, often staying the night if the weather got bad. On those nights, Josiah was confined to his tiny hideout. We kept to our routines, so not even best friends knew the workings of the Railroad, but it troubled me. I ducked inside when I saw anyone coming and longed for a return to normal when I could visit with a neighbor without a care.

In spite of this tension, Josiah proved amiable company. He took his meals with us, sitting at the end of the table nearest the stairs, always ready for a quick escape. I even mentally practiced removing the extra plate before opening the door when someone knocked. Josiah tried to help with whatever work there was, inside or out. Of course, he couldn't help outside during the day, but after dark he often went to the barn to help Jesse and Nathaniel milk, feed and bed down the animals. He was generally cheerful, though not much given to idle talk.

His curiosity about Pennsylvania and Quaker beliefs led to a lot of questions. I think he found us a little strange but was too polite to say so.

"Ma'am?" he asked one morning as he dried the breakfast dishes. "Could you teach me to read?"

"Why, yes. I'm sure I could, and it'll help you pass the time. We can start right away." I paused. "Please don't call me 'ma'am'. My name is Ann, and I'm younger than you."

He smiled and nodded. "Miss Ann."

"No. Just Ann."

We started daily lessons on a roof slate with a slate shard for a pen. Josiah carefully formed his letters, biting his tongue as he painstakingly followed my models. Busy though I was, I was glad to encourage his desire to learn.

"Nobody I knew could read and write, 'cept white folks," he observed, his brow furrowing as he put a flourish on the last of a line of 'L's.

"No. They wouldn't want to know that their slaves might be more capable even than they," I said, with an edge to my voice. "That would make it hard to perpetuate the myth of the Negro as a simple child in need of a white man's care."

Josiah nodded. "You the only white woman I ever met who talk so plain. You different from other white women," he remarked.

"Not so different from other *Quaker* women, Josiah. We believe in educating everybody. It makes us better people." I handed him a cloth to erase his 'L's.

"You strong an' tough. You knows more'n some white men, sure 'nough." He wiped the slate and handed it to me for a new model. "Where you keep your fine clothes, ma'am?"

"It's Ann, not ma'am," I reminded him.

"Ann."

"I don't have any, if by fine you mean fancy and colorful."

"Why not? You be poor?"

"No, Josiah, I'm not poor. Friends don't believe in fancy clothes. We're plain people. No frills or laces or bright colors." I handed the slate back to him with a line of 'M's for him to copy.

"Why, ma'am? . . . I mean Ann."

"We think it's a way people try to put themselves above others. We really do *believe* all people are equal. Quakers aren't opposed to wealth, but we think it should be used to do good, not feed vanity."

"Who vanity?"

I smiled. "Vanity's not a person. It's an attitude. A pre-occupation with self and appearances. Quakers think being vain about who you are, what you have or how you look is wrong. It leads to all sorts of bad things."

Josiah studied my face, trying to grasp all this, so foreign to him.

"You don't be like no other white woman I ever met," he repeated, shaking his head. "All I knew was Massa's wife and daughters. Massa's wife, she mean to me 'cause I'm Massa's son, my momma said." He paused to watch my reaction. "She made Massa sell my momma away, but he refuse to sell me. Don't say I'se his son. Don't say nothin'. But he treat me well. Give me a job workin' horses. Say I the best horse trainer he ever seen.

"Your master was your father?"

"Yes, Ma'am. That happen a lot." He spoke carefully, concentrating on his awkward imitation of my 'M's. His face was pleasing, if not outright handsome, though I hadn't formed the thought until now. Chiseled planes. I wondered if the African people had any gods like the Greeks.

He spoke again, pulling me back to reality. "Sometime they hate they child, but my Massa don't have no other boys. Just three girls."

"Those girls were your sisters! Did they know that?"

"No'm, Miss Ann. Nobody done told 'em. I sure didn't. Afraid I be sold if I done that."

"When did your master's wife have your mother sold?"

His face clouded. "When I'se six. I cried for her every night for a month. Cook raise me. She kind, but she not my momma."

"Why did you run, Josiah?"

"Massa die. Fall off his horse comin' home from town. Folks say it apoplexy. Never know'd what hit 'im, I reckon." He held up the slate for my approval of his 'M's. I nodded. "Once that happen, all hell break lose. Massa's wife hate me. Want me gone. I gotta run or get sold, an' who know what that mean?"

"So you ran. How did you know where to go?" I leaned forward, savoring this rare chance to get to know one of our charges. Most of the time they came and went like shadows.

"Black folk on the plantations talk among theirselves all the time 'bout gettin' away. They always say, follow the north star. Even sing songs about it. Follow the rivers 'n creeks. Watch. Wait. Other free Blacks'll help you if they can. Pass you along the road." The slate was forgotten now as he spoke of his escape.

"You were a long time getting here from Virginia."

"Yes 'm, Miss Ann. I 'bout got caught three, four times. Had to lay low in the creek bottom couple days till they call off the dogs. Not many free Blacks in Virginny, and they's afraid, too, now. Could be kidnapped back in."

"Oh, Josiah, how sad!" The thought that some people would deliberately kidnap free blacks and sell them back into slavery made my blood run cold. "You did eventually find help, though."

"Yes'm. I hit out for Washington 'cause I know'd free Blacks be there. I was hidin' in the bushes by a creek when along come a black man drivin' a wagon. I was so hungry, I had to stop him. He hide me under some sacks and take me to his brother, Harry Rutherford." Now Josiah stopped to pour himself a drink of water from a pitcher on the table.

"That man put me on the road. I go from Washington to Leesburg to Winchester, then north to Cumberland and on up here. I travel a little every night. Sometime it get hot and I lay low a few days. Them last folks, they nice, but they sick. I knowed soon as I seen them. Hadn't been for you, I'd a died."

Uncomfortable with his intense gratitude, I looked away. "Well, come spring, you'll be on your way again. To Canada and your own life."

"Yes'm. I got me a wife back in Culpeper County. Name Lettie. She mistress's personal maid, so she won't be sold. I gotta get her out, soon's I can get us a place in Canada."

"A wife? Oh, Josiah! Any children?"

"Not yet. We didn't want to born no more slaves. But Lettie anxious. Cry like a baby when I run. Cry 'n cry, like she gonna die."

I touched his hand. "I know, Josiah." I looked up as he brushed away a tear.

I'd never seen a man cry before. Amos had not, when Mama died. Not where I could see him, anyway. If Jesse ever did, it wasn't in front of me. I felt a lack of intimacy with men. Touched by his openness, I gave way to impulse and covered his hand with mine. The contrast of our skin color stood out. I went to move my hand, but he held it, shoulders shaking as he gave way to sobs. I lifted my other hand and touched his shoulder.

"Oh, Josiah. You'll get her back. You'll build a life. There'll be freedom and home and babies. Have faith. God has brought you this far. He will not forsake you."

&

Jesse arrived that evening, a mince pie and a bundle of mail in hand, including two letters from Elias. He wrote regularly, at least once a week. These were from last week and the week before. They were brief. He was well and learning a lot. He'd bought two likely looking brood mares. He was anxious to come home. He had something to tell me. He'd see me in about three weeks.

Mid-December. Just before Christmas. I flew into a frenzy of preparation for his homecoming: cooking, cleaning, baking. I should get some cloth and sew a new dress to wear for him. What should I get him for Christmas? We'd never exchanged gifts before, but this year—after he'd told me his "news"—I was sure we would. I wanted to make this Christmas special.

Will McKitrick came often and stayed late, hampering Betsy's worth as a helper. I went on about my work whether he was there or not. He and Betsy courted in the new parlor while I worked in the kitchen producing Christmas confections or sewing by lamplight.

I made linen shirts for Papa, Jesse and Nathaniel for Christmas, and for Betsy a set of table linen. But I thought more about my gift for Elias than anything else. It should be appropriate. Not too intimate. I settled on a pair of fine-knit wool stockings he could wear to Meeting, and maybe, depending on the season, on our wedding day.

As I cast on stitches for his gift, I hoped next Christmas would find me in my own home with a husband to care for, and, perhaps, knitting booties.

Chapter 6

1854 –Christmastime

I **worked every spare moment making my Christmas gifts, as everyone did.** Amos and Jesse spent so much time working in the barn, I knew better than to go there unannounced. Betsy made a wedding shirt for Will, another excuse for them to be together, for the fittings—as though they needed another excuse! Betsy knitted, sewed and stitched endlessly when she and I weren't cooking, washing or cleaning.

The work made the time pass quickly, and I became more breathless with each day that brought Elias closer to home. I could think of little else, even lapsing into daydreams at Meeting.

I helped Josiah learn his lessons with the same distraction I applied to my chores. An apt pupil, he made quick progress from his letters to words to sentences. There was little for him to read, except the Bible, so he began with Genesis and resolved to work his way through to Revelation. It was fine practice, and enlightening, but I wished for a geography so he could learn about Canada, where he was headed, and Africa, whence his people came. Maybe Nathaniel could find one in Bedford. A Christmas gift.

By mid-December I was excited almost to distraction in anticipation of Elias's return. But mid-month went by and no Elias. Christmas was coming on fast. He wasn't writing anymore, so I took that to mean he was on his way, or soon would be. By the 20th, unable to stand it any longer, I pulled on my coat and boots and trekked through the snow to Ben's house. Rebecca welcomed me at the door, her face flushed, very pregnant with their fourth child, two-year-old Alice, clinging to her skirts.

The kitchen was filled with warmth, the smell of spices and currants, and the chatter of children. I longed for such a scene of my own. Curious as I was about Elias, I tried not to be too forward. After all, there was nothing formal or public about our relationship. It was simply a match everybody expected would happen sooner or later. So I worked to conceal my sense of urgency.

"Oh, Ann. How good to see you," Rebecca greeted me. "I need some adult company. Ben works all the time with Elias gone, and when he's not with the horses he's in the barn making Christmas gifts. I barely see a soul except these little ones from dawn to dusk."

"I thought as much," I replied. "At least I have *plenty* of adult company. Too much, sometimes. I'm beginning to think Will McKitrick is something to dust."

"Heavy courting, is it?" Rebecca laughed. "Tell Betsy to be careful or she'll end up like me: four babes in seven years and no end in sight!"

I tied on an apron to help with the baking. "You're well suited for it, Becky. You thrive on motherhood."

"That I do, but it doesn't mean I couldn't use some relief." Little Alice peered at me from behind her mother's skirts.

"You'll be a rich dowager soon enough. Are you thinking this one will be a boy?"

"I hope. For Ben's sake. Three daughters in a row is enough for any man. He needs a son." I rolled the cookie dough as Rebecca took a pan out of the oven.

"I guess he misses Elias much, then. Only women to talk to and no one to share the load."

"He does," Rebecca continued. "But Elias should be along any day now. I thought to see him before this. Have you heard from him?"

"Not for a couple of weeks."

"See? He's on his way, of course. We'll see him shortly. He'll probably surprise us on Christmas Eve or Christmas day."

The two older girls, four-year-old Ruth and six-year-old Jane, sprinkled the cookies with sugar and pressed nuts into the dough. Baby Alice fell asleep on the settle by the fireplace.

The talk eased my anxiety. Rebecca should know if Elias had changed his plans. My purpose accomplished, the afternoon passed slowly. I would rather have returned home to the pile of work waiting for me there, but Rebecca was in need of talk and would think it odd if I left too soon. So I stayed until near dark, when Ben came in from the barn, stomping snow off his boots.

"Ann! You've been a stranger this winter! What keeps you away so much?" he asked.

"Lots of work. Papa, Jesse, Nathaniel, Betsy and her beau."

Ben laughed. "Yes, many's the time I've seen Will McKitrick's horse in Papa's barn."

The little girls tumbled over one another, bidding for their father's attention. "They'll soon be like us," he grinned, "overrun with these."

"Betsy'll be glad for it."

"And you, Ann. Your turn is likely coming home from Chambersburg right now."

I blushed, my eyes downcast. "Maybe so. I'd best be going. Betsy will think I've abandoned her."

I pulled on my boots and coat for the long walk through deep snow and purple shadows to the farm. It was so cold the snow squeaked under my boots. As I looked down toward the creek, I saw Sawyer Hartley trudging through the snow like me, only he was dragging a fresh cut pine tree behind him. I wondered what Christmas would be like in that hardscrabble cabin by the creek. The moon was already rising when I stepped up on our back porch and stomped the snow off.

When I opened the door, I found the whole family seated at the table. I took off my coat, hung it on a peg, tied on my apron, and helped Betsy serve the meal.

"What's new with Ben?" Jesse wanted to know.

"Working on Christmas, same as us," I replied. "Rebecca looks well but ready to pop. I guess they'd like a boy this time."

Papa cleared his throat. "Must needs."

"Any sign of Elias?" Jesse asked.

I shook my head.

"Ann would have told us in a second if there were," Betsy laughed.

My brothers smiled mischievously, while Papa ate in silence. He never mentioned Elias to me, preferring, I suppose, to wait for the fact.

Christmas came. No Elias. Still, I struggled to contain my disappointment. There was Meeting and dinner and visits with family and friends. Mary and Noah Poole came from Osterburg on the sledge with their five children, and Ben and Rebecca came with their girls. The new parlor was full to bursting with talk and laughter, and I served our guests, struggling to keep my mind off Elias. It was the first time in years that almost the whole family was together. Only Rachel was missing. Living in Altoona, apparently, but no one had heard from her since she'd become Mrs. Jacob Schilling.

Christmas was hard for Josiah, for though I carried platefuls of food to him, he was confined to the space under the eaves with only a candle and his slate to occupy him. We gave him his new geography book in the morning, and he tried manfully to read and study it all day. But I knew he was lonely, thinking of Lettie.

He couldn't write to her. Any letter would be intercepted by the mistress. Anyway, Lettie couldn't read. On one of my trips up to check on him, Josiah asked me to write Lettie's name on the slate, and he spent the afternoon under the eaves laboriously copying it over and over, along with his own name, Josiah.

New Year's day came and went. The weather was cold, the snow up three feet on the side of the barn. Folks traveled by sleigh, harness bells jingling merrily in the cold air. Still no sign of Elias. I expected his parents had surely heard from him by now, but Rebecca didn't speak of it, so I took that to mean they hadn't. Faced with this, I was careful to keep my feelings to myself, but I was distraught with fear and worry. Was he sick?

Had something happened to him? Who could I ask? Where could I turn?

Deep inside came a gnawing fear that he was somehow lost to me. That he wasn't coming home at all. That he'd had a change of heart. 'Change of heart?' I asked myself. Who knew his heart? Surely, not I. There was really nothing between us but speculation. No understanding. No promise. Certainly no betrothal. It was all in my mind, fed by the idle talk of well-meaning outsiders. They'd nourished my hopes, and I'd assumed that something would come of walks in the woods, frequent visits, letters passed back and forth.

Now I divided my anguish between fear for his safety and fear that I really had no claim to him at all. The latter was worse.

Then, on the afternoon of the 8th of January, I heard harness bells, and, with a sinking feeling I could not explain, I knew Elias was home. Papa and Nathaniel had gone to Bedford on business; Betsy and Will McKitrick were off skating on the pond at Dunning's Mill. Only Jesse and I were home.

A pair of fine looking black horses pulled the sleigh into the dooryard. There sat Elias, up front, wrapped warm against the cold. At his side sat a young woman. She smiled shyly from under a new wool bonnet, stepping daintily from the sleigh with Elias' help. At first I thought she must be a cousin up from Chambersburg to visit. But when I saw the look that passed between them coming across the dooryard, I knew.

"Jesse, Ann, I want you to meet my wife, Melissa Finley," Elias grinned.

Jesse recovered first, striving to sound natural. "Well, eh, Elias, you old fox," he said, with a careful sidelong look at me. "You never let on a thing." He smiled, taking both of Melissa's small, daintily gloved hands in his. "I'm pleased to meet you, Mrs. Finley."

Her eyes sparkled, even as she demurred. "And you, Mr. Redfield," she smiled. She was young. Not more than twenty. And pretty. She turned to me. With great effort I recovered my composure enough to smile.

"Yes! Melissa, is it? What a joy to meet you."

Melissa reached up and kissed my cheek. "Ann Redfield. I'm privileged to meet you. Elias has told me so much about you. He admires you so. I only hope I can come close to following your example."

Befuddled, I stepped back. I couldn't look at Elias, who blithely took his wife's arm and steered her toward the front door.

"We can't stay long," he announced as they entered the parlor. "We're making the rounds of introductions. We've got at least three more stops before dark."

"Yes, yes." I replied. "It must be a whirlwind for you. But surely you have time for some pie. I baked this morning."

Elias lit up at the prospect of pie. "You'll see, my dear," he said to Melissa, "what I mean by 'best cook in the settlement'." He looked at me. Our eyes met for the first time, mine questioning, his unreadable. He turned to his pretty new wife, attentive to her every need.

Well, I asked myself, what *could* his eyes reveal? 'I'm sorry, Ann. I went away and fell in love? I didn't mean to hurt you, but I couldn't help myself?' What could he say? What could anybody say? What is, is.

Leaving Jesse to entertain our guests, I excused myself to the kitchen to make tea. Seeking refuge, I stepped blindly through the low door to the old cabin, almost bumping into Josiah, who stood in the kitchen, looking lost.

"Josiah!" I whispered. "You'd better get on upstairs."

"I was waitin' for you to come, Ann. So if I made any noise, no one would pay any mind."

"Well, you'd best go before someone takes it in their head to come out here."

"Yes'm. That be Elias Finley you so worried about?" He moved toward the stairway door.

Sorry now that I hadn't been more discreet, I whispered, "Yes."

"Who that woman?"

"His wife."

Josiah looked at me, dumbfounded, his hand on the door latch. "He wife?" he whispered. "Did you say he wife?"

I turned my back, pumped the kettle full, and set it over the fire. I got out four plates, placing them noisily to cover the sound of Josiah's ascent. I cut the pie, made that morning from cherries I'd put by last summer. My hands shook. I stopped and held myself around the middle. I opened the cupboard and got out the tin of tea, took down Mama's best teapot from the shelf, and filled it with boiling water. Cups. Saucers. Sugar. Cream. Tears. I wiped them away, fighting for control. I put the tea things on a pewter tray Nathaniel had given me for Christmas, carried it into the parlor, and placed it on a table.

We ate quietly, Melissa chattering lightly about how beautiful Bedford County was. "This is the farthest west I've ever been. I've been east to Gettysburg, York, Lancaster, Chester and even to Philadelphia, but never west before."

Between sips of tea she looked around the parlor. When her eyes fell on Elias, I saw the exchange of loving glances. The visit was brief. Elias didn't want the horses to get chilled. After a few more niceties, they were on their way.

I cleared and rinsed the dishes, then dried my hands on my apron, took my coat from its peg, and stepped out into the waning afternoon. With nowhere else to go, I stumbled along the snowy path to the barn. Inside the cold, dark building I climbed the ladder to the hay mow and fell on my knees in the hay.

From deep inside me came a moan that grew and surged and swelled to a scream—agonizing, full of pain, longing and disappointment.

Inside the house, Jesse heard it. So did Josiah.

Chapter 7

1855

After that, nothing was right. I struggled with anger, hatred, jealousy—unfamiliar feelings. I was wrestling with angels, and I was exhausted. Exhausted with pretending I didn't care when all I wanted to do was scream, rend my clothes, or sleep.

Jesse watched me, concerned, for he knew better than anyone how I'd dreamed of marrying Elias. I found myself trying, even with him, to pretend it wasn't such a big disappointment. When First Day came, I couldn't bear to sit in Meeting in silence, knowing that the thoughts of many were on me. Couldn't bear Elias Finley standing to introduce his new wife. Couldn't bear to stand by after Meeting while congratulations were heaped upon the happy couple.

I rose early that morning, intending to overcome my distress, but when it was time to bank the fire and put on my bonnet, I hesitated, searching for an excuse to stay home.

"Papa, I'm not feeling well today. I think I'll miss Meeting."

Amos looked at me, expressionless, nodded and picked up his hat. Betsy squeezed my hand as she followed Papa and Nathaniel out the door. Jesse stopped and looked into my eyes.

"You'll have to go back sometime, you know."

"Yes, I know, but I can't, yet."

"It'll be harder if you stay away too long."

"I'll be careful not to do that," I promised. "Only don't pity me, Jesse. I can't bear that. I'll be all right."

"I know you will. I'm put out with Elias right now. There's nothing to be done but accept it, but it was wrong, the way he treated you." He touched my arm.

"Elias has a right to marry whomever he pleases. He wasn't promised to me."

"Not in words, maybe, but . . ."

"Hurry on, Jesse. They're waiting for you."

He turned, set his hat on his head, and followed the others out the door.

The snow was so bright on that cold January day that it hurt the eyes. I cleaned up the breakfast dishes and put meat on to roast. I left a bowl of oatmeal on the table for Josiah. He would come down once it was safe. I poured myself a cup of tea, climbed the stairs to my bedroom, and got back into bed with my journal. For the first time since Elias' return, I tried to give vent to the surging, boiling emotion within me.

I wrote feverishly—used real words like hate and mean and liar and deceiver. I wished ill upon Elias, gave vent to all the angry, bitter, hateful feelings that swirled in my brain. But when I read it, I didn't feel better. I felt ashamed for the meanness and bitterness.

I heard Josiah go down the back stairs to the kitchen. After a while, he came back up and stopped by the low door that joined the old cabin to the new. He stood there for a full minute, listening. I listened, too. Then I heard him go into Jesse's room. I hoped he wouldn't crawl back under the eaves. It was such a beautiful morning. A man should be free on a day like this. Through my grief and anger, I thought of him and was ashamed for raging about Elias when a man like Josiah had so little. I pushed the journal aside, got up from the bed, and went to the low door.

"Josiah," I called softly.

"Yes'm."

"Don't hide yourself away on so beautiful a day."

"No'm. I'm lookin' out. It sure enough beautiful," he agreed. "Who that woman out there?"

"Woman? What woman?" I opened the door and stepped down into Nathaniel's room. It was warmer here, because of the heat from the kitchen. I moved past Nathaniel's bed into Jesse's room.

"She gone now. Out behind the barn. Look like she lookin' for firewood or somethin'. Had a bundle on her back."

Pru Hartley. Couldn't be anybody else. "More likely food than firewood," I replied. "I'll have to count my chickens when I go for the eggs." I stood looking out the window for a long time, but Pru didn't reappear. She'd probably gone straight down over the hill. I turned to Josiah, who sat on the floor with his back to the wall of his hiding place. He smiled.

I sat down in Jesse's rocker, facing him, hands in my lap.

"You all right, Miss Ann?"

I straightened, smiled brightly. "Of course, Josiah. Why do you ask?"

"You stay home from Meetin'."

"Oh, yes. I'm a little headachy today. It will pass."

"'Bout Mr. Finley?" he asked.

I frowned. "Mr. Finley? What about Mr. Finley?"

"He brought him home a wife."

"Yes. Yes, he did, but why should that matter to me?" I wanted to assure myself that Josiah didn't think . . . didn't think what?

"Josiah, what *can* you be thinking?" I asked, rubbing at the ink stains on my fingers.

"I think you loved him and expected to marry him."

"No, Josiah. It was nothing like that. We were just friends. That's all."

Josiah smiled and shook his head. His hands hung limp from forearms resting on his knees. "I understand if you don't want to talk to me."

"Talk to you? Why wouldn't I want to talk to you?"

"'Cause I'm a slave. Or was. Ain't no more."

"Do you think I see you as below me? Is that it?"

He nodded. "Yes, Ma'am."

"No, Josiah. Don't ever think that. You know we're all equal in the eyes of God."

"Equal in God's eyes don't mean equal in man's eyes."

I studied his face, anxious to reassure him. "You're a curiosity to me. I've never known a Negro before. Never talked to one at all, let alone about my feelings." I toyed with a thread on my apron pocket. "I wonder how you see the world. What you think about things."

"Don't try and figure me out like I'm so different from you." He sounded offended. "I'm a man with black skin. You can't clump us all together and put us in a box on a shelf and expect us to stay where we're put. We're people, just like you." He looked at me, his eyes dark. "And I know hurt when I see it. You're hurt, Miss Ann. You can talk to me or not talk to me, but I know hurt."

He watched me struggle for control. I'd come over here to distract myself, not to give in to the pain. A tear slowly made its way down my face. I brushed it away but another followed.

"I wanted to be his wife," I whispered. "I thought he wanted that, too." Now the tears flowed freely. I fumbled in my apron pocket for a handkerchief.

Josiah reached up and took my hand. I let him hold it as I talked—babbled really—about my feelings for Elias Finley. "He never said . . . I just thought . . . I know he cared for me. What happened? What happened?"

Reaching up, he pulled me toward him on the floor. I let myself move until I knelt facing him, between his knees, his hands on my shoulders. He gazed steadily into my eyes.

"He fell in love," he said. "He didn't mean to hurt you. It just happen. Sometime people fall in love of a sudden. They don't plan to, but they do."

"He completely forgot about me," I said, thinking of Melissa Finley's pert little body and sunny face.

"He didn't forget you. He just want her more. Can't help himself."

Now I leaned into him and let myself cry. The smell of his body, like leaves in the fall, comforted me.

"I hate him. Hate his deceit. How could he do this when he knew I was waiting for him? How could he forget about me so easily?"

"I know you hate him now. Her, too, prob'ly. But someday it be all right. You'll understand. Most times folks do things that hurt other folks not 'cause they want to hurt but 'cause they's a hunger inside that's not bein' fed." His words brushed my ear as I leaned against him.

"I know you're right, but it hurts."

"Hurts 'cause of your own heart, or 'cause of what other folks think?"

"Both, I think. I feel so foolish and that makes the hurt more."

"That'll pass. Most folks too busy with their own cares to bother much about yours."

I sat back on my knees and looked at him. "You're very perceptive."

"Perceptive? What that mean?"

"It means you understand things without being told. You read what's inside of people."

"Oh. You surprised?"

"A little. I'm still trying to puzzle you out."

"Puzzle me?"

"You're so intelligent—so dignified, and yet your race isn't known for . . . "

His expression darkened again. "Not by whites. Slaves have they code 'bout how to act 'round white folk. We don't show ourselfs. No sense in that. They jus' get suspicious. Gets you watched, whipped or sold. Black folks carry their dignity inside. Save it for each other."

"But you've shown me your dignity."

"I trust you."

I turned and settled in with my back against his chest. The awkward intimacy satisfied a hunger, even as my brain struggled with inhibition. "Tell me more about your life."

"Not much to tell. A slave's life goes on—one day about like the last. I love horses, and Massa see I have a way with them.

So he give me responsibility for his horses. I train 'em, break 'em, breed 'em, tend 'em when they sick. I make Massa plenty of money breeding and training horses." His speech quickened with pride.

"That's what my brother Ben does. He and Elias are partners." Elias again.

"I live in the first cabin on the row, closest to the big house with cook 'til I was twenty. Cook, she thump me on the head with a wooden spoon, I get out of line. Massa not nice to me, but not mean either. Missus full of hate, and I know why. It's not my fault, but I can't help her. I just stay out of her way." I could feel his breath on the back of my neck.

"The girls nice enough. They like to ride, and I keep their horses for them. Groom 'em. Exercise 'em. Massa trust me to pick out good horses for them." He propped his cheek on the palm of his hand.

"Massa give me quarters in the stable. Three rooms. Nicer than most slave quarters. Some of them jealous. They know I Massa's son, but talk is, I ain't the only one. I don't know about that. Massa, he never tell no slave nothing."

"What was his name?"

"Frederick Colton."

"That's your name, too, you know."

"I guess so. Folks say a free man got to have two names, so I guess I'm Josiah Colton."

"When did you get married?"

"You mean jump the broom? Two year ago. Lettie, she beautiful. Make a man's loins weak, she so beautiful. I sorry to leave her -- long for her every night. Maybe never see her again." He lifted his hand from his knee and brushed away a tear.

There it was again—intimacy I'd never shared with another man. The deep emotion—hurt, anguish, longing, only shared willingly with a loved one.

The awareness frightened me. Abruptly, I stood and moved toward the door, left him sitting on the floor. "I'd better see to dinner. The family'll be home soon."

I hurried down the back stairs to the kitchen, pulled on my boots, and went around to the root cellar for potatoes, carrots and an onion. The cold air on my face wakened me as from a dream, and I breathed so deeply it hurt my lungs. Back in the kitchen, I pared the vegetables for a meat pie, made pastry and rolled it out. I shredded the meat, mixed the vegetables, and added a few spices, covered it with the pastry, and set the dish to bake.

I worked with supreme effort to keep my thoughts away from the man upstairs. All the while I wrestled with my old angels—anger, jealousy, hatred—and some new ones: fear, desire, lust.

Chapter 8

1855

After dinner, the men retired to the parlor, where a roaring fire warmed the room and those above it. Betsy and I cleaned up the kitchen and talked about the weather. A storm was coming, bright as the morning had been. As we wiped the dishes, I questioned Betsy about what was uppermost in my mind.

"What happened at Meeting?"

"Same as always." Betsy was unforthcoming.

"And Elias?"

"He was there, introduced his new wife. People smiled and nodded, and that was that."

"Did anyone ask after me?" I prodded.

"Becky did. She's worried about you. After all, he *is* her brother and Ben's partner."

"Anyone else?"

"Oh, Aunt Alice Grainger wanted a recipe of Mother's. She thought you might have it."

The talk was unsatisfactory. I couldn't conceive of going along as though nothing had happened. Surely, people understood the sky had fallen on my head. Well, maybe it was better if they didn't. Maybe I could hide it more easily than I'd thought.

The afternoon passed quietly. Jesse and Nathaniel took the sled down to Uncle Sammy Grainger's. Will McKitrick and Betsy left soon after dinner for a visit with Mary in Osterburg. Amos fell to snoring by the iron stove in the parlor, and I took up my needlework.

I thought of Josiah, alone up in Jesse's room, and, overcoming my shyness over our morning encounter, I called to him.

"Josiah, come down in the kitchen where it's warm."

He came, smiling, appreciative of the warmth and the company, but watched me carefully.

"Sure wish I could get outside," he mused, standing by the window that looked out toward the creek. "I ain't never seen so much snow before. Virginny don't get hardly much snow, and it ain't never this cold."

"You'd better get used to the cold, Josiah. You're going to have more of it, and snow, too, in Canada."

"How far Canada?"

"Not so far. Only a few hundred miles as the crow flies. But it'll take some time to get there because the Railroad doesn't go straight, and there are still dangers along the way."

"Wish I could go on now," he said. "Can't hardly stand no more of this."

"I know it's hard, staying inside, hiding all the time."

"Yes'm. I'm nigh crazy with hiding out. Worry about how I'm gonna do when I get there."

"There are Friends there, too, and other free Negroes. Whole communities of them. They'll help you get settled."

"What they do? Farmin'? What they grow in Canada?"

"No tobacco or cotton. They grow grain—wheat, oats, some corn. They keep animals, gardens, orchards."

Josiah smiled. "You think I can get a horse of my own?"

"Certainly. You'll probably have more than one. You'll be settled in and prospering in no time."

"Then I find a way to get Lettie."

The mention of his wife jarred me. Why? Why shouldn't he talk about his wife?

"You will. The Free Blacks have a whole network for helping others get to Canada."

Josiah's face lit up. He was serious most of the time, but his smile, when it came, was simply brilliant. I caught myself thinking of him as a man again but pulled back, frightened by my own vulnerability.

"Would you like some more bread pudding?"

"Yes, please, ma'am. You sure good cook."

I was flattered. Jesse was the only one who praised my cooking. The others took it for granted.

"You the rock in this family," he continued. "You the one they all depend on."

Now I was embarrassed. It seem puffed up to think of myself so.

"I just do what needs to be done," I protested, dishing out the bread pudding.

"Where they be without you? When Miss Betsy gone, you be alone with all the work."

"They work hard, too, Josiah."

"Mr. Jesse and Mr. 'Thaniel need theyselfs a wife."

"Well, I'm sure, in due time. That'll leave me alone to take care of Papa. Then what?"

There was a sudden stomping on the back porch. Someone had come up on foot! Josiah moved, cat-like, for the stairs. He was up in Jesse's room before Ben came through the door.

"Good day, Sister," he said, brushing snow from his sleeves. "Missed you at Meeting."

"Hello, Ben. Yes, I was feeling low."

"Wouldn't have anything to do with my partner, would it?"

I looked down. "No. No, nothing like that."

Why couldn't I just own up to it? Say 'yes, as a matter of fact it does'. Why this pretense when both of us knew what Ben said was true? He wasn't an enemy. He was my brother. Why couldn't I be honest with him? There it was: another angel to wrestle. Pride.

"Well, Becky and I think it was wrong. He should have at least written to you. He had to know you were waiting for him. We all did."

His words brought me close to tears again. Turning away, I asked, "Eat a bowl of bread pudding, Ben?"

"No, thanks. I came over to talk to Pa. Where is he?"

"Right here." Amos stood in the parlor doorway in his stocking feet, his gray hair tousled.

"I've got a horse down. Can't seem to get her up. Could you come over and take a look?"

Amos nodded and sat down to pull on his boots. Ben watched, still talking about his horse.

"Where's Elias? Can't he give you a hand?" Amos asked.

Ben looked sidelong at me and colored. "Honeymooning, I expect."

Amos nodded. He rose, pulled on his coat, and stepped out with Ben into the January afternoon.

I stood with my hands pressed against the table behind me, my mind racing. I imagined Elias and Melissa in each other's arms. The image of the newlyweds, snug and happy in Elias's little house, making love, made me sick. I stood alone in the kitchen, fighting nausea. Then I remembered the fine wool stockings I'd knitted Elias for Christmas. They were upstairs in my trunk, still wrapped in colored paper from the mercantile in Bedford. I put down my spoon and mounted the stairs.

"Josiah!" I called.

His muffled reply told me he was in his hideout. Reaching quickly into the trunk, I retrieved the stockings and crossed the room, ripping away the wrapping. Through the low door, down the steps, I walked resolutely into Jesse's room where I stopped by the wall under the eaves.

"Josiah, it's all right. Ben came over to get Papa to help him with a horse. I have a present for you."

He opened the panel and looked out. On my knees beside the hideout, I gave him the stockings.

"Here. You'll need these in Canada."

Josiah took them. He knew who they were meant for. He'd seen me knitting them in December. His eyes searched my face.

Then he reached out, took my arms, and gently pulled me into his private world. It was tiny, but surprisingly warm; light from one candle gave it a soft glow. I went willingly, eagerly into his arms. He cradled me there, murmuring softly, "Oh, Annie. Annie. He should not have hurt you so."

For the second time that day, I cried softly into his chest. "I hate him, Josiah. I hate him beyond hate."

"Hate a good thing to get out, Miss Ann. Let it go. Let it go, now. Scream it out like you did in the barn."

He'd heard. Well, so be it. I had nothing left to hide. I screamed into the hard flesh of his shoulder. The strength of his arms rendered me helpless, and I cried. Long, hard sobs, until I was spent, lying weak in Josiah's arms.

He took up the corner of a quilt and wiped my tears. I lay against him until I stopped shuddering and drifted toward sleep. I was awakened by his kiss, tentative at first, then softly yearning. When I opened my eyes, I saw a tear in his. Oh, Josiah.

Our coupling was slow and gentle, full of tenderness and love. Yes, love. Love born of sadness, loss and loneliness, but love more real than any I had known. I gave myself willingly. When it was done, we lay in each other's arms listening to the wind play against the roof.

"Josiah?" Softly.

"Ann?"

"Whatever else happens, let's never regret this. No one else will understand how it was."

"No regrets. Now or ever," he promised.

Sleigh bells in the distance signaled Jesse and Nathaniel's return. I knew I had time while they unhitched the horses, fed them and put them up for the night.

I knelt before Josiah and dressed, watching the candle light play on his dark, muscular body. The word magnificent occurred to me. It was not a word a Quaker woman used, but I was glad to have occasion to know what it meant.

I kissed him lingeringly, gathered my skirts, and crawled out of the hiding place. Josiah reached out and touched my hand as I straightened up and stepped into the room.

In my own room I brushed back my hair and wiped my face with a cold cloth. But for that, I looked the same in my tiny mirror. Papa didn't approve of mirrors, but I had one, given to me by Cousin Eva Blackburn. What Papa didn't know, Papa didn't know. I studied my face, my eyes, my mouth. Strange how unchanged I was. Then I tucked the mirror away in a drawer, adjusted my skirts and went down to the parlor just as Jesse and Nathaniel entered the kitchen.

"Where's Pa?" Jesse asked.

"Over at Ben's. He's got a horse down."

"It's getting dark. I'll go walk home with him,"

"I'll go with you," Nathaniel offered.

"Go by the road. The snow's too deep in the fields. We'll eat in about an hour, so don't dawdle." They were gone again in a moment, and I was alone. I wondered again at the way things went on unchanged.

Once supper was under way, I gave in to the need to see Josiah one more time. I crept up the stairs to the hideout, where he sat practicing his writing by candlelight. He smiled when I opened the panel.

"Just one more kiss," I told him.

A half hour later I was back in the kitchen, when my brothers and father returned, noisily stomping snow off their boots. The reason for the noise was soon clear; they weren't alone. The Bedford Constable, Peter Ackroyd, Smith and Weaver Hartley and two strangers followed them in.

"You can look all you want," Jesse said loudly. "You won't find anything."

"What?" I asked. "What is this about?"

"About a slave, Ma'am," Constable Ackroyd said. "A fugitive slave I hear tell you're hidin'."

My hand went to my mouth. "A slave? Hiding a slave? Who told you that?" As though I didn't know the Hartleys had something to do with it.

"Can't say, Ma'am. These here two are slave catchers from Virginny. Say there's a three hundred dollar price on that un's head."

The slave catchers were low-looking men. Unclean, unshaven, ragged, and they smelled. I couldn't help myself. I sneered at the whole company. "Well, it always does come down to money, and this lot looks like they need some. Perhaps for drink!"

The constable moved around the kitchen, looking for places a man could hide. He poked here and prodded there, looked behind and under, then nodded to Jesse.

"You the one they say helps 'em. On that Underground Railroad. You Quakers is a defiant bunch. Let's see the rest of the house."

Jesse led them into the parlor and took his time lighting a lamp. They clumped through the room, the three Redfields silent while the others touched things and pushed things aside. Then they tramped up the front stairs into my room. My heart was running wild. Josiah had to have heard, and Jesse was giving him plenty of time to get safe, but still panic ruled my mind. I heard them move into Betsy's room and back out. Then down into Nathaniel's room. The slave catchers were getting surly now.

"You nigger-lovers think you can fool us, but you can't. We got ways 'a knowin' about you," one of them growled.

I could hear them above me now, eight men, standing in Jesse's little room while Josiah cowered behind the false wall. They stood around for eternal minutes. I heard furniture moved, bumped against the wall. Fear caught me anew, and I pumped water into a basin to distract myself. The racket of the pump outdid the pounding of my heart.

They clumped down the back stairs, Jesse leading with the lamp, Amos and Nathaniel following our 'guests'.

"Now the barn," the constable growled. It was a cold night, and this was hateful duty. Whether he was for or against slavery, he had to pursue runaways and co-operate with slave catchers because of that miserable Fugitive Slave Law.

"Sure," Jesse obliged. "Let me get my coat."

In a half hour, when my father and brothers returned, I parted the kitchen curtains and watched three shadowy figures ride out of the dooryard. Two others turned down over the hill on foot. They disappeared into the night, but I was haunted by the fear that they would turn around and ask for another look. Jesse stood in the shadows behind me.

"They'll be back," he said. "Maybe tonight. We've got work to do." I awaited his instructions.

"Wait a while after supper. Then take Josiah over the fields to Ben's. Watch out for the Hartleys. "

"What if the constable comes back and I'm not here?"

"We'll tell him it's Rebecca's time, and you got called to care for her. The snow's getting deep, so follow Ben and Pa's tracks across the field."

Two hours later, Josiah and I, wrapped in warm coats, stepped out into the January night. There was no moon, and, grateful for the darkness, we held onto each other and trudged through the deep snow in silence. We watched warily for any sign of the Hartleys or their slave catching friends. Dimly lit, Ben's house looked as though no one was home when we approached. I knocked softly and tried the door. It opened, and we entered.

Ben, sitting at the table, rose when he saw the situation. "What do you need?" he asked.

"Shelter for the night. Jesse will do something else tomorrow."

Rebecca, huge with child, stood with the three little girls, in their nightgowns, clustered around her skirts. They'd never seen a black man before, and Rebecca would convince all but six-year-old Jane that this was a dream. Jane could be trusted not to speak of it.

Ben took Josiah up the ladder to the loft where the children slept, while Rebecca and I distracted the little girls with finger play. He returned alone and sat down again at the table in silence.

"I'll be leaving, then. Jesse will do something tomorrow," I assured him. Ben wasn't opposed to the work we did, but he was clearly worried about his family.

I thanked them for helping. Rebecca nodded as I tied my scarf tighter around my face and stepped back out into the snow. I trudged the half mile home, watching the shadows, trembling with cold and fear, my former troubles lost in new turmoil. This was life and death.

Chapter 9

Morning dawned in a storm, blown in overnight. Heavy snow before daylight.

"This storm will likely keep the slave catchers inside. Virginia boys aren't used to this kind of weather," Jesse announced at breakfast. "But I've gotta move Josiah on. He's not safe with the Hartleys nosing around."

Nervous and distraught for more reasons than Jesse knew, I agreed. I plunged into work to keep my mind off my fears. "What are we going to do, Jesse?"

"I'll wait until dark and move him then."

I knew better than to ask where or how. I was confident Jesse knew this business, but my fear for Josiah grew out of all reason. Out in hostile territory in the worst month of winter, his chances of reaching Canada safely were slim. Exposure to the elements alone could doom him, to say nothing of being hounded by slave catchers. "It's a bad time to travel," I ventured.

"Yes and no," Jesse replied. "At least the enemy will think so. I hope they'll think I'll wait for the weather to break, so they'll let up while it's bad and keep an eye on me as soon as it warms up."

Someone was stomping snow off their boots on the back porch. Who could be out there so early? Jesse rose and opened the door to Ben's six-year-old, Jane.

"Aunt Ann," the child said. "Papa sent me to get you. It's Mama's time."

Taking the child on his knee, Jesse talked to her at the breakfast table while I scurried to pack a little bag of medicines and put on my boots and coat. We stepped out into a world of blowing snow, barely able to make out the path. We walked slowly, bent against the wind.

"Aunt Ann?"

"Yes, dear."

"Who was that black man you brought to our house last night?" She spoke close to my ear so I could hear her above the wind.

"His name is Josiah. He's running away from slavery."

"Why did you bring him to us?"

"Because some bad men wanted to take him back. Uncle Jesse is hiding him from them." I held her arm as we made our way through the deep snow.

"Oh. Is he going to stay with us for a long time?"

"No. Uncle Jesse will take him away soon."

"Papa put him in the trunk."

"The trunk?"

"Yes. Mama's trunk. He took her things out of it and hid them under my bed. Then he put the black man in the trunk."

My heart ached to picture Josiah cramped inside a trunk. Still, I was glad to be going to him. Rebecca needed me, that was certain, but I would feel better being under the same roof as Josiah.

"Will those bad men come back to get him?" the child asked, fear in her voice.

"We hope not, but we'll be careful if they do. No matter what, you mustn't say anything about the black man to anyone."

"I know. Papa told me."

We were near Ben's house now; it was barely visible through the falling snow. I heard a horse whinny. Out on the road, I could barely discern three figures on horseback riding slowly toward Redfield Farm. Oh, Jesse. Be careful.

I looked at Jane, my finger to my lips. We stood immobile in the blowing snow as the men passed within thirty yards of us. Silently we moved on.

At Ben's house I found Rebecca curled up on her side in the bed in a corner of the main room. Ben and the other two little girls were seated at the table. I took off my wraps and warmed my hands at the fire before going to Rebecca. She was resting now, between contractions. To my somewhat unpracticed eye, this looked like a routine birth, but I hoped for someone who knew more than I to confirm that.

"I'll take the girls over to Rebecca's mother's and bring back her sister, Hannah. She's a good midwife. Between the two of you, she'll be in good hands," Ben explained.

I nodded. "The girls can stay with Grandma Finley until it's over. I'll keep things in order here until Hannah arrives."

"I've got some bricks heating for our feet. I'll go hitch up the team if you'll get the girls dressed." Ben was on his way out the door.

All three children were soon bundled up, waiting for their father. I wrapped the hot bricks in feed sacks and handed them to Ben when he returned.

They were barely gone when Rebecca was seized with another contraction. I held her hand and wiped her brow, spoke to her softly, and hoped that Hannah would get there in time. It could be a couple of hours before Ben returned. Travel, even in a sleigh, would be slow today. I prayed the baby would wait.

Once Rebecca's pain subsided, I cleared away the breakfast dishes, washed them and straightened up the room, all the while thinking of Josiah on the floor above.

"Did Josiah get breakfast yet?" I asked.

"No, I don't think so," Rebecca replied.

I cut a slab of cornbread and poured molasses on it. Gathering my skirts, I climbed the ladder to the loft. Everything looked normal. The trunk was pushed against the end wall, the children's beds unmade. I moved quickly to the trunk and spoke.

"Josiah. It's Ann. I brought you some breakfast."

Slowly the trunk lid lifted and Josiah stood up. Stiff from lying cramped all night, he stretched his aching muscles.

"How it look out there?"

"Snowing hard."

"Anybody about?"

"No." I couldn't bring myself to tell him there was. "Jesse says the weather will likely keep them in today."

"How Rebecca?"

"Her pains are still pretty far apart. Ben went for the midwife."

Josiah ate the corn bread slowly. His eyes sought mine, and he touched my hand. Meeting his touch, I raised my eyes to his and yielded to his kiss. Then, recovering myself, I rose to pull up the quilts on the little girls' beds.

"You can probably stay out for a while. Rest on here if you like." I indicated one of the beds. Afraid of arousing Rebecca's suspicion, I descended the ladder after a last lingering look at Josiah.

Rebecca's pains were closer together now, and I prayed fervently for Ben to hurry up and get back. There was a knock at the door. I hadn't heard anyone ride up, but horses moved silently through deep snow. Moving aside the curtain, I saw three horses standing outside, and, heart in my throat, I opened the door.

"Mornin' Ma'am," the constable said with exaggerated courtesy.

"What do *you* want?" I replied curtly.

"Wanna have a look around. Been to *your* house already. Stopped your brother and checked his sleigh, too. That leaves this house," he said, moving to enter.

I tried to block his way. "You can't barge in here like this! That woman is having a baby!" I indicated Rebecca, pale and wan in the bed.

The three men jostled me aside and entered anyway. "Just wanna have a look, Ma'am."

I stood by the open door, my eyes blazing. "The least you could do is close the door. Or didn't your mothers teach you common manners? Where are your friends, the Hartley boys? Couldn't get them out of bed yet?"

Ignoring me, the three moved about the room, looking in cupboards and behind furniture. One got down on his hands and knees to look under the birthing bed.

I eyed them with contempt. "Things must be bad where you come from, that you'd stoop to this level just for money. How can you stand yourselves? Look at you! Harassing a woman giving birth! You are scum. You are lower than snake shit!"

The constable looked uncomfortable but moved toward the ladder, giving me cause to start in on him again.

"What are you going to tell your children when they ask what you did today? That you searched a child's bedroom and terrorized a woman in pain so you could help a couple of thieves capture a man and return him to slavery? Is that what you'll tell them?"

Ackroyd turned his back and climbed to the second rung. Rebecca screamed out in pain. "Oh, Ann! It's coming! It's coming!"

I rushed to her side, reaching for her hand. Rebecca writhed in pain, thrashing on the bed.

The two slave catchers backed toward the door. The constable peeked over the edge of the loft, and dropped down to the floor as I jumped up and grabbed the fire poker.

"Get out!" I screamed. "Get out before I bash your ignorant heads in!" I flew at the retreating men, brandishing the poker, leaving no doubt that I was good for my threat. The three pushed through the door and I slammed it behind them, shoving the wooden bar in place.

I leaned against the door, breathing heavily, the poker still in my hand. Then I crossed to the fireplace and shoved the end into the coals. If they came back, I'd be ready.

A quiet moan came from the bed, bringing me back to the task at hand.

"Rebecca? Are you all right?"

The reply was weak but triumphant. "Yes, I'm all right. We ran them out, didn't we, Ann?"

I laughed with relief. "Well, you fooled me, too!"

I pulled a chair up to the bed and reached for her hand. "Oh, Becky. You're a good person. Bless you."

Rebecca smiled.

About a half-hour later Ben returned with Hannah, who relieved me of the midwifing duties. At about two o'clock in the afternoon, a lusty wail could be heard all the way to the trunk in the loft.

"Well, Ben, you've got your son," I announced, taking the child carefully from Hannah. I wiped him with a soft cloth.

"And another one, to boot!" Hannah added as a second wail joined the chorus. "Twin boys!"

Ben moved to his wife's side. "Thank you, Rebecca. Thank God for you."

The work of bathing and dressing the babies fell to me, as Hannah ministered to her sister's needs. In a short while all was quiet in the Ben Redfield house. The babies and their mother slept. Hannah gathered her things and looked at Ben.

"It's stopped snowing. Think you can get me home before dark?"

"I can try. I'll stop and tell Jesse to come over so you women aren't alone in case our 'friends' come back."

"I doubt they'll be back today. But leave the girls with their grandmother for a few days. Rebecca needs some rest," I directed.

With Ben and Hannah gone and Rebecca and the babies asleep, my attention returned to Josiah. He'd had nothing to eat since morning. It must have been almost as wild a day for him as it had been for me. I was sure he'd heard everything. I poured some soup in a bowl and climbed to the loft.

"Josiah," I whispered softly. "Josiah."

Again the trunk lid opened and he stood, but his cramped limbs would barely hold him. He sat on a bed, his hands shaking as I handed him the bowl. He took it, but set it down immediately. Taking me in his arms, he whispered, "Oh, Ann. Ann. You a marvel of a woman. How can I ever repay you? You saved my life."

I trembled in his arms. The fear that I stared down earlier did its work now. I collapsed against his chest, crying softly.

"Josiah, I love you."

He held me, crooning in my ear. "You some woman, Ann Redfield. Some woman, indeed. How'm I gonna pay you back for all this?" A sharp rap at the door.

"That'll be Jesse." I climbed down the ladder and crossed to the door. I looked out to assure myself that it was, indeed, Jesse before I slid back the wooden bar.

"Had a busy day, Ann?" he greeted me.

"Somewhat," I replied.

Jesse stopped by the cradle in which two tiny heads reposed. He smiled and moved away so as not to disturb them and their sleeping mother. He sat down on a bench and pulled me down beside him, talking in subdued tones.

"I have a plan for Josiah, but I need your help."

I nodded.

"I'll use Ben's sleigh when he gets back. You and I will pose as husband and wife. I'm taking you to your dying mother's bedside in Johnstown."

"Johnstown! Jesse, that's a long way."

"It's the nearest safe drop off. We'll hide Josiah in back and cover him with feed sacks and the buffalo robe. Having you along will reduce suspicion about traveling at night."

"All right. I'll go home and get us some food. You stay with Rebecca. I think she'll sleep. Josiah's upstairs." I pulled on my boots and tied my bonnet as I spoke.

Jesse opened the door. "We'll come by for you as soon after dark as it's safe."

I stepped out and followed the path through the deep snow, lost in thought about Josiah, the slave catchers, and our despicable neighbors. Amos and Nathaniel were in the kitchen when I arrived.

"Twins, is it?" Amos asked, his face crinkling into a rare smile.

"Twin boys, Papa. Both perfect. Jesse wants me to go with him to take Josiah to Johnstown."

"When?"

"Tonight."

Amos nodded. There was no safety around here anymore.

I put supper on the table, and we ate in silence, waiting for Jesse, who arrived around seven. I joined him in the sleigh with a sidelong glance at the pile in back.

"He's all right," Jesse assured me as we moved out into the night. The snow had stopped around three, and others had made tracks ahead of us, so the going was smooth enough. We talked little as we rode, mostly about family. When Betsy was coming home. What Ben and Rebecca would name the babies. How proud Amos was of twin grandsons.

The trip was long and cold. As the sleigh runners cut quietly through the snow-covered world, my thoughts were with the man in back. He must be terrified after two close calls. I was. I spoke when Jesse spoke to me, but my mind was on Josiah.

We arrived at a farmhouse near Geistown, east of Johnstown around midnight. Jesse jumped down and climbed the stairs to the porch. He knocked at the door and waited. I could tell by his movements when the door opened, but no light appeared. Conductors had to be cautious in the middle of the night. Fugitives could be moved any time of year, but snow made tracking them easier, so they usually laid low when it snowed.

Jesse returned and removed the coverings without a word. Josiah appeared, wearing an old coat of Ben's. He leaned over and touched my shoulder as he let himself down from the sleigh.

"Good bye, Miss Ann. Thank you," he whispered.

"Good bye, Josiah."

Jesse escorted him to the house. The door closed, and Jesse returned to the sleigh. He turned the horses around and headed home. That was that.

Chapter 10

1855 – Early Spring

I knew I was pregnant by the middle of March. I knew it before that—by mid-February—but tried not to believe it. Two months of daily bouts of nausea were evidence enough, if I needed more. I can't describe how I felt when I knew. A sickening fear—isolation, resignation—closed in on me. So alone. I looked desperately for someone to turn to. Someone to help. But there was no one, so I determined to keep my secret as long as I could and carried on as though nothing were amiss.

I took to walking alone along the roads or in the woods, with no particular destination, as though there were some answer out there, if only I could find it. One afternoon, I found myself in the creek bottom near the Hartley place. I didn't want to pass too close, but once I realized where I was, it was too late. Pru had spied me.

"Ann Redfield! What makes you come calling?" she hailed from the broken-down porch. It was almost as though she welcomed a visit.

"Afternoon, Pru. Just passing through. How've you been?" I tried to sound pleasant.

"Fair to middlin'. You still got that nigger hidin' out up at your house?"

"Whatever *can* you be talking about?" I tried to say it lightly, but Pru was having none of it.

"You know right well what I'm talkin' about. I saw his black face lookin' out at me one day in Jan'ry. Don't think I didn't!"

"Is that why your brothers came to our house looking for a runaway? Honestly, Pru, you're mistaken."

She spit on the porch. "Mistook, hell. I know a nigger when I see one. You Redfields better watch out. Folks got their eye on you."

I moved past the house, fighting the urge to run. "I'm on my way to Alum Bank to pick up the mail. Want me to bring yours?" I asked, knowing full well that the Hartleys never got mail—and couldn't read it if they did.

"No need. But you might bring me a pound of sugar and some tea while yer about." She preened in the doorway, feigning gentility.

I felt hateful toward her. Her and her whole low-class, ignorant, evil family. A child eyed me from behind her ragged skirt. More of the same, I thought. I hastened on down the path, careful not to step in anything.

The declaration of intention to marry for Elizabeth Redfield and William McKitrick was read at the Second Monthly Meeting (February) and again at the Third (March). No obstacles to the union were discovered, so the wedding took place in Fourth Month (April).

I did what I could to lose myself in the preparations for Betsy's wedding. I cleaned, sewed, baked and cooked until I was numb. Will McKitrick had bought a little house in New Paris to accommodate his family and his shoemaking business, so that had to be cleaned and painted, curtains made, furniture moved. Betsy and I worked hard at both houses, and I was grateful, for the work kept my mind off my situation.

Friends arrived from miles around at the Dunning Creek Meeting house, for both the Redfields and the McKittricks were well known and respected. The weather, unseasonably warm for mid-April, delivered a lovely day for the wedding dinner at Redfield Farm. I got up at dawn, worked before the service, worked after the service, welcomed guests, served food, refilled plates, cleaned up after, and fell into bed exhausted at about eleven o'clock, satisfied that I'd given my sister a fine wedding.

I felt let down afterwards, with nothing to distract me. I could no longer ignore my pregnancy, even if it wasn't yet apparent to others. I didn't regret loving Josiah, of that I was certain, but how I could do right by this child was a fearful concern. Waves of panic overwhelmed me, and I struggled with an urgency to act. Such an urge is common in times of crisis, but sometimes there's nothing to be done but accept what is.

Things were quiet along the Railroad for a while after Josiah's departure, but activity picked up as the weather warmed. Jesse was more open with me about his activities, knowing he would likely need my help again. I welcomed the openness and yearned for a chance to do more.

Ideas for moving fugitives swirled around in my brain, along with fear for Josiah and worry about my own future and that of the tiny life inside me. My resolve strengthened. I could no longer stay on the sidelines. I would do all I could for as long as I could to end this horror. I didn't fear for my own safety, and my status as a woman could be turned to advantage.

Just a week after Betsy's wedding I told him, "Jesse, I want to do more than just occasional help with the railroad. I mean not just sometimes; all the time."

Jesse looked at me in silence. "I'll call on you when I must, but I can't put you in harm's way."

"No, Jesse. Not just in emergencies. I want to be your full and trusted partner."

"Ann, this is man's work."

"It is a work of deception and craftiness, and I can deceive as well as the next."

Jesse sat on the back step, petting our old dog, his legs stretched long in front of him. I already knew more than he wanted me to know—more than was good for either of us. He watched me, deep in thought, struggling with his sense of right. Then he relented. "All right. We'll work together."

"I'm not the only one around here involved in this," he told me. "There's a little network of Friends and Free Negroes. Our passengers mostly come up through Cumberland, Maryland, but some come from the east, too."

I listened carefully, intent upon remembering all he said.

"I have several routes I can send people on. I try to vary them, just in case. My biggest problem around here is the

Hartleys. They're onto me, but fortunately, they're not that hard to deceive."

"I know. Pru always seems like she's spying on us. She shows up at odd times, sneaks around when she thinks I don't see her."

Jesse nodded. "I've seen her, too. The boys worry me more, out to make a nickel they don't care how."

"Everyone detests them, not just the strong abolitionists. Most people's sympathies are with the runaways." My own contempt for the Hartleys knew no bounds.

"Even Old Ackroyd might be more sympathetic than he looks, but he's bound to enforce the Fugitive Slave Law. The Friends try not to hold it against him."

Amos and Nathaniel were coming in from the barn, so I moved to change the subject. They were with us, but only on the edge of things. They didn't want or need to know the details.

The runaways came alone, in pairs, or in small groups, sometimes guided by one who had made it successfully to Canada and returned South to rescue others. Most of the time they were able young people, with the strength to run and hide, sometimes for weeks without relief. But occasionally they were children, even babies, exposed to grave danger by those who loved them and were willing to risk all for freedom. Conductors gave babies paregoric to render them unconscious and, therefore, silent. A few old folks made it, too. Helped along by their children or friends, they gave their last effort for the opportunity to die in freedom. It touched my heart to see them, so afraid, so dependent on the charity of others.

April gave way to May, and the planting began. With it came a long-awaited letter from Rachel. She was married to Jacob Schilling and living in Altoona. Work was plentiful, and they had bought a house not far from the booming railroad shops. Most of the men in town worked on the railroad, but Rachel was glad Jacob didn't, because the shop workers got so dirty. Jacob came home covered with plaster dust, which he called 'clean dirt', and that, to Rachel's mind, was better than the sooty grit from the trains. She described their brand new house with three bedrooms upstairs and three rooms downstairs (parlor, dining room, kitchen), a big attic, cellar, and porches front and back.

"Sounds like a big house," Jesse observed. "S'pose they'll be filling it up with children pretty soon."

"Mayhap," Amos replied with no expression. He hadn't spoken of Rachel since she'd left us. Not a word.

The news from Rachel was welcome, but I still watched anxiously for a letter from Josiah. I'd often told him the name of our post office: Alum Bank. His reading and writing had progressed to a passable state, so I waited and expected to hear from him. Not to would indicate trouble.

Weeks passed with no word. I worried that he hadn't made it. Distress bought all kinds of evil to mind; I shook myself to dispel the fears.

Then in early June, Jesse announced that he was going to Alum Bank, if anyone had any letters to post. The mail hadn't been picked up that week. Mary wrote often from Osterburg, and now that the lines of communication had been reopened, letters flew back and forth from Altoona. I gave him letters to both of our sisters as well as to friends in Menallen and Redstone Meetings.

He returned late in the afternoon with a smile. "Here's one you'll welcome," he said. "From Josiah."

My heart leaped at his name. He was all right! He'd made it to Canada. The letter was short, but neatly and carefully printed on white paper, purchased at a stationer's.

DRESDEN ONTARIO
DEAR JESSE,
I AM WELL HOPPING THIS FINDS YOU THE SAME. I REECHED CANADA IN FEBURY. SOME UTHER SCAPED SLAVES TUK ME IN. I WORK FOR A BLACKSMIT. TELL ANN I AM LERNING MY LETTERS BETTER. THANK YOU FOR MY LIFE.
YOUR FREND, JOSIAH COLTON

I committed Dresden, Ontario, to memory and answered his letter that evening. I told Josiah about Betsy's wedding and the farm and the planting. I told him how Ben's twin boys thrived. I told him Ben's mares had foaled five times that spring. I did not tell him about his child who grew inside me and whose presence was getting difficult to conceal. I did not tell him about my loneliness now that Betsy was gone or my bleak prospects for anything but more of the same. I did not tell him about my fears for him and for our child.

Jesse posted the letter the next day. It was time to get in the first crop of hay, and that meant we'd all be busy again. Rebecca was the closest woman to me now. We helped each other as much as we could, but with five little ones to care for, Rebecca's resources were strained. Haying meant feeding the men, so we pushed ourselves to the task, but there wasn't enough energy between the two of us to do it all. Rebecca broke first.

"I'm going to ask Ben to get us some help. I know of two girls, twelve and fourteen, whose family started west and their mother died. You know them: Robert Hill's girls."

I nodded.

"Robert sent the girls back to his sister, Ethan Rouzer's wife, but they don't have much and seven children of their own. I'm going to ask Ben to offer to take them."

"Your house will be full to the rafters!" I laughed.

"It'll be a crowd, but help is needed."

Ben agreed and, by the following First Day Meeting, made arrangements to take in Deborah and Abigail Hill, two pale, thin-faced girls with sad eyes—but obedient and willing workers. Rebecca sent them over the next week to help me cook for the men in the fields.

Deborah was quick to see what had to be done, and worked without much talk. Abigail, the younger one, needed more direction and was not at all given to silence. She spoke often and without benefit of forethought, and yet she was the more likable of the two and rapidly became my favorite.

The three of us managed to feed the men with ease, and I was sorry when it was time to send the girls back to Rebecca. I'd miss their company.

"Don't worry, Ann," Abby assured me. "I'll come over for visits when I can."

"I'll look forward to that."

They'd been gone for about a week when Abby returned one day with a pail of wild strawberries she'd picked for me.

"You can make preserves like my Mama used to," she offered. "I can help, if you want."

"Thank you, Abby."

"Rebecca wants to know if you want to go over to Oak Shade for cherries next week. She says we can help each other pick and put them by for both families."

"Yes. Tell her I would. Maybe Jesse can take us now that the haying's done."

I washed and capped the strawberries while Abby went to the spring house for a pitcher of cream. We sat down across from each other and ate bowls of strawberries and cream.

"Ann?"

"Yes, Abby."

"When's your baby comin'?"

I was caught short. I thought to deny it, but that was only to put off the inevitable. "In October—Tenth Month, I think."

"Oh."

I wondered how many people had already surmised the truth. Did everyone know? Or was Abby just perceptive? I glanced down at the pronounced thickening about my middle. Try as I might to conceal it, there it was. If Abby noticed, everyone else probably did, too.

"You ain't married, are you?" With childlike innocence, Abby prodded.

"No."

"Who's the Pa?"

"Nobody. Nobody you'd know."

"He gonna marry you?"

"No." I cast about for a way to change the subject, but Abby was persistent.

"Hmmm. What's your *Pa* say about that?"

"Abby, please. It feels like you're a committee."

"Guess you'll be facing one soon enough. I feel sorry for you. That won't be much fun."

"Which? Facing a committee or having a child out of wedlock?"

"Neither," the girl asserted. "Don't worry, though. I'll still be your friend and come help you with your baby."

"Thank you, Abby. Now, could we talk about something else?"

"Yes'm. We can. Do you want me to keep it a secret? About him not marrying you?"' She looked me squarely in the eye, her pale face serious.

"Yes, Abby. If you will. For now."

"Okay, but there's bound to be talk. You'll be read out of meeting, you know."

"I know, but there's nothing I can do."

"Nothing?"

"Nothing."

Chapter 11

1855 – Spring/Summer

Neither **Amos nor Nathaniel commented on my increasing girth.** If they noticed, and I couldn't conceive of their not noticing, they went about their business as though they hadn't. Only Jesse talked to me about it, one warm evening as we sat alone on the back porch.

"Ann, are you with child?"

"Yes."

A long pause. Jesse sat silent, obviously taken aback, even though he had to have known the answer. I waited for him to speak again.

"How did it happen?"

"A moment of foolishness, Jesse. I can't explain it any other way."

"But who? When?" Jesse could think of no prospective lover or opportunity that fit the puzzle. He looked blank.

"I'd rather not say, for now. Please be patient. I have a lot to think about."

"All right. But I expect the man to step up and marry you. If not, you'll be disowned and publicly humiliated. He could prevent that."

"I know I'll be read out of Meeting. I can't help that. But he can't step up. He doesn't know."

"Doesn't know you're pregnant? Well, if he has eyes, he can see."

"This will take care of itself in its own good time."

He sat quiet for a while, studying his hands. "When will the baby get here?"

"As near as I can tell, sometime in Tenth Month ."

"Are you well? Do you need anything?"

"I'm fine, thank you. I'll call on you if I need to, but up to now, I've had no problems." I rose to go inside.

"Does Papa know?" he asked, looking doubtful.

"I think he chooses not to."

"He'll be put out if you don't marry. Put out if you do marry, too."

"I know. I think that's why he chooses not to speak of it."

"Ann, you *must* tell me who the father is." Jesse pleaded. "Someone needs to make him see what he's done."

I patted his hand. "Thank you, Jesse, but no."

"It wasn't Elias, was it? If it was Elias, I'll wear him out."

"No. It wasn't Elias. It pains me to talk about this. Please, let's drop the subject."

He left me standing on the porch and walked out through the yard into the twilight, his hands in his pockets, until I couldn't see him any more in the evening shadows. I watched him go, sad to be the cause of his pain.

The work of the railroad went on in spite of my problems. Jesse was called out of bed at least once a week to take care of business. We never knew how many would come—or when. Because safety was more important than speed, we had to be ready to keep them for a day or two when times were tense.

These poor people, speechless with fear, touched my heart. They did what they could to thank us. Once I found a pearl-handled knife stuck in one of the barn beams, left there as a token of gratitude. There was seldom a chance even to learn names. I treated wounds, blisters, dog bites, bee stings, and poison ivy. I gave what I had of stockings, shoes, or clothing and provided as much food as my larder could spare.

Handbills circulated bearing descriptions of escaped slaves, and advertisements were scattered through the Bedford Gazette, promising handsome rewards for the recapture of 'property'.

The Quaker settlement was well known for its strong antislavery stance, so we were the recipients of more than our share of attention from doughfaced trash. But we were good at what we did. No charade or subterfuge was beyond us. We did what was needed to pass our charges along safely.

Once in a great while we heard from passengers who'd made it to Canada. The letters were few, for most slaves were illiterate. I also acted as a go-between, posting letters from Canada back south. I sent them on to a Friend in Virginia who did what she could to see that they were delivered. Free blacks in the South, many of whom could read and write, passed information from escapees to others still in servitude. Some of those who had made it to Canada made a trade out of writing letters to be passed along.

One of these was Josiah. He posted his letters to me, counting on me to send them on. He always enclosed a note, giving news of his situation and asking after us. I responded in kind, but kept my condition to myself.

⚒

One hot evening in late summer, there came a quiet, tentative knock on one of the kitchen windows. The door was open, but runaways wouldn't show themselves. Jesse rose and stepped outside. Around the side of the cabin, three young black men and two women cowered in the darkness.

"How did you get here?" he asked.

"Man drop us off this mornin' down by the creek. Show us your house. Say this be safe. We lay low 'til dark. You a Friend?"

"Yes, I'm a Friend," Jesse replied. "Come with me."

He led the troop to the barn and ushered them into a makeshift room under the hay. About four feet square and about as high, it was big enough for five people, tight, used only in times of real peril. Most of the time it was safe to sleep in the hay.

"You hungry?" Jesse asked.

"Nothin' to eat today except berries," he was told.

"I'll get you something."

He returned to the house, where I was already warming leftovers from supper. I'd long since fallen into the habit of cooking extra in case we had guests. I put pieces of cornbread in a bucket, my system for carrying food to the barn without raising suspicion. If anyone were really watching, they might wonder at the number of buckets I carried to the barn, but I hoped no one was watching that closely.

As Jesse stepped out the back door with two buckets of food, he almost ran into Abby, coming across the porch.

"S'cuse me, Jesse," she said, stepping aside to avoid a collision. Then, "Where're you goin' with all that food?"

Jesse turned and looked helplessly at me, then stepped off the porch and headed to the barn without a word.

"Hello, Abby. What brings you out so late?" I put on a causal air.

"Rebecca sent me to stay the night. Said you needed me to help make pickles tomorrow."

"Oh, yes. I did ask for your help, but I didn't expect to see you until morning."

"She thought you wanted to get an early start. Where's Jesse going with all that food?" she asked, looking out the back door.

"Oh, he's just slopping the hogs."

"This late? That looked like pretty good food to be feeding to the hogs!"

"Abby, be still! You're going a mile a minute and I have a headache. Let's just get to bed early, shall we?" I took off my apron and hung it on a peg.

"Yes'm. Fine with me. But I still don't know why you'd feed good cornbread to the hogs."

"It was moldy. Now, you can sleep in Betsy's room. You know where it is, so hurry along. I'll be up shortly. I want to say good night to the rest."

I listened to her progress up the back steps, then went into the parlor, where Amos and Nathaniel sat reading by lamplight.

"We've guests," I told them.

Nathaniel laughed. "It's hard not to notice when Abby is here."

"Not just Abby. Others, too."

Amos nodded. "You'd best keep an eye on that girl. She could get you in trouble."

Nathaniel agreed.

"I know. I'll try to keep track of her."

I returned to the kitchen and set the table for breakfast while I waited for Jesse. I wanted to be sure he knew Abby would still be around in the morning.

When he returned, he made no effort to hide his irritation at Abby's presence. "You'd best get rid of her early, Ann. She might figure us out, and she talks too much."

"I'll do what I can, but sending her home early is liable to pique her curiosity. Better to do the pickles in the morning, like we planned."

"I'll want to move this group on tomorrow night. I might have to split them up. Send some over to Windber and some up the valley to Hollidaysburg. I've used Johnstown a lot lately."

"I'll have Abby gone by suppertime."

"All right. Keep her out of the barn."

I took my worries to bed. Abby's curiosity alone was cause for concern, but her loose tongue was worrisome, indeed.

In the morning, Abby picked cucumbers while I mixed the pickle brine. Working together, we washed the cucumbers, packed them in three big crocks, and poured the brine over them. Then we set the crocks in the spring house, covered with wooden lids. In a few weeks, we'd have pickles.

Abby chattered about happenings in Ben's house. She was a likable child—open, guileless, without malice, but much given to idle talk.

"Do you like going to Meeting, Ann?" she asked.

"Yes, I do."

"I don't. I think it's boring. All those people just sitting there, not talking. I like it when somebody stands up and rants once in while. Gives 'em hell. That's fun, but most of the time it's just silence. I can't abide silence."

"Yes, I know," I smiled.

"I like it when Jesse gets up. At least he has something to say. Not like Friend Marsh and Friend Thomas. They're boring, droning on and on about how people don't keep the Quaker ways. Jesse fires them up, tells 'em to disobey corrupt laws like that Fugitive Slave Law. Folks say Jesse doesn't just talk about it. Folks say he really helps runaways. Does he, Ann?"

"I can't say, Abby."

"Oh, I guess not. You'd have to keep that a secret, huh?"

"Jesse's ways are Jesse's business. If he wants us to know things, I guess he'll tell us."

"I think he helps them. Anybody as full of the fire as Jesse is, has to be doing, not just talking." Her eyes shone with admiration. "Do you think he needs any help? With the runaways, I mean. I could help him."

"There goes your imagination again," I said, trying to head her off. "Next thing, you'll be making up knights and dragons."

"No, I won't. I'd rather help Jesse." Silence. "Ann?"

"Yes, Abby."

"Does Jesse have some runaways out in the barn right now? Is that who he was talking to last night?"

"Abby, don't talk nonsense. Jesse's against slavery. That doesn't mean he spends all his time saving slaves. Now let's go out to the garden and see what's next to put by."

Abby walked across the yard beside me, but her eyes flitted back and forth to the barn. Her mind was clearly not on the garden. I sat down on a bench and patted the place beside me for her to sit.

"Abby, listen carefully," I said, firmly. "To you, helping slaves run away from their masters is an adventure. But it is neither fun nor romantic. When it is talked about at all, it is with great secrecy. That's because lives are at stake."

My eyes held Abby's, intent upon making the girl understand. "You must learn to curb your tongue—to think about what you're saying and who will hear it before you speak. If Jesse *were* involved, and I'm not saying he *is*, you could cause him trouble, injury, even get him killed with your talk. Now, you don't know any facts, Dear. You may think you do, but you don't. So please don't speculate out loud."

Abby sat quietly for a long time, studying her shoes. "I'm sorry, Ann. My Mama always said I talk too much. I'll try to keep quiet."

I patted her hand, then got up to pick lima beans. Abby joined me, and we worked silently for a while.

"Ann? Last night on my way over here, I saw Jesse take those people into the barn. I know I shouldn't have, but I followed him. Heard him tell about the room in the hay mow. I'm sorry. I shouldn't have done it, but I couldn't help myself."

I rocked back on my heels and studied the pale, scrawny girl in silence. A tear stole down her face. I put my arms around her thin shoulders and held her close. "It's all right, child. You did what anybody else would have done. Now you just have to find a way to keep what you saw to yourself. Do you think you can do that?"

"Yes,m. I'm sure I can."

Chapter 12

1855 – Summer

Jesse came in shortly after I'd sent Abby home. My agitation was obvious.

"You look like you found a rattlesnake in your bed."

I winced. "There's a problem."

"What kind of problem?"

"An Abby problem. She saw you take them to the barn last night."

"Oh," he breathed. "That *is* a problem, given Abby's wagging tongue." He sat down, frowning. "I've been thinking about how to move them on, and I'll need your help. But how can we be sure that girl won't blurt something out and ruin it for us?"

"I explained the danger to her, and she promised to keep quiet. She's a good girl and very smart. But I'm afraid she'll forget and let something slip."

"Who knows what she'll say or who'll hear it and repeat it? If Ben's girls get hold of this, anything could happen." Jesse rubbed his forehead.

"Tell you what. I'll split this bunch up. They're not related to each other, so it's okay with them. I'll take the three men to Windber in a wagonload of potatoes tonight. Hide them in sacks, among the potatoes."

"It's early for potatoes."

"I know, but it's early for anything in sacks. If anyone presses me, I'll say it's the end of last year's crop."

I was confident he knew what he was doing. I had to be. "What about the women?"

94

"Dress them up in Quaker dresses and mourning bonnets and you drive them in Ben's buggy to Hollidaysburg."

"In broad daylight?"

"I figure Quaker women in mourning won't raise much suspicion."

"I guess not." I was daunted by the thought of doing this alone, but anxious to earn Jesse's confidence.

"It'll take five or six hours. Do you think you're up to it?" he asked, with a look at my protruding belly.

"Sure."

"That's what we'll do, then. I'll give you the name and directions for the drop-off at Hollidaysburg. Can you find enough clothes?"

I was one step ahead of him, working out the details in my head. "I'll fix my own mourning bonnet, and I think Mama's old dress and bonnet are still in the trunk upstairs."

"They should fit the younger woman. She's slight. I don't know about the older one. She might be too big for your clothes."

I giggled. "Mama would be proud for us to use one of her dresses so."

Jesse smiled. "That she would."

When Amos and Nathaniel came in from evening chores, Jesse let them in on the plan. Amos objected to my going alone. "She needs someone with her. I should go, or Nate." A show of concern with no mention of my condition.

"More than one person should stay here in case something happens to me," Jesse asserted.

Amos nodded.

"There is someone who could go with me," I offered, a bit timidly.

"Who?" Amos asked.

"Abby."

"Abby? That prattling child? We can't let her know about these things!"

"She already knows, Papa. She saw Jesse take them to the barn last night."

"A fine turn of events."

"Maybe we can make it an advantage," I went on. "Maybe if we let her help, she'll see the importance of keeping quiet."

"Right, Sister," Nathaniel put in.

"I don't see that we have much choice, and she *could* be an asset. It's wise to have someone along in case anything goes wrong." Jesse rubbed his forehead again. "I'll go over and borrow Ben's buggy and team for you."

"Ask if Rebecca has an extra black dress and bonnet. And bring Abby over here for the night so I can prepare her," I told him.

Amos took supper out to the Negroes, and Nathaniel helped load the potatoes in the wagon. When Jesse returned, he unhitched Ben's team and put them up for the night, and I took Abby aside to explain the plan to her. About an hour after dark, Jesse hitched up the horses and helped the men into sacks. Nathaniel made sure all the sacks of 'potatoes' were settled in, and carefully arranged.

"Since I'm going as far as Hollidaysburg do you think I could go on to Altoona and see Rachel? Maybe stay the night?" I asked Jesse as he checked his load.

"Good idea. She'll be glad to see you, and it'll give you a chance to rest from the trip." He hopped up on the wagon seat, clucked to the horses and drove out of the barn.

I climbed to the loft and called to the two women, who emerged from the hay and followed me into the house. Once inside, I gave them hot water and soap and left the kitchen while they bathed. Abby and I took a lamp up to my room. I opened a trunk, and Abby held the light while I rummaged through Mother's clothes until I found the black dress and mourning bonnet. The fine black netting sewn to the brim was almost opaque and would serve our purpose well.

Back in the kitchen, we helped the two women try on the clothes. Mama's dress fit the smaller one—a little tight, but it would do. The taller one wore Rebecca's black dress as though it were made for her. Their faces were invisible behind the veils, so the only skin showing was their hands. My gloves fit the larger woman, but Mama's had to be split in the palm to fit the smaller one. Once they were outfitted, we took them up to Jesse's room where they could sleep more comfortably than in the barn.

Abby'd been close to silent the whole evening. Being a part of so important an event was working its magic on her tongue; she was a model of self control. Maybe even 'speechless' was the word. We passed a sleepless night as somewhere out west Jesse and the three others bumped and rattled through the darkness toward Windber.

As soon as the sun rose, I was up and busy in the kitchen. Jesse wasn't back yet, and we ate breakfast in silence. Amos did the chores and hitched up Ben's team to the buggy. We women attended to our attire, critiquing one another, offering advice about how to move, stand and sit in the mourning clothes. I decided that Abby, due to her age, needn't wear a bonnet. *Someone* should have unobstructed vision.

By seven o'clock the four of us were seated in the buggy for the twenty-five-mile trip. Amos nodded to me as we prepared to leave.

"Papa," I said, "Abby and I are going on to Altoona to see Rachel. We'll stay the night with her and come back tomorrow."

"Suit yourself," was all Amos said. The sting of Rachel's departure was still there. He opened the barn doors and I drove out into the early light, black-draped bonnet in place.

It was very cool—almost cold, early on—but as the sun rose higher it burned off the morning chill. The front of the buggy was open, but the back seat was enclosed on the top, back and sides, giving our passengers shade and less visibility. Abby chatted with them as we drove, helping to pass the time. The older woman hoped to find her husband in Canada. He'd run a few months earlier. The younger one was a pitiful soul. Only about fifteen, she was just running. Didn't know where or to what. Her whole family had been sold away, and her master's son was showing a little too much interest in her, so when the chance came, she ran.

We drove through St. Clairsville and Osterburg—right by Mary's house without a glance to the left or right—before many people were astir. Then on through King, barely a village, and Sproul, not much more, to Claysburg by mid-morning. That was a tense passage; there were lots of people about, but none took special notice of a Quaker buggy and women dressed in mourning black.

Later on we passed through East Freedom and stopped for lunch in a picnic grove outside Newry. There was no one around, so we lifted our veils, and ate in comfort.

We got to Hollidaysburg at about 1:30 and, following Jesse's instructions, turned down Montgomery Street to a large, yellow brick house surrounded by a lawn and an iron fence. I turned the horses in, following the gravel drive to the back of the house. No one was about, so I stepped down and went to the back door. After making sure I couldn't be seen from the street, I knocked. The door was opened by a woman, obviously a maid, with a forbidding countenance.

"I'm here to see Mr. Thaddeus Burns, please." My voice quavered a little, and I struggled to keep calm. It was my first underground trip alone, and the responsibility lay heavy on me.

"Mr. Burns is out. He won't be back until four," the maid said without the least sign of friendliness.

"Oh. What time is it now?" My weak confidence wavered in the face of this cool reception.

"Just after two," came the crisp reply.

I didn't know what to do. "Is Mr. Burns at work?"

"Mr. Burns is in court. He's an attorney." There was no help from this sector.

"Thank you. Thank you very much," I stammered. I returned to the buggy and drove the horses on through the U-shaped driveway and back out to the street.

Beside me, Abby scanned the town. "That white steeple up there might be the courthouse," she offered.

"Yes, but even if we find the courthouse, how can the man help us if he's in court?"

"Well, I guess we could drive around and find a picnic grove or something and wait it out." Abby looked perplexed.

"You ladies lost?" A man walking down the street stopped by our horses' heads.

"No, thank you. We're waiting for someone," I replied. It was hot now, and the dark clothes were stifling. I wished I could at least take off the bonnet. My silent passengers must be melting. Only Abby's head was bare, her blond braids glistening in the sun.

There must be some place we could rest and keep out of sight for a few hours. Not knowing what else to do, I turned right on Montgomery Street and followed it down over the hill toward the canal. At the end, I turned left, crossed the canal and proceeded through a little community identified on a signpost as Gaysport. Here the houses were farther apart, each with a small barn and some livestock. We moved slowly. The horses needed a drink. As we passed a neat looking farmstead, we saw a woman picking beans in her garden. I stopped the buggy, climbed down, and went over to talk to her.

"Pardon me, Ma'am. Could I water my horses at your trough?"

The woman rose and smiled from under her sunbonnet. "Certainly you may. Just drive in and let them drink."

"Thank you, Ma'am."

"You look tired," the woman said, observing my protruding belly. "Do you have far to go? You can stop here and rest for a while if you want."

"That would be nice, but I think watering the horses will do," I replied cautiously. I climbed back up and drove the horses in at the lane, stopping by the trough. The horses drank like they'd never tasted water before.

The woman came along, carrying her basket of beans. "Can I get you something to drink, too? I've some fresh root beer on hand."

I hesitated, but a look at my drooping passengers made me accept. "Thank you. Yes."

We sat in the buggy under a huge Chestnut tree, grateful for the shade. In a few minutes our hostess was back with four glasses of root beer on a tray. As I loosened my bonnet, I realized my passengers couldn't do the same. I hesitated, but Abby jumped down and took the tray from the woman's hands. She ran around to the other side and handed a glass to me and a second to one of the ladies in back. Returning, she handed the third glass to the other passenger and took the fourth herself.

She turned to our hostess. "Is that a rose garden I see out back?" she asked. "Would you show it to me? I just love roses." She neatly lured the woman way from the buggy, giving the rest of us a chance to drink. In a short while they were back, Abby having been given the full tour.

"They don't mind waiting," Abby was telling the woman. "Their sister, my Aunt Hattie, died, and they've come for the funeral, but they don't care much for her husband, so the later they get there, the better."

"Oh? Where did their sister live?"

"Out by Duncansville," Abby replied, remembering another sign post she'd seen.

"Four women traveling alone," the woman remarked with a worried frown.

"Oh, don't worry 'bout us. Ma's sisters are widows. Pa couldn't get away from the farm, but we get on fine without any men," Abby assured her. "Well, thanks for the refreshments and the tour. We'll be goin' now." She climbed back up in the buggy, waved to the woman, and I turned the team toward the road. As we moved slowly back up the road to town, we looked at each other and sighed with relief

Back in Hollidaysburg, close to four o'clock, we turned in again at the Thaddeus Burns house. This time a young man opened the door.

"Are you Thaddeus Burns?" I asked, relieved not to have to deal with the maid again but still wary of dealing with someone I didn't know.

"No, I'm his son, Daniel. How can I help you?"

I looked at his open, young face and decided to trust him enough to begin the conversation.

"I've a delivery for Mr. Burns from Jesse Redfield."

"Of Alum Bank?"

"Yes."

"Come in! You've come a long way today," he smiled.

In the parlor, I explained my errand as Daniel listened, nodding. His kind response reassured me, and my apprehensions melted away. When we emerged from the house, he drove the buggy into his father's stable. Inside, he helped our passengers down and ushered them into the tack room. They took off their bonnets, their faces glistening with sweat.

"As soon as it's safe, I'll take you down to the cellar," he told them. "This is a pretty quiet town. No one will even notice you're here. We'll move you on tomorrow without any problem."

I sighed with relief, and Abby giggled nervously.

"You say you're going on to Altoona?" Daniel asked.

I nodded.

"Well, you'd better go, then. It's only about a half hour, but you look like that's about all that's left in you."

"Do you think you can find them some other clothes for tomorrow? I want to keep those in case we need them again. I can stop for them on my way home."

"I'm sure we can. I'll leave them with the maid so you can pick them up."

I must have grimaced at the mention of the maid, because Daniel laughed. "Once she knows the nature of your business, she'll be your friend for life."

We thanked him, said goodbye to our charges, and followed his directions to Altoona, which proved to be the boom town Rachel had described, full of building and bustle. The railroad was changing life as we knew it, and Altoona was a hub of activity, building locomotives and railroad cars as fast as its workers could turn them out.

We had no trouble finding Rachel and Jacob's house, and Rachel, radiant with the joy of marriage, was delighted to see us. Of course she was taken back by our costumes and my condition, but I parried her questions until she gave up asking. Then we talked and giggled like school girls. There was so much to catch up on.

Jacob arrived soon after we did and, with a long and meaningful glance at my belly, said, "Looks like some of us have been busy."

I blushed, wondering whether this visit was a good idea. But I longed be with my sister, so I bore his leering and unkind remarks without comment. Fortunately, he went out for a drink with his friends soon after supper and left us alone.

We spent the evening in quiet talk, Rachel anxious to show off her home and Jacob's prosperity. Giving only the essential details about the real reason for our trip, I caught Rachel up on the Quaker settlement since her departure. Abby mostly listened, speaking only when spoken to, leading me to marvel at the change in her. The talk went on until quite late, about everything except the most obvious: my impending motherhood.

Chapter 13

1855 – Fall

A **beautiful autumn came to Bedford County.** The flow of fugitives dropped off somewhat, but still they came, singly or in pairs. Because of my condition, Jesse took care of most of it by himself, with occasional help from Abby, who had brought her meager belongings and taken up residence at Redfield Farm after the July trip to Hollidaysburg.

"Ann needs me," she said.

I took to staying inside as my time neared, but still attended Weekly Meeting. My condition was obvious, and it was only a matter of time before a committee would be assigned to look into my case. I accepted this as a matter of fact. Friends were not vindictive, but transgressions must be dealt with.

I loved being a Quaker. Our plain ways suited me. I was comfortable in myself, going about life in concert with my inner light. I loved the silence of Meeting, and I loved it when someone, moved by strong conviction, held forth about some issue. This sharing of sense and sentiment bonded us in ways that other religions couldn't. I loved the doctrine of equality: Man was not above woman, nor was any man above another. I loved the Quaker tradition of educating girls as well as boys, an uncommon practice in those days.

So I accepted that the Meeting would have to take action. I expected them to be fair and was resigned to abide by the result. If I was read out of meeting, I could apply for reinstatement. It was simply a matter of time . . . time, I knew, during which I would be expected to ponder the gravity of my actions and resolve not to repeat them. Little enough recompense since I had done aught else but ponder the gravity of my actions since January.

One afternoon as I was going over this in my mind I looked out the window and saw Pru Hartley standing in the yard, hands on her hips, staring at the house. What could *she* want? I opened the door, and stood in the doorway, shading my eyes. "Hello, Pru."

She stood in that challenging posture, daring me to step outside. I wasn't sure what to expect, given that almost every interaction we'd ever had had been mean spirited. I stayed in the doorway.

"Well, they's right about you. You *are* standin' behind a baby, sure 'nough. Big as a house, I'd say."

I colored. Pru certainly had a way of saying what was on her mind. I stood dumbfounded, not sure how to respond.

"Whatcha got to say fer yerself now, Missus Prim and Proper? Didn't git *that* by follerin' the Quaker teachin's now, did ya?"

I had a notion to go inside and slam the door, but I couldn't seem to make myself move. It was as if I felt her abuse was somehow my due. I stood in dumb silence for long seconds before I found my voice. Actually it was William Penn's voice I found. "See what love can do."

"Sounds like you're weary, Pru. Why don't you come inside and have a piece of bread? I baked this morning." It was a spineless response in the face of her tirade, but I didn't feel like a fight. I hoped kindness would turn away wrath.

To my surprise, she moved toward the porch, looking almost shame-faced. "Don't mind if I do. Ain't et yet today."

She stepped into the kitchen, accompanied by a strong body odor, and sat down at the table, casting a scrutinizing gaze about the room. It was the first time she'd been in our house since Mother died. Mother felt sorry for the poor, neglected Hartley children, and had done her best to ease their way. She'd invited them to her Quaker school, and, even though their attendance was sporadic and their attention short, she'd made over them every time one of them showed up. I hadn't been as charitable, given that Pru antagonized me at every turn, and I usually did my best to avoid her.

"Where are your children today, Pru?"

"To home! Where else would they be?"

"Can you leave them alone? Aren't they young for that?"

"Don't you go tellin' me how to raise my own young 'uns!" She scowled with indignation. "We'll see how you do. You an' yer high and mighty ways!"

Ignoring the insult, I cut off a big slice of bread and buttered it. Pru was looking for a fight, and I was resolved not to give her one. I put the bread in front of her and poured hot water for tea. Obviously ravenous, she looked around the room as she stuffed big chunks of bread into her mouth. I wondered if she was looking for something to steal, then admonished myself for my lack of charity.

Watching her eat, I felt a slight compassion—very slight. She was ragged, dirty, and half starved. Her dress was torn, and her only wrap against the cold was an old shawl that had to have been her mother's. She wore shoes barely worthy of the name, so run down and cracked her bare feet showed. She saw me watching her and drew herself up.

"I'll have another slice," she announced "and honey on it, too."

I rose to get it for her, wondering where this visit was taking us. "Could you use some potatoes and carrots? We've got more than we need. Our garden was huge this year."

"I'll take 'em if ya got'em," she replied between bites of bread. I gave her a feed sack and told her to help herself in the root cellar on her way home. Then I wrapped up the rest of the bread in a cloth and handed it to her. "Here. Your children will likely want some of this."

Pru didn't know how to show gratitude. There was always a threatening edge to her thanks. Like you owed it to her, and if you didn't give it there'd be hell to pay.

She guzzled down her tea and picked up the bag. "I'll be goin' now. You take care, honey." She wiped her mouth on the back of her hand and was gone. I watched her after she came out of the root cellar, making her way down the hill with the sack on her back. She really was a sad soul, in spite of her meanness. Ever since her drunken father died and her brothers had wandered off, she was alone, at the mercy of whoever or whatever happened along.

&

I kept up my correspondence with Rachel, Mary, other Friends and relatives, and, of course, Josiah. He wrote about once a month, his writing improving with each letter. He was now teaching other ex-slaves and their children to read. He asked me to recommend books for him, and I did so gladly, even sending him a copy of *Uncle Tom's Cabin*, a book passed from hand to hand among the Quakers and often discussed after Meeting. The fact that it was written by a woman made it more meaningful for me.

Josiah's letters were full of the joy of freedom and the loneliness of his solitary life. Once or twice he mentioned meeting someone who had passed through our hands, for ex-slaves loved to share the stories of their escapes. The connection gave us both joy. He asked after my health, and Jesse's, ever mindful of his debt to us, ever grateful for the gifts of life, freedom, and literacy.

I walked the half mile to Ben's house at least twice a week to visit Rebecca. Ben had built on last summer; they needed more space to house five children. The house was now simply two log cabins joined by a large kitchen. There was much finishing to do, and Ben worked on it as he had time. Rebecca was delighted with it and proud of the five sturdy children who filled it.

Visiting Rebecca was awkward because she, like everybody else, wondered when and by whom I'd gotten pregnant. But, true to her nature, she waited for me to open up. I couldn't bring myself to talk about Josiah, even to her.

Elias built a house about a half mile on the other side of Ben's, and Melissa, being a stranger to the area, also relied on Rebecca for friendship and advice. At first it was awkward when the three of us chanced to come together—mostly for me—but after two or three meetings, we settled into a comfortable, if not intimate, friendship.

Melissa was only twenty, far from all that was familiar, and much in love with Elias. A naïve girl, she didn't suspect my earlier devotion to her husband. I liked her more than I thought I could, given the circumstances.

One day in mid-October, while Rebecca and I had our heads together over a quilt, the door opened and Melissa entered, unannounced. "Brrrrr! I think Bedford County is colder than Franklin County." She unwrapped a scarf from around her bonnet, smiling at us. "I've wonderful news," she revealed. "I'm going to have a baby!"

Rebecca made a great fuss, congratulating her and promising to pass along baby clothes and a cradle, while I forced a smile and a hug. Melissa, full of chatter, sat down to quilt. She talked almost without ceasing, mostly about Elias, giving personal and intimate details that made me squirm. Yet she was so innocent and trusting that even I had to like her in spite of everything.

"Oh, Annie, our babies will be friends! They'll play together, grow up together. And who knows? Maybe even marry!"

I cringed at being called Annie, but I smiled and nodded at Melissa's innocent speculation. She was so child-like, I understood how Elias fell in love with her, even though the wound still hurt.

After a short time, I rose and called to Abby, visiting in the kitchen with Deborah, and we started back through Ben's newly planted orchard for home. All the way, I was quiet, thinking about Elias and what might have been. I knew I didn't love him anymore. Knew the infatuation had died abruptly in January, but I still longed for the fullness of life that included a husband, a father for my child, more children, and a home of my own. None of that was possible now. No man would want me.

We arrived home to find Papa and the boys in a political discussion with Will McKitrick, who'd stopped for a visit on his way home from Alum Bank.

"I tell you, war is coming," Will was saying. "The South isn't going to give up their slaves, and the North won't stand by and let them spread slavery to the new territories. Sooner or later we'll fight."

"The South will see the light before that," Amos assured him. "They're losing property daily. They can't continue with a system so flawed."

"It depends on what the western states do," Jesse added, "if they come into the Union for slavery or free."

"I think Will's right," Nathaniel asserted. "All three of us could end up fighting."

"Quakers are pacifists!" Amos thundered. "No son of mine will take up arms! Mark my words. If war comes, *thee will not go!*"

I moved to turn the conversation in a different direction. "Will, has Betsy made apple butter this fall?"

Amos looked at me, offended at my interruption, then back to Nathaniel. "Hear me, now, Nathaniel. Thee will not go!"

Will turned to me. "Yes, she and my sister Virginia made a huge batch last Tuesday. Do you need any?"

"No. I was going to send her some, but it sounds like she has plenty. Tell her Pru Hartley's in a bad way. She could probably use some if you have extra."

Will scowled, but promised to tell Betsy. "She told me to invite you for a visit. Will you?"

I hesitated. I missed my sister, but my time was near. "Maybe another time, Will. I've too much to do this week."

"All right. I'll bring her along next week." Picking up his hat, he nodded to Papa and the boys and left.

Standing in the middle of the kitchen, I was suddenly doubled over by a long, contracting pain. I reached for the table to steady myself, trying to look normal. I fooled no one. Jesse jumped up.

"Is this it? Are you laboring?"

"I might be," I nodded. "It's time and the pain is great."

"Should we send for help?"

"Just send Abby for Rebecca. She'll know when it's time to send for Hannah."

Abby was out the door before I finished. I clung to Jesse's arm, and when the pain subsided, I climbed the stairs alone. Jesse followed, just in case. He helped me sit down on my bed, watching intently for signs of more pain.

"Ann," he whispered desperately, "Please tell me who the father is. I'll go get him, whoever or wherever he is. He should be here."

"Never mind, Jesse. There's nothing you can do. Just leave me now. I'll get myself into bed."

Reluctantly he went back downstairs. I changed into my nightgown and crawled heavily into bed. I had no idea how long this would take. I only knew that I needed help and wanted it to be over. They would know soon enough who the father was.

Then Abby was back with Rebecca, who pulled up a chair by my bed, held my hand, and spoke softly to me.

"You'll be fine, Sister. I'm here to repay your services, hoping this delivery will be free of constables and slave catchers!"

I laughed. Rebecca had no idea of the irony of it. I labored through the afternoon, Abby and Rebecca hovering close. At about five o'clock, Rebecca called down to Jesse to go for the midwife. By the time he returned more than an hour later, things were progressing rapidly.

Hannah took charge, and with the help of Abby and Rebecca, delivered me of a strong, healthy son with lots of black hair and broad features. His skin, light at birth, darkened somewhat, but, being three quarters white, remained a soft creamy beige.

It was quiet in the house, except for the baby's lusty cries. Relieved to have the birthing over, I was keenly aware of the silence that greeted my son's birth. Hannah took the child downstairs and bathed him in the presence of his awestruck grandfather and uncles.

Rebecca ministered to my needs and sought to comfort me. "Now I understand a lot of things," she told me, tucking a blanket around my legs.

"I wanted to tell you, but I couldn't make myself."

"No need. The heart has its reasons."

"I'm relieved it's over. I know there will be those who look down on him and me, but I hope not you."

"Don't worry, Sister. Not I."

Abby carried the baby back upstairs after his bath, and, true to her nature, talked when no one else would. "Well, ain't he a strong one! Just look at the grip he has on my finger! He's a cute little feller. Don't look nothin' like his mama, though, does he?"

Amos and the boys followed her into my room. My father looked at my baby, wrapped in a warm blanket. His face revealed nothing. "Healthy one," he stated. "You?"

"I'm fine, Papa. Rebecca's a good nurse."

Hannah looked at the baby with curiosity. "So that's where you came from!" she smiled, looking into his bright eyes. He was undeniably beautiful and full of life. "What could one do, but love such a bundle as you?"

Jesse took the child and inspected him closely, while Nathaniel looked over his shoulder. Neither knew what to say. Whatever his origins, the baby fairly glowed with health and strength. He opened his mouth and yawned widely at his two dumbfounded uncles.

So came into the world Samuel Redfield Colton. He would not take the last name until later, but I kept it for him. He suckled aggressively and thrived from his first day. I couldn't help but smile at his strong survival instinct.

"You've come to the right place, my son," I whispered in his tiny ear. "Here you will be cared for and nurtured. Here you will grow to be a man and make your mother proud." Words more full of hope than assurance.

Jesse took Rebecca and Hannah home, returning around midnight. Before retiring, he mounted the parlor stairs to my room to check on me. I was awake and spoke to him. "Now do you know why I couldn't tell you who the father was?"

"Josiah. But why, Ann?"

"Why, Jesse? Who knows why? He touched me when I needed touching..."

"But he took advantage!"

"No, Jesse. I went willingly. I'm not sorry, nor should you be."

"I don't want you to be sorry. Sam is beautiful. But your life—and his—will be hard."

"I don't pray for an easy life. I pray for the courage to endure what comes. Sam and I will be just fine."

"I have no doubt of it, Sister. Good night."

He rose and went through the low door into Nathaniel's room and on into his own. I lay in the darkness thinking about my baby and his father. I wished Josiah could know about him. Now, more than ever, I was filled with a mixture of joy and fear. The Lord giveth, and the Lord taketh away.

Chapter 14

1856

After Sam's birth, life returned to something close to normal. A healthy, happy baby, he brought joy with his smiles, gurgles, and outright belly laughs. Even the normally taciturn Amos talked to him and tickled him under the chin. Jesse and Nathaniel took turns bouncing him on their knees, and Abby picked him up and cuddled him at the least whimper. As my strength returned, I was more than up to the task of motherhood.

Outside Redfield Farm, the world was not so kind. Among the Quakers, Sam was an oddity, viewed from afar and without comment. New babies were cause for celebration and an excuse for visits from far and wide. No one came to see Sam except Aunt Alice Grainger, and when I took him to Meeting, people didn't fuss over him as they did other babies. It wasn't that they intended to be mean, it was just that they found his existence perplexing. It forced them to face the true meaning of equality, which they did, slowly and thoughtfully. After a time, they came around, one by one, speaking to me, asking about Sam, and then talking directly to him. His smile won them over, and he was soon a favorite with the dowagers. It wasn't the Quakers I feared. I knew they would be good to Sam, whatever they thought of me.

The Meeting would charge me soon enough. In the meantime I attended regularly and was diligent in my devotion to Quaker truth as my Inner Light gave me to understand it. The day of reckoning came at First Month Business Meeting after Sam's birth. Alice Heaton rose and placed before the company the matter of Ann Redfield, who, it was obvious to all in attendance, "had committed the sin of fornication with a man who was not her husband, having produced a child out of wedlock."

I sat silent in their midst, holding my baby close. I'd heard such charges before. Sometimes the accused rose and begged forgiveness. Sometimes they were absent at this and every other meeting, showing their disdain for the Society. I chose to let the Meeting do what it had to do.

No one responded to the charge; there was no need to object. All knew my circumstances. Now it was necessary only to appoint a committee. I knew how these things went. I'd sat through enough of them in the past—not fornication, perhaps, but marrying out of the order, or marriage by a 'priest' or dressing or behaving in a manner not in keeping with Quaker principles.

The charges were made and a committee appointed to investigate and report back, after which an appropriate penance was imposed. Most of the time, the penalty for a serious breach like mine was disownment—removal from official membership in the Society of Friends. A disowned Quaker could still attend Meetings, but had no right to speak. I could petition for reinstatement after an appropriate time, and it would be granted if I were perceived to be repentant.

So while it was humiliating and embarrassing, it was, in all probability, not permanent. I accepted the process as necessary to the good of the order and submitted without protest. I knew no other life and didn't even consider rebellion. I saw the punishment as deserved, even though I knew, given the same conditions, I would do it again, regardless of the outcome.

It was wrong to have loved Josiah because he wasn't my husband, but I knew fear, anguish, and suffering did strange things to the human mind—blurred the boundaries and changed perceptions. I understood the Society's need for order and the necessity to stand solidly against such behavior. But no human being is all good or all bad; we're all capable of either or both.

I was a loyal birthright Quaker, in spite of my error. I loved the order and, even though I'd deviated from its teachings, still held them dear. So I was prepared to pay for my transgression and move on.

I stayed close to home that winter, taking Sam out only to go to Meeting or to visit Rebecca. One afternoon when I was home alone, there came a knock on the door. I peeked through the window and saw Pru Hartley standing on the porch. Pru usually didn't knock. She stood in the yard until I noticed her and went out to see what she wanted. Knocking would indicate she wanted to come in. I sighed. Might as well get it over with.

"Afternoon, Pru."

"Afternoon. I was out this way, and thought I'd stop an' see yer young'un."

I knew all she wanted was to confirm the rumors, but I let her in. Pru had no position in the community, but she relished the chance to be first with any tidbit of gossip, as though it gave her a moment's respect.

Sam was sleeping in his cradle by the window, and I nodded toward him. Pru was quick to size up the situation.

"By God, he *is* a nigger! They said he was, but I never believed it. You, Ann Redfield! You Miss Perfect Quaker Lady! Humph! I might'a knowed. You ain't as high an' proper as you claim."

I stood dumbfounded. What had I ever done to deserve such venom? I struggled to find my voice. "That's enough, Pru. You've no right to come into my home and berate me."

"Oh, excuse me, Miss Perfect Quaker Lady. Did I offend you? I'm so sorry!" she whined.

"Please leave, Pru. Get on home with you. You've no room to talk."

She turned and faced me squarely, her eyes bright with spite. "I'll leave when I'm ready, and not before. You always did think you was better'n anybody. Now we'll see what your nigger savin' has got you."

I reached behind me for the broom, swung it around to face her. "You will go *now*. I won't put up with any more of this. I don't know why you have to be so mean all the time. I've never done anything to you!" I moved toward her.

She stepped aside and raised her arm as though to parry a blow. I hadn't thought of actually hitting her. I simply wanted to get rid of her. Now I moved toward her, threatening.

"Get out! Get out, or so help me, I'll thrash the life out of you!"

She edged her way slowly to the door, eyeing me warily. "No call to get so nasty."

"Nasty! I'll show you nasty!" I flew at her as she slid out the door. When I was sure she was gone, I sat down in Papa's chair in front of the fireplace, head in my hands and cried. Sam, awakened by the commotion, cried, too. I picked him up and held him close, rocked and soothed him, while my own heart pounded. This was just the beginning.

&

Mrs. Mills and Mrs. Baker, my committee, would counsel me about my error and interview relatives and close associates about my character. Then they would report back to the Monthly Meeting, and my punishment would be pronounced. It was public humiliation, but without malice. Friends would take no joy in it.

They arrived on Fourth Day, Mrs. Mills driving the buggy with Mrs. Baker at her side. I invited them into the parlor while Abby, on the edge of defiance on my behalf, tended Sam in the kitchen. We three sat facing each other in the parlor.

Mrs. Mills asked the first question. "Do you affirm or deny the charge of fornicating with a man who was not your husband?"

"I affirm it," I said softly.

"Do you affirm or deny that your child was the result of this liaison?" She looked down at a paper in her hand.

"I affirm it."

"How long did this go on?" Still looking at the paper.

"Only once. In First Month, a year ago."

"Bad luck." It was the first time Mrs. Baker had spoken.

I looked directly at her. "No, Ma'am."

"Are you saying what you did was right?"

"No, Ma'am. But you referred to luck. It was neither bad luck to be loved by that man nor to have his child."

Mrs. Baker straightened up. "Are you, then, proud of your actions?"

"Not proud, but not ashamed. Grateful. For the chance to love and have a son."

The two women were obviously perplexed. They'd expected contrition, humility, meekness. I displayed none of these. While I acknowledged my error, I refused to disavow Josiah or Sam.

"Do you intend to part from your past error?"

"Part from it? How can I part from it? I have a child. It will be with me always."

"Do you intend to repeat it?"

"I do not, nor did I *intend* it in the first place."

"Ann Redfield, your sin was great. You compound it now with arrogance. Pride is as great a sin as adultery," Mrs. Mills pronounced.

"That may be," I replied, "but my transgressions are my own. I don't blame others nor make excuses. I acknowledge my sin. Now it is for the Society to decide my fate."

The two women looked uncomfortable. There seemed little else to say, so they rose and I escorted them to the door.

"We have yet to question others on your character," Mrs. Baker reminded me. "That will take a week or more. We will report our findings at the next Monthly Meeting."

I nodded. I stood on the front porch and watched them drive out of the dooryard. It occurred to me that I might have been more accommodating, but I dismissed the possibility. Let the process continue to its natural conclusion.

Abby had been listening at the door and was now barely able to contain her anger. "Who do they think they are?" she fumed. "I'll bet they've done as bad or worse. Wait till they ask *me* about your character. I'll give them an earful!"

"Oh, Abby, calm down. They're not malicious. They're just doing their duty as they see it."

"Well, I can't wait till I get a chance to sit on a committee for one of them or their daughters. I'll teach *them* about pride!"

"No doubt you will," I laughed.

Abby set the table for lunch. Amos had ridden out to visit Betsy and Will in New Paris, and Nathaniel was in Bedford on business.

Jesse came in from the barn and stopped to warm his hands by the fire before picking up Sam. The baby smiled and wriggled his delight.

"I saw your committee come to call," Jesse observed. "How'd that go?"

"All right. They have their job to do."

"Yes. Well, I'm sorry you have to submit to that."

Looking down at the baby in my brother's arms, I replied, "The world has a long way to go, Jesse. Even Quakers. Sam shouldn't have to pay for my sins, either, but he will."

"I know," he replied. "The Friends will accept him, but there will be many who won't."

I sighed. "A man is a man. None better than the next. What is it in him that needs to create hierarchies?"

"I don't know. There's always a pecking order, though, and man isn't the only animal that does it. They all pick on the weak or the different."

"Yes, but man is supposed to be guided by reason. Yet he gives in to the folly of thinking himself better than others."

"Makes you wonder what God had in mind when he planted that seed."

Abby listened to our conversation, a frown furrowing her brow. "Well, Sam shouldn't have to start out that way. He's as good as any other baby. Wouldn't it be awful if some of those slave catchers kidnapped him and sold him to be a slave?"

I hushed her. She gave voice to what we all feared, but saying it made it more terrible.

Jesse laid the baby in his cradle and sat down at the table. "It won't ever come to that, Abby. Sam will be safe. We'll keep him safe." Listening to Jesse's words, I wondered how.

The committee's work was done by the next Monthly Meeting, and the charge was read to the whole congregation. "Ann Redfield found guilty of fornication by having a child in an unmarried state, and is therefore disowned."

Even though I knew it was coming, I was stunned by the pronouncement. I ached in sorrow for my father, brothers and sisters, embarrassed by my public humiliation. Bringing shame on my family was my greatest regret.

We rode home from Meeting in silence. Amos, Jesse, Nathaniel, and I. Abby snuggled down in back under heavy quilts with Sam. No one spoke, not even Amos, for whom the hurt was greatest. But it was heavy on our minds.

Chapter 15

1856 – Late Winter

"Ann," Jesse offered when we were home in our kitchen, "would you like to go away until this blows over? Spend a week or so with Mary and maybe some time with Rachel?"

I considered the idea. It *would* be good to get away for a while, and I'd enjoy visiting my sisters.

"Do you think you could get on without me?"

Jesse nodded, and Abby piped up, "Of course! I could keep house while you're gone. It'd be fun!"

So Sam and I went visiting. Jesse took us in the sleigh to Mary's new, large farmhouse in Osterburg. Full of children and noise, the house was the center of a prospering farm. Mary and Noah Poole had five children, twenty cows, seven hogs, four horses, numerous chickens, and seventy acres of land. Their lives were full, but not too full to welcome Baby Sam and me.

Kind hearted Mary took to Sam with the same generous love she lavished on her own.

"Oh, Ann, he's beautiful," she exclaimed, taking Sam from my arms. "I'm so glad you came. We've had so little time together in the past nine years."

"We've a lot to catch up on! What a houseful you have, Mary! How do you keep up with it all?"

"One day at a time, so Noah tells me," she said with a smile. Then, looking at Sam, "This little one. Bright as a new penny. He'll keep you hopping, Sister."

I smiled. Sam was beautiful. No argument there.

"The change of scenery will do me good. Don't worry, though. I'll do my share of the work. Company lightens the labor."

Mary nodded and nuzzled Sam's neck.

Noah Poole, round faced and ruddy, teased and joked with me and his children at every turn. "Do you know, Ann, I love your sister still? But she's never still!" He laughed as though his joke were new. It was a delight to see Mary so happy with such a good-humored man.

After a few days in Osterburg, I wrote to Rachel, asking if we could visit her in Altoona. Her response came quickly:

Dear Ann,

Jacob and I would love to have you and Sam come for a visit. We miss our dear family. Please try to get Mary and Noah to come along. They could use some time away, and it would such a treat to see them.

Love, Rachel

Mary and Noah, delighted by the invitation, arranged for Noah's brothers to do the chores, and two of his sisters volunteered to care for the children.

"You see, my dear," Noah told Mary, "how easy it is to get away? We should do it more often!"

We arrived in Altoona late on Third Day, grateful for Rachel's iron stoves in both the kitchen and parlor. Grates in the ceiling opened to let the heat rise into the upstairs rooms. Rachel, expecting her first baby in May, was still radiant. As she matured, her beauty reminded me more and more of Mother's. Maybe that was why Rachel had such a special place in Amos's heart. She was so happy to see us. Except for Abby's and my quick overnight last summer, she'd seen no family since leaving Bedford County.

Sam was sleeping when we arrived, and I couldn't help but notice Rachel's eyes fall when she first looked at him. Nothing was said, but my stomach felt cold. Could my own sister be hateful? When Jacob arrived home from work and saw Sam, he was clearly disturbed.

"I had no idea you had a Nigger baby," he said, making no effort to hide his disapproval. "Bad enough he's a bastard, but a black bastard to boot!"

"Jacob!" Rachel moved to silence him, her eyes pleading. He backed away from Sam as though the child carried something contagious.

Noah Poole stepped forward. "No need to be coarse about it," he told Jacob.

"I told Rachel that slave saving operation would come to no good. Now you've got yourself in a mess! What are you going to do with that one?" Jacob continued, with a quick jerk of his head toward Sam.

Rachel winced. "Jacob, please. You've been drinking," she whispered.

I drew in my breath sharply. "I'm sorry Rachel. I shouldn't have come. I had no idea Jacob would be so unkind."

"You expect me to have Niggers in my house like they were as good as me?" he challenged.

"Sam is as good as any human being on this earth—and better than some!" I spat out the words, looking squarely at Jacob Schilling.

"Now, now, let's not be throwing insults," Noah said, feverishly trying to salvage civility.

Jacob stalked out of the room, with a meaningful glance at Rachel. "I'll be out for the evening, my dear," he said.

After he left, we sat in silence for a while. What could I say? Finally I found the strength to voice my decision. "Rachel, I can't stay. I'll go back to Osterburg with Mary and Noah tomorrow."

She looked down at her hands, helpless in her lap. "It'll be all right, Ann. He probably won't say another word."

"No, it won't. It will be uncomfortable, at best. I didn't mean to bring tension into your home."

Mary nodded. "Maybe it's best that Ann and Sam come home with us," she said softly.

Dinner was passed with minimal conversation, and as soon as the dishes were done, I excused myself to go upstairs and nurse Sam. I laid him to sleep in a cradle Rachel had borrowed from a neighbor, hoping desperately that he would be a good quiet baby through the night and not give Jacob further reason to berate him.

Mary and Noah stayed downstairs with Rachel, talking quietly in the parlor until bedtime, but I stayed with Sam, afraid of another scene. I picked the sleeping baby out of the cradle and rocked him, long into the night, wishing I could spare him such insults for all of his days.

In the morning, I waited until I heard Jacob leave for work before I carried Sam down to breakfast. I was relieved at Jacob's absence and sensed that the rest were, too.

"I'm sorry about Jacob," Rachel told me. "He has some strange ways."

"Mean ways, I'd say," Mary chided.

"He's good to me," Rachel defended. "But sometimes, when he's drunk liquor, he doesn't care what he says."

"Does he drink liquor often?" Noah asked.

Rachel looked down. "Not that often," she said softly.

"Never mind, Rachel," I told her, trying to hide the anger and bitterness inside me. Jacob Schilling and I would never be friends. I would avoid him when I could and keep our interactions brief when I couldn't. My resentment went deep, and I struggled not to extend it to my sister.

We drove back to Osterburg with little talk. Noah was concerned for Mary, who, given her kind nature, would worry over the hurtful events and over my poor baby. Mary was concerned for both Rachel and me, one married to a hateful drunkard and the other struggling to raise a mixed race child in a white world. Holding Sam close, I marveled that anyone could look with malice upon one so innocent and beautiful as he.

When we arrived at the Poole farm, Mary invited me to stay on for a few days to give my hurts some time to heal. I sent word to Jesse to pick us up on the following Second Day.

"Don't worry, Ann. God will punish a man like Jacob Schilling," Mary told me, trying to sooth my feelings and brighten my spirits.

"I hope He doesn't include Rachel in that," I replied. "I fear for her. I wouldn't have taken Jacob for so mean a person. He surprised me."

"And me. Rachel didn't indicate any unkindness to her, though she did seem uncomfortable with his drinking."

"As anyone would. I wish for a husband, but not one that drinks. There are worse things than being unmarried."

I picked up the chubby, wriggling Sam, who was cooing and gurgling to the delight of Mary's two daughters. Overwhelmed by a need to protect him, I was anxious to get back to the safe familiarity of home. Travel wasn't as much fun as I'd hoped. This first foray out into the wider world had been hurtful for me, if not for Sam.

"I worry for this little one, Mary. If one man can say such mean things, what might others say and do? I wonder at what point in his life he will realize that, to some people at least, he is a lesser human being. What a sad day for a child."

"I know, Ann," Mary responded, struggling for comforting words. "Maybe things will change someday."

"No, they won't. The mean-spirited won't go away. There will always be those whose charity and compassion extend only to the end of their noses. All we can do is try to cope and be a comfort to those they oppress," I sighed.

Jesse's arrival on Second Day was a relief for me.

"Aunt Alice Grainger died on Sixth Day," he told me gently. "The funeral was yesterday."

"Oh, Jesse, no!" Tears welled up in my eyes. "She was my favorite aunt -- The only one to visit when Sam was born."

He nodded and laid an awkward hand on my shoulder. "I know. Amos'll miss her, too. She was his favorite sister." He sat down at the table as Mary set a plate of chicken and noodles in front of him. "Abbott Conway's wife had a baby. A boy."

"Another boy. How many is that, now? Five?"

Jesse nodded between bites of chicken and noodles. "The Lester sisters are back from Menallen. Elias' little brother, James, is goin' west as soon as the weather breaks." Jesse told this in a wistful voice that reminded me of his lifelong dream of doing the same. I wondered if he ever would.

"Ready, Ann?" he asked, pushing back his empty plate. "I want to get started as soon as we can. It's clouding up; looks like a big storm coming."

"I've been up and packed since dawn, Brother," I replied, indicating my bags by the door.

Jesse loaded the sleigh, helped me in, and handed baby Sam to me. Wrapped snugly in heavy quilts, we bid Mary, Noah, and the children goodbye and set out for home.

It felt good to be back with Jesse. He soon had me laughing over Amos' latest bout of consternation with the Democrats. "Papa heard they were probably going to nominate James Buchanan for president. You know how he feels about anyone who placates the South. I thought he'd burst a blood vessel, he was so mad!" Amos took his politics seriously and expected others to do the same.

"How's Rachel?" Jesse asked, carefully giving the horses their head in picking their way up an icy slope.

"She's well. Her baby is due in Fifth Month. They have a nice house in Altoona, but I don't think city life would be for me. It seems to suit Rachel."

We left it at that. The conversation moved on, as I was determined to leave the sadness behind and not spread it to Jesse, for whom Sam was a special angel.

Chapter 16

1856 – Early Spring/Early Summer

After I chased her out with the broom, I didn't see much of Pru Hartley that winter, but I knew times were hard for her. Jesse saw her over at Alum Bank looking for handouts almost every time he went to the Post Office. I couldn't help but have hard feelings for her, even though my Quaker upbringing stressed charity for all. But I pitied her poor children, and it was for them that I decided to pay a visit.

The Hartleys never had much, but things looked worse than ever when I walked down there one March afternoon with a basket of food over my arm. The snow had melted, but the wind was fearsome enough to cut through all but the warmest clothes. No one was about when I approached, but two skinny dogs set up a chorus of barking. I wasn't sure they would let me get up to the house, so I stood outside and called.

"Pru! Pru Hartley!"

Pru stepped out on the porch and yelled at the dogs. Her dirty blond hair hung below her breasts, but didn't cover the ragged dress hanging beneath. She wore a pair of men's boots, probably left over from her father, and her three scrawny, big-eyed children stood silent behind her.

"Whatcha want?"

"I came to pay a call. Thought I'd bring you some goodies." I referred to the heavy basket over my arm, which I was more than anxious to let down.

"We don't need none of yer charity!" she replied defiantly.

I'd already planned to leave the basket and go on home if it came to that. "Got some bread in here, and some jam. Some pickles and a little jerked beef."

The children looked up at her, their faces white with hope. They were hungry. Pru looked from them to me. "Jest leave it."

"All right. I did want to talk to you, though."

"What you wanna talk to me fer? Ya run me off with the broom last time."

I moved toward the porch. "I shouldn't have done that, but you were insulting my baby."

"Warn't no insult. A nigger's a nigger. I jest called him what he was."

Her words cut me again and I was tempted to turn around and leave, but a look at the faces of the children stopped me.

"Let's leave it, Pru. Do you want this food or not?"

"These here young'uns could use it," she allowed.

I stepped toward the porch, but Pru took a position between me and the door. "That's far enough," she said.

I set the basket down on the edge of the porch, and the children immediately descended upon it. They tore the bread apart and crammed it into their mouths without even opening the jam. Pru stood back for a short while but soon reached in to grab her share.

The children looked like lost waifs. Two boys and a girl, obviously from different fathers, little resemblance among them. They were dirty and almost naked, so ragged were their clothes. I thought of Sam, warm and cozy in his cradle while such as these starved and froze. My anger toward Pru melted some. She'd had a hard life. In my heart I'd thought she deserved it, but no. Not even she deserved this.

"You got enough wood to burn?" I asked, looking for smoke from the chimney.

"Ain't got none less I get it, an' I can't haul much. These here ain't got no shoes." She indicated the children.

I could see that. "Where are your brothers these days? I haven't seen them around in ages."

"Sawyer's gone off to be a peddler, carryin' a pack. Ain't heard from him since last summer. Cooper comes around sometime, but he's got him a woman down to Cessna, so he don't care about us."

There it was. A woman alone, with no one to plant, hunt or haul wood, No income. One could condemn or one could help. It wasn't a choice. For whatever reason, Pru needed help. I watched them eat until the basket was empty.

"I'd best be going now, but if you'll come up our way later today, I'll find some more for you."

I'd known Pru Hartley all my life, but that was the first time I ever saw even an inkling of warmth or kindness about her. She smiled—through broken teeth.

&

I kept count of fugitives passing through each month, and by the third week of Seventh Month in 1856 there had already been sixteen. Jesse and I were hard pressed. Once or twice we had to call on other Friends for help. Slave catchers roamed the roads and hills. Every farm was suspect, especially a Quaker farm. We moved carefully because we never knew who might be watching.

On the 25th day of Seventh Month, a group of nine arrived from Schellsburg around 11 p.m., rousing Jesse out of bed. He settled them in the barn and promised to move them along the next night. Before first light, my father and brothers went to the barn, each carrying a 'toolbox' or a bucket containing breakfast for our guests. After sun-up, Jesse rode out to consult with others about where he could send so large a group. He returned home perplexed.

"The route's clogged," he told me. "No place to send so many at once. I'll break 'em up and send 'em on a few at a time. Hope we don't get such a large group again for a while."

Abby and I stood ready to help. "Isn't there a conductor in Claysburg?" I asked.

"Yes. Joseph Dickerson takes them from time to time. Puts 'em on the Clearfield route."

"Abby and I could take two or so to him today, in the wagon, and bring back a load of peaches from the Pavia orchards."

Jesse considered the possibility. "I guess we could hide 'em under hay and gunny sacks, as usual," he said. "Let me talk to 'em about splitting up and see who's willing to go."

He was back from the barn within ten minutes. "Two are husband and wife. They're willing to split off from the rest if they can stay together."

"All right," I agreed. "If we leave right after noon, we can be back before dark."

Abby and I were getting to be old hands at this, but Sam created a problem. At nine months, he was too active for a long wagon ride, so I went out to the barn to pick a babysitter.

"Please, Ma'am, I can do that," one of the remaining three women volunteered. She was a tall dark-skinned beauty, a little younger than I. Her movements were graceful and assured, unlike so many whose backs were bent by overwork.

The problem was how to get her from the barn to the house unnoticed. She was almost as tall as Nathaniel, so I carried out a suit of his clothes and a broad brimmed hat in a gunny sack. I told her to put them on and walk with long strides, head down, hands in pockets, to the house.

Once inside, she shed her disguise, and I told her the plan for transporting the couple and explained her role in it. Then Abby brought Sam to meet his 'nurse'.

The black woman's eyes widened when she saw him. She looked questioningly from me to Abby and back at Sam. Disinclined to explain, I hurried on with preparations to move man and wife. Jesse loaded the wagon with empty baskets covered with burlap bags. The couple lay curled up among the baskets, hay scattered over them, covered by the burlap in a carefully arranged helter-skelter. Abby and I packed food, instructed the black woman on Sam's care, and drove off toward Claysburg. The men stayed to tend the farm and prepare for Jesse's nighttime trip.

We presented a pleasant picture of farm women on an errand, bumping down the road to Claysburg. Outwardly calm, inwardly tense, we were keenly aware of how completely our charges depended on us. When we arrived, around four o'clock, I was relieved to hand the couple over to Joseph Dickerson in the shelter of his orchard.

"We're going back through Pavia to get some peaches," I told him.

"I've got peaches right here," he replied, indicating his heavy trees.

"To sell?"

"Yes, Ma'am."

"What a piece of luck!" I told Abby, reaching for the empty baskets.

The wagon was soon loaded with succulent, ripe peaches, courtesy of Joseph Dickerson and his four strapping sons. I noticed Abby watching the boys and realized, with a tinge of sadness, that she was growing up.

We were soon on the road home. The heavy load made travel slow, and we arrived barely before dark. We smiled at each other as we climbed down from the wagon, quietly proud of our accomplishment.

Sam was sound asleep in his little bed when we got home. We sat down to supper, shared with Sam's nurse, as though it were just another day on the farm.

After the meal, Jesse and Nathaniel unloaded the baskets of peaches on the back porch while Amos ambled down the path to Ben's. He returned with one of Ben's teams and hitched them to the wagon inside the barn. Two of the fugitive men and two women were loaded into the wagon, concealed under several old, unused bee hives. The imagined presence of bees was enough to put off most interlopers. The slaves lay together in a tight little space behind and beneath the hives.

Nathaniel, who rarely participated in our Railroad operations, rode along with Jesse that night. His sentiments, though strongly opposed to slavery, didn't usually spur him to action, and no one was ever forced.

After they left, I thanked the black nurse and sent her back to the barn.

"That no hardship, Ma'am. He a joy to care for."

"Did you do that kind of work where you came from?" I asked, curiously attracted by the woman's obvious refinement and intelligence.

"No, Ma'am. I was a personal maid to the mistress."

"Oh," I replied. "I *thought* you had some kind of house position."

House servants didn't run as often as field hands did, because their lives were much easier. In the inevitable hierarchies that people invented, house servants were above field hands. Their access to refinements and discarded luxuries made their lives more comfortable than those of common slaves. As a result, they often developed more loyalty to their masters than to their fellow slaves. I wondered why this woman would run.

"What made you come north?"

"No one want to be owned by another, even if they nice. My mistress nice to me, but she hate my man 'cause he *her* husband's son. Master die. Mistress fixin' to sell my husband, so he run. I go to be with him."

I caught my breath, my heart racing in my breast. "What's your name?" I asked, struggling to keep my voice calm.

"Lettie."

"And where did you come from, Lettie?"

"Virginny. Culpeper County.

Chapter 17

1856 – Mid-summer

The next morning, Abby and I loaded all but two baskets of peaches back in the wagon and set off with Sam to distribute them to friends and family. We dropped off peaches at Ben's house, Elias Finley's, Uncle Sammy Grainger's, making our way around to New Paris, where we dropped off the last of them with Betsy, who had just returned from a week in Altoona with Rachel.

Rachel's baby, a boy, had been born in May and named, to Amos' distaste, James Buchanan Schilling. Rachel basked in the joy of first motherhood. According to Betsy, all was well there, so I kept my feelings about Jacob Schilling to myself.

"I liked visiting Altoona, but I was just as happy to get back to New Paris," Betsy asserted. "It's such a big city, and it's noisy all the time—houses being built, the trains, the horse traffic. They're paving the streets as fast as they can, but the building outstrips them. Jacob is speculating in real estate. He's bought four lots and plans to build houses on them and sell them. Rachel may end up a rich woman."

I listened with interest but found it difficult to take joy in Jacob Schilling's accomplishments. No one but Mary and I knew of his insulting behavior, and it was best kept that way, so I tried to look interested in all the Altoona talk, but I still felt an unspeakable resentment against Jacob.

As Abby and I drove home, my mind was on other things. Lettie. Josiah's wife. The woman I'd wronged. I struggled against a wave of panic, along with other urges I could not acknowledge—even to myself.

I pictured Josiah's joy at being reunited with Lettie, and tried to be glad for them. They had a fine future together, living and raising a family in freedom in Canada. Envy rose in me, even though I tried to put it down, for my own future promised none of that. I thought about Sam growing up, the only Negro in the settlement, never knowing his father, and my sadness for him deepened. Abby interrupted my thoughts.

"You know what, Ann?"

"What, Abby?"

"I like that woman we got now. That Lettie. She's a good person. I can tell by the way she takes to Sam."

Her words struck me deep.

"Yes. Yes, she's nice."

At home, we turned the wagon over to Jesse, who was going to transport the rest of the fugitives that night. He spent the afternoon building a false bottom in the wagon so the runaways could lie flat on the real floor, safe under whatever Jesse chose to be hauling. He'd wanted to do this for a long time. The heavy traffic increased the need for more secure measures. So he made the false bottom using wood from an old outbuilding Amos had torn down last winter.

Abby and I started on the peaches, but it wasn't long before she came up with the idea of bringing Lettie in from the barn to help. She ran upstairs for Nathaniel's old clothes and scurried out to the barn to help Lettie with the disguise.

Thrilled to be out of the barn, Lettie joined us in putting the peaches by and tending to Sam. Watching her play with Sam, I felt a twinge of jealousy. He took to her right away, even though he was at an age where the only two women that suited him most of the time were Abby and me. Usually he cried and reached out to me when a stranger held him, but now he sat content on Lettie's lap, touching her face and smiling as though he recognized her from some past life.

"He a beautiful baby," Lettie said in a quizzical tone. Her eyes studied my face for a clue to the mystery. Clearly I was his natural mother, but . . . I tried to divert attention to other matters.

"Jesse thinks you'll be moved on tonight," I observed.

"Mmmm. I can't believe I be this close to my Josiah," Lettie returned. "Maybe I be with him this time next week."

At the mention of Josiah's name, I turned cold again and became extremely agitated, unable to concentrate on the peaches or even to sit still. Without the name, I might have pretended that this was some other woman. Some other Lettie from Virginia. Now the knowledge intruded on my fragile tranquility.

I felt a need to be alone, so I excused myself and headed to the privy. At least there no one would see me tremble and quake at meeting Josiah's wife. I sat down on the closed seat, fully clothed, held my head in my hands, and cried. Guilt, shame, anger, fear, jealousy, and need poured out of me. I was confronted with the gravity of what I had done and overwhelmed by a need to somehow make it right.

My conscience pushed me to confess. To tell Lettie all of it. But why? Who could benefit from the telling? *I* would, in an immediate sense—in relief from my guilt. But that was all, and it would be selfish to lay this thing between Lettie and Josiah, especially because of Sam. No! I could not, *would not* tell Lettie. Whatever she thought about Sam, let her think it. With great effort, I pulled myself together and went back to the house.

Jesse came in as we were cleaning up the last of the peaches. "I'm done. I think I can get these last three in there and move them on tonight."

I was relieved that Lettie—and hopefully my own emotional turmoil—would soon be gone. As I wiped up the kitchen, Lettie donned her disguise and returned to the barn. It had started to rain, and I took that as a good sign, for it meant less traffic on the roads.

We ate supper in silence, aware that this night held danger for Jesse. He acted light hearted about his missions, but we knew the dangers he faced.

"I could go with you," Nathaniel offered.

"You're needed here to help Father with the chores. I'll be all right," Jesse replied.

I felt uneasy about this mission, but dismissed it as anxiety over my guilt and shame. After dark I went to the barn to help. The rain continued, likely to keep the law and the slave catchers off the roads.

The rest of the fugitives were safely loaded, lying down in the bottom of the wagon, and the false floor was dropped in, giving them little room to move. My eyes met Lettie's as Jesse dropped the floor in place. The new wagon floor was cluttered with tools, parts of farm implements, an old crock, and a couple of buckets. Wagon junk.

As Jesse stepped up on the driver's seat, I handed him an old, oilskin slicker from a peg by the door. He wrapped it around his shoulders and clucked to the horses. With clear reluctance, they stepped out into the heavy rain.

The rain continued all night, the gray dawn not much lighter. I awoke with a start, but, seeing Sam sleeping warm and snug in his little bed, I pushed aside my feelings of dread. I dressed and went downstairs, leaving Abby to tend to Sam when she awoke. I poked up the fire and added a log. Its warmth lightened the room and lifted the dampness.

I lit a lamp and prepared breakfast. Amos stirred in his bed in the corner. Pulling on his trousers and shoes, he arose.

"Jesse?" he asked.

"No sign. I didn't hear him come back."

"Probably stayed over at the next station."

"Yes, probably."

Abby brought the baby down to the warm kitchen and dressed him. Nathaniel was the last to join us, fully clothed, with a hearty appetite. We breakfasted in silence, except for Sam's gabbling and pounding the table with a wooden spoon.

The heavy rain continued throughout the morning. Amos and Nathaniel did the chores while Abby and I cleaned up the kitchen and made the beds. The dreariness seemed to penetrate our souls. I warmed the Sad Irons, and Abby swept up the kitchen. The smell of the hot irons on cotton brought welcome warmth against the dampness.

Dinner passed much the same as breakfast—each of us eating silently, lost in private thoughts. Amos and Nathaniel read while I ironed and Abby made a stew for supper. The tension increased as the day wore on with no word from Jesse.

The normally taciturn Amos gave voice to our fears. "Seems like he should have been back by now."

Nathaniel grunted. "Unless he stayed over till morning and got a late start."

"If he's not back by suppertime, best you get Ben and set out," Amos returned.

They lapsed into silence again, the drumming of the rain incessant on the roof. Sam pulled himself up to the bench beside the table and slammed the teapot lid down on it, beating out a baby rhythm, our only distraction through the long afternoon. By four o'clock it was almost dark again, and when the men went out for evening chores, the mud in the barnyard was up to their ankles. They came in, mud-stained and bedraggled, for supper.

After the meal, Nathaniel stood up. "Think I'll just go myself. No need to bother Ben."

"Take Ben with you. No tellin' what you'll find," Amos ordered.

Nathaniel's departure did little to take our minds off our fears. We'd been lucky all these years. We hadn't kept an accurate record, but probably a hundred or more fugitives had passed through our hands without serious mishap. Jesse was definitely in trouble. It remained only to find out what kind and how bad. I heard Ben and Nathaniel ride past, their horses' hooves sucking mud.

I sat up sewing by lamplight until eleven o'clock. Abby'd taken Sam up early and retired herself. Amos sat on his bed in the corner of the kitchen, staring into the shadows. Outside, the rain still fell on the water soaked ground.

Around two o'clock I was aroused from a shallow slumber by what I thought was a shout. I took up the lamp and hurried to the door. The night was dark and wet, but it had stopped raining.

Outside, a sad and broken procession made its way to the barn. Nathaniel drove the wagon, its side broken in and one wheel wobbling precariously on its hub. Ben rode beside, leading Nate's horse. Jesse was nowhere in sight. I ran forward to open the barn door and lit two lanterns as they drove the half-shattered wagon in. Then I saw Jesse, lying on his side on the false bottom, his face white, his left shoulder hunched awkwardly toward his neck.

"Jesse!"

"Wait, Ann," he said weakly. "Let them get me to the house."

Ben unhitched the horses, inspecting their legs with concern. Nate and I lifted Jesse out of the wagon; he cried out in pain despite our efforts to be gentle. Ben helped Nate carry him into the house and lay him on Amos' bed. Papa stood bewildered, watching his two sons carry the third, disturbed by his muffled groans.

I did my best to make him comfortable. I knew his injuries were beyond my meager medical knowledge. Jesse needed a doctor. Nate promised to ride for one at sunup. Meanwhile, I treated the obvious cuts and bruises, while my brothers returned to the barn to tend to the horses. Around three o'clock I heard Ben ride past on his way home.

Then the door opened and Nate entered, guiding Lettie before him. "We almost forgot about her in the rush to take care of Jesse and the horses," he said. "She can tell you what happened."

Lettie shivered in her torn, muddy dress, a big blue bruise on her cheekbone. I took a basin into the parlor so she could wash, then hurried to find her some clean clothes. About a half hour later, as she sat at the table eating a bowl of oatmeal, she began her tale.

"We goin' up a big hill. Could feel how steep it was. Then lightnin' or thunder, something spooked the horses, and they into buckin' and rearin'. Felt like the whole wagon turn upside down." She looked at us, wide-eyed between mouthfuls of oatmeal. "Mr. Jesse fall back off the seat. I couldn't see. I was under the floor. Wagon start slippin' sideways. Take the horses, Mr. Jesse, us and all off the road and down over the bank."

She stopped eating, her eyes bright. "Them horses cryin' and the wagon broke. We was all knocked heck west and crooked. False bottom fall out and me and the other two scatter in the mud." Her face darkened. "Field hands. They's not hurt too bad, and they think Mr. Jesse's dead, on account of the wagon on top of him and he head bleedin. So they lit out. Figured stayin' bring nothin' but trouble. I'm not sure he dead, so I try to get the horses free so they can help me get him out."

I listened breathlessly as Lettie recounted the story, her eyes on our faces.

"It bad, Miss Ann. I got the horses on they feet—I learned about horses from my Josiah—but they so spooked, they no help, so I tie them to a tree and pull everything out of the wagon. Make it light so's I can move it. No such luck. Jesse, he lie there moanin' and it just keep rainin'."

She passed her empty bowl to me. "After while the horses settle down, and I rope them to the wagon an' get them to commence pullin'. I push from the bottom side, and finally the wagon upright, on a steep slant. Then I try to help Mr. Jesse, but he bad hurt." Her normally animated face was slack, expressionless.

"I want to run. Figure it's my only chance, but then I think if I was hurt, he'd do what he could to help me. I knowed his folk would come for him. Just had to wait. Waited all day in the rain. Nobody on the road. No sign of them two niggers. They lit out without even sayin' goodbye." Her contempt for the others was clear.

"We was down over the bank, so a body could pass without seein' us. I pull Mr. Jesse under the wagon and hunker down and wait and pray."

"Oh, Lettie! If you'd run away, too, Jesse might have died," I cried.

"I couldn't run off and leave him after he almost died tryin' to save me."

Nate took up the story. "It was over past Pavia, halfway up the mountain we found them. By the time we got there, they'd been lying out for the better part of a day. Lettie heard us coming and climbed up on the road to hail us."

"I wa so scared and cold and hungry by then, I didn't care if it was slave catchers or who it was."

"Ben and I used the team and our horses to pull the wagon back up on the road. It was pretty broken up, but we figured to try and get it home. We hid Lettie again and loaded Jesse on top of the false bottom. Took us a couple of hours to get back."

Looking at my baby brother's face, wan in the lamplight, I thought how young he was. Jesse'd been in this thing even younger than Nate, but somehow Nate seemed too young for it tonight.

I sent him off to bed and Lettie to sleep in my room. I passed the rest of the night tending my brother. My heart ached to look at him, so broken and bruised, in so much pain.

I was in deep discomfort having Lettie back. Shame on me. Were it not for her, Jessie might have died. But now, with Jessie laid up, how was I going to move her on? Panic rose at the thought of having her around for who knew how long. Despite her kindness, courage and decency, I just wanted her gone.

Chapter 18

1856 – Late Summer

Abby rose with the sun the next morning and wandered into the kitchen to a strange sight: Jesse curled up on his side on Amos's bed; Amos asleep in a chair, lost in open-mouthed snoring; and me on a bench at the table, asleep on my arms.

The doctor came late in the morning, but he couldn't do much to ease Jesse's pain. He thought there were broken ribs, a broken collarbone, and a shoulder that he described as "smashed." A concussion compounded Jesse's discomfort with a raging headache. There was little to do beyond wrapping his rib cage, setting the shoulder and collar bone as best could be done, and putting his left arm in a sling to hold both in place.

Tearing long strips of cloth from an old sheet, the doctor trussed up the shoulder and collarbone amid groans of pain from Jesse. He showed me how to wrap the strips, watching me as I worked.

"I want to be clear about his chances," the doctor said, looking squarely at me. "If one of the ribs punctured a lung, he could die. His shoulder? That's a matter of chance. He could mend nicely, or he could have a useless left arm."

"Yes, well, it's in God's hands now," I replied.

The wagon was needed almost daily around the farm, so that afternoon Amos and Nathaniel repaired it. The horses, though scraped and bruised, had suffered no broken bones, so they would recover. The day gradually cleared, and by evening, the summer storm was only a memory.

I worried over Jesse. I wondered how we would carry on the work without him. But I had more immediate concerns. I was pondering the future—my own and my child's.

My head buzzed with thoughts about moving Lettie on; the responsibility was now mine alone. I shuddered at the thought. How could I do it? And yet I must. Slowly, a plan took shape in my mind. I mulled it over for a long time, not sure I could make it work. And yet I must.

First I wrote to Josiah and told him Lettie was with us and about the accident and Jesse's condition. I ended the letter with a revelation I never expected to make. I told him about Sam. My heart poured out on the paper—how strong, healthy, and beautiful Sam was and how he brought so much joy to us.

I didn't tell him about being disowned by the Society of Friends, or about the likes of Pru Hartley or Jacob Schilling, or about the strange looks in peoples' eyes when they saw me with a Negro child. He would already know about that. I ended by promising to get Lettie to him as soon as I could. The letter was long, the envelope fat. Nathaniel remarked on it when I gave it to him to post. No one but I knew that Lettie was Josiah's wife, and that was just as well, for now.

The next step needed Betsy's help, so on Second Day I rode off to New Paris on Nathaniel's horse, leaving Sam with Lettie and Abby. I told them my errand was to tell Betsy about Jesse's ill fortune, but that was only part of it.

"Sister, I need your help," I told Betsy, after relating the story of Jesse's wreck. "I need some fancy clothes."

Betsy's eyebrows went up. "Fancy clothes? Why, Ann?"

"I just need them, Betsy. I'll explain later, but . . . please, can you get me some? Something very unQuaker-like. Just one outfit. For me."

"I think I can," Betsy replied. Will's Aunt Edith had married out of the Society and lived in Bedford with her lawyer husband and two grown daughters. The girls were extremely fashionable, giving Betsy hope that she could get an outfit for me. "It'll take a few days, but I think I can do it." Betsy knew enough about the Railroad to cooperate without asking for an explanation.

I returned home, satisfied that part two of my plan was in motion. Now I wrote to Rachel for railroad schedules and fares between Altoona and Pittsburgh. My next concern was money. I had but little, so I needed help. No one else in the family was very well off, except Uncle Sammy Grainger. Jesse always went to him with Railroad problems because Uncle Sammy had resources and was sympathetic to the cause. I waited for a chance to go see him.

The following First Day, Amos, Nathaniel, and Abby left for Meeting, Abby protesting, torn between boredom with Meeting and a need to socialize. I urged her out the door, looking forward to some time with Jesse.

"You're looking better today," I told him as he struggled to sit up. He winced in pain but moved more easily than before.

"I think I could use a good wash," he replied, easing his way out of bed. It was the first time he'd tried to get up.

I pumped water and set the kettle over the fire. Watching me, Jesse reflected, "We ought to get an iron stove in here, Ann. It would make your work a lot easier."

I nodded, helping him to the table, where I'd set out a bowl of oatmeal with honey. While he ate, I went upstairs for some clean clothes. I filled a basin with hot water and washed his hair. I felt the bump on the side of his head where the concussion was.

"Does that hurt?"

"No. Just a little numb when you touch it."

Next I stropped his razor and set out his mug and soap to shave him. I did all right for my first attempt at shaving. Only nicked him once. When that was done, I poured a basin of fresh, hot water and helped him wash. I left him for a few minutes while I brought out clean sheets and changed his bed. Then I helped him put on his pants, shirt, and stockings. That was about all he could handle for one day, so he lay back down. He grinned. "Pretty much an invalid now, huh?"

"You'll mend," I told him, whether I believed it or not.

It was a warm, sunny day, so Lettie took Sam into the parlor and opened all the windows to air out the room. I did the same in the kitchen, but there the windows were small. Still, the sunshine and fresh air were welcome.

"I've got a plan to move Lettie on," I told Jesse.

"What's that?"

"I'll dress up as a fine Southern lady and take her on the train as my maid, as far as Pittsburgh."

Jesse nodded. "Then what?"

"We'll take a coach north to Erie. That way she'll be safe all the way to the lake. If I get her that far, and buy her a ferry ticket, she could be in Canada that night."

"I suppose so, but why would you go to all that trouble when you could just send her on to the next station and be done with it?"

"Because she saved your life, Jesse. You could have died out there on the mountain. And . . ." I hesitated but knew I must silence his objections. "because she's Josiah's wife."

"His wife?"

"Yes."

"How do you know?" Jesse leaned up on his good elbow.

"From what he told me about her and what she told me about him."

"Does she know we took care of him, too?" We spoke softly so as not to be overheard.

"No. I thought it best not to tell her."

"Then she doesn't know Sam is Josiah's son?'

"No."

Jesse lowered his head, thinking. He liked Josiah and Lettie, too, and he understood my need to make something up to her. "All right, if you can arrange it, I'll support you. But how will you get enough money?"

"I'm working on that."

"I have a little cash, but not that much," he offered. I wish I could help more. Wish I could go with you, but this shoulder's going to keep me down for quite a while."

I patted his good shoulder. "You've already done enough. More than enough. I should be able to take care of this on my own."

A few days later, I rode Nate's horse to Fishertown to see Uncle Sammy Grainger. He greeted me at the door, energetic in spite of his eighty years. "Ann! It's been so long since we've seen you!"

"I should have come sooner, Uncle."

Uncle Sammy was a loving soul. Married to Amos's oldest sister, he'd spent his life in good-humored service to others. He and Aunt Alice were childless, and so took a great interest in the lives of their nieces and nephews. Aunt Alice was the first to visit me after Sam's birth when others were hesitant to call on a sinner.

Now Uncle Sammy asked after my siblings and I dutifully reported on each, with extra details about Jesse's troubles. Uncle Sammy didn't go to Meeting much anymore, so he hadn't heard about Jesse. He listened intently to my account of the accident and Lettie's heroic behavior. While we drank a cup of tea, I revealed the reason for my visit.

"Uncle Sammy, I need some money."

"You do, dear? Whatever for?"

"To get Lettie to Canada."

I explained my plan and outlined the steps I'd already taken. "I want to repay Lettie for saving Jesse's life."

The old man was thoughtful. "Child, I probably shouldn't tell you this, but you are a legatee in my will."

"I am?" My voice faltered.

"Yes. You and all your siblings. So I suppose I could advance you a sum against your inheritance for this."

"Oh, Uncle Sammy! Thank you so much!"

My plan moved forward. The railroad fares and schedule arrived from Rachel early the next week, and Will McKitrick rode up with a bundle on his saddle on Sixth Day. Now it was left to ask a favor of Ben. That afternoon I took the path through the orchard to his house. As I crossed the yard, I saw him in the doorway of the barn and waved.

"Ben, I need your help. I'm moving Lettie on soon, and I need a way to get us to Bedford. We'll take a coach from there to Altoona. I won't be coming back right away, so I'd like to borrow your buggy and a team to take us to Bedford, but I can't return it."

"I could take you," Ben offered.

"No, Ben. You have enough to do. I was hoping to borrow the buggy and leave it at the livery. Then maybe Nate or Elias could bring it home when they go to town."

Ben looked puzzled. "Sure. You can do that," he said.

Walking back through the orchard, I went over the plan again in my mind. In Altoona, we could stay the night with Rachel, in spite of possible hostility from Jacob Schilling. This was more important than his antics. I thought it through, one step at a time. It should work. A southern lady traveling with her maid.

I missed Meeting again the next First Day so I could pack a small trunk, try on my "Southern lady" finery and outfit Lettie in one of my old dresses. I slept little that night, wrestling with nightmares when I did. Dawn finally came, and I went to awaken Lettie. Then I returned to my room, dressed in the dark so as not to waken Abby, and quietly picked up the sleeping baby and carried him downstairs.

Placing the child in Lettie's arms, I put a cautionary finger to my lips and nodded toward the door. Lettie carried Sam to the barn, where I hitched up Ben's team to the buggy. Inside the barn, Lettie let out a cry.

"Miss Ann! Where we takin' this baby?" she asked.

"We're taking him with us."

"Why, Miss Ann?"

"Because, Lettie, he's going with you."

She looked at me in horror. "Goin' with me? Why?"

"Because Josiah is his father."

"He father? My Josiah? How?"

"Get in the buggy, Lettie. I'll explain it as we drive."

Lettie glared at me through dark eyes. "*My* Josiah?" she asked again.

I opened the barn doors and we drove out into the early light. Sam still slept in Lettie's arms. We traveled in silence for several miles, Lettie looking angry, lost and hurt.

"Josiah came through on the Railroad, like you, only he was ill when he arrived. Gravely ill. So we kept him until he recovered—well into winter. He was with us for about five months."

"And you? And Josiah?" Lettie faltered.

"Oh, Lettie, I am sorry. It happened only once, and neither of us meant for it to happen. I was so sad and he was so lonely. Please forgive us, Lettie. We didn't do it to hurt you."

Lettie looked down at the sleeping child in her lap. She touched his fat cheek with the back of her finger. A tear wended its way down her face. She looked over and saw that I was crying, too.

"How can you give him up?" she asked. "How can you send him off without he Mama?"

"Because his life here would be hell, Lettie. I'm sending him for the same reason you don't stay here and Josiah didn't. Sam deserves better."

Sam stirred in his sleep, reached out a chubby hand and grasped Lettie's finger. I saw, and felt a pang of jealousy. We rode on in silence, each of us looking at a world blurred by tears.

"Lettie, I can't take back what I've done. I can only try to do what's best now. Sam will be better off. Josiah won't be deprived of his son, and you—I am giving you my most prized possession—because I trust you to be a good mother to him."

"Does Josiah know about Sam?" Lettie asked.

"He does now. I wrote to him a few weeks ago so he wouldn't think you were coming with someone else's child."

"Thank you for that."

Lettie looked down at Sam, who was by that time awake and looking for breakfast. He smiled at her, and she snuggled him until he giggled. I drove on, my jaw set, my will determined, now that the wheels had been set in motion, to see the plan through.

Chapter 19

A little after nine o'clock we rattled down a dusty Bedford street to the livery. We left the buggy and walked to the stage coach stop, Lettie three steps behind, carrying Sam and the small trunk. This bothered me, but we needed to keep up our pretense.

On the stage ride, amid shaking and jostling toward Altoona, we took advantage of the opportunity to practice our roles, as we shared the coach with two gentlemen and a lady. Altoona seemed even bigger and busier than six months earlier. Sam was a handful by now, very tired of restraint. We arrived at about four o'clock and walked the three blocks from the stage depot to Rachel's house.

Jacob Schilling was still at work, so Rachel and I had a little time to talk. It was tempting fate bringing Lettie and Sam into his house, but the circumstances called for tempting fate. Let him say one word.

James Buchanan Schilling, three months old, lay asleep in his basket. His cousin, Sam, nine months old, crawled on the floor seeking mischief. Lettie sat quietly in a corner of the kitchen, watching. I'd warned her there might be some unpleasantness with Jacob.

Rachel made tea, nervously chattering about baby James. She knew I was shepherding Lettie to freedom, and clearly wondered why I'd brought Sam along, but I evaded her questions.

"Well, you do look the Southern Lady," she commented. Rachel didn't mention it, but I think my clothing gave her pause, even though she, herself, had given up plain dress.

Rachel smiled at Lettie. "I heard how you helped Jesse and stayed with him until Ben and Nate came. Thank you for that."

Lettie nodded.

A scrape and a rattle outside told us that Jacob had returned from work, and was stowing his tools in the shed out back. I shot a look at Lettie, and Rachel rose and led her upstairs along with Sam and our trunk.

"Jacob is a good man," she explained to Lettie, "but drink makes him mean sometimes. Best we don't wave you in front of his face."

"We got to stay hid?" Lettie asked, looking doubtfully at Sam.

"No. Just try to stay out of his way. He'll probably go out after supper, and he leaves early in the morning, so you may not see him at all."

Jacob took off his shoes and shook the plaster dust out of his shirt on the back porch. Rachel was back before he came in and stepped out to speak to him, I guessed to prepare him for visitors and warn against an outburst. As I watched them talking on the porch, it occurred to me that Rachel looked a little worn. Not the same beautiful girl who had ridden away in the dray wagon two years before.

Jacob entered and nodded to me, sitting at the table with my cup of tea. "Fancy dress for a Quaker lady. For a minute I thought you one of them uppity society belles," he observed.

"Yes, it does feel strange," I replied, trying to sound cordial.

"What do you think of *this* guy?" he asked, pointing with pride at his sleeping son. "Ain't he a fine one?"

"Oh, yes," I smiled. We talked politely for a while, mostly about Jesse's accident. The talk was pleasant enough, reminding me that I had once thought well of this man.

The dinner conversation centered on the weather, Altoona's growth, and baby James. If Jacob was curious about my mission, he didn't ask. After the meal, he rose abruptly and announced he was going out and would be back late.

When he was gone, I asked, "Where does he go when he leaves like that?"

"To a saloon, most likely," Rachel replied.

"Does he do that often?"

"Two or three nights a week. He meets his friends there. They play cards, tell stories, do business. Jacob says that's how he learns about business deals."

This was a world I knew not at all. Coming from a place where men drank moderately, if at all, in the company of other Friends, and business was conducted after Meeting, I found Jacob's behavior strange, if not abhorrent.

"Does he drink a lot?"

"Not usually. Sometimes." Rachel twisted a handkerchief in her hands.

"Is he mean when he comes home?"

Her eyes widened in protest. "No. No. He's a good man. He works hard. He needs a little fun, is all."

I nodded and forced a smile, mindful that I was taking advantage of my brother-in-law's hospitality. I didn't believe Rachel's denial, and could only hope Jacob didn't abuse her.

I went to the stairway and called Lettie down for supper. She came, carrying Sam, a squirming armful. While Lettie ate, I fed Sam and played with him. The three of us made short work of cleaning up the kitchen and retired to the parlor. The talk was good for me. It kept my mind occupied.

"Ann," Rachel began, "your hair is too plain for your dress. You need a more stylish hair arrangement."

"Oh, yes!" Lettie agreed. "Miss Rachel, you got a curling iron? I could make Miss Ann look like a real fine Southern lady for the rest of our trip!"

The curling iron was brought out, stuck down a lamp chimney, and Lettie worked her magic. I wasn't comfortable with such 'making up', but submitted because it improved my disguise.

"Oh, Ann, you look beautiful," Rachel exclaimed, showing me the looking glass. I held it up and was pleased, in spite of myself with what I saw, my dark hair swept away from my face in long curls.

Lettie bathed Sam, dressed him for bed, and carried him upstairs. Rachel and I talked for a while on the front porch in the warm August evening. Rachel thought I was taking Sam along as part of the charade, and I let her go on thinking it for the moment.

"I know you want to repay Lettie for helping Jesse, but this escorting her all the way to Erie seems like more than necessary," Rachel observed.

"Maybe," I replied, "but I'm too far into it to turn back now."

"Well, you needn't put Sam through all this. You could leave him here and pick him up on your way back."

I hesitated. I could still change my mind. Leave him here and come back for him. Sitting in the dark, I struggled with the urge to accept her offer. But the thought of people like Jacob stopped me. No.

"Sam isn't coming back," I said softly. "He's going with Lettie to Canada."

"Ann! Oh, Ann! How can you do this? How can you hand your baby over to a stranger?" Rachel's voice broke as she spoke.

"Lettie is taking him to his father. She's Josiah's wife." I had held up as long as I could; now the tears came. I let go and cried as though I would never stop. Indeed, I would not. Ever. Rachel understood and did the only thing she could. She cried with me.

We retired at ten o'clock, and this night I slept, exhausted from travel, grief, and lack of sleep. Jacob Schilling's comings and goings didn't wake me, and in the morning it was Sam's baby talk that roused both Lettie and me from sleep.

The train to Pittsburgh left at ten o'clock, and our little party was on the platform, tickets in hand, waiting, when the iron monster steamed into town. It was still a marvel—the noise and speed of travel. One hundred miles in only four hours seemed impossible!

The stylish Southern lady with her long curls and fancy dress boarded the train, speaking softly to her colored maid with the fat, smiling baby. Anyone seeing us would think us real. It was the first train ride for all of us. I'd never imagined any of this—the dress, the hair, the train, the long distance from Bedford County. Sadly, there was no joy in it.

I listened to the rhythm of the wheels, each turn bringing separation closer. I tried not to think about it, but Sam's antics made the trip even more poignant. He crawled from one lap to the other, smeared the train windows with baby handprints, pounded his wooden rattle against the back of the seat, and shouted joyfully at the other passengers. By the time we reached Pittsburgh, everyone in the car knew his name: Sa-um.

In Pittsburgh, we caught a ride to a small hotel, where we rested against the most difficult part of the journey—a hundred and twenty-five miles by coach on rough roads through strange country, every step bringing the parting closer.

Thinking back, I don't know how I got through those long days. Sam was beside himself. Bored and needing action, he resisted us with vigor I hadn't seen before. We stayed the last night at a small hotel in Meadville. The owner was reluctant to accommodate a black woman and child, but my acting the offended Southern lady wore him down. Besides, there was no other lodging in town, so he showed us to a tiny attic room and admonished us to stay out of sight and keep the baby quiet.

Three days of travel had worn us out. Sam had to be wondering what had become of his cozy little bed and all the familiar folk. I wished we could get out and walk about, but we settled for opening windows on two sides of the attic and letting a gentle breeze refresh the room.

The parting lay before us like a chasm. We still hadn't talked much about it. Talking led to tears, and we could ill afford to draw attention to ourselves. But this night was our last chance to get it all said.

For Lettie, the knowledge of intimacy between Josiah and me still stung. "Josiah never been with nobody but me," she said.

"I know, Lettie. He's not that kind. Please try to understand. He's such a good man, and he loves you. I know he does."

I told Lettie about Elias Finley and how full of anger and hurt I was that January day. Lettie nodded.

"That Mr. Elias, he wrong headed. He fall in love with a pretty face when he got a good woman waitin' for him."

"That's what Josiah said. Life takes strange turns. Makes people do things they can't explain."

"Josiah be so happy to get Sam, Miss Ann. He want babies bad, but not as a slave."

"Yes. He told me that."

"Sam's lucky to have you for his momma. Not many can love they babies enough to let them go."

"Oh, Lettie, I don't know if I can. When I think of it I want to grab him up and take him back home with me."

Lettie rose to her full height. "Ann, you decided with a clear mind. It best for Sam. We both know that. You can, because you not sending him to strangers. You sending him to Josiah. To he daddy." We sat down on the bed beside the sleeping baby, clung to each other, and wept.

In the morning we set out again, arriving in Erie at about three o'clock. I rented a room in a small hotel near the lake and went to find the ticket office for the ferry. The boat would leave at eight the next morning and would arrive five hours later at Port Stanley, Ontario, just after 1 p.m. I purchased a one-way ticket and made my reluctant way back to the hotel, looking in the shop windows to distract myself.

A gold watch with an engraved case in the window of a jewelry store caught my eye. Such an adornment was not for plain people, but I'd been masquerading as a Southern belle for so long, I was beginning to think like one. I opened my reticule and counted the coins. There was ample to get me home, thanks to Uncle Sammy's generosity. Once there, what need had I for money? I entered the shop and, in my best Southern drawl, asked to see the watch.

It was beautiful to look at and heavy in my hand. The merchant counted its features on his fingers, extolling its accuracy and long guarantee.

"Can you engrave the back?"

"Oh, yes, Ma'am."

"Today?"

He looked at the clock with knit brows but gave in.

"I think so. Tomorrow would be better, though."

"Tomorrow will be too late," I said, slipping out of my southern drawl.

"Yes. Ah, what did you want it to say?"

I told him, watched him write it down, checked his spelling, paid him half the cost of the watch, and left, promising to return at half after five o'clock.

That evening in the hotel, Lettie and I played with Sam until he fell asleep. Then we looked out at the wide lake that represented everything Lettie longed for in life and everything I had to lose.

Lettie, past worrying about Josiah's infidelity, showed concern for me. "You sure you still want to do this?"

"Don't want to. Must."

"You could still take him back, you know."

"Take him back to what? A place where he could be kidnapped into slavery? A lifetime of being the only black child around? What happens when he's old enough to marry and the white fathers won't let their daughters near him? What then? Oh, Lettie, he's a strong, intelligent human being. He should grow up in a family with brothers and sisters. He should belong and not have to doff his hat to anyone."

Through the long night we sat up, watching the reflection of the moon on the lake, feeling the breeze rustle our hair, listening to Sam's innocent breathing.

We rose early and dressed mechanically, speaking very little. We breakfasted in the hotel dining room, where, again, I had to speak up in my maid's behalf, then started the long walk to the dock. I knew how it must feel to be a prisoner on the way to the gallows. I wished for a mourning bonnet to hide my face. I wished for my old, comfortable Quaker clothes and my old, comfortable Quaker home, which I knew would never be the same after this day.

Too soon and with heavy hearts, we came to the dock where the Lake Erie Ferry was taking on passengers. We stopped by the gangplank. I reached into my reticule, found Josiah's address, and pressed the paper into Lettie's hand.

"Have Josiah write as soon as you get there. I'll be sick with worry."

"I will. I promise."

"This night, Lettie. This night you will spend in Josiah's arms." Unable to help myself, I broke down. Sam put up a wail in sympathy.

I found a handkerchief and wiped my eyes, so wanting his last memory of me to be happy. I reached into the reticule again and gave Lettie enough money to get her to Dresden. Then I brought out the watch and showed it to Sam. His eyes lit up and he reached a chubby hand for it. He grabbed it, inspected it, turned it over, and put it in his mouth. The engraved back shone in the morning sun.

TO SAMUEL REDFIELD COLTON
With Love From
Mother
8 AUGUST 1856

The lake steamer's whistle blared and the boatman called, "Board!"

Lettie stepped away and walked up the gangplank, carrying Sam, still holding the watch, with the little trunk on her shoulder. She didn't look back, and that was well. I stood alone, my heart broken, unable to move, unable now even to cry. I watched the boatman lift the gangplank, heard the engines pound as they built up steam. Then, slowly, dreamlike, the boat pulled away from the dock. They were standing at the rail,

Lettie waving and Sam looking around at all the people. The boat's whistle blew three short bursts, picked up steam, and moved quickly northward.

I watched it pull away, rapidly diminishing against the vast lake. I found an unclaimed trunk and sat on it, watching my life slip away. The boat ebbed to a tiny speck on the horizon.

"Over there, my baby. Over there you'll be safe and loved and free. Oh, God," I breathed, "Bless him. Keep him. Help him know why I did this."

Chapter 20

1856 – Late Summer/Fall

The journey home alone with my thoughts was as hard as leaving Sam. Bumping along in a coach or railroad car was numbing to my body but not to my mind. I felt his presence, heard his laugh, saw his face reflected in the train windows and in my dreams. When I reached home after ten straight days of travel I wanted to sleep but feared the inevitable dreams of my baby.

Except for Abby, the reaction at home was quiet acceptance. Amos listened, nodded, and sat down in silence. Nathaniel, likewise, listened wordlessly and went out to the fields on the pretense of checking the corn. Jesse's eyes revealed unspeakable hurt that kept me from talking to him about Sam for months. But Abby couldn't control her young emotions. Her hands went to her face, her mouth agape. Heartrending cries escaped her throat. They'd guessed that I was sending Sam on, but Abby had refused to believe it. Now, faced with reality, she collapsed in grief, threatening to pull me down into a darkness I could not let myself enter.

"Abby. Abby, listen. You must face this. You must. Sam is with his father now. He's part of a family and a community that will love and care for him. Let up, Abby. I need you to help me get through this."

She raised her haunted, tear stained face. "Oh, Ann. It feels like he's dead," she moaned and went back to sobbing.

I resisted the urge to join her. Instead, I tied on my apron and threw a log on the fire. Work would be my salvation.

Abby was more than a week getting over the outward signs of grief. Sometimes I envied her ability to give herself over to it. It might not last so long that way.

A letter came from Josiah a few days after I got home.

"I'm so glad to see Lettie, I sweep her off her feet. Then I saw the child. Oh, Ann. How can I tell you the feeling? Lettie say, 'Ann send him on to be with his pappy. His life better that way.' I could hardly talk for joy, and love for this baby. Lettie is hurting, that's sure, but we be all right. We be fine. How Sam so lucky to have two mamas love him so much?"

I drew comfort from his words, but as I looked up from the letter, I felt Jesse watching me.

"What is it?"

"Heavy rains while you were away. Creek was up for more than a week. Pru Hartley's little Nancy fell in and was swept away. They found her yesterday, a mile downstream."

I stared in disbelief. Nancy couldn't have been more than five. Tragedy piled on top of tragedy.

It may have been my own grief that moved me, but I had to go see Pru. I walked down over the pasture path to the creek, then crossed over the log bridge to her cabin. This time I went right up and knocked at the door. Dogs be damned.

Pru opened it, looking out of haunted eyes. "What *you* want?" she asked.

I reached out and hugged her, struggling to hold myself together. She stood mute, her head down, not returning my hug. We stood so for a long time. Then, slowly, she put her arms up around me. Grief bonded us. Old hurts and slights melted away.

"Do you want to talk?" I asked, leading her to a chair by the table.

"Yes," she whispered. She sat silent for a while, examining her palms as though they held the answer to her grief. "I done it. Sure as if I held her under. I wasn't watchin'. She was always playin' in the water. I forgot the creek was swollen." She sighed.

Her two thin, solemn-faced boys stood behind, one on each side of her chair.

"I lost my baby, too," I told her.

Her head jerked up. "How?"

"I gave him up. Sent him on to Canada to be with his father."

"What'd you do that for?" she asked, incredulous.

"I think you know."

She sat looking at the floor, her hands in her lap. The old chip on her shoulder was gone. She turned and spoke gently to her boys. "You go on now and play. I want to talk to Miss Redfield." The boys obediently filed out.

"Did you think I'd turn him in to the slave catchers?" she asked wearily. "Is that what you was afraid of?"

"No, Pru. I didn't really name any one fear. There were so many. I just wanted his life to be better."

"'Cause I wouldn't of."

I patted her rough hand.

She raised her eyes to mine. "We both know how hurt feels, then."

I nodded. I looked around the bare cabin, changed in the wake of tragedy. The floor was swept. The furniture was neatly arranged. Dinner bubbled in a kettle over the fire, and the windows were even clean. It was just as threadbare as ever, but the old slovenliness was gone.

"Work helps ease the pain, doesn't it?" I asked her.

"I can't think of aught else to do. It don't make it go away, but it gives me a measure of peace."

Neighbors had come together to help in the wake of Nancy's death. They pulled down an old shed and chopped it up for firewood. They patched the roof and chinked the logs. The place looked almost presentable. Jesse and a work crew from Meeting had built a new chicken coop and brought in a rooster and several hens. Someone else had given Pru a goat for milk. Sad that it took such a tragedy to bring folks together.

"Anyone dig you a root cellar yet?" I asked on my way out.

"No, but I expect to set my brother Sawyer to it next time he comes."

"I thought Sawyer'd gone to be a peddler."

Pru nodded. "He passes through once in a while. Stops to see if I need anything."

"Well, put him to it next time he comes. I've got more potatoes, carrots, beets and turnips than we can ever use. You're welcome to all you need."

Pru forced a sad smile. "We can use 'em. That's sure."

I visited her regularly for a few weeks, letting her talk about whatever she wished. I was surprised at how sensible and mild she was. One day as I was leaving, she stopped me. "Would you go to the burying ground with me on First Day?"

"Sure, Pru. I'd be honored."

&

In the meantime, more fugitives came our way. Without warning, late in September, a party of five turned up at our door around midnight. The responsibility fell to me. I put them up for the night as comfortably as I could in the barn. In the morning Jesse and I discussed the next step.

"We'll keep them moving," he said. "We can't hold them here for even a day. The weather's changing fast."

"One of our Johnstown links is shut down now that Prospect has gone west," I replied.

"I'm thinking we could at least get them to Noah and Mary in Osterburg today, and they could be moved to Hollidaysburg tonight. Noah will know how to arrange that."

"Take them to Osterburg in broad daylight?"

"I think so."

"Well, you can't drive the wagon in your condition. I'd have to drive it."

"No. There's been too much talk about us since the accident. Slave catchers would suspect the wagon."

I sighed. "Yes, I guess the false bottom has done its job—for this year, anyway. So what do you think to do?"

"Send Abby over to Ben's to borrow his white mare," Jesse directed. No sooner said than Abby was out the door, throwing a shawl over her shoulders as she went.

"You put together some food while I tell them the plan."

When Abby rode in a few minutes later, barefoot, on the white mare, Jesse waited for her to dismount, but she sat tall astride the horse, not moving.

"Come on down, Abby. I'll take it from here," he said.

"No," Abby replied.

"No? What do you mean, 'No'?"

"I mean you aren't healed enough to be doing this." Abby looked directly into Jesse's eyes. "I can do it."

"You don't even know the plan, Abby."

"Well, you could probably explain it to me in a minute if you weren't so hard headed."

I turned away, smiling.

"You think you're the only capable one around here, but Ann and I have had our share of adventures, so just tell me what to do and I'll do it."

Jesse frowned, hesitated, then relented. "Okay, Miss Abby. Here's what you do. You ride from here to Osterburg, along the ridge road down to Bob's Creek. The Negroes will be up in the woods, following, just out of sight. On the white horse, you'll be a beacon for them. If you meet anybody on the road, say you're on an errand for Rebecca, taking some things to her aunt in Osterburg. Folks won't bother much with a young girl traveling alone."

Abby saw the beauty of the plan and nodded vigorously. "Okay. Set them into the woods. I'll be back before dark," she promised.

I handed up the food basket, and Abby set it in front of her and nudged the mare with her heels. Slowly, the white horse turned and walked out to the road. Jesse called the black men out of the hay mow and took them down through the barn to the cornfield a few feet beyond. They went through the tall corn and up over the hill. From the ridge above the village, they could watch Abby's progress until she turned right, out of the village on the road to Weyant. Then they trekked through the woods halfway up the ridge, keeping her in sight as they went.

Jesse returned to the house, worn out from even so small an exertion. He sat down in a rocking chair on the porch, his arm still in a sling.

"I hope she doesn't run into trouble," he said doubtfully. "She's only a child, really. Barely thirteen."

"That's an advantage. Anyway, Abby can talk her way out of anything. She'll be all right," I assured him.

Jesse nodded, but he was restless all afternoon—sitting down, standing up, pacing. Watching him, I thought about all the times I'd done the same, worrying about him. Changing places gave a person pause – made them realize what others went through. That was a good thing.

When Abby returned, all excited and pleased with herself, she recounted her trip. "I rode real slow, kept looking over my shoulder to keep track of them. Couldn't see them very well for the leaves."

She was breathless with the telling. "I kept riding 'til I got to the edge of Osterburg. Then I held the mare back for a few minutes in case they'd fallen behind. Mary was right surprised to see me."

Listening to Abby's story, Jesse smiled. He was happy with her performance.

"I went right up to her and asked if her man was around and she sent one of her daughters for Noah on the run."

Abby watched Jesse's face as she continued. "Noah Poole came round and I told him what was going on. He wanted to know where they was now, so I told him they was still up in the woods. Told him they wouldn't come down until dark. Told Mary to hang a bedsheet over the upstairs porch railing when it was safe to come down."

Abby wasn't given to pride, but I could tell she felt good to have an important role in the Railroad work.

"Mr. Noah Poole was very nice," she said. "Mary gave me supper, and they invited us over for a visit soon. They said one of their neighbors could move the Negroes on to Hollidaysburg without any trouble. They were glad to help. Mary's real worried about you, Jesse. She said to tell you to give your shoulder all the time it needs to heal."

Jesse smiled, shaking his head. "It's a close network. When you're among Friends, you're among friends."

Abby prattled on, filling us in on every detail of her adventure. "I met the Conleys on the way to Pavia. I told them I was on an errand for Rebecca. I'll fix it with her when I take the mare back, so she'll know what to say."

Jesse and I listened with measured pride to Abby's ramblings. "Abby," Jesse told her, "you did a fine job today. I'd trust you with anything I own."

The girl smiled and shuffled, her eyes downcast, clearly delighted to have Jesse's respect.

"She's a rare gem," he told me when Abby'd left to take the mare back. "No bigger'n a minute, but full of the fire."

⌘

Ever since my disownment, I'd felt detached, though the Friends hadn't entirely abandoned me. I still attended Meetings, and sat silent through the Business Meeting. It was different, though. The knowledge that my actions had brought shame on my family burdened me. I needed spiritual growth, communion with other souls. I wanted to belong in the full and complete way I'd belonged before, so in late September, I decided to ask for reinstatement. It had been eight months since my disownment, and I hated the prospect of a long, cold winter without the full fellowship of Friends. So I sat down at my writing desk and composed a carefully worded letter acknowledging my error and asking for reinstatement. When I finished, I sealed the letter and left it on my desk for a few days to see how I felt about it in the passage of time. When Papa and the boys left for Meeting the next First Day, I begged off but asked Jesse to hand the letter to the Women's Business Meeting.

Late October brought the Meeting's response: 'Ann Redfield may resume her place as a member of the Meeting in good standing.' My relief was surprising, even to me. I'd no idea how important it was to be readmitted to the community of Friends.

Chapter 21

1856 – Fall

As the leaves turned and temperatures dropped, I looked for ways to lose myself in preparations for winter, still grieving for Sam. I canned, pickled, dried corn, made apple butter, and helped with the hog butchering. Work eased my grief, or numbed it. Hard work brings weariness, and sleep comes to the weary, or so I hoped. Abby kept up with me, sighing occasionally, and asking only once how much dried corn five people could eat in one winter. As Sam's birthday approached, the emptiness forced me out and away from the house. So I made the rounds of family and friends with preserves, pickles and compotes. Rebecca saw what drove me when I stopped there on my way back from visiting Betsy one October afternoon.

"Working your way past Sam's birthday?" Her tone was compassionate. "Best to keep the grief at bay."

I nodded. Rebecca knew me well. Even this day she lightened my load.

The twins were two already, and Rebecca was pregnant again.

"I'm hoping the Lord will see fit to send me just one this time," she mused. "He must know I'm stretched to my limit around here. If it weren't for Deborah, I don't know what I'd do."

"She and Abby are worth ten hired girls," I agreed. "What a piece of luck, getting these two." I shot a glance at Abby, helping Deborah shake out the bedding. Redfield Farm agreed with her, and she with us. She was almost a little sister.

Rebecca picked up one of the twins and sniffed his britches as he struggled to get free. "Have you seen Melissa Finley lately?"

"No. She hasn't been to Meeting in months."

"Ben says Elias is worried about her. She doesn't take to motherhood very well. Says the baby is a burden and wants Elias to take her home to Chambersburg for the winter."

Rebecca wasn't given to idle gossip, especially about family, so I took the situation to be serious.

"Maybe Abby and I should stop by and see her. She's probably lonely, Rebecca."

"I expect she is. She used to come often, but not since Lucy was born. I send Deborah and Jane over to visit sometimes. But I worry about her with winter coming. Elias may have trouble on his hands."

"I've some preserves left over. We'll stop and see her this afternoon, before we go home."

"Yes. She'd like that."

I left Ben's dooryard, turned right, and drove the short half mile to Elias Finley's house. The door opened as we approached, and Abby and I were greeted by a disheveled Melissa, holding a squalling, soiled baby.

"Hello, Melissa. We brought you some pickles and preserves." I forced a smile, struggling to keep the dismay out of my voice.

The young woman looked at us, expressionless. "That's nice" she said dully. "Elias will like that."

I handed her the basket and stood aside, expecting to be invited in. But Melissa stood silent, the crying child on her hip, studying me. Abby shifted nervously from foot to foot.

Melissa looked from me to Abby and back again. Then she shoved the screaming baby into my arms and closed the door. I held the little one close to stop her crying, then knocked softly. Melissa didn't respond, so I opened the door and carried the baby inside, followed by an uncomfortable Abby.

The house was dark, the shutters closed. Abby opened them, revealing a scene of complete disarray. The fire was out.

Dirty dishes cluttered the table and dry sink. Clothing lay strewn around the furniture and the floor. The baby's cradle, soiled and smelling foul, was turned on its side, and the jumble of dirty quilts on the bed in the corner looked like a hoorah's nest.

Wondering how Elias could let things come to such a pass, I started the fire and set Abby to washing dishes while I gave the baby a bath and found clean clothes for her. Lucy was scrawny for six months, and her skin was raw and chafed from lack of bathing. Abby scurried over to Ben's for a nursing bottle and some goat's milk, which I warmed and fed to the child. She fell into a contented sleep in my arms, giving me sharp reason to miss Sam again. I lay her down in the clean cradle, and she slept, snug under a crocheted shawl I found tucked away in a cupboard. Melissa lay curled up in bed, facing the wall, oblivious.

We set the house to rights and bundled dirty clothes to take home for washing. We swept the floor, took out the ashes, wiped the windows, and set the kettle on to heat again. Still, Melissa didn't move or speak. I approached her with caution, anxious not to add to her distress.

"Melissa, come now. Let me clean up this bed. Abby'll draw a bath for you. You'll feel better once you're clean."

The young woman shrank back. "No. Elias will see me. Every time he sees me, he wants me. I can't bear to get pregnant again."

"Elias is out working with Ben. He won't be home for a long time."

"Don't let him touch me!" Melissa cried, holding the dirty quilt up in front of her. "Please. I want my mamma."

When the baby awoke, I sent Abby home with her and sat down to wait for Elias. When he returned, near dusk, I accosted him sharply.

"Elias! How could you let things go this far without asking for help?"

He hung his head. "I kept thinking she'd get better."

"Well, now you're in a fine pickle. You can't keep this up any longer for fear she'll hurt herself or the baby."

"What can I do, Ann?" he asked helplessly. "I want to do right by her, but she's in such a black state, she won't have anything to do with me."

"Take her home, Elias. Take her back to Chambersburg, where things are familiar. Her mother will know how to handle her. She has sisters, doesn't she?"

"Yes. Two still at home."

"Good. They can nurse her, take care of Lucy, whatever is needed. Now go tell Ben, and get yourself ready. Leave in the morning. I'll let Abby go along to take care of the baby, but you'll have to send her back right quick."

He nodded woodenly and turned toward the door. He hesitated, looking around the room, now neat and clean. "Thank you, Ann. I was at my wits' end, thinking what to do. It's been a long time since the house was this orderly."

"Go, Elias. As a matter of fact, stay over at our house tonight. Get a bath and a change of clothes. You look like horror yourself. I'll stay here and see to Melissa."

Obediently, he lifted the latch and stepped out into the October evening. When he'd gone, I looked around at the forlorn little house and sighed. All the bright hopes so quickly dashed.

I was hungry, but there was little to eat. I wondered how they'd gotten this far without cooking. They must have survived on dried meat and apples. No wonder the baby was scrawny. What kind of milk could come of dried meat and apples? I picked bugs out of the meal, mixed up some cornbread, and heated water for tea while it baked. When it was done, I ate it with a dollop of my own peach preserves.

Then I awakened Melissa and watched over while she ate and the water warmed for her bath. I spoke softly, reassuringly, to the girl, who stood in dejected silence, head down, allowing herself to be undressed. I bathed her, washed her hair, put a clean night-gown on her, and sat her in a chair by the fire while I stripped the bed. I scoured the house for clean linen and soon had the bed ready. Taking Melissa by the hand, I led her there without protest.

"Please don't tell Elias," Melissa mumbled as she crawled into bed, curling up, knees almost to her chin. "He'll be mad at me."

"Don't worry, dear. Elias isn't mad at you. He's going to take you home."

"Home? Home to Mama?"

"Yes, home to Mama." I tucked the blankets around her.

"When?"

"Tomorrow. First thing in the morning."

"Oh," Melissa sighed. "Mama will know what to do with the baby. She cries all the time."

"Yes, dear. Your mama will take care of you both."

I sat with her until she fell asleep, then set about getting things ready for the trip. First, I found clothes for the three of them. There wasn't much clean, but I packed what I could. Then I washed the dishes, banked the fire, put out the lamp, and undressed in the dark.

I lay down beside the sleeping girl, wakeful for some time, struck by the irony of this unaccustomed familiarity with Elias Finley's life. Time was when I would have been all aflutter at the mention of his name. Now I felt sorry for the helpless, inept creature that he was.

The next morning I dressed, fed the fire, and prepared breakfast before awakening Melissa. She'd slept through the night and awoke looking less gaunt. There were still dark circles under her eyes, but her color was better. She even noticed the house was clean. But it wasn't until Abby and Elias arrived with Lucy that the young mother even realized the child was gone.

"Abby, did you pack a satchel for yourself?" I asked, mindful of trip preparations. I handed a basket of food and a couple of wool blankets to Elias.

He'd brought up the buggy, pulled by his finest team, which gave me to wonder if his desire to be seen driving fine horses outweighed his concern for his frantic wife and poor neglected baby. I pulled Abby aside.

"I'm not sure Elias grasps the weight of the problem even yet. Don't let him make light of her condition. Make sure her mother knows it's serious."

"Yes'm, I will. You can count on me," Abby assured me, throwing a look of contempt at Elias as he loaded the satchels in the buggy. When Melissa saw Elias, she shrank visibly, hunched over, and pulled her shawl around her. I helped her into the front seat, where she sat, head down, contemplating her hands. Abby took the baby in back. I made sure everyone was tucked up and warm, then stepped aside as the horses pulled out of the yard, down the Fishertown Road.

When they were out of sight, I went back into the house, gathered the soiled linen, put out the fire, and closed the latch. I walked the mile to Redfield Farm, carrying the bundle of laundry on my back.

Chapter 22

1856-1857 – Late Fall/Winter

A few days later, my brothers greeted me at breakfast, dumb grins on their faces, making me wonder what they were up to. Even Amos seemed amused. Around eleven o'clock, the source of their mischief was revealed when a dray wagon drove into the yard, carrying a cast iron kitchen stove. I stared as Nathaniel helped the drayman unload it.

They placed it in front of the fireplace that had served the family under this roof for more than fifty years, then removed enough chimney stones to install the stovepipe. I looked at the stove and my brothers in disbelief.

"Well, I never thought I'd have such as this to cook on."

Nathaniel laughed. "Figured I could fool you, Ann. You'd never guess what we were up to."

"You, Nathaniel? This was your idea?"

He nodded. "Went to Bedford and bought it yesterday. It's got a boiler built right in so you don't have to heat bath water in the kettle, and you don't have to wait for it, either."

I was amazed at the joy he took from stove mechanics. I turned to Papa. "Were you in on this, too?"

Amos nodded. "And Jesse," he replied.

I smiled. Their desire to cheer me up was touching.

Not long after we got the stove, Pru Hartley stopped by. Winter was coming on, and I guessed she'd need our help again.

"Mornin', Pru."

"Mornin'."

"Isn't that a new dress?"

She nodded. "Ain't that a new stove?" She stood by it, looking at it from every angle. She opened the oven and peered inside. She opened the warming cupboards. She lifted the lids and watched the fire. "Fine one, too," she said.

"Nate, Jesse, and Papa bought it. It pleases me."

"I'd guess." She seemed on the verge of one of her tirades, but resisted the urge and turned her attention back to her dress.

"Got this from the poor committee. Shoes, too." She stuck out a foot, shod in a fairly new looking black leather shoe. "Store bought. All of it. Who'd give away such as this?" she asked.

We both knew. Some woman had died and the family gave away her clothes to ease their grief. I smiled as Pru twirled before me, showing off her fine attire.

"Now all I need is a coat. Ain't had one in years. Shawls don't work good outside."

"We'll see. Maybe we can get you one. I'll ask around." Ever since the death of her daughter, Pru's edge was mostly gone, although I still wasn't sure it had gone far. She kept herself and her boys cleaner and neater now. She was, for the most part, polite and courteous, even though I could tell sometimes it galled her. She was sending her boys to Aaron Groves' Quaker school, as charity cases. She assured me that didn't mean she was joining the Society again, just that she wanted them to be able to read, write, and cipher.

"How's Jesse?" she asked, changing the subject.

"Well enough, but his arm's never going to be the same. He can barely lift it from the shoulder."

"He *looks* real good."

"Yes, but he won't be much help on the farm anymore."

"He still messin' with that Underground Railroad?"

I stopped and looked at her. Why was she so interested in Jesse's Railroad work? She sensed my suspicion and hurried to reassure me.

"Don't worry. I ain't gonna turn you in or nothin'. I know Jesse didn't hurt his arm fallin' off the hay wagon, is all."

I was still put off by her questioning, and my impatience found its way out. "What was it you came for, Pru?"

"No call to git uppity. I was jest askin'. Besides, I might could help you some with that."

"I thought you hated black people." My spine was alert for her next move. Where was she going with this? I could tolerate her, even like her a little when she behaved, but I didn't know what to think now.

"I jest hated bein' poor. Still do. An' hated seein' folk like you make all over those niggers when my need was at least as great." She sounded spiteful, and a little sad.

I knew Jesse would never hold still for letting a Hartley in on anything we did, but I thought I'd question her to see where she was going with this. "What do you mean, help?"

"Well, to begin with, I wouldn't tell my brother Cooper anything I knew about you Redfields. He's helpin' a slave catcher from Maryland ever' chance he gits. Makes him a little money at it. I could close my eyes, is what I mean."

"You must think we're into this pretty deep."

"I reckon."

I eyed her warily. I couldn't tell how much of what she said came from knowledge and how much was speculation. Given the Hartley family history, I couldn't help but note that none of them ever got out of bed early enough to keep track of much of anything. Still, suspicious as they were, Jesse and I needed to be more than careful.

"What would it take to keep you from talking to Cooper?"

"A new coat would help for this winter. Like that green one I seen you wearin' a week or so ago. That'd do."

My coat wasn't new. It was a hand-me-down from Aunt Alice Grainger. Uncle Sammy had given it to me after she died. I liked that it had been hers. Liked the way it fit. Liked how warm it was. Suddenly I realized where this would lead. "No. I'm not giving you my coat. You're reading far more into this idea of the Underground Railroad than is real. I'll see if I can get you a coat from the poor committee."

Her eyes narrowed. "Well, I can't help it if Cooper and his friends come callin'."

"Let them come," I said wearily. "They've been here before."

&

I told Jesse about Pru's thinly veiled threats when he came in from the barn. "Nothing new there," he replied. "Cooper Hartley's just like his old man. Take a nickel any way he can get one."

"Yes, but it seems to me this business is getting meaner every day," I complained.

"Traffic increases, and so does the anger in the South. They mean to make the North enforce the law. Gives people like Cooper reason to hope they can get rich."

"I'd hate to be a constable. Even if they're sympathetic to the runaways, they have to help the slave catchers."

"Yeah. I've often wondered about old Ackroyd. Whether he's really as hateful as he acts. For all we know, he might be helping fugitives, too." Jesse grinned at the thought of the constable running his own delivery system.

"You know, though, Jesse, I'm always surprised at the number of Bedford County folk who side with us. They aren't all dough-faces like the Hartleys."

Jesse picked up his hat and set it on his head. "We can be glad of that!" he said. "Now I've gotta go talk to Ben. Come along?"

I looked around at the mound of washing I had to do and declined. "Tell Rebecca I'll try to visit toward the end of the week."

Abby and Elias returned on Second Day of the first week in November. According to Abby, Elias seemed completely befuddled by Melissa's condition, left all interaction with her to her family, and made his own exit as quickly as possible. Abby voiced her anger.

"He doesn't care a whit for her *or* the baby in hard times," she grumbled. "All he wanted was a pretty wife, but he doesn't

173

want *any* of it if there's trouble attached." She clucked her tongue in disgust.

I must admit, at first I felt a certain 'serves you right' satisfaction in Elias' troubles, though I felt more compassion for Melissa than I expected. Elias deserved some comeuppance for the way he'd treated me. He'd turned to me in his time of trouble. That gave me satisfaction, but I kept it to myself. Chastised myself for my pride.

Melissa was gone the whole winter. Elias went to Chambersburg for short visits, but time wasn't kind to the couple. Melissa, though seemingly well enough when with her family, showed no inclination to return to Bedford County as Elias' wife. Her fears of pregnancy, childbirth, being saddled with many children, submitting to her husband's needs—in short, the common lot of women everywhere, made her hide when Elias came to see her. So she stayed in Franklin County, and Elias didn't push for her return. He wasn't happy, but he was learning that there are some things a man can't control.

Watching the sad relationship play out, I thought myself lucky to have lost Elias Finley. He seemed less and less like husband material. I laughed at such thoughts. What did I know of husbands?

Elias lived alone, worked steadily with Ben and kept to himself except to attend Meeting. Rebecca did his laundry and sent Deborah over once a week to keep the house in order. Elias took his meals at Ben's, slowly slipping into a solitary life. By spring, it was apparent to all, except perhaps Elias, that Melissa would never return. His life was suspended—a married man without a wife. He didn't speak of her unless someone asked, in which case he turned away questions with as little explanation as possible. Embarrassed by his situation, he tried to avoid it by ignoring it.

As I watched the unraveling of my former suitor's life, a surprising sympathy began to form. My anger faded, and I was left with only sadness for both Elias and Melissa and their little daughter, Lucy. I could blame neither for their failure, for I understood such tragedy played out in peoples' lives more often than anyone could guess.

Though distracted by Elias' troubles, I was still in the depths over Sam's loss. I thought about him constantly—how old he would be, what he would be doing. Walking. Talking. Josiah wrote about once a month, letters full of Sam's accomplishments. I was grateful to be included, even remotely, in his life. I knit him mittens, a cap, and a tiny muffler to keep him warm in cold Ontario. For Christmas, I made him a warm coat out of a length of blue wool I'd been saving. Little by little, I pulled out of my grief. The knowledge that he was well, happy, cared for, and loved took some—but not all—of the sting out of losing him.

It was mid-winter before I could talk to Jesse about sending Sam away. I knew he understood why I'd done it. Still I needed to talk to him. One January night as we walked home from Ben's, I broached the subject.

"I want to talk to you about Sam."

"No need, Ann. I know."

"It matters to me what you think."

"I think you did what you had to do."

"Yes. But my heart went with him. I never wanted to be anything but a good mother. I couldn't have loved him more."

Jesse stopped, looking at me in the snowy moonlight. "You've no need to explain to me, Ann. I knew when you took him that you'd come home alone. I knew why. I wanted to help you get through it if I could. Now I'm sorry I wasn't strong enough for you to lean on. It took a while to control my own grief. But I knew we'd talk when the time was right."

"Thank you for knowing I was beyond talking for a long time." I stopped in the path and turned to look at him.

"Sure."

"Jesse?"

"Uh huh?"

"Where does my life go from here? We both know marriage isn't in my future. What now?"

"I don't know. Maybe someday someone'll come along for you. Time changes people's perceptions. But I know this. You're the one we all rely on in times of trouble. No matter who's in need. No matter what the need. Look how Elias turned to you when his life came apart. And me. What would I do without you now that my arm's crippled? Somehow that's got to come back to you."

We walked along the snow covered path in silence. Then, without warning, Jesse broke into a run, slowing a second to scoop up a handful of snow. He turned and pelted me with a snowball, then another. Protecting my face with my arms, I scooped up my own snowball, heaving it directly at his face. Now he was running at me, throwing an armload of snowballs one after the other. I ducked behind a tree quick, to make him miss. Then I let loose a torrent from the shelter of the tree, pelting him with a series of well-placed globs of mushy snow. Jesse came through the onslaught, head down, determined to roust me from my fortress. He grabbed me from the side, wrestled me down one handed and washed my face in the snow.

I screamed, then laughed as the cold, wet snow went down my neck. "You, Jesse. Drat you, Brother. That's not fair!" I complained. "You're stronger than I."

"Sure it's fair, Annie. We all have our weaknesses."

Chapter 23

1858 – Summer

One evening as I sat alone in the kitchen, reading, I heard a quiet tap at the window, almost like a scratch. Someone was outside. I rose, turned out the lamp, and walked out on the back porch. Fugitives often came under cover of darkness, so, though cautious, I thought I knew what to expect. I stepped off the porch and around the side of the house. There was no moon, another reason to expect fugitives. All was dark and strangely silent. I felt a presence. Peering into the darkness, I asked, "Who's there?"

"A friend." There was no mistaking that voice. Josiah! In a moment I was in his arms, enfolded like a baby, rocked slowly back and forth.

"Josiah! What are *you* doing here?" I asked, through sudden tears. "What about Sam? And Lettie?"

He held me close for a long time, breathing into my hair. "They fine. They send they love."

"But why? Why are you here?"

He held me at arm's length. "Got some business down in Virginny. Won't take long."

"Business in Virginia? What business?"

"My mamma. Goin' to bring her out."

"Oh, Josiah, no! What if you get caught? What if something happens to you? What will Sam and Lettie do?"

"Sam and Lettie and *Ann*," he added.

"Ann?"

"Two months old," he grinned. "Named after her guardian angel."

The tears came again. "Are you and Lettie all right? About Sam, I mean."

"Yes, Ann." He looked levelly at me. "We all right. Lettie a good woman. I told you that. She love Sam like her own."

I looked up at him, my emotions on edge. "Now what is this about your mother? I thought you didn't know where she was."

"Didn't. Early spring a man come to Dresden from Shenandoah County, Virginny. Place called Mt. Jackson. He from the same place my mamma on. We talk long about where it is and how he come up from there to Cumberland and the rest of the way."

I led him into the kitchen. "How do you know it's really your mother?"

"Her name Mandy. She a house slave, personal servant to the mistress. Like Lettie. My mamma brought up in that. She the right age, about fifty. Man say she always talkin' 'bout her little boy Josiah, that she got sold away from."

I smiled at that. "She'll be surprised to see how her 'little boy' has grown."

I re-lit the lamp, pulled the curtains so we couldn't be seen from the road, and set a cup of coffee on the table for him.

"You recall Jesse's accident."

Josiah nodded. "Sorry to hear it. Good man, Jesse. Helped a lot of folk."

"He's not the same man he was. His left arm isn't entirely useless, but it's pretty weak. He doesn't do much of the heavy work anymore."

"Where he now?"

"Over in Osterburg, visiting Mary and Noah Poole."

"Can't linger here. Gotta get down into Virginny soon as I can, grab my mamma and get back."

"Does she know you're coming?"

"No. Couldn't risk tryin' to get word to her. The less people who know, the better. Gonna find the plantation, camp out as close as I can and try to contact her."

"I'll be worried sick about you. This is such a dangerous business, and Sam needs you, Josiah."

He nodded. "I know, but I couldn't let my mamma die a slave, and me knowin' where she is."

I sighed. I understood that deep sense of responsibility only too well. "All right. I can move you down to Cumberland maybe tomorrow or the next day. I know someone who trades there. He brings people back with him when the need arises, but I doubt if he's ever taken anyone down."

"Thank you, Ann. I knew you'd help. If I'm lucky this shouldn't take but a week or so. Hope to move right back north through the same stations I come on."

"I *hope* you're lucky. Otherwise, I'll be sick with worry. You can sleep in Jesse's room tonight. He'll be back in the morning." I went upstairs to find him some linen, struggling with the desire to fall asleep in his arms. When I returned to the kitchen I found Papa and Abby, back from a visit to Ben's.

"Josiah's here," I told them.

"Josiah? You mean him, *Josiah*?" Abby blurted. "What's *he* doin' here?"

"He's headed back south to bring his mother out."

"How long's *he* gonna be here?"

"Not long. I'm going over to see Tyler Pell in the morning— see if he's going to Cumberland anytime soon."

Abby looked hard at me for any sign of intimacy between Josiah and me, but I kept that well concealed in my heart.

"What's he say of Sam?" she wanted to know.

"That he's well and happy and that he has a baby sister."

"That's good!" Abby cried, as though that made any further attraction between Josiah and me impossible.

I went to bed with plans for Josiah's trip in my head, but sleep eluded me. I couldn't get him out of my mind. I longed to share my bed with him, to be held as only he had held me. Morning was slow in coming, as was relief from the yearning.

I cooked breakfast for Amos and Nathaniel, and more for Josiah when he came downstairs. Abby watched us with a vigilance that would have impressed a hawk. I assigned her to the spinning, took the horse Nathaniel saddled for me and rode away to the Pell farm near Fishertown.

Tyler Pell was in his field when I arrived; I walked between the corn rows to talk to him. Tyler had a truck farm, and Cumberland, Maryland, was his best market. Yes, he was going to Cumberland later that day to get a head start for tomorrow's early market. Yes, he could conceal a man and deliver him into safe hands, if there was anyone fool enough to want to go back. Yes, he could be counted on to provide transport back on market day a week, under cover of darkness. He was known on the road between Cumberland and Bedford, so it shouldn't be a problem. I thanked him, promising to deliver the 'package' early that afternoon.

At home, I went to the barn to unsaddle the horse and found Jesse and Josiah, sitting on a couple of upturned logs, talking like conspirators. Jesse had drawn a crude map on the barn floor with a horseshoe nail and was apprising Josiah of safe houses on the way south.

"Once you're in Cumberland, Pell can settle you with Jeremiah Hobbs. He's been a conductor for years and will know the safe houses down probably as far as Romney, at least. You'll be in the mountains, mostly on seldom traveled roads. That's good in some ways and not so good in others," Jesse counseled him.

I joined them, nodding to Jesse. "Mary's well, I hope."

"Well—and looking forward to a visit from you."

"I see you two have laid out a plan."

Josiah smiled. "Ann ain't happy about me goin' south again. She worried about Sam."

"With good reason," Jesse replied. "I wouldn't try what you're doing, but I wish you success and Godspeed."

"Josiah, do you need anything for the journey?" I asked.

"No, thank you. Knowin' where to go and who to count on all I need. The rest take care of itself."

I remembered my errand. "Tyler Pell's leaving this afternoon for Cumberland. Jesse can take you over to his house in the wagon, and he'll hide you among his vegetables for the trip."

"That be fine. Thank you, Ann. I should get to Mt. Jackson in two or three days. Then contact my mama. If she willin', it take a day or so to set up a plan. Her bein' house help, we run at night, soon as she's off, to give us a start before they know she gone. I'm still hopin' to be back here in a week."

Jesse listened intently to Josiah's plan. It had to be loose. There was no other way, but loose bothered Jesse.

"Wish I could take you down, like Ann traveled with Lettie. Like a Southern gentleman and his slave," he told Josiah.

The conversation stopped. Josiah looked at Jesse with hope in his eyes. I looked at both of them with fear.

"I know the road to Cumberland," Jesse continued. "I could get you that far as well as Tyler Pell. From then on, we'd just let ourselves be passed from one safe house to the next. What do you say, Josiah? Should we try it?"

Josiah's face broke into a huge grin. He shook Jesse's good hand. "You 'n me, together, we can do it just fine."

I kept silent, sure that expressing my fears wouldn't change any minds. I excused myself and went back to the house already planning for their needs. Jesse would need some fancy clothes. Maybe Betsy's brother-in-law would have something. It meant a day or two delay until we could fit the two of them up for the masquerade. My hands wouldn't stop shaking as I prepared the noon meal. Why did men insist on courting danger?

Two days later, two days and nights filled with worry and longing, we saw them off on the road to Cumberland. Then I settled down to the hardest waiting I've ever done.

Jesse looked so fine, dressed in gentlemen's clothes. Josiah chafed at donning slave's overalls again. They took Ben's buggy and a good team. Not the best, so as not to attract too much attention, but a good, solid, reliable team. The plan was to travel in daylight. No one would question a white gentleman with a Negro headed south. When they got to Mt. Jackson, Jesse would approach the owner of the plantation—actually it was little more than a farm, according to Josiah's source—saying he was returning south with a runaway, and ask for hospitality. Josiah would be chained up in the barn while Jesse was wined and dined, but it would be his chance to contact his mother.

The next morning they would thank their host for his kindness and move on south. They'd hide out during the day and meet Josiah's mother after dark, headed north.

It should work. I knew it should, but that didn't slow my fears. Abby was no help. She was as worried as I. So we went through each day distracted, jumpy, a little tense with each other.

After Jesse's last mishap, Nathaniel and Amos were all too aware of what might happen. Nathaniel seemed more concerned than Amos, probably because he, as a young man, might have been the one to accompany Josiah. He would have, if asked, but it was not Nathaniel's way to volunteer.

I tried to reckon how far they'd go in a day and where they should be at a given time. If their plan worked, they would leave Mt. Jackson on Seventh Day evening, an advantageous time, because slaves had First Day off, and Amanda wouldn't be missed until Second Day morning. With good luck they could be fifty to seventy miles away by then.

Going over it in my mind, I saw them reaching a safe house that first night before midnight. On First Day they could probably move north unmolested along a little traveled mountain road, all the way to Romney if they were lucky. The Cumberland Friends could be counted on to provide fake bills of sale for Amanda and Josiah, in case anyone asked.

According to my calculations, the soonest we could expect them back was the following Third Day. I told myself such dispatch was unlikely, that something surely would slow them down, but in spite of myself, I started to look for them on Third Day. I kept an eye on the road, stopping work to gaze through the trees, trying to will them home. By evening, I had to struggle to keep worry at bay. To keep busy I crocheted a little sweater for Baby Ann. I slept that night, but fitfully, awakening, listening at every sound.

Fourth Day was a more reasonable expectation. Given a smooth path, they could easily make it back by that evening, but they didn't. I was of a seriously worried mind by then. Finishing up the sweater wasn't enough to calm my fears. That night I didn't think I slept at all, but I must have. Some.

By Fifth Day morning, I was fighting waves of panic. I snapped at Abby, and Abby, also full of fear, mostly for Jesse, snapped back. Amos had long since retreated into a shell of silence, and Nathaniel took to riding out the road to the south in hopes of meeting them. Nothing.

I spent another night in anguish, crying quietly in my bed. I made plans to go to Canada and bring Sam back. I made funeral plans for the three of them, sure the Friends would let me bury them at Spring Meadow. I got out of bed, knelt and prayed as I had never prayed before, bargaining with God, promising anything I could think of, if only they came home safe.

On Sixth Day evening just after dark, Abby, out on the back porch, let out a whoop.

"Ann! Ann! They're here! They're comin'. Someone's coming! It must be them!"

Chapter 24

1858 – Mid-summer

As the buggy turned in at the gate, I held a lantern aloft, straining to count the occupants. Oddly, it looked like four. In the barn, I closed the door as Nathaniel helped two black women out of the buggy. Josiah stepped down and walked around to the older woman's side. The other black woman, hardly more than a girl, hung back, fearful.

"Mamma," Josiah said with a smile, "this Ann Redfield, Jesse's sister I told you about."

The small black woman's face lit up. "You save my boy," she whispered, tears glistening in her eyes. "An' he save me. Thank the Lord. This my daughter, Lovely."

Oh, Josiah, you have a sister!" I laughed, giddy with relief at seeing them whole and healthy. "We'd best get the three of you settled for the night. I know you're tired. We'll hear your story in the morning."

Josiah led his mother and sister up the ladder to the loft. Nathaniel took care of the horses, and Amos and I helped Jesse unload the buggy. Josiah elected to stay in the barn, so we walked to the house, Jesse with his good arm on my shoulder. "This was as much adventure as I need in my life," he said wearily. "I can't wait to get out of these dandy clothes."

I slept that night, the deep sleep of relief from the darkest fears. Next morning my mind was already laying plans for moving them on. I cooked enough breakfast to satisfy hearty appetites.

Jesse came down dressed in his farm clothes, looking pleased with himself.

"Let's take breakfast out to the barn so you can hear the story while we eat," he suggested.

Abby helped me carry the food in baskets and buckets to the barn. Nathaniel upended logs in a circle, and we sat to eat, plates in our laps.

"All right, Jesse, let's hear it," Nathaniel prodded.

"Well, we got down there fine in two and a half days. Found the place. Not a big plantation or anything—more like a big farm, an orchard farm. They grow fruit—apples, peaches, pears, and some grapes."

"Fine peaches. Fine grapes," Amanda added with pride.

Jesse nodded. "Amanda'd been there for twenty-five years. It was hard for her to leave."

"Yes'm," Amanda said. "That a long time. Mistress good to me. I help her raise five children. They just like my own." She looked at Josiah and smiled. "Not *quite* like my own," she corrected herself. "No one like your own babies!"

Her words touched my heart, and my eyes involuntarily fluttered to Josiah, locked on his, and fluttered away.

Jesse continued. "The owner, a Mr. Robert Tull, was happy to have company and showed me the finest hospitality. I felt a little mean, coming there to rob him like I was, but I went right on playing the Southern gentleman. Josiah was chained in the barn all night."

Josiah nodded. "Pure torture, puttin' on those chains. But I whisper to the slave what chain me that I need to talk to Amanda."

"Ole Joe come to me at the back door," Amanda put in. "Say someone in the barn want to see me. I say I busy and go back in the house. Still, I wonder who it be. Back in my cabin about eight o'clock, Ole Joe come round again. This' time I say, 'What you doin' knockin' at my door again?' All he say 'You gotta come.' So I gets my kit and go to the barn, thinkin' maybe somebody hurt or ailin'."

Josiah mimmicked his feisty mother coming to the barn with her basket of herbs and potions, expecting to treat a sick slave.

Then he looked at her with such tenderness. "I saw her, I 'most cried."

Amanda's face wrinkled as she held back tears. "I cry. Almost cry my eyes out. Never expected to see that one again."

"Take me fifteen minutes to settle her down so I can tell her the plan."

"' And then I told him about Lovely. He say no worry. We take you both."

"Mama married one of the orchard workers. He die two year ago," Josiah explained. "He a bit older, but good to her. Lovely's daddy."

Lovely sat quiet, hands in her lap, listening to the others tell the tale.

"She the reason I run," Amanda said. "She seventeen. Got a chance for a good life. This one," she indicated Josiah, "he tell me I got two grandchildrenn. Oh, joy. I lost five babies of my own. Thought I lost six, but God give me this one back. That why I run. Mistress Tull be heartbroken now I'm gone. But I got to save my best for my own."

Now Lovely spoke. "I find out I got a brother, a nephew and a niece. All at once." She smiled, her young face alight with the joy of freedom.

Jesse took up the story from there. "The next morning I fetched my Negro from the barn, thanked my host, and headed south. About five miles on, we found an abandoned tobacco shed, so we drove in there and sat out the day. After dark, we headed on north, hoping Amanda and Lovely'd be waiting when we reached the Tull place."

"We's ready," Amanda crowed. "We's waitin' by the line fence. All pack up and dress for the trip. Long come the buggy. Stop. We step in like ladies, and we gone!"

"That night was fine." Jesse continued. "We traveled until around eleven and came to a little place called Lost City. It is a lost city, for sure. Not much city at all—only about a dozen houses tucked away in the mountains. A mile or so beyond there was the Easterbrook place, a station. They put us up for the night. The next day is when it got worrisome." He and

Josiah exchanged glances. I sensed a bond between them, and was glad for it.

"We started out around eight o'clock so it'd look like we were off to church. Things went along fine until early afternoon when we met three slave catchers headed south. They stopped us and demanded papers. I had false papers for Josiah and Amanda, but none for Lovely. I took my time getting them out, thinking to hand over what I had, and try to explain away what I didn't. I thought they might be illiterate louts, and I was right. They only glanced at the papers and asked me where I was going."

Jesse stood in the center of the circle like a performer, all eyes on him. Dust particles danced in the rays of morning sun shining through the barn boards. "I said I was a slave dealer from Harrisonburg, on my way to deliver these three to a buyer. I didn't like the look of them, but I hoped they'd buy my story and let us go. Then one of them says, "He's a weak lookin' specimen, ain't he?" Meaning me. "We could just knock him on the head and take these three for ourselfs. That buck alone'd fetch four hundred over to Winchester.""

Josiah stiffened at the memory. "I reach for the ax handle stowed under the buggy seat. If I's goin' back into slavery, I's goin' fightin'.""

"I tried to talk some sense into them," Jesse continued. "Bought us some time. Told them my brother, a constable in Harrisonburg, expected me back in a day or so. Said he wouldn't rest 'til he saw them hanged if they touched me. Then I clucked to the horses and drove on past. They sat in the track until we'd gone maybe a quarter mile; then they commenced to following us."

Amos, Nathaniel, Abby, and I sat in rapt attention. Amanda looked from one to another, eyes alight, fully enjoying the telling.

"I knew there was a safe house a few miles ahead, but I hoped our friends would turn back so they wouldn't see us stop there. I'd been told to look for a red brick house with a blue and white quilt hanging out a second story window. If the quilt wasn't there, we were to move on. Found the house but no quilt, so we kept on going."

He took a drink of coffee, his breakfast untouched atop his log seat. "The next place I knew of was maybe twenty miles on, past Moorefield. I don't mind tellin' you, I was scared. Then here comes a wagon down the track, with an old black man driving. He stops and we talk."

Jesse emptied his coffee cup and set it down on the floor, wiping his mouth on the back of his hand. "I say maybe he should turn around and travel with us. He's from a nearby farm on his way to his master's son's farm with a sow he wants bred. The sow stinks. He says the slave catchers won't bother him, but if we turn in at the next left, there's folk there that'll help us. We thank him and move on."

Now Jesse sat down on a log, rubbing his thighs with rough hands. He looked up at the open door in the hay mow. "The next left was maybe a mile farther on. Barely a path leading back into the woods. I hoped I could trust the man's word. I turned the team in. The track meandered for maybe another mile into a hollow in the mountain. Finally we came to a house and barn and some outbuildings." Nate stood up. "Gee, Jesse, how'd you know it wasn't a trap?"

"I didn't. Sometimes you just have to hope and trust. I couldn't see if our friends had followed us or not, so I pulled up to the house and knocked on the door."

"The owner was a country doctor with five slaves, Tate Woodruff. He took a chance, helping us. He took me into his house and sent the other three to the slave quarters. He was deeply conflicted about slavery, said he'd often thought of freeing his. He'd allowed one to buy his freedom, and that one was saving to buy his wife away, too."

Josiah spoke up. "He a good man. He slaves, they stayed 'cause they cared for him."

"I told him how Josiah had run all the way to Canada and come back for his mother," Jesse continued, "and about our three friends following us. Told him I needed shelter and time to reorganize."

The barn was silent except for Jesse's voice. It seemed as though even the animals were listening in rapt attention.

"That a strange place, that farm," Josiah put in. "Them slaves knew they could run. Knew the workin's of the Railroad. Knew the where and the who and the how. But they loved the doctor."

"I asked him if he was afraid my Negroes would make his dissatisfied—make them want to run, too," Jesse went on. "He said yes, but slaves were always going to be dissatisfied, so he didn't think it would matter much."

Josiah was obviously interested in Woodruff's slaves. His voice grew quiet as he talked about them. "They were one family, the slaves. Man, wife, grown daughter (wife of the one who'd bought his freedom), and two sons, ten and twelve. Never known any other life. Doctor bought 'em as a young couple and kept 'em together 'til he bought the young man, thinkin' to start a new generation." His face showed his consternation with slaves who might run but didn't.

Jesse went on with the tale. "If the slave catchers were still around, I figured I could throw 'em off if I drove back out in an empty buggy and turned south. The doctor thought it was worth a try, so I did it."

Josiah interjected here. "We saw Jesse drive away, Mama and Lovely afraid he'd gone and left us. I wouldn't blame him. His life in danger, but I knowed he wouldn't do that."

"I got out to the road, and there they were." Jesse grimaced at the memory. "Guess they figured I'd just turned off to trick 'em. I smiled, tipped my hat and turned south, back the way we'd come. They followed me, again about a quarter of a mile back. I drove all the way to the Easterbrook place. I can tell you I was nervous. I went in to Easterbrook's to see if my friends would get tired and leave, but they didn't. Easterbrook and I watched them from the parlor window, hanging around out on the road. It looked like they were fixing to follow me all the way to Harrisonburg."

Listening, I made a firm decision never to let Jesse go off south again. Life was dangerous enough right here in

Pennsylvania. I wondered how I would have acted in the same circumstances. If I'd have been as calm as Jesse.

"Mr. Easterbrook was pretty sure they were trying to wait me out to see if I went back for the slaves. So I decided to lay low for a few days, hoping they'd get tired of that game. The Easterbrooks set up a plan to let Josiah know what I was about. Mrs. Easterbrook and their two daughters set off to Moorefield to shop the next day. On the way they stopped at Dr. Woodruff's and told Josiah to stay put until he heard from me."

"I's glad to get any word," Josiah added. "I's thinking on heading out by myself with Mama and Lovely. Feared Jesse was dead."

Jesse nodded and continued. "In the meantime, I thought the best way to shake those three for good was to drive to Harrisonburg, as though I really did come from there. Easterbrook was afraid they might jump me anyway, especially if they thought I'd been paid for those slaves. So he and his oldest son went with me, each of us with a shotgun across our knees. When those louts saw the shotguns, they followed us for a short while and then turned off as though they had business elsewhere."

"We stayed overnight in Harrisonburg on Second Day, then drove back to Easterbrook's on Third Day without seeing them again. I set out as early as I could on Fourth Day morning, picked up my charges and headed for Moorefield. We pushed on through the night to Romney. I was through with daylight travel, even on those mountain roads."

"The nights scary, too," Amanda added.

"Depends on what you scared of, man or beast." Josiah laughed.

"Once we got to Romney, we were passed from one station to the next, mostly at night, and here we are," Jesse concluded. "We met a good batch of conductors on this trip." He picked up his plate of cold eggs and continued eating with a ravenous appetite.

The story over, Amos stood up and stretched. "I hope this has been a lesson to thee, Jesse, not to bother with this anymore." He shook a finger in Jesse's direction. "It gets more dangerous every day. We were worried near to death about thee."

Jesse nodded between bites. "I know, but it'll give me some good stories to pass on to my grandchildren."

"If thee has any. They don't come without effort, you know," Amos observed, heading for the ladder to the lower barn. "Now I have chores. Nathaniel?"

"I'll be down in a minute," Nate assured him.

"Well, you're safe, thanks be to God," I pointed out. "But we still have to pass you on to Canada. We need a plan."

Suddenly, Lovely tensed, her eyes wide. "Shhh! They's a horse outside."

Chapter 25

1858 – Mid-summer

The group fell silent. A horse whinnied. The sounds of creaking leather and restless hooves penetrated the barn. Nathaniel looked out, turned, and waved the Negroes away. Jesse herded the two women up the ladder, and Josiah, lithe as a cat, sprang to the side of the barn door, lifting a corn knife from a peg.

"Hello, the barn," came a call. "We know you're in there. We know you got niggers, too. Send them out and we won't be no trouble to you."

Jesse looked out a dusty window. "Oh, God!" he breathed. "It's them! They must have followed us all the way from Virginia!"

"I'll handle them," Nathaniel said, waving the others back as he squeezed out the door. "What do you want?" he asked.

"Clear what we want. Now hand 'em over."

"I don't know what you're talking about," Nathaniel said.

Inside the barn, I pulled Abby aside. "Go downstairs and out through the barnyard. Keep the corn crib between you and them. Once you're out of sight, run and get Ben and Elias. Tell Papa to lay low."

Abby nodded and climbed down the ladder. She moved quickly, and seconds later I peeked through a crack and saw her edging the yard, skirts hiked up, running like a deer.

Once Abby was clear, I stepped out beside Nathaniel, who was still arguing with the slave catchers. They were a rough looking lot—grimy, ragged, unkempt, smelling of tobacco, liquor, and horse manure. Their poor, neglected mounts looked as though they'd been pushed hard and fed little.

"What is this about?" I asked with authority. "What do you mean, coming here making wild accusations?"

"Ain't no wild accusations. We been trackin' that guy with the crippled arm all the way from Harrisonburg. Thought he lost us, but he didn't."

"There are no Negroes here."

"Yes, they is. We seen them turn in here last night. Seen you greetin' them with a lantern. Figured we might as well get some rest and wait till mornin' to take 'em back."

I figured the trio for a father and two sons, weary from the long ride. There was a sharp meanness about them. I didn't doubt they meant to get what they came for.

"You can search the barn if you like," Nathaniel offered, hoping the hiding place wouldn't be discovered.

"I ain't going to search nothing," the older man maintained. "You're going to give them over is what's going to happen. We know you're with that Underground Railroad. We know every place you stopped since Harrisonburg." His saddle creaked as he shifted his weight.

"We paid the Easterbrooks and the Woodruffs and all your other friends a visit after you left, and we don't think they'll be so eager to help you in the future." He leaned forward in the saddle, smiling down at me with crooked, yellow teeth. "'Specially that Mr. Easterbrook. He looked pretty bloody, last I saw."

Inside the barn, Jesse and Josiah exchanged glances. Jesse moved to the side of the door opposite Josiah, an ax handle in his good hand.

Now one of the sons dismounted and strode toward the barn. "Enough talk," he said. "I'm going to get them." He walked up to the door, gun drawn, slid it open and stepped inside.

Josiah moved with quick deftness. Before the lout could turn his head, his right arm was twisted behind him, the corn knife at his throat. His gun clunked to the barn floor.

Jesse, who hadn't moved, now stepped outside. "We've got your boy," he said. "If you want him back, you'd best leave off and head south. We'll send him after when we're sure you're gone."

The older man looked at his second son, rage in his eyes. "Dammit, Ab, why'd you let him go in there like that? You know he's stupid."

"That's okay, Pa. Let's just burn down the barn. They'll all come runnin' out like rats when it gets too hot in there," he grinned. "Zach might be stupid, but he can take care of hisself in a fire."

The old man considered the idea, but thought better of it for the moment.

"Naw, they might kill Zach. Besides, them Niggers might roast rather than go back. Then what'd we have? Nothing. I want that reward money." He took a crumpled handbill out of his shirt and showed it to Jesse. "Here. Look at that there. What's that say?"

Jesse's earlier suspicion was confirmed; they couldn't read. "Reward $200 for the return of two Negro women, Amanda, 49, and Lovely, 17, escaped from Shenandoah County on the night of July 27. Both women are dark, of medium height. May be traveling in company of a white man and a large, light-skinned Negro. I will give reward for their safe return. Robert Tull, Mt. Jackson, Virginia."

"Two hundred dollars! You've worked long and hard for a mere two hundred dollars!" I jeered.

"That ain't all. I figure that buck'll fetch three, four hundred easy on the block. No questions asked."

A surge of terror passed through me.

Inside the barn, Josiah let the blade of the corn knife bite into Zach's neck. Blood trickled down his shirt.

"Tell your papa to leave off," Josiah whispered. "Tell him I'll kill you right now if he don't turn around and ride out of here."

"Pa!" Zach bawled. "Pa! He's cut me. This nigger's gonna kill me, Pa."

The father looked frantically at his other son. "Do something, Boy! Go in there and get him out!"

Both men now had rifles at the ready. Nathaniel, Jesse and I stood helpless between the two horsemen and the barn. From inside the barn, Zach's loud caterwauling penetrated our brains.

"Pa! I'm bleedin'! Make 'em stop, Pa!"

Suddenly, from behind the three horses, a shotgun blast ripped the air, set them to rearing, and knocked the older man to the ground. Horse and man were peppered with buckshot, both screaming in pain. Ab had all he could do to stay astride his terrified horse as it tore around the side of the barn and down toward the creek, his rifle flying from his grasp.

Behind them stood Amos Redfield, shotgun breached, reloading. "Nobody gonna take nobody nowhere from this farm," he said tersely. He walked up to the old man lying prostrate on the ground. "This one'll live," he told Nathaniel. "See to the horse."

The blast brought Ben and Elias at the run, each armed with a loaded shotgun. Amos looked around at the carnage in his yard. Josiah brought the bleeding Zach out of the barn, corn knife still at the ready. I knelt over the old man, examining his buckshot riddled backside while Nathaniel ministered to the unfortunate horse and Jesse gathered up their rifles.

"So it has come to this," Amos said, evenly. "To violence, here in my own yard. Those people who *will* have slaves have no idea how far reaching is the pain and suffering they cause. Or for how many generations to come. It is shameful that Friends be forced to take up arms in defense of the helpless. God forgive us all."

The cut in Zach's neck was minor, as were his father's wounds. Ab wandered back from the creek, sheepishly leading his horse. The three stood cowed by the sheer determination of the Redfield family. They mounted and rode off to the south with full knowledge that if they ever came back, somebody would get killed. I knew it, too. My father, my brothers, even Elias, left no doubt about their determination.

Jesse put a hand on my shoulder as the contemptible louts rode away. I turned to see a steely resolve in his eyes. "We've got to move them on right away. If I know anything, those curs'll be in Bedford visiting the constable within the hour."

"I know. But how can we move them in broad daylight?"

"The old wagon. I haven't used it since Lettie. Come on. Let's go. We've no time to waste."

I hurried inside to gather up provisions for Josiah and his family. We never knew where they would go next, or whether they'd find food or shelter. The way north was safer than the way south but still fraught with danger.

Nathaniel stayed in the barn to help Jesse hitch up the horses and get Josiah, Amanda and Lovely packed in the narrow wagon bed. Literally packed in. Lying flat, head to toe and toe to head.

I was back in the barn within ten minutes, hoping to speak to Josiah one last time, but I was too late. Nathaniel stepped up. "I'll go with you, and we'd better take the shotguns, too, in case our friends decide to follow us." He swung up on the wagon seat beside Jesse, and I opened the barn doors.

"Which route will you take?" I asked, anxious to know where to look in case they didn't return.

"A different one than usual. I don't feel as safe as I used to."

I nodded.

"Maybe Pavia to Beaverdale. Haven't used that one in a while."

I winced at the reminder of Jesse's accident on the Pavia road. "Well, at least it isn't raining," I said. "Please, Jesse, can't I go with you?"

He looked away without argument. I took that as consent and reached for Nathaniel's hand to pull myself up. The need to get moving hung heavy in the air.

"Jesse?" Abby asked, her face full of hope. "Can I go, too?"

"I don't see why not," Jesse replied, to my surprise.

"Abby, there's no need," I began, but Jesse interrupted me.

"It's fine, Ann. I want her to go."

Just after noon the wagon with its seven occupants—four up and three down—rumbled past Amos, standing alone in the dooryard, and turned toward Alum Bank. It was a typical early August afternoon—hot, sultry and still. We lumbered along the Pavia road and on up the mountain. Jesse pointed out, as near as he could tell, the spot where his accident happened.

"Makes my arm hurt just to think about it," he said.

We came to the outskirts of Beaverdale around five o'clock. Jesse slowed the team, peering at the gateposts. When he found the mark he was looking for, he turned in and drove the wagon up to the barn, open at both ends. He climbed down and turned toward the house but was met by a tall, stoop shouldered farmer with a loping stride.

"Afternoon. I'm Mathias Pierson. Got a package for me?"

"Jesse Redfield. Yes. Three of them."

"Good. I'll take care of 'em," he said, with a nod toward the barn. "Where'd you come from?"

"Near Alum Bank."

"That's a long way. You need some supper?"

"That'd be fine," Jesse nodded.

"Come in and rest. Hot coffee and food'll do you good."

Jesse and Nathaniel helped our host lift the false bottom, releasing Josiah, Amanda, and Lovely. I would have taken my meal in the barn with them, but Mathias Pierson was deceptively quick in his movements. They were safely behind a false wall in the tack room before I could reach Josiah's side. My eyes sought his in the dim light. As the door closed on the tiny room, he reached out and touched my hand, held it, then let go. Mathias Pierson led the way to the house.

Mrs. Pierson put out a hearty supper, and I ate, in spite of the lead in my heart. We left soon after, hoping to get back before midnight. The ride home was long and lonely for me, but relief at having sent Josiah and his family on soothed my loneliness. Still, I would worry until I heard they were safe in Canada.

Chapter 26

1858

Amos, Jesse, Nathaniel and I. It was getting as comfortable as an old shoe. No change on the horizon, though I guessed I shouldn't expect it. We sat outside of an August evening, reading the mail Nathaniel had brought.

"Getting Josiah, Amanda and Lovely to Canada was easier than getting them out of Virginia," Jesse observed, reading a letter from Josiah.

"That's good. My emotions needed a rest." I opened a letter from Altoona. "Rachel's had her baby. A girl, Ellen Louisa!"

Amos smiled. "How many's that make, now?" he asked, counting on his fingers. "Fourteen grandchildren!" It was clear he took pride in it, despite his Quakerly ways.

"And more to come, I'm guessing. Jesse'll probably up and marry one of these days." Nathaniel shot a glance at our older brother.

"To say nothing of you!" I swatted at him with a rolled up newspaper. It was left unsaid, but I was destined to remain a spinster. Used goods.

A week later, Abby and I took the buggy over to Betsy's to return Jesse's borrowed clothes, and she gave out the news that she would be adding to the total of grandchildren in about six months. Joy for her! Oh, well, at least I'd known Josiah and borne Sam, and my life was full. Complaint wouldn't help.

That evening, I brought up the idea of a little trip. "Jesse, Fall is a good time to visit. How about taking me over to Mary's so she and I can go on to Altoona to visit Rachel and see the new baby?"

Jesse was willing, so I wrote Mary, and the plans were made. Visiting Mary was always fun, especially if Jesse stayed for a day or two. We talked and laughed well into the night. Our adventures with Josiah's family seemed almost humorous now that all was well. And hearing Jesse tell it with his own gestures and voice inflections did make me smile. His imitation of Zach bawling to his Pa that Josiah was like to kill him had Mary and Noah laughing out loud.

"Our older sister seems quite happy," I told Jesse.

He agreed. "Plenty of hard work, tempered by laughter and fun."

"That Noah is such a tease. I wonder that Mary doesn't swat him now and then." I didn't say it, but watching the Poole family made me envious.

In contrast, our visit to Rachel revealed the kind of tension I'd long suspected. Rachel followed Jacob's directives without question, since it was obvious that not to do so would bring wrath upon her.

"Jacob makes *all* the household decisions," Mary observed to me, "and Rachel carries them out like an obedient servant."

I nodded. "I've never seen a man so interested in *everything* to do with his family. He has an opinion about every detail. The children, the house, the cooking, even Rachel's clothes!"

"Especially Rachel's clothes." Mary scowled. "All it takes is a look from him and she's off to change!"

"Well, she doesn't complain, but I'm sure this is not at all what she dreamed of."

"Yes," Mary agreed. "It seems a hard life for one who was as flighty as a butterfly. Her beauty is fading. Her eyes have lost their luster. I can't say marriage has agreed with her."

Still, Jacob Schilling prospered. His investments paid off handsomely. Despite her lack of personal freedom, Rachel had a beautiful, well appointed home and all the modern conveniences. But Jacob forbade her to travel, so she saw her family only when we came to visit her. Mary and I winced at his controlling ways but kept still, except in confidence with each other.

"Most of her sentences begin with 'Jacob says' or 'Jacob thinks,'" I told Mary on the way home. "How sad! I'd stay unmarried for eternity before I surrendered my thinking to any man."

Now there was an amusing thought. Time was, if Elias Finley had smiled at me, I'd have agreed with anything he said. Surprising how a few years of living changed one's perspective so. All I knew was, once a perception changed, there was no going back.

&

I didn't have time to think much about either of my sisters once we got home. Fall was closing in fast, and I had my hands full with putting food aside for the winter. Abby and I made the rounds again with whatever canned or preserved food we had extra for anyone who seemed in need.

On the way home one day, we met Pru Hartley and her brother Cooper walking along the Pleasantville road. I hadn't laid eyes on Cooper Hartley in years, but he still looked tough to me. Slouching. Not given to bathing or shaving.

"Well, Cooper Hartley. Where have you been keeping yourself?" I greeted him in my brightest, friendliest voice. The Hartleys were always on the lookout for a slight. Better not to give them an excuse.

"Been around. Here and there." He leered at Abby's budding young womanhood. "Who's my little friend here?"

"I'm Abby Hill, and I'm not your friend. So you can just stop staring."

Cooper stepped back. "Nasty little snake, ain't you? I didn't mean nothing by it."

Abby straightened her spine and looked away. Needing a quick diversion, I looked to Pru. "Need any tomatoes to can, Pru? I've got more than I can use this year."

She sidled up to Cooper, made a point of slipping her arm through his. "No, thanks. My brother'll be takin' care of us for the present."

I looked to Cooper. "So you'll be staying around for a while?"

"Long enough to make me some money roundin' up niggers," he said pointedly. "Been livin' down to Maryland. Got a lot of friends getting' rich catchin' runaways. Figure this'd be good territory to start up on my own." He looked me straight in the eye.

I thought of Josiah and Sam, safe in Canada, thank God. Cooper Hartley meant to do us harm, no doubt of it.

"So, you'll be looking out for Pru and her boys? That's nice. They need a man around."

"Got one now," he said, puffing out his chest. "Man enough to handle what comes." He spat a stream of tobacco juice, leaving a little trickle at the corner of his mouth, and turned his attention to Abby again. "Ain't you Robert Hill's girl?"

Abby's nod was barely an acknowledgment.

"Your old man was a piece of work, now wasn't he?"

Abby looked down at her lap. She rarely mentioned her father, and when she did, it was only brief, in passing. Now she picked up a handful of her skirt and twisted it with white knuckles.

"Owed me some money, that one. Died afore he paid me my debt. I might be collectin' it yet, though," he said, leering at Abby.

I felt a need to move on before my temper got the better of me. It was a lifelong tenet of survival not to rile the Hartleys. Though I hated being hostage to their evil ways, I knew better than to poke a snake.

"Well, nice to see you, Pru. You take care, now, and if you change your mind about those tomatoes, let me know."

"Not likely."

I flipped the reins over the horse's rump and drove away, not too fast, but not too slow. At home that evening I told Jesse about the encounter, but, true to his nature, he was unconcerned.

"Cooper Hartley'll have to go to school before he can catch me," he said. "Not that I'm proud. I just know a fool when I see one."

"He was very interested in Abby. Said her Pa owed him money."

Jesse turned to face me. "He'd best stay away from Abby. Now, get your bonnet and shawl. We've got visitors."

A man and wife had been passed along from Everett, and Jesse was careful not to keep people around for too long with the Hartleys watching our every move.

I gathered some quilts. These late August nights could be cold. I picked up my bonnet and shawl and a lantern. Abby came down from upstairs. She yawned. "Where are you goin' so late?"

"Business. Got to keep ahead of the Hartleys."

Abby moved to get her shawl and bonnet from the peg. "Where you takin' them?"

"Over to Mary's, I guess. It's too late to do much else. No need for you to go," I told her.

"There's always a need for more folk. Make it look like you've got a reason to be out. Besides, more heads make the thinking go better."

Jesse was already in the barn, hitching up the wagon, and I didn't feel like arguing, so I hurried out the door with Abby behind me. Jesse nodded to us as he swung up on the wagon seat. I let the wagon out and pulled myself up beside him. Abby was settled among the quilts in the back, barely visible to either of us.

The night was dark, but the moon came up late, brightening the road ahead. Still the forest, close on both sides of the wagon track, was hardly penetrated by the light. Shadows closed in, wrapping themselves around us.

Suddenly, from the woods on the left, we heard a horse snort. Then the forest was alive with movement. Five riders stepped out on the road in front of us. Jesse and I hadn't agreed on a 'story'— careless of us. Now we searched our minds frantically for any reason to be out on the road this late at night.

"Hold up!" came a sharp command from the darkness. "Constable Bennett here. What's your business?"

"Evening, Constable," Jesse spoke slowly. I frantically cast about for a 'story'.

Then from the wagon bed, "Pa? Pa? Where are we? My head hurts, ever so much. I'm burnin' up, Pa."

I crawled over the wagon seat to Abby's side, ministering to the 'sick' girl. Abby moaned. "Pa? How far is it yet to the doctor's? I'm so sick."

The horsemen backed up a few steps. "What's the matter with her?" one of them asked.

"Don't know," Jesse replied. "Some sort of fever. Came on all of a sudden."

I talked quietly to Abby. Gentle, comforting words. "It's all right, dear. Don't you worry. We'll get you there. You're going to be all right."

The horsemen were nervous. They backed a little farther away. Jesse let the team move a few steps toward them.

"Hey, stay back!" one of the men said. "We don't want what she's got!"

"Best you step aside, then," Jesse told him. "Sooner I get her out of here, the safer you'll be."

The five riders turned, passed back into the trees and were gone. Jesse clucked to the team. In back with Abby, I kept up a stream of encouraging words, mostly for those below.

We continued down the road, surrounded by night sounds and the smell of damp leaf mold. The sky was beginning to lighten when we arrived at Mary's farm near Osterburg. Jesse drove around behind the barn, and we unloaded our charges into the corn crib and covered them with corn cobs. We worked silently and quickly, grateful that Noah kept his dog inside at night. When the fugitives were safely stowed away, Jesse unhitched the horses and led them around to the lower barn. Abby and I entered the hay loft and lay down to await the dawn.

When he returned Jesse smiled at us in the gray dimness. "Abby, you sure can think on your feet," he said. "I always want you on my side, girl!"

Abby wiggled like a happy puppy.

When we heard Noah and his son Adam come in to start their chores, we called down to them and lowered ourselves on the ladder.

"Brought you some presents. In the corn crib," Jesse explained.

Noah nodded and turned to his milking. "Adam, go tell your mother. They'll be hungry."

"I can do that," I offered. "Come on, Abby. Let's go surprise Mary. Two visits in two weeks! Aren't we the gadabouts!"

Chapter 27

1858-1859

One day about a month later, Abby came back from Ben's, all breathless with news. "Elias's been called to Chambers-burg. Melissa's down with pneumonia and it don't look good."

Elias left the next morning, astride one of his best riding horses. He waved—almost gaily, I thought—as he rode by on his way to the Fishertown road.

"That Elias," I grumbled to Jesse at breakfast. "He's hardly visited his wife these two years now. Even Lucy doesn't seem to hold any attraction for him. He doesn't care about anyone but himself!"

But Jesse saw him only as inept. "He's not a bad sort. A lot of the time he doesn't know what to do, so he doesn't do anything."

I was unconvinced. I saw Elias as selfish, but Rebecca also spoke of her brother in a charitable tone.

"Elias doesn't mean to be hurtful. He's immature at worst. Can't find room in his head for others' needs. He means well, but he doesn't see beyond his nose. He's been that way since he was a boy, which some say wasn't so long ago."

"I wonder that I didn't see it when I thought to marry him," I mused. It was sure I didn't care for Elias anymore, leftover resentment from his marriage to Melissa tainting my view, but I wished him neither well nor ill. He was as much a part of the landscape as any other Friend. No more. No less.

Melissa died in September. It was not unexpected, but still very sad. I remembered the beautiful young girl, so much in love with Elias, who had unknowingly destroyed my world. Despite wanting to dislike her, I'd found her a kind and pleasant soul. The tragedy of her marriage and short life made me sad.

A few days later Abby brought more news from Ben's. "Elias is still down there. She lingered a long time, poor thing. I guess he'll be home in a week or so. Ben's sorely overworked without him."

"What about Lucy?" I wondered. "I suppose he'll leave her with Melissa's parents."

"He will, if I know Elias," Abby replied.

Apparently, Abby didn't know Elias, for a week later he arrived on horseback with his little daughter bundled in front of him. Abby, Rebecca, and I looked at one another, in disbelief.

"What is he thinking?" I asked. "How's he going to take care of her when he couldn't even take care of Melissa when she needed him? Who does he think is going to help him?"

Elias' first move was to hire one of the Conley girls to care for Lucy during the day. The rest he did himself, asking Rebecca or me for advice but doing for his child with a new found sense of responsibility. Elias and Lucy became a familiar pair at social gatherings, Meetings, or family affairs. She wore store bought clothes and shoes. She learned to ride a horse before Christmas. She followed her father to the stables and listened to horse talk before she could reach up to feed a horse an apple. A beautiful child, she favored her mother but was fully able to speak for herself, stronger than Melissa had ever been, and the center of her father's world.

I watched Elias's struggles in raising Lucy with detached interest and not a little amusement. One day, he asked me to teach him how to braid the little girl's hair. Long and blond, it had flown free since babyhood, but now Elias worried (like an old hen, I said to myself) that it would get caught in something and cause her injury. Elias and I had a good laugh as his clumsy hands fumbled to braid hair as soft as silk and just as slippery.

"Aunt Ann does it better than you, Papa," Lucy told Elias. "Her braids are tighter. Yours feel like they're falling out."

Elias chuckled at the criticism. "I do pretty well for a mere man, don't you think?" he asked with a wink.

Abby watched with interest as Elias, a little at a time, wormed his way back into my life. "He's just making excuses to visit you," she said. "Wants another wife, most likely."

I pushed that idea to the back of my mind and tried to be helpful when Elias came around—for Lucy's sake, I told myself.

Consciously or not, I protected myself against a repeat of my earlier humiliation.

One evening the following summer, Elias brought Lucy over for a visit, seated, as always, in front of him in the saddle. Elias handed her down to me, dismounted and tethered his horse. Abby and I had canned peaches and saved several big, juicy ones for eating. I sliced one into a bowl for Lucy and sat down with Elias to watch her enjoy the treat.

"I've been thinking about my house," Elias began. "Thought I'd build on, maybe double the size, add a porch on back, and put in some new windows."

"Time you paid some attention to that," I observed dryly.

"I've drawn up a plan." He spread a rolled up paper on the table before me. "Thought I'd show it to you. Get your ideas."

I studied the crude drawing and made some suggestions, agreeing with some of Elias' plans, vetoing others.

"When do you expect to start?" I asked.

"Tomorrow."

"Tomorrow? That's quick!"

"I want it done by harvest. So we can enjoy the winter in it. I want it to be a fine home for Lucy. A cook stove in the kitchen and a heating stove in the parlor. I'm even thinking about running water in the kitchen instead of a hand pump. These new pumps they have can do that."

I was skeptical. Running water seemed a little prideful to me.

"Or I can leave it a hand pump, if you'd like that better."

"I would," I replied before the implication of his remark dawned on me. He watched me, an expectant half smile on his face.

"Will you, Ann?" he asked.

"Will I what?" I countered.

"Marry me. Be a mother to Lucy. Be mistress of my house."

I rose and walked away, stepped off the porch and out into the yard. I couldn't say I hadn't thought about it. It had been in the back of my mind since Melissa died, but I wasn't ready for the actuality of it. My feelings about Elias had been here, there, and everywhere since the January day he'd driven up with Melissa at his side. I'd loved him, hated him, resented him, pitied him, disdained him, enjoyed him, laughed at him, even respected him. Now I looked among all those feelings for something solid, unchanging—something to make me want to spend the rest of my life with him.

Elias sat quietly on the porch with Lucy, giving me time to think. I couldn't get my mind around the idea of actually being his wife. Too much water under the bridge. I walked all the way to the edge of Ben's orchard and looked over at my brother's house, bursting at the seams with a big family growing bigger. Ben and Rebecca's seventh child was due before Christmas.

It was all I'd ever wanted—a husband, a home, a family. Now, here it was, mine for the taking. Lord knew, I had no other prospects. What was stopping me? I didn't know. I couldn't name it. But there it was in front of me like a huge boulder in the road. I couldn't marry Elias because I didn't love him. All old hurts aside, I knew him too well to ever love him like that. Like what? Like I loved Josiah. I turned and walked back to the porch to give Elias my answer.

Apparently Elias was bent on having him a wife, for two weeks after I rejected his offer he proposed to Deborah Hill, Abby's 18-year-old sister. Rebecca was more than a little put out with him for taking away her hired girl, but Elias reminded her that someone was bound to do it some day. It was simply a matter of time.

I watched the new addition to the Finley house take shape amid much talk about the suddenness of the marriage proposal.

"Deborah accepted Elias with all speed," Rebecca observed to me. "Guess it was more than the poor girl dreamed of. Going from nothing to a fine, new house, the wife of one of the respected men of the community. More than she ever expected from life."

"I hope it turns out that way. For her sake."

No one could blame Deborah for marrying Elias, even if it was more for convenience on his part than anything else. Their intention to marry was announced at Meeting, with appropriate committees assigned. The union took place in October, just after harvest. Sitting in the Meeting House, watching Elias take a wife, I was at peace with my decision.

Even though I kept my rejection of Elias to myself, Jesse surmised what had happened and couldn't resist the chance to tease.

"That sure is a fine house Elias is building for his bride," he gibed. "It's not every woman gets a chance at a catch like Elias. Sure would look fancy riding to Meeting in a fine buggy at Elias's side. Yep, I bet there's many a woman wishes she'd had a chance to land that one!"

"Yes, many. If Deborah had rejected him, there's always Pru Hartley! Get thee behind me, Jesse!" I chided. "You need a wife yourself, but I doubt anyone would have you, even Pru. Mayhap we could advertise in the Bedford Gazette and see what turns up!"

Chapter 28

1860

Uncle Sammy Grainger died in March. I was deeply touched by his passing, indebted to him as I was for his help in sending Sam to Josiah. Jesse confided that he'd been the one to start the Underground Railroad in the Quaker settlement. I hadn't known that, but come to think of it, he was always there on the fringe of things. He'd stepped aside years ago for younger men, but the Railroad work was only part of his legacy. His death brought change to Redfield Farm.

First there was Uncle Sammy's will. Each of his sister Martha's children shared equally. It wasn't a huge sum, but enough in every case to make a difference in a life. I learned I'd received only about a quarter of my share, and was pleasantly surprised with more. Ben spoke of using his share to buy more breeding stock, but Rebecca raised an eyebrow.

"We need a bigger house for these seven and a half children!"

Ben grinned and quietly agreed. Mary and Noah Poole used their legacy to buy some adjoining land they'd wanted. No one knew what happened to Rachel's money, but we speculated that Jacob Schilling put it to good use in his investments. Betsy and Will built onto their house in New Paris, more space for the shoemaking business and raising two boys. Nathaniel invested his money in railroad stock, and I asked him to do the same with mine, thinking primarily of Sam's future. Jesse put his share away without a word about his plans.

Ever since he was a little boy, Jesse'd talked about going west. He'd read about it, studied it, even planned for it. Now, given the wherewithal to actually do it, he dallied, unable to make the decision.

"Jesse, do you think you'll go west now that you can?" I asked him one April evening.

"I don't know. There's still so much to be done here."

I knew he meant the Railroad. "But there are others who can take over for you. I'd hate to lose you. I'd miss you like everything, but this is your one chance." He sat opposite me on the back porch, whittling at a stick with his pocket knife.

"I know. It's what I've always wanted. Matthew Miller writes that life is fine in Indiana. He's got a hundred and sixty acres. Planted apple trees. Near a place called Edinburgh." There was longing in his voice.

"Then do it, Jesse. Don't stay here and be a martyr for the Railroad. You've already given your left arm to the cause."

I heard myself say the words, but my heart ached at the thought of his leaving. He'd always been *my* Jesse, two years ahead, sensible, level headed, self assured. What would I do without him? Who would I turn to when the world got too much for me? Who would tease me out of the doldrums, make me laugh at myself, take me in hand when I needed it?

Of course I wouldn't stand in his way. No one, least of all Jesse, would ever know how alone I would be without him. If anyone had a right to follow his dreams, Jesse did. But for me, a future taking care of Nate and Papa was an empty prospect.

He smiled. "You're right about the arm. Maybe I better go while I still have one good one." He rose to go inside but stopped at the sound of someone approaching on horseback. The visitor was Constable Ackroyd from Bedford. The April night was damp and cool, so Jesse invited him inside.

"You folks seen any runaways hereabouts in the last day or so?"

Jesse smiled. "Don't suppose I'd tell you if I did," he replied.

"Well, normally I wouldn't be askin', but there's a problem you should know about.

"What's that?"

"Some folks down in Chaneysville was robbed and beat up pretty bad by a rogue fugitive on Monday night. You need to be careful who you take in, is all."

Jesse stepped back. "Oh."

I looked at him questioningly, then remembered my responsibility as a hostess. "Thank you for the warning. Can I get you a cup of coffee? Something to warm you on the ride home?"

"Don't mind if I do," he replied, taking off his hat. Abby pulled out a chair for him. I poured the coffee and cut a piece of apple pie left over from supper.

"I figure he might try to hook up with the Underground Railroad around here, if he knows of it. Pass the word around the settlement. I shouldn't be talking to you like this," the officer told us between bites of pie. "But this one's a mean one."

By the time the constable left, I was fidgety. There was something on Jesse's mind, but I had to wait until everyone else had gone to bed before I asked. Abby was the last, leaving Jesse and me finally alone.

"Jesse, what is it?"

"There's one in Spring Hope tonight. At Ezra Warner's. Came up this afternoon alone, asking for a hook-up. Ben was down horse trading with Ezra, and he told me when he stopped on the way home."

"We've got to warn Ezra."

"Could be the constable already has."

"Is Ezra a known conductor?" I asked.

"No. He just took the man in out of pity."

"Then no one would know to warn him. We'd better do it, Jesse."

He stood rooted before me, a pained expression on his face. "I hope we're not too late."

I understood his chagrin. It was one thing when *he* was in danger. He chose the path. But it was something else entirely when others were at risk. The prospect of anyone getting hurt had always daunted him. I reached for my coat, handing Jesse his. Together we hurried to the barn with a lantern.

Jesse stopped me at the barn door. "I'll go alone. It'll be faster on horseback," he said. "No telling what I might find."

"I can't sit here waiting. Saddle Nate's mare for me. I'll hike my skirts."

We rode through the night toward the tiny village of Spring Hope, south of Fishertown. It was only about ten o'clock, but there was no light in the farmhouses we passed. When we reached Ezra Warner's farm, it, too, was dark. No one answered Jesse's knock. He pounded on the door hard enough to rattle the windows, but no one answered. He came back down the steps.

"I'm going to look in the barn."

I climbed down from my horse to follow him. Jesse found a lantern on a peg and lit it. We looked around the barn floor, moving toward the hay mow. Then I noticed feed sacks spread over some barrels and motioned to Jesse to have a look. I held the lantern high, and Jesse yanked the sack off one of the larger barrels. Inside, hands clasped over his head, crouched a black man.

"'Don't take me back. Please, Massa,'" he pleaded. "'Please don't take me back. I'll do anything. Please, Massa!'"

"Where is the Warner family?" Jesse demanded.

"Gone away. Say to stay here. They be back tomorrow. Send me on then. Please, Massa. Don't send me back. I's cold an' hungry, but I's free."

His pleadings sounded sincere, but I puzzled over the whole Warner family being gone.

"Where did you come from?" Jesse asked.

"North Carolina. Halifax County. Been runnin' two weeks now, tryin' to find the Railroad. Some folks help me, but they don't know how to hook up. Mr. Warner say he know a real conductor."

"Which way did you come up from Maryland?"

"'Long Wills Creek. Through Hyndman and up to Mann's Choice."

"That where you were this morning?" There was skepticism in Jesse's voice.

"Yassuh."

"How did you get here from there?" He spoke sharply, watching the man's every move with suspicion.

"Just kept the morning sun on my right and kept walkin'. Kept to the woods mostly. Mr. Warner, he workin' in the field. I ask him do he know the Railroad. He say yes. Bring me here. Say he got to go to town tonight—something about his wife's father sick. Say he fix things and be back for me in the morning."

I nodded. Ezra Warner's wife was a Baldwin. Aaron Baldwin's daughter. They lived in Schellsburg, and the old man was on his deathbed. I knew that.

"All right," I said to the black man. "Stay here. Help will come tomorrow. Don't move or make a sound until either Ezra or Jesse, here, comes for you."

We re-covered the barrel and put out the light. Outside, we mounted the horses and turned toward home.

"If he came up through Hyndman, he can't be the one who did the damage at Chaneysville," I offered.

"*If* he came up through Hyndman," Jesse countered.

"I'm inclined to believe him."

"I don't know. He *could* be the lost soul he claims to be, in which case he really needs our help. *Or* he could be a wily criminal who knows the geography well enough to take us for a walk in the woods."

"You don't think he's hurt Ezra and his family, do you?"

"No. That part sounds right. He'd be gone already if he'd hurt them."

We rode toward home in silence, wondering what to do next.

Jesse was thinking out loud. "I'll get up early and go see Ezra. Between us we can decide if this one's lying or not. If he's not, we need to move him on tomorrow night. There's no room to fool around, what with Cooper Hartley watching our every move."

The next morning Jesse was gone before sunup and back in time for a late breakfast. He seemed confident, after talking to Ezra, that this was a runaway in need, not a criminal. He'd promised to return that night to move the man on.

Jesse's confidence was enough for me. Relieved that the Warners were all right and comfortable with Jesse's plan, I went about my chores with little thought.

What *was* on my mind was the idea of Jesse's going west. A sister has to expect to lose a brother, some time or other. I was lucky to have kept him this long. That was true, but it didn't help. My heart was still heavy.

As soon as supper was over, Nate and Jesse went to the barn to hitch up the team. I gathered food and blankets, and tied on my bonnet.

"Where are you off to?" Amos asked.

"Making a delivery to Giestown."

"Hope it's not that killer one," Abby piped up.

"It's not, Abby," I replied with more confidence than I felt. "Besides, nobody got killed."

"Oh, no. Excuse me. Just beaten and robbed," Abby replied.

"All right, Abby. That's enough."

"I'm going with you," she said.

"Why?"

"So there's somebody there with some sense. Somebody who doesn't necessarily think the whole world is filled with good people. Or that *all* fugitive slaves are kind and benevolent. Honestly, Ann, just because they've been slaves doesn't make them all saints."

"Thank you for enlightening me, Abby. Now, if you think Jesse and I aren't up to the task—in need of your protection— get your bonnet."

Amos smiled behind his newspaper.

We set out through a night warmer then the last, made our pickup in Spring Hope, and backtracked through Fishertown to Alum Bank, then on over the mountain toward Geistown. After cresting the mountain, Jesse stopped to let the horses catch their wind. There was a rap on the false wagon floor, and Jesse stepped back to lift the trap. As he peered down into the darkness a huge, swift, black fist slammed into his face. Caught unawares, he was thrown over the side of the wagon to the ground.

Abby screamed and jumped down to Jesse's side, leaving me face to face with the man, now standing in the wagon bed, reaching for my arm.

"Two!" he yelled. "I get two white asses in one night!" With a loud, grating laugh, he grabbed my hands, held my back against him and shoved me down under the false bed. He slammed the trap back in place and jumped down to grab Abby's arm before she could run. He yanked her back up into the wagon and slammed her down on the floor so hard she lost consciousness. Then he lifted the false floor and dumped her in on top of me. I lay there, too dazed to think. I could hear him panting, smell his sweat. He sat down in the driver's seat, took the reins and drove the startled horses on down the mountain toward Ogletown.

Under the false bed, I felt feverishly for any means of escape or defense. All I found was one square horseshoe nail. It had to be enough. I lay on my back, Abby still groggy at my side, and waited.

After about a mile, the wagon jolted as the horses veered off the road to a stop. The man stepped into the wagon bed and lifted the trap, leering at us, helpless and barely conscious under the floor. Staring at the menacing silhouette above me, I felt for Abby, found her hand and squeezed it. The nail tucked into the waist of my apron was all that stood between us and savage rape.

Our tormenter slammed back the trap and crawled down into the wagon bed, opening his pants. Panting and moaning grotesquely, he looked from one of us to the other, trying to decide which to do first. I struggled to stand up; it was enough to make me his choice. He grabbed my arms and pinned them beneath me, wrestled me to the false floor and lay on top of me, slapping and punching my face with his free hand. I struggled, but his strength was too much for me. As I lay helpless under his weight he reached down and pulled up my skirts, wrestling himself between my legs. Suddenly, Abby jumped on his back, grabbing at his face from behind. He rolled over on her, releasing his grip on me, and I reached for the nail. I raked it over his face, digging and tearing at the flesh, trying to rip it into his eyes. He grabbed my wrist with an iron grip, but Abby reached around again from behind and grabbed one of his nostrils, holding and tearing as though possessed. He thrashed at the two of us, knocking us heavily against the sides of the wagon, but still we fought him. The horses, spooked by the terrible noise, circled and ran headlong back up the track the way they had come.

We got to our feet, one of us on either side, fighting fiercely. With a wild swipe of his arm, he knocked me out of the wagon. I landed with a thump on my back in the track, seeing stars. Then as the demon lurched to the driver's seat to stop the terrified horses, Abby jumped out, too.

She ran back toward me, her white apron a blur in the darkness. I stumbled, limping, toward her. We crouched behind a boulder, clinging to each other, trembling. Our hands searched frantically on the ground for anything we could use as a weapon. The fugitive stopped the horses, jumped down and walked back along the track looking for us. We held our breath, watching him.

He lurched past within a few feet of us. "God damn white bitches," he mumbled as he staggered along in the darkness. Suddenly Abby sprang out behind him and smashed a rock into his skull. I heard the sickening thud. The man grunted and fell forward, blood soaking the back of his head.

"Let's go," Abby cried, grabbing me by the arm. We ran blindly up the track and climbed into the wagon. Abby took the reins, and I looked back for the first time. I saw nothing in the blackness, heard nothing but the creaking of the harness and the squeaking wagon springs. We moved slowly through the night, back up to the summit. There lay Jesse, sprawled on the side of the track, looking like death itself. We strained to lift him into the wagon and slapped the reins against the horses' rumps. Neither of us spoke until we reached home well after midnight.

In the barn, we unhitched the horses and inspected ourselves by lantern light. The damage was ugly but not life threatening. Jesse, on the other hand, was seriously hurt. He lay in the bottom of the wagon, still unconscious.

Abby ran into the house to get Nathaniel, who appeared in his underwear, groggy from sleep. "What's this?" he asked.

"Jesse's hurt bad, Nate. Help us get him inside," I implored.

We carried Jesse into the kitchen and laid him on Amos' bed, a sad replay of that other night a few years ago. Amos, roused by all the activity, questioned us.

"What happened? What's wrong with Jesse?"

I pumped water and built up the fire in the stove as we told the tale to Papa and Nate. Abby and I inspected our injuries by lamplight. We looked a fright, but not as bad as Jesse, who lay lifeless on Papa's bed.

Nate was pale with fear for him. "I'll go for the doctor at first light."

The two men retired to the attic rooms while Abby and I bathed. We shed our filthy clothes and washed our aching bodies, trying to remove all evidence of our attacker. When we'd washed every inch of ourselves, even our hair, we put on clean nightgowns and went up the parlor stairs to my room. There, lying in the dark, we held onto each other and cried. I cried because my faith in the goodness of man had been shaken to its roots. Abby cried for Jesse.

Morning had long since broken before either Abby or I awakened. Amos had taken care of the chores while Nate rode to Schellsburg for the doctor. Jesse, though conscious now, still could not move his feet and legs. He said his hands felt numb.

Abby and I each had a black eye and many cuts, bruises, and scrapes. Soreness was setting in with every twist of the back and raise of an arm.

Dr. Telford examined Jesse and found what he thought was the problem. In the fall from the wagon, he'd struck the back of his head, low, near his neck, on a rock. The bruising and swelling put pressure on his spinal cord, causing the paralysis. The doctor hoped it was only temporary, that once the swelling went down, Jesse would be able to walk, but it would take a long time and plenty of bed rest.

"Do you have any ice?" Dr. Telford asked.

"Yes, the ice house is full this time of year," I replied.

"Good. Chip off pieces and hold them on the back of his head. It'll numb the pain and reduce the swelling."

Abby rushed to get the ice, returning in a few minutes with a basin half full. She sat beside Jesse, gently turned him on his side, and applied the ice to his aching head.

"You look like the wrath of God," he told her.

"It was wrath, but it wasn't God's" she replied.

"What happened out there?"

"He tried to rape us."

Jesse moaned, and tears came to his eyes.

"Rape?" he rasped. "What did you do?"

"We fought him off. I think I killed him."

"How?"

"I bashed in his skull with a rock."

"Oh, Abby!" Jesse's voice broke. "I'm sorry I got you into this."

"You didn't. I volunteered," she corrected him. "And it's a good thing I did, because if there hadn't been three of us, you and Ann might be dead by now."

Jesse's face—contorted by a broken nose and two black eyes—looked at Abby's cut, bruised, and swollen face with gratitude and shame.

"You're some woman, Abby Hill," he said.

From then on, Abby took over nursing Jesse. His recovery was slow, aided by Abby's constant attention. When he could stand, she took him out on the porch and read to him. When he could walk, she took him first to the barn, then over to Ben's, hovering over him at meals and between. I saw what was developing, but chose not to speak of it. This was their business, not mine. I waited to be told, certain that I *would* be told.

Nate rode to Bedford to drop a word to the friend of a friend to tell the constable to send somebody over to the summit on the Geistown road to investigate a dead body said to be there. Word came back in a couple of days that there was, indeed, a body. Nothing more was asked or told.

Jesse convalesced through the spring, slowly regaining movement and feeling. I allowed myself to hope that he might shelve his plans to go west at least for a while. But change was in the air.

Chapter 29

1860 – Summer

Jesse put off his departure for the west while he **recuperated,** but it was soon apparent that he still intended to go. Abby hovered over him, protective as a she-wolf. I moved aside when I saw the unmistakable look of possession her eyes. Jesse was too foggy-headed to read the female maneuvering that went on about him. All he knew was that Abby looked different. Like a woman. By June, he was ready to tell the world. He was going to Indiana and taking Abby as his wife.

Abby and I attended to the inevitable sewing of linens, a wedding dress for her, and a wedding shirt for him. Time rolled by too quickly, try as I would to put the impending departure out of my mind.

Maybe I could get them to take me with them. No. How silly. Papa needs me. Nate can fend for himself or marry, but I can't abandon Papa. It's a childish notion anyway. What would Jesse and Abby want with me?

I awoke on the wedding day almost giddy with excitement until I remembered that it was Abby and Jesse getting married and moving on, not me. The whole family, including the bridal couple, boarded Ben's carriage for the ride to Meeting. There we met Mary and Noah with their shiny-faced brood, hardly able to contain their good natured silliness long enough to sit still for a wedding. Betsy and Will McKitrick arrived with their two boys, already long and tall. Once they saw their Poole and Redfield cousins, there was no containing them. I loved these family gatherings—they happened too seldom. The only one missing was Rachel, who had given birth in May to her third child, John Tyler Schilling. She wouldn't have been allowed to come in any case, but Rachel was in my thoughts that day.

Jesse was clearly eager to get to Indiana and the life he had thus far put off. Abby's beauty, though late in coming, was in full bloom. She was so deeply in love with Jesse, it shone from her eyes. My own feelings aside, I couldn't help but be glad—for Abby to have found love, and for Jesse, too. But, oh, the emptiness I faced as a result.

They left the next day to take the cars from Altoona to Pittsburgh, then on to the prairie of central Indiana. I thought them well suited for the adventure they faced. No lack of courage between them.

Nate drove them to Altoona in Ben's best carriage. Amos and I rode along to stay the night with Rachel and Jacob Schilling. It was the first time Amos had seen Rachel in six years, the first time he had met his three Schilling grandchildren, and the first time in all of his sixty-four years that he slept under any roof but his own.

Jacob was still at work when we arrived. Rachel and the children met us on the porch of their home on 10th street. The three blonde-haired, blue-eyed, solemn faced children eyed us shyly at first but soon warmed up to their Uncle Jesse's pulling nickels from behind their ears and their Uncle Nate's horsie rides. Little Ellen was especially attractive to me, being less of a reminder of Sam than the boys.

Abby and I helped Rachel with supper, and the family sat down, nine strong. Rachel beamed. "I'm so glad you came! You'll never know how much I've longed to see all of you. I'm glad not to have missed out on *everything*." Her joy was contagious, and we were soon laughing and talking as of old.

As soon as the meal was over, Jesse stood up and motioned to Abby. "We'll be going now," he said.

"Oh, yes," Rachel responded. "The Logan House! It's near the railway station, a few blocks down 10th street."

The bridal couple took their leave politely, obviously anxious to be alone.

Jacob Schilling rose and turned to Nate. "Come on, little Brother. Time you learned the wonders of the big city."

Amos watched them go with a yawn and mumbled something about going to bed with the chickens, if he could only find some chickens, and retired early, giving Rachel and me a chance to talk more freely than we had in years.

"What will you do when they're gone, Ann, with only Papa and Nate to do for?"

"Truth to tell, I'll be lost without both of them."

"Why don't you come to Altoona and live with us for a while? Maybe you would meet a nice man and get married."

"Thank you, Rachel, but no. Someone has to take care of Papa. Nate will marry soon enough, but I can't leave Papa. Besides, Jacob wouldn't want me around."

"Whyever not?"

"I'm a little too saucy for him, I think."

Rachel sat quietly, studying her hands in her lap. "He's not such a bad man. He has his good qualities."

"No doubt he does, but our personalities would clash, I'm afraid." I looked directly at her. "How are you doing, Rachel? You look well enough, but I miss my old sister. Where's she gone?"

"One grows up. Three children and a husband tame the child pretty quick."

"Is he good to you?" I pressed.

"Yes." Rachel hesitated. "Most of the time. But I always toe the line. If I anger him, he can be beastly. Not that many men aren't the same. When you live as close to your neighbors as I do, you know that."

"Maybe so, but I worry for you. You're not the carefree girl I grew up with, and my guess is it has more to do with him than the children."

"The children are my joy. Jacob is my keeper."

"As I suspected. You know you could leave him and come home to us, especially with Jesse leaving."

"Oh, no. I could never do that. The children need their father, and Jacob's a good provider. We want for nothing. I would find life in the old place hard," she said. Then, apologetically, "I've learned to like my comforts."

I studied her, hoping my worst fears were groundless. But I knew in my heart that Jacob Schilling and I would clash mightily, given the opportunity. I lay awake long into the night, brooding over the impending loss of Jesse and Abby and over Rachel's plight.

In the morning, the family gathered for breakfast without the newlyweds. I helped Rachel dress the children, and we set out for the station, Baby John in a fine new wicker perambulator, young James riding on Uncle Nate's shoulders, and prim little Ellen holding my hand. Jesse and Abby waited on the platform, their joy in one another impossible to mask. A shudder passed through me when I saw them. How could I ever say goodbye?

We engaged in light conversation as the locomotive steamed up and passengers from the east alighted. Jesse saw to the loading of the trunk, then rejoined the family. He took both my hands in his and looked into my eyes. I couldn't return his gaze without tears, so I looked away.

"Good-bye, Ann," he said softly. Pulling me to him, he gave me an awkward hug. "I'll miss you."

Unable to speak, I stood encircled by his arms until he let me go. Then I turned and hugged Abby.

"I love you like a sister, Ann," she said, holding back her own tears. "I know how much Jesse means to you. I'll take good care of him."

They stepped aboard the train, and we watched them settle in. Jesse opened the window and talked to us as they waited to pull out. I found myself wishing the train would just go. It was a full five minutes before it rumbled out of the station, building up steam for the long haul up the Alleghenies. I looked away as the rest watched it disappear. In need of distraction, I tucked Baby John's blanket around him and took little Ellen's hand. When I saw Amos wipe a tear from his eye, I reached out with my other hand and took his arm. It felt small and weak. He looked, suddenly, like an old man.

We said goodbye to Rachel and the children around ten o'clock and drove south out of the city toward Bedford. Nate tried to distract Amos with farm talk, but got only mumbled responses. I stared at the road ahead, afraid to speak lest my emotions overflow.

At home, Nate put up the horses and I tied on my apron to prepare supper. I looked around at the empty house, tomb-like in its silence. So much of life had happened here, and now, it seemed, it was gone for good. Suddenly, I missed Sam and Josiah overwhelmingly, so much that I had to find a way to see them.

Sam was almost five now and, according to reports from Josiah, was growing tall, handsome, and smart. Hearing about him in letters was better than not, but I needed to see him. Urgently. I wondered how Lettie would take to a visit from me. For a few days. To satisfy the longing.

That evening I wrote to Josiah by lamplight:

Dear Josiah,
I take my pen in hand to write to you, hoping
these lines find you in good health. Jesse
and Abby are now man and wife. They left this
morning for Indiana. I find myself alone and
in need of distraction. To be direct, I wish to
come visit you and especially Sam. Do you
think Lettie could forbear such an intrusion?
Please speak to her for me. I await your
response.
Yours, Ann Redfield

The next day, without waiting for the letter to be posted, I asked Nate to arrange for some of my money to be made available. I laid out my itinerary, following the same route I'd taken with Lettie and Sam four years earlier, only this time there was a train between Pittsburgh and Erie, so the trip wouldn't take as long.

Josiah's response was two weeks in coming:

Dear Ann,
I am overjoyed to hear of your wish to visit
us. Of course you are welcome. Lettie is
delighted and looks forward to seeing you. She
can't wait to show off our home and family.
Please, by all means, confirm your plans and
advise us when to expect you.
Yours, Josiah

I marveled at Lettie's forbearance and resolved to convey to her my deep appreciation. I wrote to her that very night, trying to put into words what I had held so long in my heart.

Her response to me put the matter to rest for all time.

Dear Ann,
I take my pen in hand with the help of my husband who
writes better than I do. But these words are my own.
There are those who would find our relationship strange,
awkward or unacceptable. We can not care for their opinions.
I cling to the things I know. I know you are a good person. I
know Sam is a darling child. I know Josiah loves me. I know
we, all of us, need to care for one another. I know you respect
me or you would not have given Sam to me. So where is the
need for rancor? Where is the need for bitterness? Life moves
forward. One step in front of the other. You saved Josiah's life.
You gave us both our freedom. You gave us our son. What
more can we ask of you?
Lettie Colton, Freewoman

The next day, when I told Nate and Papa of my plans, Amos responded, "Say hello to my grandson for me." It was his way of saying he forgave me my trespasses.

&

The travel was almost as long, jolting, and dusty as the first time, with the addition of a plague of motion sickness from the lake crossing. I arrived at Port Stanley, Ontario, weary and travel-worn. There was no coach to Dresden. The only option was to take a coach to London, a train to Chatham and hire a driver to take me and my trunk the rest of the way.

I arrived in the little Canadian town just after six o'clock the next day. It was a tiny hamlet, so it took only two queries to find Josiah Colton's house. I was dropped off at a neat cottage, fenced and trellised, with a new coat of paint, a thriving vegetable garden, and flowers in every available space. I smiled my approval, paid my driver, and directed him to carry my trunk to the door.

I was greeted by Lettie, smiling, a child on her hip and another clinging to her skirt. Her warm welcome erased any fears I had about lingering hurt or jealousy. I was graciously gathered into their home without reservation.

"Sam! Sam! Come here, boy! There's someone here to see you!" Lettie beamed in anticipation of showing off my son to me.

A tall, sturdy, light-skinned child stepped out of one of the bedrooms. "Good evening, Ma'am." He extended his hand.

I took his hand in both of mine, fighting the urge to sweep him up in my arms. "Good evening, Sam. I'm Ann Redfield, a friend of your family. I'm so happy to meet you."

The boy, smiling broadly, looked at me expectantly. "Aren't you the lady who sends me presents?" he asked.

I nodded.

"Did you bring me anything?"

Lettie swiftly pointed out his breach of manners, with apologies to me. "He's been trained better, but sometimes he forgets."

I smiled, still holding Sam's hand. He stepped toward me, laying his head on my hip. "I'm sorry, Miss Ann Redfield," he said. "But I hope you did bring me something."

I knelt and looked into my son's face, where I saw traces of Josiah, and traces of Jesse, but his curly black hair and deep brown eyes shifted the balance in favor of his father. Three quarters white, his skin was pale in comparison to Lettie's and

Josiah's. I found him extremely handsome and wished Papa and the rest could see him.

"Yes, Sam, I think I can find something for you in my trunk," I smiled, turning to bring it in the front door. I was met by Josiah, coming up the walk. Smiling broadly, he swept me off my feet and swung me in a circle.

"Welcome to Canada, Ann! Welcome to Freedomland!"

I laughed out loud at the sound of his voice.

"Lettie, let's eat! I'm a hungry man," he bellowed, lifting my trunk, which looked diminutive perched atop his muscular shoulder.

We sat down at the table, the baby in her cradle and Sam and little Ann perched up on boards over chair arms. I couldn't help but feel pride in my role in getting this family to 'Freedomland.'

"Where are Amanda and Lovely?" I asked.

"Lovely got married in the spring, and Mama moved over there about a month ago. Lovely is with child and not having an easy time."

"How long are you staying with us, Miss Ann Redfield?" Sam wanted to know.

"Just a few days. Until mid-week."

"Oh. Why did you come here?"

"Mostly to see you, Sam," I answered honestly.

"Now that you've seen me, are you going home?"

I laughed. I longed to enfold him in my arms, cling to him. He was so beautiful it almost stopped my heart. How had I found the courage to give him away? How would I find it again, to leave him for a second time?

After the meal, I opened my trunk and presented gifts to the whole family, even baby Athena. There were clothes and toys and sweets for everyone. In truth, I had packed very little for myself. When I finished handing out the gifts, the trunk was nearly empty.

I watched Lettie herd the little ones off to bed, grateful for the generosity of her heart, for her being strong enough to stand back and let this be. I wanted nothing more than to watch from afar as my son grew up and to be allowed a small measure of significance to Josiah. Somehow Lettie knew it without being told, and I am forever indebted to her for that.

While she attended to the children, Josiah invited me into the garden for some fresh air.

"You're doing well, Josiah. Your home and family look prosperous."

He smiled. "We do all right. What do you think of our boy?"

Calling him 'our boy' gave me a turn. To acknowledge our relationship so was a joy to me. "I think he's a fine, bright, healthy boy in good hands. I think the universe turns on his whim."

Josiah laughed. "I try not to let him know that."

"I'm glad I came. It's good to see you free and happy. I'm not sure how much we'll have to do with the Railroad now that Jesse's gone."

"Even if he were still here, I'd think you'd be a *little* fearful. All of you."

I turned to him, my chin trembling. "Oh, Josiah! It was awful. So awful to be abused by someone we were trying to help. Abby and I were badly beaten, but Jesse! I was terrified for him. Afraid he'd never walk again." The tears came and I made no effort to hide them. There was no need. "That's why I had to come and see you. I had to see the good that's come of it. Every time I looked at Jesse, I saw the bad."

Josiah sighed. "Folks want charity to fall on worthy ground. But don't let one bad time outweigh the good. Don't let it stop you or even slow you down. Those poor slaves need you now more than ever. Come. Come with me."

Josiah led me out the garden gate and down the main street of Dresden. Along the way he pointed out the homes of former slaves he'd seen come to Canada and make a good life. He was so sincere, so grateful, so sure of the importance of our work, I took heart and dried my tears.

As we walked along in the gathering twilight, he introduced me to his friends and neighbors, and they responded with joy and gratitude. One old man held my hand in both of his and looked long into my eyes, tears channeling down his wrinkled face. "Freedom be the greatest gift," he said.

When we returned to his house, Josiah took my hand. "Come inside. I've something to show you."

In the parlor he pulled a book from the shelf, one I had heard of, but never read, Bunyan's *Pilgrims Progress*. Inside the back cover he showed me a series of tick marks, in groups of five, four uprights and a diagonal.

"These are people I know you've helped," he said. "I took them from your letters. Each time you wrote of a Railroad event, I marked down the number of people you saved. I did this for Sam. I want him to know what his mother did—some day."

I looked at the tick marks through gathering tears. There were more than a hundred and fifty.

"I'm sure there are some I've missed. Do the work, Ann. Don't let one poor, sad, twisted soul stop you."

"I feel like a man with one arm without Jesse."

"Then use your other arm."

I raised my chin, looked into his eyes and nodded.

Chapter 30

1861 - 1862

One day in late April, Nate burst in from Alum Bank with the mail, his young face alive with the news he carried.

"War. They've gone and started to fight. Down in South Carolina." Amos and I stared at him. "Well, don't look so surprised. Tension's been building for years. I knew it would come, soon as we elected Lincoln."

More disbelief than surprise. I sat down at the kitchen table to think. Nate added details about the shelling of Fort Sumter in Charleston Harbor and Lincoln's call for troops. Amos sat on a straight chair, rubbing his hands over his thighs, his face red, listening.

"Are they *all* quitting the Union?" I asked.

"All those ones that went after the election. Virginia went, too. Probably the rest'll follow."

It felt like someone had died. "I guess we had our part in it, Jesse and I," I mused. "I don't regret it, but I hoped it would never come to this. I hate slavery, but I hate war even more."

Nate stood in the middle of the kitchen, an odd excitement in his eyes. "Guess this'll shake things up around here."

"Shake things up! More likely tear us asunder." Amos warned. "It's hard enough to keep the Quaker principles without this."

"Some'll join up, no matter if they get disowned," Nate allowed. "Some won't, even if you promise them a kingdom. And some'll find a way around taking sides and come through at a profit!"

Amos shook his head. "None of mine. None of mine."

The next week, Papa rose at Meeting and ranted against the war. No one spoke for it, even though, as Nate said, in their hearts they welcomed an end to the constant bickering and compromise. "Quakers don't embrace violence!" Amos thundered. "Let the non-Quakers traipse off to Bedford to enlist. We'll still be here when it's over." But, when, early in June, news came of the rout of Union troops at a place in Virginia called Manassas, concern heightened and enlistments increased. More than a few seats on the men's side of the Meeting house were empty come July.

Through the spring, Nate and I held long evening talks about the war, out on the porch, after the work was done. Something was going on in my little brother's head, for sure.

"Joseph Blackwell up and left last week to join the Army," Nate told us. "Seems to be a pattern. Working in the fields one day and gone the next."

I nodded. "The fathers want to hold to Quaker principles— and their sons—but war has the power to pull them in."

"For some it does." Nate looked thoughtful.

"Not for you, I hope." I'd been wary of him since the war began, hoping he wouldn't take it in his head to go.

"Well, I'll tell you one thing, I won't be farming this time next year. I hate it. Pa and I trying to make up for the loss of Jesse. It's too much. When harvest is over, I'm moving on."

His words alarmed me. "What will you do?"

"I don't know yet, but not this."

Amos stepped out from the kitchen doorway. We didn't know he was listening. "I hope *thee* are not thinking of going to war."

"I can't say, Papa."

"Can't say? What does thee mean, thee can't say? No son of mine will take up arms! I won't have it!"

"Ben and Elias could take over our land," Nate continued, ignoring Papa's wrath. "They need it for oats and pasture. Keep it from lying fallow."

"Would you join their operation, then?" I pressed.

"Maybe. Or I could take my legacy and join Jesse in Indiana. He could probably use my help."

My heart sank. Not another one to go west! "Why don't you open a business in Bedford? You have a talent for numbers and the like."

"I've thought about that. Maybe a mercantile. I don't know what I'll do. But I lack Jesse's patience. I can't keep myself at a task I hate, and right now, I hate this."

I never gave liking or hating a task much thought. If it had to be done, it had to be done. If I didn't do it, who would? The idea that one had to like one's work was foreign to me and, I was sure, to Amos. But it certainly mattered to Nate.

In those tense times, I relied more on Rebecca's friendship and confidence. She invited me over to help can tomatoes for both households, and I welcomed the distraction, even if it was for talk of war. Rebecca and I and her three girls worked through the day in the summer kitchen, the heat and the smell of tomatoes heavy in the air.

I confided my fears about Nathaniel to Rebecca. "I'm afraid he might be thinking of going to war,"

"Nate? Has he said anything?"

"No, but that doesn't mean he isn't thinking of it. I wish he'd just find him a wife."

Rebecca smiled. "That'd be a relief for you. Now what's got you worried, anyway?"

"I don't know. He's restless. Ever since the war began."

"He has his hands full. But so do Ben and Elias. This war is making a labor shortage, I'll tell you that." Rebecca ladled hot tomatoes into the waiting jars.

"Nathaniel will do what he will," she reminded me. "You and Amos can only watch. But, surely Nate, of all people, won't choose war. Slow to decide, even slower to act. I can't conceive of him volunteering."

But the nagging fear would not go away. It was Nate's to decide, but I held my breath and prayed.

One August afternoon, Pru Hartley's oldest boy, Thomas, wandered down from the woods, a dead squirrel dangling from his belt. "Wanna buy a squirrel?" he asked, holding up the limp body. Out of pity for the scrawny, dirty-faced child, I offered him two bits, even though Nate could get me a squirrel anytime.

"How's your mother?" I asked.

He lay his gun on the ground while he untied the squirrel. "Down with the grippe."

"Oh? Does she need me to make a call?" I was locked in a dance of wariness with Pru. To embrace her was frightening. To ignore her was worse.

"She'll be all right, but it's hard now Uncle Cooper's gone."

"Gone where?" I hadn't seen Cooper Hartley in months, but that counted as good.

"Gone for a soldier. Joined the Rebs. Says he has to fight for slavery." The child's face showed no expression. Neither approval nor disapproval. "Been huntin' runaways all these years. Can't get his mind around the idea they might free 'em. Wish I was old enough."

I shuddered to think that a man could love slavery enough to go to war for it—and gain a boy's admiration to boot. I put a coin in Thomas's hand and took the squirrel. "Tell your mother to stop by when she's feeling better." The boy went his barefoot way down over the hill to the hovel by the creek, shotgun slung over his bony shoulder.

Nathaniel didn't wait for the harvest. He enlisted in September, in Company F, 37th Regiment, Pennsylvania Reserves. They formed up at Camp Wilkins, near Pittsburgh. He joined for three months, but the government went back on their promise, and the 37th was mustered in for three years. He bragged in his early letters about how they'd thrash the rebels and be home by Christmas. I winced at his brashness. Later, he put me in charge of his financial ventures, which, I soon learned, were extensive. "If I don't come back," he wrote, "it's yours to do with as you see fit." 'Don't talk nonsense' would have been my response had he been within reach. But he was decidedly out of reach now and maybe forever.

One more empty chair. Papa and I looked at each other from opposite ends of a table as wide as all creation, remembering when there were nine. Two was such a sad number.

I tried to talk about family matters to ease the emptiness. "Mary writes that her Martha is opening her own Quaker school this fall." Amos nodded, barely acknowledging me.

"They're keeping a close eye on Adam. Fifteen years old and full of romantic notions of war. Mary's afraid he'll run off and join up one of these days."

Amos sat silent at the other end of the table. His face clouded. "You'd think he'd been raised better." He took a drink of coffee, made a face, and wiped his mouth.

"I'm sure Mary and Noah have done their best. She's always going on about how hard it is to raise good Quakers with the world intruding all the time."

"The world will always intrude. That's why we have to be strong. Not give in to impulse. Think things through."

I knew he was talking about Nathaniel. He was beside himself with impotent rage. I watched his shoulders droop as he struggled with tasks he'd once done with ease. Getting old.

I was so lonely in those days after Nate left that it felt almost good to see Pru Hartley drop by. She did so fairly regularly now that Cooper was gone and she had to fend for herself. I watched her climb up the path from the creek, bent over a walking stick, carrying an empty basket for handouts, and I steeled myself for her approach.

"Pru! You look spry today. How about some apples? I've got some good ones for sauce."

"Takes too long. I'll take some, but the boys'll just eat 'em afore I git around to sauce."

I led the way to the root cellar, pulling my shawl around my shoulders against the October wind. "What do you hear from Cooper?"

"Naught. He can't write, and I don't read much better. 'Spect I'll see him comin' up the road when this's over."

I nodded. Pru picked up apples and dropped them into her basket, without a care for bruising. She helped herself to more than I would have given, but I reminded myself that we had plenty for two. Pru evidently thought so, too, for she poked around the root cellar in the dim light and helped herself to whatever she wanted. Potatoes, squash, onions, carrots, beets. I truly wondered how she expected to carry it home.

"Let's get in out of this cold and have a cup of tea," I invited. The warm kitchen smelled of fresh baked apple turnovers.

"Think I'll have one of 'em with my tea," Pru ordered, pulling a chair up close to the stove. "What do you hear from your brother?"

"Jesse? Or Nate?"

"Jesse. Nate's gone? Where to?"

"Nate's gone to the war. Left in September. Jesse's well. They're expecting a baby in December."

"I never did know what he seen in that scrawny, pasty-faced girl. Bet she won't give him any strong babies!"

I struggled to ignore this attempt to bait me. Remember who you're talking to, Ann. Don't let her get your goat.

"He still messin' around tryin' to save niggers out there wherever he is?"

"Indiana. He's in Indiana. Has an orchard. Apple, cherry, and peach trees. You do hold fast to the idea that we have something to do with helping fugitives. With the war on, I doubt that there *are* many any more."

Pru scoffed. "If'n I know Jesse Redfield, he's still in it. Out there savin' the world for the Quakers." She picked up the biggest apple turnover as I poured her tea. "Bet if he hadn't messed up his arm he'd be carryin' a gun with the rest of them. Well, best he ain't. If my brother Cooper ever run up against him, he'd get a receipt for all the niggers he saved. Cooper's right glad to be shootin' blue bellies."

I sighed. "Pru, don't you ever get tired of it?"

"Tired of what?"

"Of raging. Constant, incessant raging."

She looked away, sat back on her chair, eating her turnover and drinking her tea. After a while, she replied, "No," picked up her basket and walking stick, and clumped out, leaving the door open behind her.

Amos and I waited for the mail, impatient for every bit of news of the war and the 37th Pennsylvania. Nathaniel wrote few letters and those he did write were brief. The luster of war faded quickly, and he complained of boredom, camp conditions, the food or lack of it, and inaction.

Let him complain, I thought. At least he's alive.

One morning in December, I trudged through six inches of snow to visit Rebecca and found her in a snit over her brother.

"That Elias! Be glad you never married him, Ann. He's so thick-headed, sometimes I wonder where he came from."

"What's he done now?"

"He's talking about joining the Army."

"Why? He's thirty-five years old."

"Don't ask me. Deborah's beside herself over it, and Ben is about as bad, but there's no talking to him. I vow it's just for the adventure. Some men never grow up."

I sat in Rebecca's rocking chair, knitting a pair of stockings for Amos for Christmas. "When does he plan to go?"

"As soon as he can find a company organizing." Rebecca kneaded bread dough in a wooden trough. "What's Deborah supposed to do, sitting alone here with Lucy and one of her own and another one on the way?"

"Wait, I guess. And pray he comes home at all."

"How does he think Ben's going to handle all the work? First Nathaniel goes off without a thought for Ben, and now Elias does the same thing. I tell you, Ann, I'm getting bitter over these men and their damned war!"

Elias enlisted in Captain Dick's Company, the 107th Pennsylvania Volunteers, in January of 1862 and departed first for Harrisburg, then Virginia. He rode away grinning like a boy off to the county fair.

Nathaniel's letters of complaint stopped abruptly that July, just after a battle called the Seven Days. Not knowing where he was, nor if he was alive or dead made us all frantic. The days dragged on; we waited for the mail. When it came, and there was nothing, we grumbled and went back to waiting. Then, in early September, a letter came.

> *Dear Ann and Papa,*
> *You haven't heard from me in a while. I and 50*
> *or so others from F company were captured in the*
> *Seven Days. They marched us to Richmond. Spent*
> *all of July and most of August in a Reb prison.*
> *Got exchanged last week. Good to be back in the*
> *thick of it again.*
> *Nate*

Rebecca and I groaned as I read her the letter. "I'll never understand men. Daughter of one, sister of four, wife of one, and mother of five. You'd think I'd get it, but I don't." We both laughed. If Rebecca didn't get it, who would?

I folded the letter and put it away. "Ever since the war began and before, I've counted myself thankful to be a woman. Men seem to have an intense desire—even an obligation—to fight. It puzzles me how some seem to welcome war, even to lust after it."

Rebecca nodded. "Some even form stronger bonds with their fighting comrades than with their wives. And to what end? To be injured, maimed, killed, or to carry horrible memories with them to their graves. She paused for a long, deep breath. "And women—their mothers, wives, sisters, sweethearts—wait and never understand, can't begin to know the closeness their men share only with their fellow soldiers. I don't have to see war to know I hate it."

But see it she would. Elias Finley died at the Second Battle of Bull Run on August 30, 1862. He never saw his third child, a son born in May and named for his absent father. I grieved for the loss of a friend. Emptiness seemed to close in. The old world was passing away and the new held no promise for me.

Chapter 31

1862 – September

Something was in the air in mid-September. Fall, yes, but that wasn't it. A feeling of foreboding haunted my days. Something terrible was happening. I could almost hear it sometimes—the roar of guns and the agonized moans and cries of wounded and dying men. I visited Rebecca to clear my mind, but that only helped until I started for home, alone, through the orchard.

At night I lay awake, tearful, filled with a nameless fear. I distracted myself with getting up, lighting my lamp, and writing letters, but nothing gave me comfort.

Around the 20th, Ben's Jeremiah rode in astride a big workhorse and slid down to tell me news. "There's fightin' down to Maryland," he said, his face flushed. "Somethin' awful. Down by Sharpsburg. Pa heard about it at the mill."

I drew in my breath. So that was what had dogged me for the past week. The war was closing in.

"Pa says the fight was along Antietam Creek. A terrible battle, they said. Thousands of men killed in one day! Worst battle of the war so far!"

My apprehension now burst into full blown terror. Something was wrong with Nathaniel. He'd been wounded there. I didn't know how I knew it, but I did. Death was hovering over him, waiting to bear him away. I had to find him and bring him home. I had to save my brother.

Persuading anyone else of my intuition was beyond me. Amos stared blankly when I told him, unwilling or unable to believe my nightmarish ranting. I left him standing in the kitchen and rushed through the orchard to Ben's house. Ben and Rebecca stood mute as I tried to enlist their support. "I need a buggy and a team. Nate is hurt. He was in that battle. That Antietam Creek battle."

Ben stared like he thought I was mad. "Where are you going?"

"East and south. South and east. Somewhere in Maryland. I'll know when I get there."

Now Ben scoffed. "How would you find Nathaniel, even if your instincts are right?"

"God will guide me to him."

"This is nonsense," Ben scolded. "You can't just drive off on a fool hope. Wait until you at least know something." Rebecca nodded, siding with Ben.

"It'll be too late. I have to go now. Today."

Ben shook his head. "I've never heard such a fool notion in my life. You're usually so sensible, Ann. What's got into you?"

"I can't explain it. It's just a feeling, but I can't shake it, Ben. It won't let me go. Please."

He shook his head and began walking toward the barn. "Then take someone with you. Don't go alone."

"Who can I take?"

"Take Adam. He's hungry for war. Maybe he can help you find it."

Mary's boy, Adam Poole, had come to help Ben in Elias' absence. At sixteen, he was a big, strong, open-faced innocent.

"What if he takes it in his head to run off and join the Army? I can't stop him, Ben."

"If you get close enough for him to see real war, maybe it'll cure him of wanting to."

Ben hitched up the buggy amid much grumbling, while I went home to gather what I'd need for the trip. I knew of Quaker families in McConnellsburg and Hagerstown, where I hoped we could stay overnight and get directions and news of where the wounded could be found.

Ben and Rebecca watched me stow my belongings in the buggy. "Sometimes I think you're mad," Ben muttered.

"There's no use talking. You'll do what you will, with or without my approval."

Rebecca was skeptical, too, but more gentle. "I worry for you, Ann. We'll look after Amos. God bless you and keep you."

Ben instructed Adam. "Take care of her. Do as she says, but try to keep her out of trouble."

Adam Poole nodded, swung easily up beside me, and took the reins, his face flushed with excitement. It would take two days hard traveling to get to Hagerstown. Sharpsburg was a few miles farther south. We could be gone a week or more. I didn't wonder that Ben and Rebecca thought I was mad.

We pushed hard that first day and made it to Saluvia, a tiny village outside McConnellsburg. We were welcomed by a Quaker couple whose name I knew by association with the Underground Railroad. The next morning, they packed us a lunch and sent us on to Hagerstown, where we sought out Adam's uncle, Matthew Poole, whose farm was situated to the west of town.

The farther south and east we went, the more intense was my certainty that this was no fool's errand. An unshakable gloom hung in the air. A sense of death and foreboding, side-by-side with beautiful autumn weather and the early turning of the leaves. Adam was good company, always willing to do my bidding, no matter how strange it seemed. He never argued or criticized but simply did as he was told. I think it was his first experience with a woman on a mission, but I suspected it wouldn't be his last.

At Hagerstown, we saw houses and tents transformed into makeshift hospitals, the first evidence of tragedy. Wagons transporting dead and wounded men clogged the streets.

I stopped a man walking by to try to make sense of the situation. "Do you know if there is anyone keeping track of the wounded? Where they've been taken?"

He shook his head. "They're scattered helter-skelter as far north as Chambersburg, west to Hancock, east to Frederick."

"Is there a headquarters where I can ask?"

"Down Prospect Street."

We made our way down the crowded street amid chaos. Adam pulled up by a house with a flag in front and several military horses standing by. I went in.

"Could you help me?" I asked a mustached man seated in a chair and writing a letter on a field desk. "I'm looking for my brother. He's with the 37th Pennsylvania."

The man shook his head. "Ma'am, I'd be lucky if I could find my own regiment, and they're camped out back." He looked worn out, exhausted. "Men from Pennsylvania, New Hampshire, Ohio, Wisconsin . . . share whatever space and care there is. They'll be burying the dead down in Sharpsburg for weeks."

My instincts told me Nate wasn't down there. He was somewhere else, his life ebbing away.

"I doubt anybody can help you. The units left behind to pick up the pieces, we're tryin' to keep track of who's who and who's where, but it's beyond us. Just go around town, askin'. That's the best I can tell you."

Back in the street, the sweet, foul smell of rotting flesh hung in the air, so strong it made me want to vomit. The hope of professional medical care was ludicrous. Townspeople gave what care they could, often simply holding a hand, wiping a brow, while nature took its course. Dressing wounds, providing nourishment, the lowest, meanest bed or shelter was most often the extent of it.

Into this morass of wounded and dying men, Adam and I plunged, frantically searching for Nathaniel. Adam's young face sobered at the sight of so many boys no older than he, broken and desperate for home. Our task was hopeless from the start. We wandered from one field hospital to another, asking, sometimes calling out, for Pennsylvania men who could tell us of the 37th. We spent three days, passed back and forth on the tiniest shred of hope, driving, exhausted, back to Matthew Poole's farm each night. Then, early on the fourth day, as we wandered disheartened between the rows of cots in the sickening air of a school-turned-hospital, I heard my name.

"Ann Redfield!"

I turned and saw Charles Conley, a Bedford County boy from Cessna, not far from home. I knew his sister, Emma—had visited their home more than once. His head was bandaged over his left eye, and his left arm was in a sling, but compared to many others, he looked almost healthy.

"Charles Conley! How good to see a familiar face! Are you badly hurt?"

"Some, but I'll be all right," he replied.

"Have you seen my brother Nathaniel?"

He shook his head. "Ain't seen anyone I knew," he said. "What're you doin' here?"

"Looking for Nate."

"I heard they took a bunch of Pennsylvania boys up to Chambersburg, but I wouldn't know where to start lookin.'"

Chambersburg! Something in Charlie's account rang true. I felt an almost magnetic pull north. I touched the boy's thin shoulder.

"I'll tell your mother I saw you."

"Yeah. Tell her I'm fine," he said, with a sadness that touched my heart. I knew with tragic certainty that he would never be *fine* again.

Three days of walking among the dead and semi-dead made Adam Poole physically sick. Boys his own age, mortally wounded, waiting with haunted eyes for the end of a too short life. Piles of amputated limbs, their former owners staring vacantly into an uncertain future. Any romantic notions he harbored about war evaporated in the foul air. Once, he left my side and bolted for the door of a makeshift, inadequate hospital. He returned, wiping his mouth on his sleeve, his young face pale. "I'll be more than glad to be gone from this place. I just hope I don't dream about it forever."

He turned the buggy north to Chambersburg, and after five hours of bumping and jolting along rough roads, we reached the town around three in the afternoon. On the southern edge, we came to a farm where increased traffic told us something was going on. Turning in at the lane, we passed a wagon carrying three partially uniformed corpses.

243

"Are those Pennsylvania men?" I asked the driver, deliberately avoiding looking at the faces of the dead.

"Yes'm, they are. Thirty-seventh Pennsylvania Volunteers. A proud regiment," he replied.

My heart jumped. "Are there more men from the 37th here?"

"Yes'm. Most of 'em is in the barn," he nodded over his shoulder.

Adam cracked the reins over the horses' rumps and drove away without even a thank you or a goodbye. He stopped the buggy by the barn and helped me climb down. I hiked up my skirts and hurried into the dark, cavernous building. In the dim light, I saw rows and rows of the most hideous and pathetic victims of man's worst endeavor. I leaned on Adam's arm as we wended our way among the wretched souls, some silent, others moaning, sobbing, a few reaching out to touch my skirt as I walked by. Most of their wounds had been treated and bandaged, but a nauseating smell oppressed us as soon as we entered.

It was futile to ask the orderlies to identify anyone. These hollow-eyed men didn't know who they were themselves, so Adam resorted to the only way he knew of finding Nate. "Nathaniel Redfield!" he shouted as he walked. I joined him. "Nathaniel Redfield!"

"Over here." The first reply was weak. I shouted again.

"Ann! Is that you?"

There he lay on a soiled blanket, his left arm gone just below the shoulder. He wore a tattered, dirty uniform, the left sleeve ripped out, his face ashen, his brow wet with sweat, mud encrusted boots beside him.

"Nate, I've come to take you home."

He looked at me with dazed eyes, struggling between delirium and reality. "I'm ready," he whispered.

I sent Adam to make a pallet on the floor of the buggy and searched for someone in charge to complete the formalities. The attending physician, weary from overwork and lack of sleep, took a look at Nate and signed the paper releasing him.

"He'll never make it, you know. He's lost so much blood, and I suspect infection has set in. But he'd die here, anyway, so take him," he mumbled, and turned back to his ghastly tasks.

I did not respond, refusing to give in to despair. Looking around, I spied an orderly staggering up the crowded aisle, carrying a bucket.

"Young man! Could you please help my nephew carry my brother outside?"

He looked at me as though I were talking out of a dream. He put down the bucket of offal and wiped his hands on grimy blue pants, once part of a proud uniform. "Yes, Ma'am. I'd be honored."

He and Adam picked Nathaniel up by the bloody blanket and carried him to the buggy. I followed, leaving the muddy boots behind. The army could have them. I climbed up beside Adam as he slowly guided the horses back down the lane. It was late, after four o'clock, but I was determined to get my brother out of there—away from the war—as far and as fast as possible.

Sometime after seven we drove into the hamlet of Fort Loudon, looking for a place to stay the night. We didn't know anyone, so I directed Adam to drive up to a neat looking cottage, got down from the buggy and knocked at the door.

"Do you have any place you could put us up for the night? I'm taking my brother home. He was wounded at Antietam."

Without a word the woman, round-faced and full of energy, swung the door wide and hurried out to see what Nate needed.

"We can make a stretcher out of the blanket." She peered in at Nate's face and struggled to hide her dismay. He was slipping in and out of consciousness, unaware of what was happening.

The woman turned to me, her face grave. "Let's get him inside." We carried him into the dining room, and laid him on the table. Our hostess, Mrs. Eckhart, bustled around the kitchen, placed bowls of stew in front of Adam and me and tried to spoon some broth into Nathaniel. We spent the night under Mrs. Eckhart's watchful eye. In the morning, she tried to persuade us to stay for a few days to let Nathaniel mend a little, but, haunted by the possibility that he would die before we got home, I chose to press on. I couldn't tell her how afraid I was. Speaking the words might somehow make my fears a reality.

The next night, we stopped at a Friend's house in Breezewood, more or less repeating the rituals of the night before. People were curious to see the wounded soldier, but once they looked at him, their faces betrayed their lack of hope. Nathaniel's breathing was shallow, his face gray. He looked like death.

That night I bent near his ear and spoke to him. "Don't leave me, Nate. One more day and we'll be home. You can hold on till then. Once we're home, you'll be all right. Just stay with me."

He slept more soundly that night. The next evening, as we drove slowly up the road from Fishertown into our dooryard, Nate seemed to know he was home. He stopped thrashing about and moaning. His breathing calmed.

Papa stepped out on the porch when we arrived. Adam jumped down to help me carry Nate inside. Papa took one look at Nate and hurried ahead to clear the way. He stood silent as we laid Nate down on the bed, his gnarled hands helpless at his sides. He didn't ask any questions. He stood, head bowed, as Adam and I tried to make Nate comfortable.

"Adam, run and get Ben and Rebecca. Papa, you unhitch the team," I directed.

Ben and Rebecca arrived within minutes, their eyes answering most of their questions for them.

"I'll ride for the doctor." Ben was down the steps and out the door before anyone could respond. I suspected he wanted to be alone when his stomach gave up its contents. Men had a hard time with these things. Rebecca and I stripped Nate and bathed him. He was unconscious all the time now, and I tried not to look at his face; it was so gray.

When the doctor arrived, he examined Nate's arm, his face grave. The dressing was soaked and foul-smelling. I took it downstairs and burned it in the stove while the doctor was still there. He shook his head.

"I don't think there's much hope," he said as he redressed the ugly amputation. "If he rallies, I'll try to make that look a little better, but I don't think it'll matter."

I sat by my brother's bedside for three days, leaving only for the direst necessity. I spooned broth into him, wiped his brow, changed his dressing, held his hand, sang to him, read to him, prayed for him, all with no response. I stayed stubbornly, willing him to get better, aware that hope was futile but hoping just the same. I kept telling myself that at least he wasn't dead. On the fourth morning, he opened his eyes, looked around the room and whispered, "I'm going to make it."

And he did. Slowly, steadily, the fever and chills subsided. By mid-October, he was sitting up. By the end of the month, he could walk. His frame was nothing but skin and bone, but his color came back, and, along with it his appetite.

Nathaniel Redfield would not die in 1862, but another of our own did. Two weeks before Christmas, Amos brought a letter from Altoona.

"Oh, good. Open it and read it to me. She's probably had her baby." I was heartened to hear from Rachel.

Amos began to read and stopped. His hands shook, holding the letter. His eyes sought mine. "She's gone," he said. "Baby was a girl. She died, too."

"When?" I asked.

"Last Saturday."

Jacob Schilling named the baby Rachel and buried her in the same coffin with her mother.

The weather was bad. Amos, beaten down by our travails with Nate and grieving for the daughter he'd lost, wasn't up to the trip, nor was Nate. So Rachel was buried on a hillside lot in a cemetery called Fairview with no one from her family in attendance.

Chapter 32

1863 – Spring/Summer

One morning in April I heard a wagon pull into the dooryard. I looked out and saw Jacob Schilling get down and lift his three children, one by one, to the ground. Much as I disliked him and blamed him, however irrationally, for my sister's death, I felt sorry for him standing there with three motherless children in tow.

He came to the door. "Mornin' Ann."

"Morning, Jacob." Uncomfortable silence. I looked past him. "Morning, children. Come on in. It's cold out there."

I poured coffee. Jacob sat at the table, sipping, looking around. "Where is everybody?"

"Everybody—that's Papa and Nate. There's not so many of us anymore. They went over to help Ben this morning."

The children stood in a row near the door, watching. "What I come for, Ann, is this. Can you—would you—take care of them until I can make arrangements?" He jerked his head toward the children. "I can't do for them and run my business, too."

I smiled at Rachel's babies, lest they think themselves unwelcome. "Of course, Jacob. I'd be glad to."

Jacob fairly jumped up and went to unload the children's trunks. He struggled up the stairs with them, reminding me of the day years ago when he and Rachel had struggled down the stairs with her trunk. Life has a way of coming round to where it started. Once the trunks were put away, Jacob drank up his coffee, still standing, wiped his mouth and turned to me. "I'd best be going. Can't afford to take much time off work." He was gone within the hour, and I knew I'd never see him again. Sympathy misplaced.

Three big-eyed, sad-faced children stood in my kitchen, watching me in silence. James, six, was tall for his age and what you might call skinny. He spoke with a lisp, unsure of himself, cautious. At four, Ellen was his exact opposite. Short, pudgy, confident, and full of pee and vinegar, according to Amos, who carried on delighted conversations with her. John, only two, was in many ways still a baby. Round, fat, full of giggles, only he of the three was completely unaware that he had lost anything. More rearranging was done to create a nursery in Betsy's old bedroom, next to mine. Suddenly, the house was full again. Spring was here; there was work to be done.

The children proved a tonic for us all. James attached himself to Nate, followed him everywhere, asking endless questions, and filling Nate's need for a 'right hand man.' Buoyed up with reflected glory, James was soon regaling his cousins with war stories, mostly made up but nonetheless attributed to Uncle Nate. Ellen was her grandfather's favorite, with a ready smile and disarmingly forthright observations about the world. John, delighted to be babied again, filled the void in my heart left years ago by Sam. While no one could accuse me of lacking proper grief for my sister, it was clear that these children were a gift.

One might think that once the war was on, the flow of fugitives would stop, but it didn't. They came in greater numbers at first, and the flow tapered off to a trickle as the war dragged on. But even after the Emancipation Proclamation, which we cheered so fervently in January, some poor, hapless creatures wandered by. No longer needing to fear slave catchers, they came in daylight, but their plight was sad beyond words.

I had put baby John and Ellen to bed one night, late in June, a few months after they'd come to live with us. James and Nate were off buying supplies in Bedford when I heard a timid knock at the kitchen door. I went to open it, but no one was there. At first I thought it was James, playing a joke, but after I sat down, there came another knock—very quiet. This time I took a lamp, thinking to catch James at his game, but even when I walked out on the porch, holding the lamp high, I saw no one.

"James!" I called. "Come, now, boy! It's past your bedtime!"

Still no answer, and, looking out at the barn, I saw no sign of either James or Nate. I'd turned to go back in the house when I heard a cry—soft, muffled, like a baby. I stepped off the porch toward the sound, which seemed to come from the spring house. Caution gripped me, but something told me to trust. I moved to the door and pushed it open a few inches.

"Is anyone there?" I asked. "Come on out. No need to hide. You're among friends." I don't know what made me think it was black folk—maybe years of working with runaways. But now there was no need to run. Still, I knew in my bones that's what it was.

Out of the shadows of the cold, damp springhouse stepped a black boy, smaller and looking younger than James. He was barefoot, even though it had been a cold, wet spring and wasn't yet fit weather for going without shoes. In the lamplight, he looked up at me with huge eyes, his face full of fear.

"Well, who are *you*, young man?" I asked gently. "What can I do for you?"

"Gideon." His reply was so quiet I barely heard him. He was thin, frail, ragged, and shivering.

"Gideon, is it? Well, Gideon, how did you get here?"

"With my mama." He almost whispered it.

"Where is your mama now?"

The boy nodded in the direction of the shadows behind the door. I pulled the door to and held up my lantern. There, curled up on the damp floor was a thin black woman not more than twenty-five years old, with two smaller children clinging to her ragged skirts. If Gideon looked afraid, the other two were engulfed in terror, and the woman was barely conscious.

"Oh, Gideon! Come, let's bring your mama inside where it's warm," I said, softly so as not to add to their fear. I bent down to help the woman up, and a piercing squall rose from the throat of the smallest child. Barely three, I guessed, and terrified of a white face. "Gideon, you take your little brother's hand and I'll help your mother and sister."

The boy obeyed, tugging the baby along against his will and amid ever louder protests. I looked into the woman's eyes as I helped her to her feet. "Don't be afraid. You've come to the right place."

The middle child, a spindly five-year-old, held onto her mother's skirt and watched me in dreadful silence, her thumb in her mouth. I led the sad little party across the yard and into the house. Once there, I nearly cried at the sight of them. Gideon told me he was seven, but he was smaller even than six-year-old James. The mother, gravely ill, held fiercely to the two younger children.

"You must be hungry," I smiled, trying to put them at ease. I had a pot of soup on the back of the stove, thinking Nate and James might be hungry when they came, so I dished it out to the little family, and they ate it and chunks of bread with surprising energy.

I let them eat in silence. While they ate, Nate and James came in, surprised at my company. I served up soup to them, and they sat down on the bench opposite Gideon and his mother.

"This is Gideon," I told them. "Gideon, this is my nephew James and my brother Nate."

Gideon nodded solemnly from behind his soup bowl, then held it up to me for more. His sister ate more slowly, her eyes on us, but spoke not a word. The mother alternated bites between herself and the little one, thus keeping his crying at bay. When they were fed, the woman looked up at me, gratitude in her eyes.

"Thank you, Ma'am," she whispered. "I don't know how much farther we could have gone. We's wore out." She held out an emaciated hand. "My name Maggie."

"Happy to meet you, Maggie. You look exhausted. What can I do to help?"

Maggie looked around at her children, now quiet in the warmth, their tummies full. "We goin' to Canada. My brother there. He can help us. You know how to get to Canada?"

"Yes, we can help you get to Canada. It's still a long way, though. Why don't you stay here with us for a while until you're stronger? There's no need to run anymore. You can travel in daylight. You're free."

"I knows I's free. But that don't keep *him* from findin' me."

"Who?"

"Abe. He want me to marry up with him. Send my children away. He won't let me be, so I run." She looked around at the two little ones still clinging to her skirt. "This be Della, and that be Andrew."

I smiled at the two children, hoping to push their fears aside. "Is this Abe fellow following you?"

"Was. Don't know if he's still. We been runnin' more than a week now. Ain't seen him since he sic his dog on Gideon."

I turned to the boy and he lifted his dirty, ragged pant leg to reveal an ugly, jagged tear in his calf. It was swollen, oozed pus, and looked to be infected.

"Maggie, you'll *have* to stay here for a while. That wound needs tending or he might lose the leg. You'll be safe here. We'll take care of you."

Nate nodded. "We won't let anyone hurt you. If Abe shows up, we'll run him off."

"He a mean one." Maggie's attention was drawn to Nate for the first time. She noticed his empty sleeve, neatly pinned up, and drew in her breath. "You get that in the war?" she asked.

Nate nodded.

"Oh, my God. Thank you. Thank you for fightin' for us. We's ever so grateful. Now if I can just get my babies to Canada, and find my brother, I be fine."

I cleared the table and drew bath water for the children in a small oaken tub. "Maggie, let's bathe the little ones and I'll see to Gideon's leg. We've lots of clothes to fit all of you."

Nate led James upstairs to bed, and returned to watch me tend to Gideon's wound. It was deep and ragged, but the child never whimpered as I cleaned and dressed it with strips torn from an old sheet. Once the younger children were bathed, I went upstairs and rummaged in our children's trunks for clothing. Maggie was combing Della's hair, holding Andrew on her lap, when I returned.

"You think that dog bite that bad?" she asked as I handed her the clothes.

"I'm sure it is." I moved to help her dress Della, but the child pulled away without a sound.

"She don't talk none," Maggie explained. "Ain't talked since her daddy left."

"Left? Did your husband leave you?"

"Had to. Abe would have killed him. Abe the overseer once the war start. He worse than the white ones. He make everyone work like dogs. Say the South gonna win and he be rewarded for bein' loyal. My husband say no, the North gonna win, an' Abe be nobody. Abe get mad, and my husband run for fear Abe gonna kill him."

"Do you know where he is?" I asked.

"No. Abe say he caught him and beat his head in, but I don't believe him. That why I go to Canada. My husband know my brother there. He might of got there somehow."

"Where did you run from?"

"Virginny. Prince Edward County. Long way from here. We hide out from the soldiers—blue *or* gray. Soldiers want to abuse me."

I drew more bath water for Gideon and Maggie and went upstairs to get my nightgown. I'd sleep in the kitchen. Once everyone was clean and settled, I lay on Amos' old bed in the corner thinking about my guests. I thought of Rachel's babies, so close in age to these but, even with the loss of their mother, so much better off. I thought of Sam, and how he might have shared their plight. Finally, after hours of racing thoughts, the Gods of sleep took mercy on me.

In the morning, Amos, Nate and I talked about what to do with Maggie and her little ones. "This Abe fellow's dangerous.

He could show up any time. Best keep a loaded shotgun handy," Nate declared.

"Not around these children. You can load it and keep it up on the rack, but not where they can reach it," I told him.

Amos agreed. "Send them along the old Railroad route as quick as you can get them there."

"I'm not sure about that, either." I mulled the situation. "Abe could try to catch up with them by doing the same. Besides, Maggie's not well. Her cough sounds consumptive. She needs time to regain her strength. I'm for keeping them here for a while. I'll write to Josiah and see if he can find her brother. She should know where she's going, at least."

"Suit yourself," Amos replied. "It's not like the old days. They can stay here in plain sight. But I don't want any of us to get the consumption."

"Unless . . ."

There was a knock at the back door, and Nate opened it to Jeremiah, one of Ben's twins. "Mornin' Grandpa, Aunt Ann, Uncle Nate. Papa wants Nate and Grandpa to come over. Someone stole one of our horses last night."

A look of alarm spread over Amos' face. "You go, Nate. I'll stay here with Ann and the little ones."

I went upstairs to awaken Maggie and her children. James was already out of bed, pulling on his britches. "Where's Uncle Nate going?" He'd seen Nate and Jeremiah walk across the yard toward Ben's.

"Hurry and you can catch up. Someone stole a horse last night."

I dressed Ellen and baby John and took them downstairs. Maggie's three children were already seated at the table. I dished up cornmeal mush and maple syrup to the lot of them. Gideon, Della, and Andrew stared in silence at Ellen and John. James had run out without a thought for breakfast.

A deep rumble rattled the silverware in the empty plates. My eyes sought Amos's. Outside, a cloud of dust rose from the road. Fearful of who or what might be coming, I shepherded Maggie and her children up the kitchen stairs and into the room

Jesse had fixed to hide slaves. Sliding the panel aside, I pointed to the space under the eaves. Maggie understood immediately and pushed the children in ahead of her. I had no idea what was happening, but I wanted to be sure these poor souls were not involved.

Downstairs, Amos stood in the kitchen, shotgun at the ready, watching a group of horsemen ride past. They didn't stop, but proceeded to Ben's as though on a mission.

"I'm going over to see what's going on." I was out the door and across the porch before Amos could respond. I hurried through the yard and up the orchard path to Ben's. I arrived, out of breath, in time to see a lot of rough looking men open Ben's corrals and herd his horses away.

Rebels! Some wore remnants of grey uniforms, but most were clothed in ragged, nondescript castoffs. Their leader sat astride his horse, pointing a long barreled pistol at Ben's family while a few of his men stood by, to see that no one interfered. There beside him on a huge roan sat Cooper Hartley, looking as ragged and unkempt as ever—but no more so than any of his compatriots. I faded back among the trees, hardly breathing for fear of being noticed.

"By what right do you take our stock?" Ben yelled.

"By this right," growled the officer, holding up his pistol. "And by right of the Confederacy."

"You can't come in here and commandeer our property!" Nate protested.

Cooper Hartley threw his head back and laughed a mean, hateful laugh. "Can if we want. Don't see none of *you* stoppin' us," he jeered. "Put you together and you barely make up one man!"

The officer leaned forward in his saddle and peered at Nate's empty sleeve. "Where'd you get that?"

"Sharpsburg."

"*Good* fer you! I was there, too. Lost a couple friends. Maybe that'll learn you not to mess with us."

Nate moved to reply, but Ben grabbed his good arm. "Keep quiet, or they'll kill us."

"With pleasure," Cooper growled, lifting his rifle.

The officer grabbed the barrel and forced it down. "Good advice about keepin' quiet. We'll be goin' now. All we come for was the horses." He nodded in Nate's direction. "Thank you, in the name of Jefferson Davis and Robert E. Lee." He spit on the ground and rode off.

I emerged from the orchard as Ben comforted Rebecca and the children. Nate stood by, helpless and frustrated, his anger overwhelming.

"Damn Rebs," he muttered. "Should have killed more of them when I had the chance."

"No such thing," I chided him. "There will be wars as long as men like you want to fight, and as long as you think you'll win."

"Yeah, well, *they* ain't gonna win," Nate declared. "We're two years into it, and no end in sight, but one of these days we'll break their backs. You wait and see. Cooper Hartley won't want to show his face around here when this is over."

The raiders were attached to Lee's Army, which had boldly invaded Pennsylvania in late June. The Army needed shoes, food, horses. This ragtag bunch was simply foraging for the cause. The clash was coming within the week, down near Menallen Meeting, at Gettysburg.

Ben counted himself lucky not to have lost more than a dozen or so horses. There were more in the south pasture and in the barn, but the raiders had been in much of a hurry, so had missed them. It was enough of a loss, but Ben was resilient.

"They missed the best of them," he observed. "Anyway, with no help around here, I could do with fewer horses to take care of." He looked around at his oldest sons, the twins, now eight. "You two better hurry and grow up. I'm gettin' worn out, doin' it all."

Nate picked up a rock and threw it against the barn. "Damn Rebs."

"It's all right, Nate," Ben reasoned. "It could have been worse. They didn't burn us out or kill anybody."

I silently thanked God the Rebels didn't know about Maggie and her children hiding in our house. It could, indeed, have been much worse.

Chapter 33

Ours wasn't the only farm the rebels visited that day. Most of our neighbors lost stock, provisions, or both. I was spitting mad at Cooper Hartley for leading them to us, but there was nothing to be done. Still, I wanted to give Pru a dressing down. After all I'd done for her over the years—without so much as a thank you!

The next day, I put on my sunbonnet and marched down over the hill to the Hartley cabin. Everything was quiet there, and no one showed as I approached, not even a scrawny hound. The yard was trampled and littered with trash, like a camp meeting. Nothing moved. I approached the porch and called. No answer. Stepping carefully around rotten boards, I knocked at the door and waited. Nothing. I called again. No reply.

Gingerly, I lifted the latch and entered. It looked like a cyclone had passed through. Not a piece of furniture stood upright; the floor was littered with broken bottles, dishes, and rags, fragments of curtains ripped from the windows. I stood in the doorway. A whimper came from the bed in the far corner of the room. Pru huddled there, wrapped in a filthy quilt, knees to her chin, rocking slowly back and forth.

"Pru! What happened?" I rushed to her side, but she raised a bruised arm to ward me off.

I could hardly make her out in the dim light. Her hair was matted and dirty, her face battered and swollen almost beyond recognition. One side hung limp, drooping, and her left eye was swollen shut.

"Who did this to you?"

She turned away, whimpering, hid her face, and went back to rocking.

"Where are your boys?" I asked, pushing aside a ragged curtain to let in more light. The window was broken.

Pru looked at me like a lost child. She put her head down on her arms and continued to rock slowly back and forth. Seeing she wasn't ready to talk, I picked up trash and righted furniture. Everything of value was gone. There was no food or supplies of any kind. The utensils were gone. The spit was bent from the fireplace. Everything that remained was shattered or splintered beyond use. The table had only three good legs, and the only thing to sit on was a chair without a back. Wanton destruction everywhere I looked.

I picked up a corn broom with its handle snapped off and used it to sweep broken glass and pottery. Pru was watching me.

"I'm gonna die," she said.

"No, Pru. You'll be all right. I'll see that you're taken care of. It's really not that bad."

"I'm gonna die."

Cold fear in my gut told me she was right. I could see enough damage to know that she'd been beaten and abused, but I had no way of knowing how much I couldn't see. I reached out to help her up.

She held onto my arm but couldn't rise. Under her on the filthy bed I saw a huge dark bloodstain.

"Pru, I'm going to get Rebecca. I can't lift you by myself. I'll send Nate for the doctor."

She sank back down into the bed and lay on her side, knees up. With every move she whimpered in pain.

"No. Stay. I ain't got long. It won't do no good to get help."

"Where are your boys?"

She looked at me with her good eye. "Gone, gone for soldiers."

"Soldiers? But, Pru, they're just little boys. They can't be soldiers." I paused, piecing the scene together. "Was it the soldiers who did this?"

Pru's head nodded almost imperceptibly.

"Rebels? The Rebels with Cooper? The ones who stole our horses?" I took her hand. "Pru. Not your brother!"

"He let 'em. They was all drunk. I don't think he could of stopped 'em if he wanted to."

Pru Hartley lay helpless and broken. I cried. In spite of her meanness, she didn't deserve this. Her breathing became more shallow as I watched. She opened her right eye and looked at me.

"They kilt the dogs," she said, and then she drifted away.

I held her lifeless hand for long minutes and thought of our years of contention. None of it mattered anymore. I pulled the blood stained quilt over her. The cabin was pitiful. Bare and beaten. I closed the door. War is a terrible thing.

&

Antietam was about seventy-five miles from Redfield farm, as the crow flies. Gettysburg about fifty-five. Too close, both of them. Some of Ben's horses probably died at Gettysburg. Better the horses than any of us.

That month of July in 1863 was almost as bad as its predecessor of 1856, when I'd given up Sam. I thought not to like the month ever again, but I was wrong. July would redeem itself.

We kept Maggie and her children with us, to protect them from this Abe fellow and to nurse them back to health. Little Della never did say one word to any of us. She warmed up some—enough to take sliced peaches from me or to let me wipe her face clean, but not to speak. Gideon's leg healed pretty quick, and by benefit of regular food he started to fill out a little. He was full of the dickens, always teasing and trying to get my goat. A likable imp who made me think of my own child up there in Canada. Little Andrew warmed up, too. He'd climb up on my lap and snuggle like a lost lamb.

It was Maggie who worried me. She was so thin, my old dress hung on her like a sack. She tried to help with the work, but her strength was about used up. Sometimes she coughed up blood, and I tried to keep her down, but she *would* get up and try to work. It was too late for Maggie. Death was waiting for her around the bend. She was determined to get back on the road to Canada, but I argued against that.

"Maggie, I know how bad you feel. You'd never make it to Canada if Canada was down by Fishertown."

"Where Fishertown?" she asked, her eyes feverish.

"Not that far," I replied. "You need to stay here so you don't get sick on the road. Your babies wouldn't know what to do. Stay here where we can take care of them."

She lowered her eyes and nodded, almost imperceptibly. Her thin shoulders drooped.

"Don't you worry, Maggie. I wrote to my friend in Canada and asked him to try to find your brother. If anyone can do it, he can. If you don't get better, we'll see that the children get there."

"Uh huh." The fight was gone out of her. She took to bed soon after and didn't get up again.

I took this time to try to wean her children away, to dull the pain they would feel when she died. Gideon and Andrew were all right, each in his own way, but little Della was a challenge. She wandered around the farm with her thumb in her mouth, dragging a rag doll, lost without her mama.

We buried Maggie in the Friends Cemetery in Spring Meadow not six weeks after they came to us. Nothing more was heard from the elusive Abe, but just before Maggie died, the constable brought back the bay gelding that had been stolen from Ben the night Maggie arrived. He said it was taken from a black man jailed for stealing another horse. We guessed it was Abe.

The week after Maggie's death, a letter came from Josiah, saying he'd found her brother and that the children's father was, indeed, with him. Once more a party from Redfield Farm made the arduous journey from Alum Bank to Erie and sent a black family across to Freedomland. This time it was Nate who accompanied them—and James, who had attached himself to his uncle like a barnacle. They put Maggie's children on the ferry, with Josiah waiting on the other side to take them to their father.

Poor little ones, lost in the world. I looked at Rachel's babies, so recently orphaned and abandoned. Well, at least they had me, and would for all time. But I needed some respite from the sadness. From the horrible stories that kept coming in the wake of the great battle at Gettysburg. Needed the company of another woman. I wrote to Mary.

Chapter 34

1863 – Late Summer

Mary came in August and stayed for a week—the first time we'd been alone together since her marriage nineteen years before. She came to comfort me and to visit her son, doing a man's work at his Uncle Ben's side. She came to talk and laugh and lighten my load. Of all of us, Mary reminded me most of our mother. Round faced and ample bosomed, cheerful blue eyes. Nathaniel, back from Erie, seemed to feel the same, seeking Mary's company like a lost child.

"He has a ways to go," Mary told me as we sat on the back porch one warm afternoon snapping beans.

"Yes. Sometimes I wonder if he'll ever get over it completely."

"It'll take time, but it'll happen."

"He and James make a pair. James is starved for a man's attention. I doubt Jacob ever paid him much mind," I commented. "But Nate has taken him under his 'broken' wing, and they both seem to thrive on that."

"This family is a little man-shy," Mary went on. "We've got plenty of boys, but able-bodied men are lacking. Ben'll wear himself out before those five sons of his grow man strong. You need to find yourself a husband, Ann."

I demurred, then giggled. "Why, yes, Mary! Why haven't I thought of that? I could just go out and say to the first eligible man I met, 'Come with me. We need a man on the farm!' Anyway, there aren't any good men left, and if this war doesn't end soon there won't be any good boys, either."

Mary smiled and reached for another handful of beans. "Well, Ben needs a partner. You should see what you can do before he wears himself out. I hate to tell him this, but Noah needs Adam at home. I'm to take him back with me." She swatted at a fly, pestering her nose.

"Oh. I can't blame Noah, but Ben'll be lost without Adam. Everything's hard with the war. I thought the rebels would be easier to beat."

I looked down the road, empty in the afternoon sun, and thought of Pru's boys, tagging along after the Rebel army, poor wretched waifs. If they had any innocence left, it was surely lost by now. Mary broke in on my thoughts.

"I'm glad Adam got a chance to see the real thing when you and he went looking for Nate. It certainly settled him down. Must have been awful, what you saw."

I nodded. "I was worried that it'd be too much for him, but he kept his head and behaved like a man." I shaded my eyes. A lone rider made his way slowly up the dusty road through dappled sunlight. Mary saw him, too, and we watched as he turned in at our gate. "Now, who do you suppose that is?"

He rounded the corner of the house and stopped, looking down from his horse. A well-built man of about my age.

"Can you tell me where Elias Finley lives?" he asked, leaning forward in his saddle. He looked travel-worn, a little downcast, somehow.

"Elias Finley is dead. Killed last year at the Second Battle of Bull Run."

"Oh? And what of his family?"

"His widow and three children live about a mile farther along, on the right," I directed, watching him curiously. I was sure I didn't know him, and it was odd, a stranger coming along, looking for Elias.

"Widow?

"Yes."

"I thought his wife died."

"His first wife, yes. He married again."

The man looked puzzled. "What about his daughter?"

"He has two daughters." I peered at him, uncomfortable with so many questions. "You mean Lucy?"

"Yes. Lucy. What of her?" He took off his hat and beat it against his knee, sending up a cloud of dust.

"She's there with his second wife."

"Oh, I should take her home."

"Home?"

"Her mother, Melissa, was my sister," he explained. "I came here to see Elias about horses and to see my niece. I'm sorry he's gone, but I should probably take her back with me to live with her grandparents. My mother would be vexed if she knew Lucy was an orphan living among strangers."

"Not exactly strangers," I corrected. "Elias's sister lives next door, married to my brother. Lucy doesn't remember any other mother than Deborah, her stepmother."

The man looked concerned. "Well, yes. Maybe so. I should introduce myself. I'm Preston Neff, from Chambersburg."

"Pleased to meet you." I got up and walked to the edge of the porch. Up close I saw a distinct family resemblance to Melissa. I offered my hand. "I'm Ann Redfield. This is my sister, Mary Poole. Can I get you a glass of cold mint tea?"

Preston Neff climbed stiffly down from his horse, still slapping away the dust with his hat. I excused myself and went into the kitchen to get the tea. I returned with three glasses on a tray and set it down on a table beside Mary.

"Mr. Neff tells me he's a widower," Mary informed me with a look that told me how providential she found this news.

"Oh? I'm sorry to hear that, Mr. Neff."

"Cholera," he replied. "My wife and three children—last summer."

I breathed a sigh. So that was his burden. "How very sad."

He looked down. "Yes. Well, one has to go on."

He drank his tea and made movements to go, as Nathaniel and James arrived from fishing at the creek. James was full of stories of fish caught, fish not caught, and whoppers seen lurking in the shadows. I watched Preston Neff listen to the boy's chatter, a smile playing at the corners of his mouth. He seemed a good-humored sort. A man who is kind to children and animals is a man to be trusted.

"War?" Preston asked, noting Nate's arm.

Nate nodded.

"War's been hard on all of us, and *we're* supposed to be pacifists!"

"I've had *my* fill," Nate replied.

"Anyone else here to help with the work?"

Nate shook his head. "You're lookin' at all the manpower we got. Pa's up in years. I wouldn't say it in front of him, but he's not much good on the farm anymore."

"So you're short of labor, huh?" Preston observed.

"Sure are," Nate said with a glance toward Mary. "My brother's pushed to his limit, and I'm not much help. Elias is gone, and my other brother moved west. You any good with horses?"

"Yes, indeed." Preston turned to me. "You knew our father was a breeder, didn't you? Isn't that what brought Elias to us in the first place?"

Nate continued, "Ben sure could use some help. Maybe you should talk to him."

So Preston Neff stayed on to help Ben the next day, proving his expertise with horses from the start. Quiet, thoughtful, hard working. Good Quaker stock.

That first evening, he sat at our table, helping James whittle a toy horse. "Would there be room for me to board here for a while?" he asked. "Ben's house is full, and I wouldn't be comfortable at Deborah Finley's, even though she has room."

I nodded, glad for the help, especially since Adam was leaving with Mary the next day. "Certainly. We can put up a cot in Nate's room, if you don't mind Amos's snoring next door. It's been compared to a locomotive."

He smiled. "I don't mind. I'm a sound sleeper."

I set another place at the table. The arrangement was in our favor, needing the help as we did, but I wondered what was in it for Preston. He worked hard from sunup to sundown, went to Meeting on Sunday, and kept to himself most of the time, except for forging a bond with Rachel's children. Clearly, he was trying to leave his old life behind.

One evening a few days later, I laid a little fire in the parlor to take the chill off the room. Preston wandered in and helped me get it going. We sat in silence for a while. I embroidered by lamplight and Preston contemplated the flames.

"I can't believe it's almost a year since Adam and I went looking for Nate," I said, to make conversation.

Preston nodded, then asked, "Ann, what happened to your husband? Did the war take him, too?"

"I've never been married. The children are my sister Rachel's. She died last December and her husband left them with us in the spring."

"Oh, I'm sorry you lost a sister. But it seems you've gained a family."

"They've been a Godsend. We all needed them." I picked up my embroidery and worked on a pillowcase I was making to send west to Abby for Christmas.

"They remind me of my own," he mused. Mine were a bit older—nine, seven, and five. Two girls and a boy. But children are children."

"I hope the reminder isn't too painful."

"No. They're good for me. While they remind me of what's gone, they also remind me that life goes on." He poked at the little fire with a stick of wood. It was one of those nights—too cool without a fire, too warm with one.

"It does, indeed." I sneaked a glance at Preston and found him watching me. I looked away.

"What about your brother who went west? I always wanted to, but life got in the way."

"They're doing fine out in Indiana. Lost a child a year or more ago, but they're expecting another one soon." I held up my thread to the lamplight to decide on a color.

"Wasn't he with the Underground Railroad? A conductor?"

I wondered who he'd been talking to. "How would you know that?"

"Ben told me. He says you were all involved, but mostly Jesse. Weren't you in it, too?"

"Some. After Jesse left, I didn't do much. Then the war came. At first the numbers increased, but after the proclamation, few came north. Things are coming apart in the South, I fear, but not soon enough for me."

He nodded. "I've always been opposed to slavery but never acted on it. The opportunity never arose and I didn't go looking for it."

"Most didn't. But you would have helped if asked. Jesse just couldn't leave it alone. Most of the time he was easy going, but slavery brought up the bile in him."

We sat for a while in silence, watching the fire wane. "Ann, how well did you know Elias Finley?"

His directness took me by surprise. "Quite well, I guess. Why?"

"My sister wasn't happy with him. It makes me curious about the sort of man he was. Melissa was such a happy child. To see her so sad at the end made us wonder. I never really got to know him, but my parents didn't think much of him either."

"Then why did you come looking for him?"

"I wasn't exactly looking for *him*. I was trying to get away. I headed west and found myself in Bedford County. Since I was here, I thought I'd stop and visit Elias, but I never intended to stay."

"Elias wasn't a bad sort. Just inept. Couldn't see any needs beyond his own, I guess." I followed the thread of Preston's thoughts. "Do you think you'll ever go back?"

"No. Probably not. I'm just wandering. Trying to lose myself."

"Lucy's glad you came. Lucky, too. She might never have known her mother's people."

"I think I'll take her to Chambersburg for Christmas." He rose to open the door. The little fire had displaced the chill. "Deborah cares for her, but she can't do for her like we can."

It was true. When all was said and done, Elias hadn't much to show for his years in the horse trading business. He was more interested in the appearance of wealth than in prudent management. Now Deborah and the children had a decent house but little to live on.

"Are you thinking about leaving Lucy with her grandparents?"

"We'll let her decide. She's old enough."

I nodded. "I don't know what Deborah will think. It's a struggle for her to put bread on the table, but she's practically raised Lucy. It'll be hard to give her up, but if she wants to stay with her grandparents, I don't think Deborah will stand in the way."

"My parents will be glad to have her, and there's an abundance of aunts, uncles, and cousins."

"Will you stay down there or come back after Christmas?" I asked.

"I guess I'll come back. Ben has a good operation going, even with the loss of some of his herd, and he really needs help. Besides, I don't have any place else to go."

"What about your farm and house?"

"My brother wants to buy my place. It adjoins our father's land. I don't want to live there anymore. Anyway, Ben seems a solid sort. I might buy in with him."

I wouldn't be honest if I didn't admit to some speculation about a future with Preston Neff. He was attractive—tall, sandy-haired, with deep-set eyes. Kind. Intelligent. But disappointment and long years of hard work with little reward made me shy. I pushed the idea away. "Will that be all right with your parents?"

"My brothers and sisters all live close. They can get along without me."

"Well, there's no question Ben needs you. I hope maybe someday you'll come to think of Bedford County as home."

"Maybe," he said. "At least for the time being."

Our conversation was interrupted by Amos, Nate, and James coming in from the barn. "Hey, don't take the last piece of pie!" Nate hollered at James. "Save some for me!"

Preston nodded toward the kitchen. "I think Nate's filling out just since I've been here."

"He laughs more now, too. He and James! Sometimes it's hard to tell who's seven and who's twenty-nine! Maybe time *will* heal all the wounds."

A wistful look passed over Preston's face. "One can hope."

James and Nate came in from the kitchen, still arguing over the pie. Amos took his chair by the window, nodding to Preston.

"James, go wash up and get ready for bed. Ellen and John have been in for almost an hour," I told him. James made a face.

"I'll wash his face for him!" Nate grabbed the boy's head with his good arm. "Let's go down to the creek and get some sand!"

James giggled, wriggling free and dancing toward the door. "Oh, you never touched me," he sassed. "You better be nice, or I'll tell Hattie Kensinger you're sweet on her!"

Nate caught him and wrestled him to the floor, one handed. "You do and I'll never take you fishing again."

"Nate, if you marry Hattie, can I be your boy?" the child asked, helpless in Nate's grasp.

"Sure, James. You're already my boy." Nate replied.

Amos, Preston and I exchanged glances across the room. Nathaniel, evidently, had plans.

Chapter 35

True to his taciturn nature, Nate didn't speak of his plans to marry Hattie Kensinger, partly, I surmised, because Hattie was not a Friend, and that meant disownment for marrying out of Meeting.

"They disowned me before when I went to war," he told me when I asked how he felt about it.

"Yes, but you were reinstated."

"Reinstated, but not rehabilitated. I'm not a pacifist. I still think sometimes a man has to fight."

"That may be," I replied. I was again glad to be a woman and not subject to the forces that drove men to violence. I had only once had the urge to fight, on the road to Oglestown that night—in self-defense.

"Anyway," Nate continued, "the Friends are falling away. Every time you go to Meeting there are fewer. Some go west, some die, some marry out, some are disowned, and some just quit. The only reason I asked to be reinstated was for Pa's sake. He was so put out with me for going to war."

I sighed. This younger brother would always be a mystery. I barely knew Hattie Kensinger, but then I barely knew Nate. He would go his own way. I had no desire to criticize anyone's religious leanings or lack of them. That part of life was wholly personal. If Nate wanted to leave the Society, it wouldn't come between us.

"Have you and Hattie decided where you'll live?" I asked.

"I'm working out a deal with old Mr. Jakes to buy his dry goods store in Bedford. Hattie's father owns a little house on Richard Street that he'll sell me on time."

"That sounds nice. Your plans are pretty firm, then."

"There's one thing I want to talk to you about."

"What's that?"

"James. I need someone with two arms to help me run the store. Hattie and I want to take him as our own."

It didn't surprise me. Their mutual need was clear to anyone with two eyes. James was rarely more than three feet from Nate's good elbow, and he did, in fact, help Nate with many of life's chores. He buttoned his shirts, cut his meat, saddled his horse, baited his fishhook. I knew some of those duties could be taken over by a wife, but James and Nate would still be lost without each other.

"I don't like to split these children up, after losing their parents, but if you promise to keep close so they really are part of each others' lives, I'll allow it."

So it was decided that James would live in Bedford as Nate and Hattie's son. The wedding took place on a cold day in February, 1865, in the Bedford Presbyterian Church. James stood up beside his uncle for the ceremony, looking older than his almost nine years. When it came time to paint a new sign for Nate's store, the wording was thus: Redfield and Schilling, Dry Goods.

One morning in April, Rebecca came running up the orchard, her skirts hiked like she was being chased by demons. I met her on the porch, fearing the worst. "It's over! The war is over! Lee surrendered yesterday down in Virginia!" Her face was flushed, her eyes alight. I hugged her, and we danced around the porch for joy. Amos heard the goings on and came in from the barn.

"Papa! Papa!" I cried. "The Rebels surrendered. The war is won!"

Amos stood speechless, head down, in the middle of the yard, thinking of a return to peace and pacifism, I guessed.

It was five days later that Rebecca was back, walking slowly this time, her face ashen. "Oh, Ann. They've gone and killed Mr. Lincoln."

I stared at her. "He was such a kind man, just what the country needed to help it heal," Rebecca lamented. We sat down on a bench under the newly budding grape arbor to try and make sense of it.

One tragedy on the heels of another. So much news in so little time. It took some getting used to.

My mind wandered to the former slaves still in the south. Now Negroes walked freely on the streets of Bedford with barely a notice. For me it felt a little strange—like I was no longer needed. I thanked God for Rachel's babies. Without them, I might have lacked a reason to live.

I wrote to Josiah, told him of my joy that the war was finally over and my hope that the former slaves would now know the joy of freedom. The Railroad was passing into history, and I reflected on my role in it with quiet satisfaction.

Josiah, free for ten years now, wrote that he was skeptical about the lot of free blacks in the South. For him, the bitter and complete southern defeat and the appalling ignorance of most slaves was a recipe for exploitation and discrimination. Still, he rejoiced in freedom for his people and worked harder to bring more of them to Canada, where the future looked brighter than in the south.

With Nate's wedding, the number around the Redfield table was again reduced by two. In some ways it felt like a little family. Grandfather Amos, Mother Ann, Father Preston, and two children. A fantasy family, to be sure, but still all I had ever wanted in life.

Preston came and went between our house and Ben's farm, asking little and working hard. Rebecca said he'd saved Ben's back *and* his sanity. I was grateful for that, but it was another side of Preston that interested me. He was a man of the world in my eyes. He'd often traveled to Philadelphia and Baltimore to attend Yearly Meetings, and he opened my eyes to the wider world of the Quaker faith. The Society of Friends might be losing ground in these western counties, but it was alive and well in the east and in far flung places like Indiana and Iowa, even California.

"You should go to Yearly Meeting, Ann. You'd meet interesting people and learn how wide the Friends' influence is," he told me.

The idea was appealing, but I hesitated. Why was he asking *me*? Would he have extended the same courtesy to anyone? I put my doubts aside, and decided to join him and a small group from Dunning's Creek Meeting for the trip to Baltimore. I still loved the Quaker faith, was proud of the pacifism, equality, moderation, and self-restraint it stood for. I'd once dreamed of attending Yearly Meeting at Elias Finley's side. Now I understood how the answer to some dreams was, 'Wait'. Going at Preston Neff's side was a far more worthy dream.

I sought a favor from Deborah Finley. "Can Ellen and John stay with you while I go to Yearly Meeting?"

"Of course! Ellen and Sarah will be happy playmates for a few days, and John loves to play big brother to my Elias. What about Amos?"

"Rebecca says he can take his meals with them."

"Yearly Meeting! Aren't you excited, Ann?"

"Oh, yes! I can hardly wait, though I've never been before. I don't really know what to expect."

"I'd love to go," Deborah said, starry eyed.

"Your turn will come," I assured her with a pat on the hand. "Life isn't over for you yet."

Thus freed of responsibility, Preston and I met the group at the Meeting House and traveled to Hagerstown, where we boarded the train to Frederick. We spent the first night in Quaker homes there and continued on the train the next day to Baltimore. Preston escorted me to the home of his uncle, Robert Neff, where I was introduced to Robert's wife, Susan, and his daughters, Mariah and Miranda. We four women fell together like old friends, talking about the issues that confronted the Society.

"You'll love Yearly Meeting, Ann," Susan Neff assured me. "Women's rights will be on the agenda this year, and high time!"

Such talk awakened interests I didn't know I had. The Neff women were open and outspoken. Their animated conversation kept me up late every night. I'd never experienced such intellectual stimulation, and I reveled in it, thriving on the energy it awakened in me.

"I've heard of these issues before—of Seneca Falls and the Declaration—but only vaguely. This is the first time I've met anyone with intention to act upon them," I told Susan Neff as we sat in the parlor one evening. Preston and Robert were still engaged in Society business and wouldn't return until late.

The next day, I listened in rapt attention as a parade of Quaker women addressed the conference, modestly self-congratulatory for the victories of abolition and the Underground Railroad, and exhorting the group to new action in the area of women's rights. "What good," they asked, "does it do black women to shed the bonds of slavery only to retain the bonds of gender? Why should any person be deprived of rights others enjoy simply by accident of birth?"

My head was still spinning three days later when Preston and I boarded the train for the trip home. At first, I was shy about addressing the topic of women's rights with him, but he brought the subject up.

"What did you think of my girl cousins?" he asked. "And their confrontational attitude on Women's Rights?"

"I loved it!" I blurted, in spite of myself. "I've always felt that women needed to assert themselves more, and I've certainly met some kindred souls!"

Preston laughed. "I knew a trip to Baltimore would unleash some tumult in the Redfield house!"

He wasn't at all threatened by the prospect of associating with a strong woman, for that is what I was – had always been. Now I was confident enough not to hide it away. We talked almost all the way back to Bedford, finding ourselves in delighted agreement on many points. I was giddy with the excitement of new ideas and new horizons, and, though I tried, I couldn't keep myself from hoping that a true union of souls might still be in store for me.

When we got home, it didn't take long for my new found inspiration to find a voice. The very next First Day, I stood at Meeting and preached—yes, preached—my first testimony on equal rights for women.

"You can not profess to believe in equal rights and still deprive the women in your own family of the right to a voice in government and a share in the decision making."

The ideas weren't new, but my call to action stirred some underlying discontent among the women and opened the way for serious discussion across the aisle.

Preston, on his side, supported me and pressured the men to put into action the equality they professed belief in. It was the liveliest Meeting in recent memory—at least since before the war, when abolition held sway. People stood outside talking in small groups well into the afternoon. I visited with Rebecca and her sister Hannah, but my eyes scanned the crowd for Preston, ever conscious of his whereabouts.

Try as I would to resist, I felt myself drawn to him. My cautious nature made me wary. Elias' treachery still lingered in memory. It was coming up on a year since Preston had appeared in our lives, and my good opinion of him had grown steadily. Still I tried to keep a tight rein on my feelings, this time not revealing to anyone that I saw him as a dream postponed, even though I guessed there was talk. There is always talk.

The summer came in full blown. Life at Redfield Farm was routine but never boring. My newfound interest in Women's Rights flourished, and I was soon the center of a small but determined group of female Friends who shared the writings of women like Lucretia Mott and Elizabeth Cady Stanton over canning, preserving, or quilting. I spoke up with more courage and frequency at Meeting. One cause is won and another takes its place. Life goes on. It is ever thus.

One evening in July after helping me wipe the dishes Preston whispered, "Let's go for a walk along the creek."

I untied my apron and patted my hair. I noted the children playing on the porch with Amos, and followed Preston across the yard and down over the hill to Dunning's Creek. As we walked, he took my hand. He'd never actually touched me before, beyond rubbing shoulders in a crowded coach or offering a hand to help me up or down. His touch sent an impulse through me, and I shuddered involuntarily.

"Are you cold?" he asked.

"No. Someone just stepped on my grave." I spoke lightly, determined to mask my joy.

We walked hand in hand down over the hill to the creek in the July twilight. We stood looking into the clear water, keenly aware of each other. He turned to face me, taking both of my hands in his. "I've been thinking."

"Really? About what?"

"About us."

"Us?"

"Yes. You and me."

"What about us?" Now my heart was pounding so hard I was afraid he could hear it.

"Well, I was thinking maybe we could marry. Raise these two children. Maybe have one or two of our own," he said, hopefully. "I've learned to love you, Ann."

My hands began to shake and I pulled away. Love! He'd said he loved me! No one, not even Josiah, had ever said that. How could I be worthy?

"Preston, there is much you don't know," I faltered.

"What? I know all about it. Josiah. Sam. All of it."

"How? How do you know?"

"People talk, Ann. They talk all the time—about everyone. I picked it up from my sister Melissa, from Deborah Finley, from Ben and Rebecca. You'd be surprised how free they are with information when they think you already know. But it doesn't matter."

My eyes searched his. I felt myself carried away by an irresistible current. Too weak to stand, I sank to the ground.

"How can a man like you love me? What do you see in me?" I asked.

"I see a woman whose dreams were dashed but who rose to the responsibilities life placed in her way. I see a woman whose life has been spent in sacrifice, who has taken risks many men would have shrunk from." He was kneeling at my side, holding my shoulders from behind. Slowly he lifted me, guiding me gently along the path until we came to the same woodlot where Jesse and I had met the two slaves twenty-eight years before. We sat on a fallen log, watching the creek bubble along, listening to the frog chorus.

Preston straddled the log, facing me. "I want you to be my wife, Ann. I won't have it any other way." He pulled me to him and kissed me.

I leaned against his chest, my head on his shoulder, breathing in his scent. It felt so good to be there. Tears filled my eyes. I'd waited so long.

"Marry me?" he asked.

"Yes. Gladly."

So the intention to marry for Ann Redfield and Preston Neff was declared at Second Meeting, Eighth Month, and the ceremony was witnessed by family and friends in September, 1865.

I was thirty-seven, and, having had only one encounter before this, I felt compelled to waste no more of my life in chastity. From our first coupling on the creek bank until our marriage, we indulged ourselves daily, adroitly avoiding Amos' watchful eye. That made it all the more delicious and the need more pressing. I fully expected to be with child on my wedding day. In fact, I wanted it that way.

Christmas of 1865 should have been the most joyful in years, but as I knew well, the Lord giveth and the Lord taketh away. Preston, Amos, and I agreed to make a special Christmas for Ellen, John and James.

Amos set out early on the afternoon of the 20th to cut a Christmas tree but did not return by supper time. I knew instinctively something was amiss. Preston and I bundled up the children and took them over to Ben's. Unaware of my fears, Ellen and John immediately fell to playing with their cousins while Preston and I enlisted Ben's help in the search. We found Amos dead in the snow up on the hill behind the house, beside a half-chopped evergreen.

Preston held me close while Ben picked up the ax and, without a word, finished chopping down the tree. Then he and Ben laid Amos on the sled. Ben and I pulled the heartbreaking burden home while Preston followed, dragging the tree.

Chapter 36

1866

Amos's will directed that his estate be settled and the proceeds divided evenly among his six surviving children, Rachel's in equal shares to James, Ellen and John. In letters back and forth to Indiana, the brothers and sisters agreed that Preston and I should keep the farm, buying out my siblings' shares. Preston left the negotiations to me, encouraging me to oversee my own financial arrangements. I was grateful for that. Once the estate was settled, we made a few modest changes to bring the place up to date.

The farm is rocky and hilly, so I set aside only a few acres for planting corn and oats. On the rest, we grew hay and pastured Ben and Preston's horses. The barn stored hay and provided shelter for our cow and a few more horses, the overflow from Ben's. Even now I sometimes stand in the barn and look up at the hay loft, remembering the people who passed through. It always seemed to me there were ghosts in there.

Slowly, the community—as the nation—returned to normal after the war, but it would never be the same. Too many men and boys had gone away, never to return. Too many had returned scarred or maimed. Some of the scars were invisible, but they played themselves out in unforeseen ways. Ways which couldn't be clearly blamed on the war. But I always thought bad behavior—abuse and insensitivity to others' pain—had its roots there.

In July, 1866, I gave birth to a baby girl whose name, Patience, was promptly shortened to Polly. Preston's joy in having a child again was as deep and wide as mine. Her name was testament to my view of life: good things come to those who wait.

October brought a long anticipated visit from Jesse and Abby, come east to buy more nursery stock. Their family now numbered five: little Margaret Ann, named for her maternal grandmother and her 'favorite aunt', and twin boys, Jesse and Josiah, the pride of their father's heart.

"I wouldn't have moved west if I'd realized how important it would be for these little ones to know their cousins," Jesse told me. I listened with hope. I still wished he'd never left.

Timed to coincide with Jesse's visit, but unbeknownst to me, was a visit from another place. One evening as we all sat down to supper, four adults and six children, there came a knock at the door. A look passed between Jesse and Preston, as Jesse said, "Ann, you're closest. Would you see who it is?"

I rose and crossed the room, brushing off my apron, and opened the door. There stood a tall, handsome Negro boy of about eleven. He smiled broadly and said, "Hello, Ann Redfield. Remember me?"

With a cry, I reached out and gathered him to me. "Sam! Where did you come from?"

Sam was joined by Josiah, Lettie, Ann, Athena, and Amanda, (or the "Three As," as Sam called them). Now sixteen people crowded around the table; introductions were made and more food brought forth. It was better than Christmas.

"I'd no idea you were coming," I told Josiah.

"I know. That was the plan Jesse and I put together."

I looked from Josiah to my brother. "I might have known!"

We made beds to accommodate six adults and ten children. When the children were finally bedded down all over the parlor floor and up in the nursery, Preston and I, Josiah and Lettie, and Jesse and Abby sat around the stove in the kitchen, talking long into the night. There was so much to catch up on that letters couldn't tell.

Once the children were asleep, I took Preston aside. "Are you sure this is all right with you? Their being here, I mean."

He smiled and kissed me on the forehead. "No need to worry yourself, wife. Your joy is my joy."

Reassured, I basked in the happiness of reunion and pride in my son.

The company stayed for a week, and the walls of the old house nearly burst with the strain of youthful exuberance. Children everywhere, from Sam on down to Polly, and when Ben's children and Betsy's boys came to visit, it seemed the whole world was full of noisy, raucous fun. Mary and Noah Poole brought their family from Osterburg after Meeting, and Nathaniel and Hattie came out from Bedford with young James and the announcement that they would soon add another grandchild to the flock.

It was Indian Summer, a brief respite before the coming winter, and we women congregated on the back porch to watch the rip, race, and tear of the bigger boys contrasted with the quiet pretend games of the girls.

"Wouldn't Mother and Father love this?" I asked no one in particular. "Twenty-two grandchildren! We have certainly flourished and multiplied!"

"I love a reunion," Rebecca reflected. "It's neither a beginning nor an ending, but a touchstone between the past and the future."

I nodded, satisfied with my part in it. We were strong, hard working, responsible people, the kind the earth needed more of. Amos and Martha were not there to see it, but that in no way diminished their role.

I sought out Preston one evening, longing to touch him and re-establish our bond. It was not threatened—no, it was strengthened by exposure to the broad texture of my family and my life before him. I simply needed to touch him—physically and spiritually—before going out among them again.

"There is very little peace to be found here tonight," I told him as we walked among the trees of Ben's orchard.

"Very little," he agreed. "Praise be to God."

Peter McKitrick jumped out of an apple tree a few feet in front of us with a shout. He was met by a barrage of crab apples flipped from sticks in the hands of Ben's twins, Jeremiah and Jonas. Somewhere a few rows over, Sam came pounding down between the trees, pelting Paul McKitrick with apples as he ran.

"I was looking for some quiet, just for a few moments," I said doubtfully.

"Yes, well, you might have to go a ways for that," Preston smiled.

"Will you take a little walk with me?"

"Of course. Are you disturbed about something?"

"No. Just needing you. That's all."

He took my hand and held it to his face. "Let's go down by the creek."

Passing through Ben's orchard gate, we followed the well worn path down over the hill. This was a favorite place for us for over a year now. We sat down on the same log we had sat on that July eve more than a year ago, quietly watching the moon reflected on the rippling water.

"It's beautiful, you know," I told him.

"What is?"

"Life. Beautiful in its beginning. Beautiful in its ending. Beautiful because it goes on. Because when you think it's over, it has just begun. One life ends and another begins, and we are all a part of it. None immune to its sufferings; none excluded from its joys. It's all there for the taking."

"I love your perspective on things." He smiled, holding my hand against his thigh.

A twig snapped off to the left, and we peered out of the woodlot to see Sam walking purposefully along the creek path. He approached us, stopping at a respectful distance.

"Ann Redfield?" he asked. "May I talk with you?"

Preston rose, with a questioning look at me. I nodded as he stepped away, passing the boy on the path. Sam moved silently to my side, and positioned himself on the log.

"Miss Ann Redfield?"

"Yes, Sam?"

"There's something I want to ask you."

"Yes, Sam. What is it?"

He sat beside me in silence, looking down at the ground. It seemed he was gathering his courage. Then . . . "Are you my mother?"

Taken aback by the directness of his question, I hesitated. "Yes, Sam, I am. But how do you know that?"

"I just know it. You had to be *somebody* special. All those letters and packages. Papa all the time talking to me about you." He turned away and looked down the path, very quiet. I watched him, concerned that this knowledge not hurt him. "I'm lighter than Papa and Lettie. That always made me wonder, especially since the "Three As" are darker, too." He reached in his pocket and brought out the watch I'd given him at the boat dock in Erie. "Then there's this."

I smiled. "When did they give it to you?"

"They didn't. I found it in a trunk when I was ten, wrapped in some baby clothes. I knew it wasn't from Lettie. That got me wondering. All the wondering pointed to you, but I didn't know why."

"Do you want to know why?"

The boy nodded, seriously. "Yes, Ma'am. I do."

So we sat alone on the log, watching the waters of Dunning's Creek while I related the story of Josiah and me and the baby, Sam.

"Your name is Samuel Redfield Colton. Did you know that?"

"Yes. I knew it, but I thought it was because you saved my daddy."

"It's a custom to give a boy his mother's maiden name as a middle name."

"So Jesse is my uncle?"

"Yes."

"That's good. And Polly, your baby, is my half sister?"

"Yes. She's related to you like Ann, Athena and Amanda."

He smiled. "I'd like a half-brother, please!"

I laughed. "We'll see what we can do." I watched his young face, his quick mind taking it all in. "I would have told you sometime, Sam. I was waiting until you were older. Josiah or I would have told you."

He was silent for a long time. "I'm sorry you had to give me up."

"I'm sorrier for that than anything else I can think of. It was the hardest thing I ever did. But, look at you! Look how you turned out—how good your life has been with your father and Lettie."

"Lettie's good to me."

"I knew she was a fine person from the start, or I couldn't have given you to her."

Again a long silence. I moved closer to my son and put my arm around him. "You're so precious to me, Sam. I don't expect you to understand all this as deeply as you will later. But I hope you'll think I did the right thing. There is ugliness in the world, and the best thing is to fight the ugliness any way we can. Sometimes that means putting what is most precious out of its reach."

Sam nodded. "I'm not mad at you."

"Thank you, Sam. I love you."

"Uh huh. I know. I love you, too."

We walked back along the path to Redfield Farm, mother and son, together.

Afterword

No one ever came back to the Hartley place. I often wondered about Sawyer, Cooper, and Pru's boys. The house fell apart. The roof caved in and the porch rotted away. The last time I saw it, someone had torn it down to salvage a few logs for a pig sty and left the rest lay. I don't get down over the hill much anymore.

Attendance at Meeting fell off after the war. So many people moved west, and cities beckoned with the promise of good jobs and an easier life. The Quaker community shrank over the years. There are only a few of us left now, but I still find comfort there. Everyone needs a place to belong, and that is mine.

My time with Preston was short. In June of '75 he was up on the hay wagon, forking hay into the barn, when he fell to the ground and never got up. They said it was apoplexy. I didn't know. All I knew was, the Lord giveth and the Lord taketh away.

Polly was the only child Preston and I had. She lives in Bedford now, married to a doctor. Has four little ones of her own to tend to, a houseful of energy and noise. She'll fret about me all alone out here on the farm now that Jesse's gone, but I've given her to understand that this is the only place for me.

Ben's youngsters are scattered all around the country. The girls all married. Jonas took over the farm, raising and breeding horses. He stops by every day to keep an eye on me. I'm thankful for that. And their baby Micah's a senator in the state legislature. Course he always did have a way about him. Friendly, likable. Kind of like his Uncle Jesse. Ben died in his early sixties, some said from overwork, but Rebecca lived on into her seventies. Died just a year ago. I sorely miss her.

James Buchanan Schilling got himself sent to West Point and became a soldier. Always was fascinated with soldiers. Last I heard, he was stationed over in the Philippines. I keep a globe on the shelf in the kitchen so I can keep track of where he goes. Fancy that. He's a captain now, and who knows how far he'll go?

Our little Ellen is back in Altoona where she started life, with two young boys to raise alone. Her husband up and died around Christmas two years ago. Hard life for a woman raising children alone. She runs a boarding house to make ends meet.

Baby John was a doctor, but he caught some kind of flu and died when he was only forty. They buried him up on that hill in Altoona, by his mother. He'd like that. Never did get enough mothering, it seemed.

Josiah's gone, too. Stopped to help a black man whose wagon was stuck in the mud and got kicked in the head by a scared horse. So sad. I grieved for him as much as any of them. But I saw to it that Sam got to go to college up there in Ontario, and he became a real lawyer and was elected to the Provincial Parliament. I hear from him regularly. He's married and has two lovely children. Lettie still lives with them. They visit now and again.

Jesse lost Abby to childbirth in 1870—brought her back and buried her at Spring Meadow. Now, there was a good woman. If I hadn't had my hands full here I'd probably have gone out to Indiana and helped him raise his children. As it was, he did it himself for five more years. Then he decided to come back and live here with me after Preston died. That was fine. No explanation needed between Jesse and me.

Jesse never did sell his land out there in Indiana. His boys went back and took over the orchard. Now he's gone to join Abby.

It feels good to know they're both here—not far away. I'll be joining them in a couple of years. That's where I've spent my life: two years behind Jesse.

About the Author

J udith Redline Coopey is a native of Pennsylvania and a student of Pennsylvania history. Her studies of family history created the background, characters and setting for Redfield Farm.

A log cabin built near Pleasantville, Pennsylvania, by her great-great-great-grandfather, Thomas Blackburn, around 1799, is rumored to have been a station on the Underground Railroad, though no documentation exists. A summer spent working to prepare the cabin for restoration provided the inspiration for Redfield Farm.

A graduate of The Pennsylvania State University and Arizona State University, she lives in Mesa, Arizona, with her husband and a beautiful German Shepherd named Mollie.